IN REPAIR

In Repair

A Novel by
ROZ PRESTON

STONEBOOK

First published in 2025
by
Stonebook

www.stonebook.co.uk

Copyright © R. Preston 2025

The right of R. Preston to be identified as the author of this work has been asserted by her in accordance with the Copyright, Designs and Patents Act 1988.

All rights reserved. No part of this publication may be reproduced, stored in a retrieval system, or transmitted in any form or by any means, electronic, mechanical, photocopying, recording, or otherwise, without the prior permission of the copyright owner.

ISBN: 978-1-0683267-0-7

British Library Cataloguing-in-Publication Data. A catalogue
record for this book is available from the British Library.

Designed and typeset in Verdigris MVB
by James Hutcheson

Printed by Bell & Bain Ltd, Glasgow

DEDICATION

For my late, beloved husband, John.
Without you I would never have experienced the music industry up close, or explored the west coast of Scotland in a Moody 35, or taken the risk to give up London life to build *Sweet Dreams* in a Dorset barn.
You were my fiercest critic and my greatest supporter.
Thank you for believing in me, for always driving me on
to be the best writer I could be.
I wish I could turn back the clock to answer the question you always asked,
'Who is this Cal guy?'
He is you, of course.

PART ONE

Chapter 1
West Highlands
March

Bright daffodils growing along the verge told her she was almost there. Only another hundred yards ...

Annie slowed down.

Once again, she asked herself the question she had been asking all the way back from the States – was she doing the right thing, coming here? Or was it just another way of prolonging all the pain and uncertainty of the past year?

Vividly she remembered the moment – almost a year ago, on this same road – when a sheep and lamb ran out in front of her car. Dragging the steering wheel hard over, she drove straight into the rocky verge. With a sickening crunch, the car had come to a bone-jarring stop, airbag punching her in the chest as it exploded open. Winded, she was trapped – pinned back in her seat.

That was the beginning.

Sometimes a single event changes everything. That crash was one of those life-altering moments. Until she confronted all that had happened since – whatever the outcome might be – Annie couldn't see how to plan for the future.

She took the narrow turning onto the track towards the coast. The sign appeared ahead. She could just drive on, back through the village, back to Edinburgh airport. No one would ever know she'd been there. But the promise she made her father was fresh in her mind, and her stepmother's advice still rang in her ears.

'If you don't try, honey, you'll never know.'

The driveway opened up. Steeling herself, heart hammering, Annie turned the wheel.

Chapter 2
London
March, one year earlier

'Good morning, everyone, thanks for getting here promptly.'

Annie looked around the conference table. Familiar faces turned towards her as she opened her briefcase and drew out a thick file of papers. Pete studied the agenda, frowning.

The Monday morning meeting of the Simpson Inquiry legal team, 8.30am, provided a chance to set the schedule for the coming week. Annie and her boss, Dame Moira Simpson, took it in turns to chair. With Moira absent at a briefing from the survivor groups, this week it fell to Annie.

'So, let's start with last week's interviews. Pete, could you kick off with the findings from Huntingdon House? I understand there are new accusations about the manager. Did you get a chance to interview the person who came forward?'

There was a ripple of movement around the table, and Annie became aware of her PA, Joanie, standing outside the glass door, holding up a mobile phone and mouthing something unintelligible. Annie frowned and shook her head. Nothing was going to interrupt this meeting. There was too much to get through, and the weekend press coverage had given her a jolt.

'Too little, too slow.' – *The Times*.

'The Simpson Inquiry drags its heels while abuse survivors wait to be heard,' the *Guardian* article began.

'Second Suicide while Simpson Shilly-shallies!' the *Mail*.

They had to ramp up the pace, Moira had said in their conversation last night. An erosion of public support could mean fewer accusers coming forward, more abusers escaping scrutiny and justice. Not on their watch, they agreed.

Annie frowned her annoyance as Pete dropped his papers on the floor. With a muttered apology he bent to retrieve them. Joanie took advantage of the pause to let herself in.

Holding out the phone, she whispered, 'It's someone from Scotland – Plockton, I think they said? You need to take it. She says it's urgent … '

Plockton? That was where Aunt Janet lived. Why would Janet be calling at this time on a Monday morning? She knew never to interrupt Annie's working day.

'Please excuse me for a moment, I'll be right back.' She followed Joanie out into the corridor, taking the mobile as she pulled the door closed behind her.

'Annie MacIntosh,' she announced in a businesslike tone.

'Oh Annie, it's Fiona – thank God I've got you. Janet collapsed … the doctor thinks it's a stroke … in the shop this morning … they're taking her to Broadford hospital … He said you should get here as fast as you can … '

Annie froze, brain in turmoil as she struggled to compute what she was hearing. Janet, her beloved aunt, the only person she could call her family – no. She was only just seventy. This couldn't be happening.

'Is she conscious? Talking?' From somewhere in the depths of her brain she summoned up all she knew about the effects of a stroke.

'I don't know, Annie – it all happened so fast. There was an ambulance in the village bringing someone home so they took her straight away ... you need to come ... I'm on my way now.'

'Of course. I'll get there as soon as I can.'

Concern furrowed Joanie's brow as she listened to Annie's end of the conversation

'I'll get you a taxi and a flight. Inverness?'

'Yes, and a hire car – it's two hours' drive at least. Oh God...'

With the calm efficiency that had so impressed Annie in her interview, Joanie swept into action, informing the meeting that Annie had been called away for a family emergency, leaving Pete to take over. Within minutes she had booked a flight. Helping Annie into a taxi to take her to City airport, she said

'Try not to worry, Annie. I'll text you the details of the car rental and I'll let the hospital know you're on your way. My dad had a stroke last year and he's fine now, you'd never know...'

But Annie took little comfort from her PA's reassuring words.

It was going to take at least six hours to get to the hospital. Six long hours. Anything could happen.

'Mark, it's me – I'm on my way to the airport. My aunt Janet has been rushed into hospital, it sounds serious ...' Annie choked back a sob, trying to dampen down her anxiety as she left a message for her partner. 'Please call me as soon as you get this. I'll be driving from Inverness to Broadford – it's on Skye, the reception probably won't be great but I need to know you've picked this up, and if you could come and join me, I'd really appreciate your support ...' She tailed off.

Theirs was not that kind of relationship. Both career-minded individuals, what they had was more an agreement than the kind of close bond that other friends seemed to enjoy with husbands and boyfriends. But in their four years together it had always worked for them, a convenient arrangement – someone to go out with, stay in with, share a bed with. Companionship, rather than a great love affair. Mark lived most of the time in Annie's Putney apartment, but still kept his own flat in Shoreditch as a place to work undisturbed. He'd spent the last few nights there, working on an investigation for his newspaper – a political scandal that he was determined to expose.

Right now, she longed to have him by her side, a large, comforting male presence. She had never felt so vulnerable. But her phone remained resolutely silent, and no return message flashed up on the screen. Typical – work first, as always. There was nothing further she could do once she was on the flight north.

It wasn't until she crossed the tarmac at Inverness airport that she realised how inadequately dressed she was for this part of the world. The weather in London was unseasonably warm and she had been expecting to have lunch in Westminster with a junior Home Office minister. Her cobalt-blue silk dress and jacket with matching suede stilettos were hardly going to be suitable for the cold, wet Highlands in early March. There was a display of Scottish knitwear in the airport shop. While she was waiting for her hire car to be brought round, she chose a lavender-coloured cashmere scarf. It was the best she could do for the moment – maybe she'd get a chance to find something more suitable once she got to Skye.

∼

'I'm so sorry, Ms MacIntosh.' The duty doctor and a nurse were waiting for her in the family room. 'I'm afraid you're just too late. Your aunt never recovered consciousness – we were hoping to get her to Inverness but she died before they could get the helicopter. She suffered an intra-cerebral haemorrhage. Quite honestly, she would probably not have survived the journey in any case – there was extensive damage ... It'll be a comfort to you to know she'd have known very little about what was happening to her. There would have been no pain. It was very peaceful. Would you like to see her?'

Annie nodded, numb.

The nurse accompanied her to a side room. Janet's friend Fiona was in a chair by the bed as they entered. She stood to meet them, wiping tears from her eyes.

'I'm so sorry, Annie.' She clasped Annie's hands. 'I was with her – she just slipped away quietly. You must have already been well on your way ... I told her you were coming ...'

Annie nodded. 'Thank you, Fiona. I'm so glad she had a friend by her side.'

An image of her mother's lonely death flashed across her mind. She had never forgiven herself for not being there. Perhaps she could have stopped it happening.

'Can I have a few minutes alone with her, please?'

'Of course.' Fiona and the nurse left the room.

Annie took the seat by the bedside, taking Janet's still-warm hand in her own. Beautiful in death, her aunt's face looked more peaceful than Annie could ever remember. She thought of Janet, eight years ago, full of life at the party to celebrate her retirement as headmistress of a large Edinburgh secondary school, telling Annie of her plan to retire to her holiday cottage in Plockton in the Highlands of Scotland.

'This is what I bought the cottage for – it's got a studio. The light is wonderful. At last I'll be able to paint full time! You really must come and visit, Annie. These last few years I've just been hanging on for this. Now I can do what I've always wanted.'

'I'm so glad you got that time, Janet. I wish I'd made the effort to come and stay with you – if I'd had any idea … but I always thought I'd do it next year, or … somehow there just never seemed to be time … '

Annie murmured the words aloud, full of regret as she stroked her aunt's greying red hair back off her face, feeling the cooling skin of her forehead, strangely smooth and unlined. She took comfort from talking to Janet as if she could still hear her words.

'I know you were so proud of me too, after losing Mum so young and everything – I'd never have got through any of it if you hadn't been there with all your wisdom … you've been such a wonderful role model for me, I just can't imagine life without you in it. Never thought I'd have to, you were always so strong. I thought you'd always be there … '

Annie began to cry as she pictured Janet as she had last seen her. Four months previously her aunt had had her first solo exhibition in a London gallery. Annie remembered Janet's delightful combination of pride and modesty as she stood surrounded by her bright, abstract canvases, red dots already peppering the white walls.

'What a life you've had – all those generations of children you inspired, and then your art … but what a waste. Too soon … '

Some time later, she was startled by the feeling of a hand on her shoulder, bringing her abruptly back to the present. 'Mark?'

But it was the nurse.

'We need to prepare her now, Ms MacIntosh. I'm sorry, but ...'

With great kindness she escorted Annie back to the family room, where Fiona was waiting. A wave of exhaustion and grief overcame her. Fiona clung to her as they both wept. Sobs racked her whole body, leaving her drained and helpless as they slowly subsided.

The darkness outside the windows surprised her. Surely it couldn't be that time already? But then she remembered the long hours of travelling and saw that it was already late evening.

There was so much to do, reminding her of the aftermath of her mother's death long years before. Memories of those dreadful days returned as she was presented with forms, details of local funeral directors, a certificate for the registrar's office that would open again in the morning.

'I can do that if you want, Annie.' Fiona's offer was kindly meant, but Annie saw the exhaustion on her face. It suddenly occurred to her that Fiona must be much older than Janet, in her eighties at least.

'No, Fiona, I've got this. I'm so grateful for everything you've done, but now you should go home and rest. It'll do me good to have something to focus on tomorrow ...'

'But you'll come back with me, won't you? I'd ask you to stay at mine, but it's a bit small – Janet's spare room is always made up and ... oh dear, Boris! I'd forgotten all about him, he'll need looking after too. Janet's cat, you know?' Annie had been unaware that Janet had a cat.

'Actually, I'm probably best to stay here. Then I can get to the registrars' office first thing – it'll be better to stay on the island.'

Fiona nodded, with barely concealed relief.

'My sister has a B&B just up the road.' The nurse broke

in. 'I'll give her a call.'

Alone for a few moments, Annie made a call herself.

'Mark, it's me, where on earth are you? Aunt Janet died,- just before I got here. It would be so good to talk to you. Will you please call back, or even just WhatsApp. Please.'

~

It took the whole of the next day, driving between Broadford and Portree, then back across the Skye Bridge to the funeral directors in Kyle of Lochalsh on the mainland before she completed all the tasks that needed to be done. With no time to shop for a change of clothes, Annie set the thought aside. The discomfort of her high heels and the lack of warmth provided by a suit designed to be worn indoors were of no consequence in the face of losing the last member of her small family.

In the late afternoon, worn out, she decided against trying to go to Janet's cottage tonight. Even though it was only a few miles to Plockton, Annie was loath to drive the narrow roads, tired, in failing light and heavy rain. Instead she went back across the bridge to Skye, installing herself in a warm café to catch up with work. Mark's continued silence preyed on her mind, but she set that thought aside too. It was too late now for him to be anything other than someone else to worry about, and if life with a single, alcoholic mother had taught her anything, it was resilience. As always, she was comfortable in her own company, reliant only on her own resources.

She called Fiona to make sure she was alright, before speaking to Joanie.

'I was too late – she died about an hour before I got there. Massive bleed in the brain, no warning ... ' Annie composed herself as renewed tears threatened.

'I'm terribly sorry, Annie. I'll let everyone here know. Are you going to stay up there or will I book a flight back? I think Moira's still hoping that you'll be here for the publication of the interim report on Thursday. What shall I tell her?'

'My God, I'd completely forgotten.' Annie could barely believe that something so important had been wiped clean out of her mind. 'I'll be back, of course I will. I just have a few more things to deal with at Janet's cottage, and I need to see Fiona again. I can do that first thing in the morning. Can you get me on a flight from Inverness tomorrow? Late-ish evening would be best. Thanks so much, Joanie.'

Last thing that night, after rinsing out her tights and underwear in the chilly bathroom and faced with the scant comfort offered by a second night in the lumpy bed at the B&B, she called Mark again. To leave yet another message.

Chapter 3
West Highlands
March

The gearbox ground as Callum shifted down approaching the bend. He mulled over the news from Plockton.

The whole community was in shock. Janet's death was so unexpected – out of the blue, no warning. An apparently fit, healthy woman, only just turned seventy, Janet was a popular member of the tight-knit Highland community she had made her home. A talented artist, a keen walker, someone who took part, helped out, working hard to fit in, making friends and earning the respect of even her most curmudgeonly neighbours. Fiona had given him the news in the village shop that morning when he went to pick up some groceries, tears welling up with sadness at the loss of her dearest friend. He wished he had given her a hug, but he knew she wouldn't have wanted that – not from him, anyway.

'What the ... !'

Braking hard as he wrestled with the heavy steering of the Land Rover, he only narrowly avoided crashing into the Renault slewed across the single-track road, horn blasting.

It must have just happened. Callum rushed to the stricken car. Rain lashed down as he struggled with the door – the wind, blowing broadside on, was pinning it shut. It took all his strength to force it open.

'Are you alright? What happened?'

The sole occupant was a woman, held fast in the driving seat by an inflated airbag.

The tremor in her voice betrayed her shock.

'I think I'm OK. Sheep ... ran in front ... '

They often did, on the unfenced roads of the Highlands. A sheep and her lamb, grazing on the opposite verge, watched unconcerned while Callum reached in to release the seat belt as the airbag slowly deflated.

'I'm going to try to help you out, but don't move if you're in any pain.'

'I'm not hurt, really. Thanks.'

Tentatively, she swung her legs free. Callum helped her step out onto the road, keeping a firm grip on her arm as she straightened up.

It was a surprise she was able to stand at all. She was wearing the highest heels he had ever seen around these parts, where wellies and walking boots were the usual footwear of choice.

'Thanks. Thank you.'

Driving rain was soaking her thin jacket, electric-blue turning indigo. Raindrops trickled down her face and glistened like tiny diamonds in the tight curls of her hair. Callum shrugged off his padded jacket, wrapping it around her shoulders as he led her to his battered grey Land Rover.

'Oh no, really, that's not necessary. I'm fine. You'll get soaked.' Her accent was unmistakably English.

'Not as soaked as you.'

Hastily he swept a mess of dog hairs and sweet-wrappers into the footwell, helping her up into the passenger seat.

'My place is down the road. I'll take you home and get you sorted out. Unless you'd prefer to see a doctor? I could take you to the surgery ... '

'No, really, I'm quite OK. It's only my pride that's

hurt. Thank you.' She smiled weakly, and he noticed even white teeth and dimples in her cheeks. She held his jacket tightly around her, shivering with what he interpreted to be shock as much as cold.

'I'll be right back.'

Callum ran through teeming rain to turn off the engine of the Renault, silencing the horn, leaving the lights flashing. In the boot he found hazard signs to post in the road. He retrieved her handbag. There was nothing else in the car, no luggage, no raincoat. Not even an umbrella.

What kind of an idiot comes to these parts in a silk suit and stilettos? Bloody stupid southerners, he was thinking as he climbed into the driving seat, soaked through, raindrops dripping into his eyes off clumps of hair plastered over his forehead. He pushed it back, turning the key in the ignition, willing the engine to start. Fortunately, still warm, it sprang into life. He turned the heating all the way up.

'I'm Callum, by the way.' He spoke loudly to be heard above the noise of the engine.

'Annie. Thank you so much, I don't know what I'd have done if you hadn't come along.'

'Aye, well you couldn't have walked far, not in those shoes.'

The loud vibrations of the elderly engine made further conversation impossible.

Manoeuvring round the stricken Renault, he drove the short distance to the turn off the road onto the track that led to his house. Bright daffodils buffeted by the gusty wind marked the entrance to the driveway. He turned in past the faded sign by the gatepost.

> Mathieson Boatyard.
> Boatbuilding and Repairs.
> Storage.

'You're a boat builder?' she asked in the sudden silence as he turned off the engine.

'Aye.'

Callum led the way into the house. Barking rang out from somewhere inside as he took back his coat to hang in the hallway.

'Quiet, boys! It's me! Settle down!' Surprisingly, the dogs fell silent.

'Give me your jacket. I'll dry it on the range.'

Obediently, Annie slipped it off. The sleeveless dress she wore beneath it seemed still to be dry, but she continued to shiver uncontrollably.

'Come in and get warm.'

She followed him inside.

The large black Aga ensured that it was always warm in the open-plan interior, a long island unit separating the kitchen from the dining and living area. The presence of a stranger made him aware of how untidy it was – surfaces cluttered with unwashed mugs and plates, books, magazines. His guitar lay where he'd left it last, on the sofa. He murmured a vague apology for the mess, hanging her wet jacket on the rail of the stove.

'Wait here. I'll get you something to wear.'

In the bedroom at the back of the house he quickly changed into dry clothes, rubbed his hair with a towel and searched in the back of a drawer for a clean sweater, which he handed her as he went back into the kitchen.

'Now, a hot drink. Tea, lots of sugar, OK? For shock.'

'Actually I'd prefer coffee, if you have any. Black, please – no sugar.'

Annie pulled the sweater on over her dress. It was one of his, black cashmere which he rarely had occasion to wear these days. Despite the fact that she was tall, it was much too long, almost completely covering the blue dress. She rolled back the sleeves and took the brightly painted mug he handed her, sipping hot coffee as he hastily cleared a space on the worktop.

'Have a seat.'

She perched on a stool at the end of the island.

'That's better, thanks – sorry to be such a nuisance.'

'Och, you're not a nuisance, not at all,' he lied.

This was the last thing Callum needed this morning. There was a boat in the shed, due for delivery to its new owner at the end of the week. The varnishing was still unfinished. He needed to get another coat on the thwarts and tiller today if it was to be ready in time. But it couldn't be helped – he could hardly have just left her to fend for herself.

'I'd best get someone to get the car off the road before it causes another accident. Rental, is it? Where do you live? I take it you're not from round here.' Worried that she might think he was making some kind of cack-handed comment about her colour, he softened the comment with a wisecrack and a quick grin. 'Not in those shoes.'

'London. I had to come up in a hurry – my aunt lives … lived here. She had a stroke … died.'

How could he have been such an idiot, not to make the connection?

'You're Janet's … I'm terribly sorry. Really, very sorry. The whole village is in shock.'

Annie nodded, biting her lip. Tears welled up and spilled over.

Callum took the mug, handing her a sheet of kitchen towel. She pressed it to her eyes, bringing her sobs under control. Tentatively Callum reached out and laid a hand on her arm. Instinctively he wanted to put his arms around her but he was conscious of her reticence – and his own.

'Poor lass. Poor Janet. No wonder you're upset.'

'I'm OK. Sorry ... Just ... She was the last one ... Of my family, I mean. It's ridiculous at my age, but I feel like an orphan, with Janet gone.'

'You need never apologise for crying when you lose someone you love. You should cry – need to cry. It won't bring her back, but it will help.'

He removed his hand with a slight squeeze of her arm.

'Thank you. You're very kind. But honestly, I'm fine.'

He got the impression that now she had brought her emotions under control, she would prefer some moments alone. He knew how that felt.

'Well, if you're sure you're alright, I should get over to the shed. I'm on a deadline. Give me the car rental papers. I'll sort that out for you and then get back to work.'

'I can do that, you don't need to ... ' Annie fished her mobile out of her bag.

'I'll do it. There's no mobile signal in the house.'

'Oh.' She searched her handbag for the paperwork.

'I'll be in the study. Behind the kitchen.'

∽

Annie sipped her coffee, hearing the soft murmur of Callum's voice talking on the phone. For the first time since her dash from the office in London, she began to process what had happened. Janet – gone. It barely seemed possible – they had spoken only a couple of nights ago, Janet bubbling with excitement about a new series of paintings she was working on, full of news and gossip about the village she loved.

Tears threatened to overwhelm Annie again. Impatiently she wiped them away, looking around for distraction.

Across the sitting room, a wall of high windows

framed a spectacular West Highland view. Crossing through the dining area – another clutter of paperwork and dirty mugs covering the table top – she made her way into the living space. What Annie had first taken to be a simple cottage revealed itself as a grand design, its soaring windows opening onto a cantilevered deck. It sat at the head of a small bay, enclosed by a stone pier at one side and a rocky headland on the other.

The earlier squall had died down, leaving the loch and mountains dappled in shafts of sunlight that danced on the water and illuminated bright patches on the steep slopes across the inlet. The colours were dramatic – greys in every imaginable shade and tone, dark rusty greens, yellow where the sun shone on flowering gorse. Pinpricks of silver and gold sparkled on the sunlit water. In the distance the high mountains of Skye were a misty blue backdrop. Above, swathes of bright sky amongst the stormy clouds of an early spring day promised better weather as an Atlantic front passed through.

It was an artist's paradise, she thought sadly, Aunt Janet's dramatic canvases vivid in her mind. Laid out before her was the source of her aunt's inspiration – scenes exactly like this one – the West Highlands of Scotland, with its rugged coastline, island-strewn seascapes and magical, ever-changing light.

A few hundred yards away, to one side of the cottage, a large wooden barn stood on a promontory. In front was the pier, with a slipway into the water. A yacht, white-hulled with a varnished mast and coach roof, was secured alongside. Behind the building a variety of boats sat in metal cradles or propped up with wooden stakes. Faded lettering on the wall read

Mathieson Boatyard
Home of the Raasay 25

A rough path led across coarse grass along the shoreline to the shed. Annie pictured Callum's commute to work, ruefully contrasting it with her own daily struggle by tube and bus through the chaos of the London rush hour.

A seal appeared in the water below the house. Holding her breath, she watched, entranced. It seemed to look straight at her with huge dark eyes before turning away in a lazy dive. The sleek grey back glistened in a shaft of sunlight as it slipped under the water.

She exhaled in a long sigh.

Just as the seal disappeared, Callum joined her by the window.

'That was Sammy. My daughter Kirsty named him. Sammy the Seal. There's an otter out there as well. She calls him Elvis, for some reason.'

Annie smiled, noticing that the tone of his voice softened as he talked about his daughter.

'It's wonderful – so incredibly peaceful. You're very lucky.'

'Aye ... I suppose I am ... anyway, the breakdown truck'll be here in a couple of hours. Jim'll take you back to Inverness – I saw that's where the car came from so I assumed ... '

'Yes, I'm on a flight tonight ... '

'Well, it won't be the most comfortable ride of your life but you'll easily catch your plane.'

'That's great, thank you so much.'

'Oh – and I also checked with the hotel – if you don't feel up to travelling after your accident they've a room free.'

'Really, that's very kind, thanks, but I need to get home. There's a big work thing I have to get back for.'

'What do you do?'

'I'm a lawyer. I'm on ... I lead the legal team on the Simpson Inquiry. The interim report's due out tomorrow.

I have to be there.'

'The Simpson Inquiry?'

'Yes – you know – historic child abuse in care homes? It's been in the news.'

Callum shrugged. His blank face suggested he knew nothing about the Inquiry, despite the national coverage as the date of publication approached.

'I don't pay much attention to the news.'

'Oh.'

Annie tried her best to hide her dismay. It was difficult to understand how anyone could be ignorant of Simpson and its dreadful revelations. Her working life was filled with witness statements detailing the abusive treatment of vulnerable young people in care. Even with her lawyer's ability to compartmentalise, lately she was finding it difficult to leave work behind at the end of the day.

'Right, well … I'd better get over the way … Make yourself at home, there's coffee in the jar, biscuits in the tin, bathroom's just inside the front door … I'll be in the shed if you need me.'

She watched as he walked across the garden – a long, loping stride, thick dark hair flying in the breeze. Two rough-coated brown terriers ran at his heels.

∽

The bathroom came as a surprise after the cluttered living space. It was feminine and cottagey, with panelling painted an attractive shade of duck-egg blue and striped curtains in the window. Bottles of scented oil were arranged around the edge of the bath, perfumed candles on the wide window ledge.

Annie washed her face and did her best to tame her hair, tying it back with a band. There were dark circles under her eyes, not only because her mascara had run – lately there had been too many sleepless nights, too much stress. Nothing could be done about her dress, hopelessly creased under the borrowed sweater, and her shoes were ruined by repeated soakings in the rain of the previous day. But all that really mattered now was getting home – to London, to Mark's strong embrace. Then she needed a long bath – with scented oil, perhaps – and a good night's sleep to prepare for the launch of the report.

Refreshed, she made another cup of coffee. It was going to be a while before the breakdown truck arrived. All thoughts of getting to Janet's cottage on her way to the airport would have to be set aside, but she would call Fiona and ask her to make sure everything was secure. With nothing to do for the first time in days, the adrenaline that had fuelled her rush north began to ebb away as the exhaustion brought on by the shock of losing her aunt so suddenly began to take over. It was tempting just to stretch out on a sofa in front of the view and fall asleep.

Good manners dictated otherwise. Work – there was plenty to do in preparation for tomorrow. Emails had been arriving in her inbox ever since she left the office. This was the perfect opportunity to deal with them. She set up her laptop on the kitchen island. But with no mobile signal, there was no connection.

'Damn. Bloody backwater. When are the Highlands going to join the twenty-first century?'

She checked her settings. There was a strong wifi signal – password protected.

Chapter 4
West Highlands
March

The flower-painted wellies Annie found inside the back door were a size too small, but better than her well-named killer heels. She wrapped her scarf around her neck and set out across the garden, following the rough path from the house. Halfway across, her phone pinged as a message came through. As she drew closer to the pier the signal grew stronger, eventually allowing texts and emails to upload. Few were urgent – the staff at the Inquiry would be giving her space, at least until tomorrow. She scrolled through, increasingly puzzled as she saw there was still nothing from Mark. Answering the most important text, she watched the line creeping slowly across the screen before the 'sent' notification came up.

One of the dogs rushed up, a tennis ball in his mouth. He dropped it at her feet. She stamped on it quickly to stop it rolling off the edge of the pier. As she bent to pick it up, Callum's voice rang out.

'I wouldn't throw it if I were you. He'll have you playing all day.'

She looked round to see him emerging from the shed in white overalls, pulling off a pair of surgical gloves.

'Varnishing.'

Annie took that as an explanation for his strange outfit. Either that, or the shed was a crime scene.

The second dog joined the first, jumping up around her with excited yelps.

'Gently, lads, no monstering. Are you OK with dogs?'

'As long as they're not Rottweilers – or pit bulls.'

Annie crouched down to greet them, scratching their ears, ruffling their coats.

'They're so sweet. What are they called?'

'Mick and Keith.'

'What, like Jagger and Richards? Not very well behaved, then?'

'No, you got that right. Maybe I should have gone for Simon and Garfunkel.'

She laughed.

'Which is which?'

'Buggered if I know. Can't tell them apart. They're brothers – Border terriers.'

Momentarily shocked by his colourful language, she said, 'I hope you don't mind – I borrowed these boots … I came to ask if I could have your wifi code.'

He looked down at her feet and broke into a smile – a lopsided grin, laughter lines crinkling around remarkably blue eyes, unusual in a man with such dark, almost black, hair.

'Course I don't mind. I wouldn't want you to survive a car crash only to break your ankles in those heels. Those are Kirsty's wellies. Sorry for abandoning you – I had to get the varnishing done this morning or the boat won't be ready for the client. I'm way behind schedule.'

～

He didn't tell her why he was so behind. That was nobody's business but his own.

It was Freya's birthday last Tuesday. They loved

birthdays, celebrations of all kinds. He had always enjoyed making a fuss of her. Squirrelled away in a box at the back of the wardrobe were all the cards she had kept over the years. There were quirky hand-drawn ones from Kirsty, cartoons from the dogs, friendly greetings from friends and relatives, and his own, reproductions of some her favourite artists – Dürer's intricate drawings, the French Impressionists, Picasso. She loved the abstract expressionists – Pollock – ('No, Cal, he didn't spill the paint!'), Rothko – ('No, a five year old couldn't do that. Look at the colour, the nuance, the way he builds it up, layer upon layer. It's like Mozart. Perfection') and her all time favourite, the artist she wished she could be, Diebenkorn. He set them up on every horizontal surface. Then he opened the bottle.

He didn't recall the first birthday after she died. Jack told him about it afterwards – the week he'd spent in oblivion. Like his own birthday, their wedding anniversary and all the other significant days that they used to celebrate together. The worst was the first anniversary of the day she died. The second had not been any easier.

He was careful never to let Kirsty see him in that state. Bad enough to lose her mother when she was only thirteen. So he made sure it was only one bottle this time – he'd had to go to Fort William to buy it, Laphroaig, his preferred malt – the local shopkeepers all knew better than to sell him alcohol. He'd still lost a couple of days. He could function after one bottle – dress himself, remember to feed the dogs and let them out – but he couldn't lay down a smooth coat of varnish when his hand was shaking too much to hold the brush.

Maybe next year, as a third set of anniversaries and birthdays came round, he'd be able to let them pass without the aid of whisky. And the self-loathing that came in its aftermath.

'I've never been in a boat shed before. Can I have a look?'

'Aye, sure.'

Annie followed him into the cavernous space.

It was the smell that hit her first – freshly sawn timber, rich and resinous, with a hint of the more chemical notes of varnish. She breathed in, savouring the unfamiliar aromas.

Her knowledge of boats was restricted to the channel ferry and the river bus, but she always thought that yachts looked very inviting when she saw them on trips to the coast, tied up in the marina or lying at anchor in the sheltered bays around the south of England.

He indicated two boats in the middle of the shed. 'These are Raasays. They're single-class racing boats. Named after the island across the sound. My uncle Alistair designed them. I took over the yard from him.'

To Annie's unpractised eye one of the boats looked completely finished, paint and varnish gleaming in the light pouring through skylights in the roof. The other was upside down, partly planked over a complex framework of ribs.

She ran her hands along the smooth side of the upright hull, admiring the way all the different parts fitted together in a display of fine craftsmanship.

A workbench ran along one wall, its surface littered with sections of joinery, shavings, tools. There was a curved plank clamped between two vices spaced out on the side of the bench.

'Is that one of the planks?' She hoped it wasn't a stupid question.

'Aye. It has to be shaped to lie snug up against the next one. See these marks here?' He indicated places where the piece was marked up in pencil. 'This tells me where I have to plane the timber down – it's trial and error until you get it just right.'

'Sounds a bit like my work. But probably more fun.'

One corner of the shed was enclosed behind a screen of dusty polythene sheeting.

'That's the glue and varnish room. It's always nice and cosy in there – my favourite place in the winter. I'd show you but the varnish is still wet. You have to keep the dust off it.'

'Hence the crime scene suit?'

'Aye, that's right. And bad varnish is a crime.'

'What makes it bad?'

'Runs, curtains, drips, bare patches, dust. You don't want to see any of those. What you try to get is a finish that's smooth as glass. Not easy.'

There were no crimes that she could see on the gleaming varnish of the finished boat.

He showed her the machines he used for shaping and finishing the raw timber, explaining what they were: a table saw, with a vertical rotating blade – 'that's for cutting long lengths into planks' – a bandsaw for cutting curves, a planer to smooth the surface down to the desired thickness.

'You have to be careful. Any one of these machines would have your fingers off before you even noticed.' Annie edged away.

Planks were stacked up here and there, more lying across beams suspended from the rafters. Racks of hand tools, drawings, clamps festooned the walls.

'My mother was a dressmaker. Those remind me of her paper patterns.' Annie indicated shapes made out of thin plywood hanging above the bench.

'That's exactly what they are. Boatbuilding patterns. Boatbuilding and dressmaking have a lot in common.'

It was a glorious muddle, but somehow it was possible to imagine the yachts he built, out on the water, lying peacefully on a mooring or sailing across the bay amongst the seals and the seabirds.

'This is amazing. How wonderful to be able to build something so beautiful – such incredibly satisfying work.'

'Aye, well, as my teacher at boatbuilding school used to say, it's 99 per cent perspiration to 1 percent inspiration. He wasn't far off, although personally I'd say he was generous on the inspiration side.'

Annie smiled, enjoying his dry humour. 'I think it's rather ... romantic.'

He chuckled, a low, throaty sound.

'I can assure you, it's anything but. Plenty of people dream about building their own boat – but then where do dust, glue, fumes, splinters, sore knees and an aching back ever feature in anybody's dreams? Never mind getting something wrong and having to start again, or the fu ... bloody thing sinking when you launch it – that happens more often than you'd think. Then there's every boatbuilder's worst nightmare – you put it in the water only to find that it sails like a dog. Nobody in their right mind builds boats.'

Annie laughed, noting his expression as he looked at the half-built hull.

'You don't look that mad to me. In fact, I think you love every minute of it!'

'Aye, well, maybe I do.' His face softened in a smile.

'What about that one?' She indicated the shrouded shape of a third boat, hard up against the wall opposite the bench. As far as Annie could see, it was much larger than the others, although only the keel, spotted with rust and flaking paint, was visible under a dusty cover.

Abruptly he turned away.

'In repair.' His tone invited no further discussion.

An awkward silence fell.

'I'm holding you up again. The wifi code ... ?'

'Sorry. Aye. You'll find the router on the desk in the study, second door on the left behind the kitchen. The password's on the back ... I'll finish off what I'm doing here ... '

∽

The dogs followed Annie back to the house, settling onto a mud-stained blanket on the utility room floor. She found her way through the kitchen into a corridor. In the dim light she identified the second door.

It only took a cursory glance to tell her this bright room wasn't the study. Wet black jeans and a jumper lay in a puddle of sunshine on the polished oak floorboards of an otherwise immaculate bedroom, dominated by a large iron bedstead on which a faded patchwork quilt was folded back to reveal snowy white linen, plump pillows and lace-trimmed cushions. On a dressing table under the window, an array of jars and bottles spoke of a woman who looked after her skin. A pale pink cashmere robe hung next to a man's fleece dressing-gown on the door through which she caught a glimpse of a walk-in shower in a stylish en suite. Feeling like an intruder in the tranquillity of someone else's private space, Annie quickly stepped back into the passageway, closing the door.

She checked the first door. A larder would be easily overlooked.

The third door opened into the study. Annie found the router half-hidden under a pile of paperwork, next to a photograph in a silver frame of a smiling woman with a heart-shaped face framed by cropped blonde hair. There was an attractive sparkle in the grey eyes that looked out of the picture with an expression of love and trust. This must be the woman with a taste for expensive toiletries. Callum's wife, probably. She turned the router round to reveal a card on the back.

Using her mobile, she photographed the string of characters that constituted the password – Cal2CMathieson1709*70. A terrible password, she thought, his name and date of birth, obviously. Which made him forty-five, the same age as Mark, only six years older than her – she'd have thought he was well into his fifties.

Unlike the calm oasis of the bedroom, the study had the cluttered feel of the main living area. Apart from the desk, the only other furniture comprised a comfortable chair draped in a plaid throw in a recess beside a floor-to-ceiling window overlooking the garden. A book lay open over the arm – Patrick O'Brien, *Master and Commander*. Along two walls overcrowded bookshelves sagged under the weight of novels, contemporary and classic, poetry, sailing books and boatbuilding manuals, row upon row of art books and catalogues, academic works on psychology and mental health. The kind of books cherished by serious readers and book-lovers.

On the third wall there were vinyl records, measurable in metres, along the bottom shelves, others crowded with CDs and DVDs. Never a great music lover, Annie recognised the names of only a handful of the thousands of artists represented here, but as a film fan she would happily spend a few days with this collection – classics and foreign language films alongside some of her own favourites – *The English Patient*, *Witness*, *Don't Look Now*.

There were framed photographs above the desk. Stepping closer, she read the family history in pictures. A young, smiling version of Callum, tall and very striking in a black kilt, with his new wife by his side, petite and pretty in cream lace, a crown of wild flowers in her spiky blonde hair. Her head barely reached his chest. A baby in a striped sleep suit lay kicking her legs in the air on a rug in front of the view Annie had admired earlier. She smiled at a series of pictures of the little girl – it was almost possible to hear the hysterical giggles as she gripped handfuls of her father's hair, sitting astride his shoulders. Annie would never have recognised him, laughing, eyes alight, so unlike the grim-faced man she'd just left behind in the boat shed. She was a leggy child, hand in hand with her mother, both wearing flowery dresses, thick socks and Doc Martens. In another the family sat close together on a sofa. Kirsty cradled two Border terrier puppies on her lap, smiling between her parents. Callum's arm rested along the back cushions, one large hand ruffling his wife's hair. Their faces were turned slightly towards each other. The love that flowed like a current between them was so clear it was almost visible.

Annie, childless only child of a single mother, felt a twist of envy.

In more recent pictures Kirsty was pictured alone, or with her father. They were very alike, tall and lean with thick black hair and clear blue eyes. Already a lovely girl, Callum's daughter would be a beautiful woman in a few years' time.

Back in the sitting room a battered guitar stood propped up against a keyboard. A sheet of heavily notated music was set up on the stand, together with a page of lyrics, written in neat italics. Annie went to look, just a quick glance before she stopped herself – she'd done enough prying into the lives of this family already.

Her own life sprang into focus as soon as she opened her inbox. Work and more work – she replied to various messages – arrangements for the event to launch the interim report, a note from the press officer listing her interviews. With a sinking heart she saw that she was to appear on the panel of *News Tonight* – alongside an as-yet unnamed government minister and a representative of the Care Commission. That might be tough.

Then a clicking sound announced a WhatsApp message. Mark. At last.

Chapter 5
West Highlands
March

'Had to go to Brussels – European Summit. Hope you're OK. Sorry about your aunt.'

Annie re-read the message, perplexed. Brussels? What about Westminster? That was Mark's patch – and his passion. Even by his standards the message was abrupt. And was that all the comfort he had to offer? Not even a miserable 'x' at the end?

'Well, thanks very much for your support.' Her tone dripped sarcasm.

'Who, me?'

Annie jumped. She hadn't heard Callum arrive, walking silently into the kitchen in his socks.

'Oh, sorry, of course not. No, my partner's had to go to Brussels … '

'Your partner. Why didn't he come with you?'

'Mark's so busy, always on a deadline. He's a political journalist. Looks like the paper's sent him to cover the European Summit.'

Callum looked blank. Annie could see he had no more idea what a European Summit was than he had about the Simpson Inquiry.

Her partner. He hated that word. Such a cold, businesslike term to describe a relationship that should be warm, full of life. Husband, boyfriend, lover – but not partner. Mark. He should be ashamed of himself. What kind of a man would let his 'partner' go through something as traumatic as the sudden death of her only relative, all on her own? He would never have …

'I came to see if you'd like some lunch. I expect you're hungry after your wee adventure this morning.' He busied himself clearing the worktop.

'That would be lovely, if it's not too much trouble.'

'Bacon roll?'

Her eyes seemed to light up.

'As long as you have ketchup. I can't eat a bacon roll without ketchup.'

'Ah. A woman after my own heart. Will this be enough?' He took a large bottle out of the fridge and set it down on the worktop. Annie smiled.

They sat up at the kitchen island, enjoying their lunch in companionable silence, looking out at the ever-changing light across the loch.

The sound of a heavy vehicle reversing down the drive announced the arrival of the breakdown truck. In a high-visibility jacket and heavy boots, Jim from the garage arrived to another chorus of frantic barking, gratefully accepting lunch before they got on the road. He devoured his bacon roll in a few large mouthfuls.

'Thanks, Cal. Appreciate that. But best no' hang around.'

Annie gathered up her bag and jacket. Reluctantly she bent to remove the wellies.

Jim caught sight of her shoes.

'Christ, ye're no' wearing them are ye? Ye'll never be able to get into the cab wi' them things on yer feet. In fact, now I look at you, thon skirt willna help either!'

Callum laughed.

'Tell you what, keep the boots and jumper on until you get to the airport. You'll be warmer.'

'Aye, too right, the heating's no' working. We'd better go, there's plenty time but ye never ken aboot the traffic round Inverness.'

They made their way out into the hallway. Jim went out to check the straps securing the Renault to the bed of the truck. Annie produced a business card from her bag. She offered it to Callum, with a smile.

'Let's do lunch again sometime. I know some of the best greasy spoons in London.'

Callum laughed as he took the card. He glanced at it briefly, setting it down on the hall table. In a drawer he found one of his own, a photograph of one of the boats under sail in the bay.

'In case you ever want a boat built ... ' Annie slipped it into a pocket in her bag.

'Thanks. And thank you for everything you've done – I don't know how I'd have managed without you.'

'Och, it was nothing. Anyone round here would have done the same. So sorry about Janet. Let me know about the funeral.'

Annie nodded. They shook hands.

She made her way out to the waiting truck, relieved when Callum turned back inside, leaving her to struggle up into the cab unobserved. It was a feat that required hitching up her skirt to the point of indecency. As she settled into her seat, he reappeared with a fleece blanket.

'You'll need this too. And these.' A bag of toffees and

two bottles of water followed.

'Goodness, you think of everything!'

'Aye, I have to. I have a teenage daughter. Bye now. Safe home. And hope it goes well tomorrow.'

'Bye. And thanks again.'

He closed the door of the cab and turned back inside. Jim put the truck in gear and reversed carefully out of the driveway to begin their journey to Inverness.

~

Callum watched until the truck was out of sight. Back inside, he tidied the kitchen and sat down at the dining table to start on some paperwork. He sorted through a few letters, but after a while realised the silence to which he was accustomed seemed more oppressive than usual. The solitude he had schooled himself to tolerate, even enjoy, since Kirsty had left for school in Edinburgh, now felt more like the loneliness that had almost brought him to his knees in the early months of his bereavement.

Annie's presence had stirred up memories he'd have preferred were left dormant. A woman's presence in the house, her scent, smile, laugh. Instinctively, he'd wanted to hold her when she started to cry, but it was so long since he had held a woman in his arms he no longer felt that he knew how.

A walk was what he needed. Since Freya's death he had developed strategies to deal with his mood swings. Exercise usually helped when he felt things turning dark.

He pulled on his boots and the warm padded jacket Annie had worn. Her lingering scent disturbed him momentarily. Putting the feeling out of his mind, he headed out along the shore with the dogs.

As always, he imagined Freya walking beside him, arm

linked through his, chatting inconsequentially about this and that. Today they would have talked about Annie. Freya would have been shocked about Janet – they had been great friends, despite the difference in their ages. A common love of art made the gap meaningless. Freya would have liked Annie too, but the therapist side of his late wife would have worried about her stress levels – how could those Londoners live at that pace? In the conversation with his late wife, he agreed.

An hour's brisk walk along the shore, dogs rushing around him chasing the ball, put him in a better frame of mind. He returned to the shed. There was a plank to finish.

The sigh of the plane cutting wafer-thin shavings off the surface of the mahogany, combined with the resinous scent of freshly cut timber, worked its usual hypnotic magic. He worked on until he was happy with the result, setting the plank up ready to attach to the hull in the morning. He checked the pieces he had varnished earlier – almost dry. Good – the boat would be ready for its new owner in Ullapool on Saturday.

By the time he returned to the house, darkness was falling. It occurred to him that the truck would have reached Inverness already. He switched on the kitchen lights.

A flash of colour caught his eye. Annie's scarf was draped over the back of a stool. Picking it up, he caught another faint hint of her perfume, something grown up – rich and spicy. It made him want to bury his face in the soft wool. He resisted, knowing the scent he breathed in would be Annie's, when what he longed for was Freya's floral fragrance, so elusive now that it had faded from the clothes that still hung in her side of the wardrobe.

Folding the scarf, he laid it on the hall table, ready to post next day. He put the business card on top.

'Don't let me forget, Freya, *mo gradh*.'

His voice echoed in the empty house.

In the mirror above the table he caught sight of his reflection. Even he could see what a mess he was. Freya would never have let him get away with it.

'Honestly, Cal, look at yourself – going around like a tramp. I'm not kissing you again until you shave that stubble off your face!' He could almost hear the laughter in her voice.

Telling himself he must book an appointment to have his hair cut and visit the dentist – momentarily he remembered Annie's straight white teeth – he decided to take Kirsty back to Edinburgh himself the following week and spend a couple of days with his brother and sister-in-law, where Kirsty lived during term time. Maybe he'd buy himself some new clothes.

Then he wondered if he could be bothered. Who cared?

He looked down, so he could no longer see the pain in his eyes. How long did it last, this terrible, aching sadness that was his constant companion, even two years after her death? Or the clenching in his stomach as sudden memories ambushed him, taking his breath away and leaving him weak and shaking. The feeling that his heart was an open wound. Would the agony of losing his wife ever leave him, or would it just gradually become more bearable?

Chapter 6
West Highlands
March

'Whit did ye make o' Cal Mathieson?' Jim asked. He turned to grin at her through his thick ginger beard.

Warm in her blanket, chewing a toffee, Annie thought for a moment.

'He was nice. Kind.'

He laughed.

'Aye, but whit did ye think o' him? Really?'

'I don't know, why do you ask? I'm sure you know him much better than me – you live here after all. It's a small place, you must all know each other.'

'Aye, but I've no' been here long and Cal – well, he keeps tae himself, ken. I've no' had a chance tae get tae know him yet.'

What did she think of him? He was quite attractive, in a scruffy kind of way – he obviously didn't take much care of himself. Although why would he, working alone in that draughty barn, building boats? She had liked his thick dark hair, and his bright blue eyes. Nice smile. Lovely voice, deep, an accent she still couldn't place, Scots but softer – islands maybe. A bit thin. She liked her men chunky, like Mark. Big men made her feel smaller.

'I thought maybe he seemed a bit ... lonely.'

'Aye, his wife died a couple o' years back – Freya. Such a shame, she was a very nice person, popular. Some kind of cancer, nasty. Looked efter her himsel', and the bairn, Kirsty. Always got her tae school on time every day. Must've been hard.'

How sad. He seemed much too young to have lost his wife. That explained the sense of an absent woman in the cottage, a feminine touch overlaid with the clutter of a man living alone.

'I'm surprised he let his daughter go to Edinburgh. You'd think he'd want her at home, under the circumstances.'

'She's very good at music. Nane o' the schools here could keep up wi' her, and she got some kind of a scholarship, I think. One of thae posh Edinburgh schools. No' that she needed it, no shortage o' money in that hoose!'

'Really? I wouldn't have thought there was much money in building boats.' Annie was surprised.

'Boatbuilding! Ye ken whit they say aboot that game – if ye want to make a small fortune as a boatbuilder ye'd best start wi' a large one!' He barked with laughter at his own wit. 'Naw – he made his money wi' the band.'

'The band? What band?'

'Christ, are ye telling me ye dinnae ken who he is? Have ye never heard o' Cal Mathieson? Guitarist wi' 2CM?'

'Goodness. No, I didn't know that's who he is. The band whose singer died? I never really liked them, couldn't have told you what they looked like.'

'Naw. I suppose ye're intae rappers an' that kinda stuff.'

Annie was used to it, the assumption that because she was mixed race she would conform to some ill-defined set of stereotypes. She'd learned long ago not to mind.

'No, not really. Classical is more to my taste. Opera, choral music … jazz, soul.'

'So ye'll no' ken much aboot 2CM – best Scottish band ever. Until Charlie died. Fuckin' tragic, that wis, the end o' them, right at the top o' their game. They were just making it in the States, playing the stadium gigs. Right up there wi' Simple Minds and U2, might even have been as big as the Boss himsel'!'

'The boss?'

'Springsteen! Bruuuce!'

'You were a 2CM fan.'

'The biggest. Must've seen them twenty or thirty times.' He began to sing one of their hit songs, "Island Nights".

'Going back to those Island lights
Back to those Island nights ... '

He was no singer. Thankfully, he broke off to add, 'Aye, bloody shame. Cal plays at the pub sometimes wi' a couple o' locals. Singer-songwriter stuff, ither people's songs, won't play the old songs fae the band. Nice enough, no' my kind o' thing. Sometimes Kirsty sings wi' him. Voice o' an angel, thon girl. Only fifteen, but she could gie Annie Lennox a run fur her money ony day o' the week. Even had a couple of guys frae a record company sniffin' around once. He gie'd them the bum's rush, though, he's no' having his lassie going tae London. No' like him an' Charlie, they ran away frae Stornoway when Cal wis just sixteen ... '

Suddenly Jim's story was interrupted as her phone sprang into life with a beep. They were within range of a mast. Texts and emails flooded in with a cacophony of trills and pings. It was open season again.

'Sorry, Jim. I'll have to deal with this lot.'

'Popular lady.'

For the best part of the next hour, oblivious to the mountainous Highland scenery, she worked her way through the messages as the signal came and went. There were documents to read, questions to answer – but nothing more from Mark.

Travelling up the side of Loch Ness, the heating began to work after all. Still wrapped in Callum's blanket, her eyelids began to droop in the warmth of the cab. Jim was eager for more gossip, but, uncomfortable talking about someone who'd been so kind to her, she excused herself and drifted off to sleep.

She woke as Jim swung the truck round the Longman roundabout on the edge of Inverness. Across the Moray Firth, the twinkling lights of the villages strung out along the south coast of the Black Isle were just visible in the failing daylight as a squall passed through on its way to the North Sea.

'Damn.'

Walking across the car park towards the terminal, the cold wind reminded her – she had left her scarf on the back of the stool in the kitchen of the man she now knew to be Cal Mathieson, former rock star.

Chapter 7
London
March

Annie's heart sank as she stepped out of the taxi. An absence of light in the first-floor windows told her that Mark wasn't back. Despite his message she had hoped he might be there to welcome her home with a big hug, a sympathetic ear and a large gin and tonic.

The flat was cold and unwelcoming. In the dim hallway light, Annie made her way to the bedroom, stepping out of her shoes with a sigh of relief. Kicking them under the bed, she promised herself she'd never wear them again. In stockinged feet she padded to the head of the bed to turn on the bedside lamp.

Mark wasn't just not home. He had gone altogether – it was clear as soon as she looked around, from the absence of all his usual clutter – books, keys, papers, sports bag. Stunned, she sank down on the bed.

Perhaps he'd just cleared up, to surprise her. She was always asking him to be a bit tidier, that was it. He'd cleaned up for her coming home.

The wardrobe was empty of his suits, shirts, shoes. Suitcase. It was as if he had never been there at all.

He must have left something, a note maybe? ...

She found it in the kitchen – spotlessly clean, no dirty coffee cups, unwashed cereal bowls, evidence of burned toast. A plain white envelope was propped up against the kettle, 'Annie' scrawled across it in Mark's untidy handwriting.

~

It wasn't unexpected. Part of her had always known their relationship would end, probably like this. She wasn't even sure she wanted to read what he had to say – what difference would it make, anyway? – a posting to another country, another woman, perhaps a combination of the two. This moment had always been going to come. She had known, because it was how all her relationships ended.

'You won't commit,' they always said.

'What about kids, a proper home, marriage?' they would say.

The truth was, she'd never felt able to take that step with any of the few men with whom she'd shared her life. They were right – she wouldn't commit. She was afraid. Basically, she didn't trust any of them, decent enough men though they were.

'It's your upbringing,' Mark used to tell her. 'It's damaged you. That crazy mother of yours. No father. You should do something, see a counsellor, get some help.'

'I'm perfectly fine,' she would reply. 'There's nothing wrong with me. I just like to keep my independence.'

'You're so cold, Annie.'

She'd heard that again and again. Much as she didn't want to admit it, at some level she knew it was true.

Dear Annie,
I'm sorry to do it this way – especially with all you're going through. A better man than me would be there supporting you, but I can't – not any more. I know that makes me a coward – I recognise that. I just couldn't do this to your face.

I'm truly sorry about your aunt – I know how much she meant to you. It's a shame that I never met her. Just another way in which you kept your family separate from me. I only ever shared a small part of your life.

It's not just that we've drifted apart, it's the Inquiry – the only thing you think about now, it's so all-consuming. I actually think it's colouring your view of all men – as if you see us all as abusers. Otherwise I think you'd have noticed how much I've been away, the late nights, weekends. Another woman would have said something, challenged it. Not you. It's as if you just don't see me at all any more. I sometimes wonder if you just wanted me for sex now and again – though hardly ever lately.

What you need to know is I've met someone. We're in love. I can see a future for us as a proper family. She edits a magazine, in Brussels. That's why I've been away so much. I asked for a transfer. It just came through – political correspondent on the Europe desk. In the end I thought it best just to go.

I know you'll hate me, but I also know you'll move on very quickly. Whatever we had, it wasn't love. I know the difference now.

Take care of yourself.
With regret, and many apologies,
Mark.

'You fucking, fucking bastard. How could you? You complete, total shit. Bastard.' There were not enough expletives in her vocabulary.

Self-pity overcame her. She sat down in the kitchen, his hateful note crumpled in her hands, and cried, overwhelmed with grief and rage. Alone, bereaved. In pain. Without even the kindness of a stranger for consolation.

∼

Annie's taxi drew up outside the hall off Parliament Square. The press were gathering outside, TV crews setting up, journalists and photographers milling around. Taking a moment to compose herself before stepping out of the cab, she put aside all thoughts of everything that had happened in the last three days. Today she had to focus.

Recognising a number of familiar faces in the crowd of media, she nodded a greeting as Joanie hurried her through to where the team were gathered ahead of the ten o'clock press conference. Interest was intense – Annie had noticed European as well as American TV stations represented outside, alongside the UK press. Abuse of vulnerable children was an issue around the globe, Simpson just one of many ongoing inquiries.

Moira caught up with her in the meeting room, gathering her up in a hug full of friendship and comfort. Annie struggled to keep her tears at bay, biting her lip.

'I'm terribly sorry about your aunt – and so grateful to you for coming back – I can't imagine how we'd have managed without you. The press office has a list of your interviews. You'll be doing some of the news bulletins – they're all going to lead with the report. Sorry about *News Tonight*, but I know you're a safe pair of hands and it won't be a hostile interview. Thank you again, Annie – for everything. You've dealt with it so well.'

'It doesn't always feel like it. I wonder if it helps not to have kids.' Moira was also childless. 'It must be unbearable to imagine your child in that situation ... '

'I've often thought about that myself.'

They agreed to meet later at Moira's apartment in Pimlico for a drink and a 'proper catch up', as Moira put it.

Watching Moira on the podium, impressively eloquent as always, Annie reflected on her own involvement in the Inquiry.

When Moira had approached her three years previously, asking her to become part of the team, she had hesitated. Moira was a rising star in the judiciary, the obvious choice for such an important role – a leading barrister, free from the potential conflicts of interest of more long-established colleagues, but with a track record that spoke of her integrity and strong work ethic. Impressed by Annie's concise briefing in a particularly harrowing domestic abuse case, Moira had invited her to lead the legal team.

'I don't think I'm qualified to handle anything on this scale. I'm just a solicitor.'

'Don't underestimate yourself. You'll be fine. Just do what you do best – examine the evidence, make the argument.'

It wasn't easy. Nothing could have prepared the Inquiry team for the harrowing stories they heard as they amassed statements from hundreds of adults who claimed they had been physically, mentally and often sexually abused as children in care homes. So often were the same groups of perpetrators implicated – doctors, teachers, the clergy and politicians, as well as council workers and care home staff, they could only conclude that an organised group was using positions of authority to gain access to vulnerable children.

The more she heard of the testimonies the greater Annie's sense of outrage grew. Many of the survivors grew up to be damaged individuals, desperate for their voices to be heard, their stories believed, yet all too often thwarted in their desire for justice as, time after time, the Director of Public Prosecutions ruled that there was insufficient evidence to bring a prosecution, or carefully built cases collapsed before they ever reached court. It had been a struggle to maintain a professional distance. Daily she reminded herself that the Inquiry gave her an opportunity to represent those affected to the best of her ability – it was all she could do. Be their champion.

Moira drew the press conference to a conclusion.

'As you are aware, a number of successful prosecutions have already been brought against care home staff. However, this is only the tip of the iceberg. The work of the Inquiry must go on. There are many more questions to be answered, both by individuals and by the organisations they represent. Further evidence will be heard and our recommendations will be drawn up, with all due care, as a matter of urgency. There is a compelling need now for transparency. Never again must we, as a society, allow a situation to develop where the least advantaged children in our communities become the victims of systematic and sustained abuse in what should be places of safety. Never again must this be allowed to happen while those in authority simply look the other way.'

Annie nodded her agreement.

It was late evening when Annie arrived at the *News Tonight* studio. She felt lightheaded, exhausted by the long day, the sleepless night and the events of the days that had gone before. The round of TV interviews had gone well – none of the news anchors had challenged the findings. Any criticism was aimed at those who had been found wanting in their duty of care. All that was required of her was to expand on aspects of the report. *News Tonight*, a programme she admired for its in-depth analysis of current affairs, would be tougher.

The presenter was well respected for her abrasive, no-nonsense style and for her modus operandi – to encourage a heated argument.

'First, for the government, we have Justin Brooke,

junior minister in the Home Office. We also welcome Samira Akbar, chief executive of the Care Commission, George Alexander, who represents the South-East Survivors group and Annie MacIntosh, head of the legal team on the Simpson Inquiry. Good evening to you all.'

She paused briefly, referring to her notes.

'Minister, Simpson blames this catalogue of failures on the severity of cuts that have led to inadequate scrutiny of the care system. What is your department doing to address this issue?'

Justin Brooke sat forward in his chair. He didn't reply to the question. Instead, he asked himself the question he wanted to answer, pointing out how much money his government spent on care, while stressing that Baroness Simpson's recommendations would be taken very seriously. In the ponderous tones of a politician with nothing of substance to offer, he insisted that lessons must be learned.

Samira Akbar jumped in.

'Does the minister not see the devastating effect that this government's cuts have on the care system? That it is the failure of his department, and the Treasury, to provide adequate funding that lies at the heart of this catastrophe? Does he not remember that time and time again, we in the Commission for Care issued stark warnings about the lack of proper scrutiny of the homes in question? Those warnings were wilfully ignored. That is why we insisted that a full inquiry be made into this scandal.'

Pleased to have deflected criticism from her own organisation, Samira sat back, allowing George Alexander into the debate. He spoke passionately about the need for the survivors' voices to be heard, their stories believed.

'While the report goes a long way, it still does not address the real issue here, which is that for years, the truth about what happened in these homes has been covered up by the very authorities who were supposed to protect the vulnerable kids they themselves put there.'

The presenter nodded at something her producer was saying in her earpiece.

'Ms MacIntosh, you have been involved in Simpson from the start. What, in your opinion, are the main changes that must come in the wake of the Inquiry's findings?'

Annie began by repeating the words and phrases she had been using all day, echoing what Moira had said at the press conference.

But then, quite suddenly, it was as if a switch was thrown in her brain. She was sick of mouthing the same words while nothing ever seemed to change. It wasn't good enough. She had to get beyond the well-worn phrases, the protocols. If anything was going to get across the seriousness of the situation they were faced with, much more needed to be said.

She turned to face full on to the camera.

'But I would also like to add to what I have been saying today. There is another lesson that must be learned here. In the wake of the Savile and Harris cases, we need to acknowledge and understand that perpetrators can get away with years or even decades of abuse by hiding in plain sight.'

'I really don't think that comparison stands up ... '

Ignoring Justin Brooke's attempt to interrupt, Annie carried on.

'Over the years, I have heard stories from those involved that have left me and my team shocked to the very core. Even to contemplate the systematic depravity the survivors were subjected to would make any one of us feel sick. Every single one of those whose testimony we have heard is damaged. Most are severely traumatised, robbed of the ability to lead normal productive lives. We have heard of repeated self-harm and suicide attempts. You will be shocked to learn that some victims – and I use that word deliberately, because that is what they were – have succeeded in taking their own lives.'

'That is absolutely tragic. Minister, would you like to … ' The presenter turned to Justin Brooke.

But Annie was determined to finish what she wanted to say. 'These people deserve justice.'

'I agree with Ms MacIntosh about … ' Samira Akbar tried to get back into the conversation.

Ignoring her, Annie carried on. She had a bombshell to drop and nothing was going to stop her now.

'New evidence has recently been uncovered, which points to an organised group using the care system as a way of gaining access to vulnerable children. We believe the activities of this group are known to the police. But many of those against whom allegations have been made are in positions of authority. I believe that is why no action has been taken against them. Some of the names mentioned are Members of Parliament. Indeed, Minister, a member of the Cabinet has been identified in multiple testimonies.'

An agitated Justin Brooke made as if to stand up. The presenter held up her hand, indicating he should wait.

'There must be a thorough investigation into all of the accused. I for one will fight with everything I have to make sure it happens. If the government and the police are guilty of covering up the facts to protect powerful individuals, that must be exposed.'

There. She'd said it. To her horror, tears of emotion were rolling down her cheeks. The minister leapt to his feet, face flushed with rage.

'How dare you imply that members of the government might be implicated in such heinous crimes! It is an outrage that you should use a public forum to make these unsubstantiated claims! I demand an apology!'

'I have nothing to apologise for,' Annie responded quietly, 'but if the statements I have heard time and time again are true, then perhaps, Minister, you do.'

George Alexander was moist around the eyes. 'Thank you, Ms MacIntosh.'

Half-listening to the producer screaming in her ear, the presenter quickly intervened to calm things down.

'Emotions are running very high with the publication of this report. Ms MacIntosh's serious allegation, if true, brings the matter right to the heart of government. Obviously the police must instigate a thorough investigation. Let us hope Baroness Simpson's recommendations are implemented in full and abuse in care homes becomes a thing of the past. *News Tonight* will continue to follow this story and bring you further insights as it develops. For now however, we have run out of time, so from all of us here in the studio, goodnight.'

It was only as a stunned assistant let her out of the studio that Annie recognised the full implications of what she had just done.

Justin Brooke caught up with her just outside the building, grabbing her by the arm. His face was puce with rage.

'How dare you make such accusations, and on national television! I can assure you, whatever your *report*–' he uttered the word with contempt '–may think it has discovered about members of the government, those false allegations will never see the light of day. Not whilst I have anything to do with it. I'll see you never work again – as if anyone who mattered would ever trust you after tonight's performance.'

'Take your hands off me,' Annie hissed, any attempt at dignity and professionalism abandoned. 'If you think I'm afraid of bullies like you, think again. I intend to make sure there's a full investigation of *everyone* who is accused and I don't give a damn if it means ruffling feathers all the way to the prime minister himself. The survivors of this … crime have given us a comprehensive list of names. And yours is one of them.'

She pulled free from his grasp.

Turning on her heel, she wrenched open the door of her waiting taxi. She watched his face as she was driven off towards Moira's flat. No longer puce, he was ashen.

Chapter 8
West Highlands
March

Callum was pleased. The new songs had gone down well, although he was the first to acknowledge that the audience, mostly friends and locals, were a soft target. It was one of the really enjoyable things about these gigs, the warmth and camaraderie of the crowd in the pub.

All a very long way from the stadium gigs of the past. Hustled on and off stage by minders, crowds of people backstage, the press, the record company, the hangers-on. The booze, the drugs, the women, the excess. Tour buses, hotel rooms. The paparazzi.

He didn't miss any of it. It was a part of his life he tried not to think about any more – it was safely in the past now – over twenty years since Charlie died.

Kirsty, home from school for a few days of revision before her exams, received a warm welcome. Her voice just seemed to get better and better, low and husky when she wanted, but with all the power of a rock singer when the song called for it.

The interest of an A&R man from London worried him. Kirsty was much too young, she should finish school before deciding whether to follow a career as a singer or a flautist, or neither. She was academically bright too, like her mother – university was an option. He wanted her to have choices – he wasn't keen for her to launch into a world which he knew all too well could eat you up and spit you out without a second thought.

Winding down with Jack and Steve after the gig, he was sitting at the bar nursing an orange juice when something on the TV in the corner caught his eye. It was Annie, on *News Tonight*. The contrast between the bedraggled woman he'd met the day before and the person on TV could not have been stronger. With her hair tamed in a tidy coil, beautifully dressed in a smart suit in a rich turquoise which set her skin aglow, she looked absolutely at home in a TV studio. Poised and articulate, she cut an imposing figure.

'Can you turn it up, Scott? Thanks.'

He excused himself and moved closer to hear the conversation. Kirsty came to stand by his side, puzzled.

'What are you watching, Cal?'

'Shhh.' He took her arm to stop her wandering away again.

On screen Annie turned and seemed to be looking straight at them as she launched her attack on the abusers of children in care homes, with the sensational accusation of a cover-up.

'Who's she? She's awesome! And so right! Those scumbags should be locked up!'

'That's Annie MacIntosh – Janet's niece. I said about her having the crash yesterday.'

Callum was stunned. As he had told Annie, he didn't follow the news, but he had made a point of reading up about the Simpson Inquiry that morning, realising that in his grief he had allowed his previous interest in current affairs to diminish. Full of admiration for Annie and what she was doing, even he could see she had just stepped way over a line.

Briefly he remembered her scarf on his hall table – he'd forgotten to post it today. It could wait. At the moment it was probably the last thing on her mind.

Chapter 9
London
March

Moira threw open the door and pulled Annie inside.

'What have you done, Annie? What possessed you? Years of work jeopardised. I thought we were all agreed how to handle this! You might have prejudiced the whole case. I just can't believe you could have been so stupid.'

'I'm so sorry. I don't know what happened, I just couldn't stop myself.' Annie slumped into a chair in the hallway, head in hands. Then she told Moira about her encounter with Justin Brooke outside the TV studios.

'Oh God. I need a drink.' Moira led the way into the sitting room. Ignoring the wine already open on the sideboard, she poured herself a large whisky, and another for Annie.

'OK, let's deal with this. I blame myself, Annie, I know what you've been through these last few days, on top of everything else, and then with Mark as well …'

'How do you know about Mark? I haven't told anyone!' She had barely taken it in herself.

'We had a drink the night you got the call about your aunt. He told me everything. He was desperate, Annie, didn't know what to do for the best. I begged him to wait until after the report came out, but he felt that once he'd confided in me, it was only right to tell you as soon as he could. Then I got a message to say he couldn't face it, he'd left a note. I was really shocked by that, what a ... anyway, I was waiting for you to tell me yourself. I should never have put you up for *News Tonight*. I should have done it myself. I am so sorry, it's me who let you down.'

Something about Moira's kindness, her understanding, reached into the part of herself that she had been trying and failing to protect for the past few days. Once again, Annie found herself in tears.

'I'll have to resign. I've made myself the story, I can't go on.'

'I can't afford to lose you, Annie. I'm not going to throw you to the wolves. I'll make some sort of statement tomorrow – pressure of work and your aunt's death ... you're taking some time off to arrange the funeral and so on. Take a break, get away. Lie low for a couple of weeks – longer if you need it.'

The rush of relief took her breath away. Annie simply nodded.

They finished the whisky, and the wine, and as the effects of the alcohol kicked in, so did their normal ease.

'I'm so sorry about Mark,' Moira said as she refilled Annie's glass. 'I thought you two were good together – it seemed to work well. To be honest, when Mark asked to meet me I thought it was to say he was going to ask you to marry him. I just don't get him going off like that.'

'Nor do I. There's hardly been any ... well, maybe he has been away from home a bit more than usual – working from his flat, he said. He seemed quite excited. I thought he was working on a big story ... obviously not. If he had asked ... ' Annie paused and considered what her response would have been to a proposal of marriage from Mark. 'Well, I suppose I'd have said yes. I thought it worked between us as well.' She paused, thoughtful. 'What about you, Moira? Why have you never married?'

'I'd have loved to marry, have kids and all that. But I just never seem to have time to meet anyone. I've done all the usual stuff, online dating, speed dating. Never worked for me – I seemed to end up with weirdos all the time.' She paused to take a sip from her glass. 'I have a theory about the men on those dating sites. They fall into three categories, in my experience. You get the ones who've never been married, some of them have never lived away from home – still living with Mum. You want to stay well away from them.'

She shuddered theatrically.

'Then you get the divorcees. I dated a few of them before I got wise. The ones who've been dumped – well, you soon get to understand why. And they're so angry, all they want to do is slag off the ex. The dumpers, seems to me that they're permanently in search of the impossible dream. Whoever they're with, there's always going to be someone better just around the corner.'

They were both laughing by now. Black humour raised Annie's spirits.

'Or there's the third kind – and if you're lucky you might just find one, but they're very, very rare.'

'Who are these precious creatures, then?' Annie topped up their wine glasses again, still snorting with mirth.

'The widowers. Decent men who know how to be husbands, men who've been married and lost wives so they know what they're missing. But they don't make it on to the dating sites because the minute the funeral's over every widow and divorcee for miles around is queueing up with casseroles and sympathy. You have to catch them fast!'

Overcome with giggles, they clinked glasses in a toast to 'the widowers'.

After midnight, Moira urged Annie to stay in the spare bedroom, but she declined, arriving back at her empty flat in the early hours exhausted, drunk and tearful. She fell into bed – and strangely, into the deepest sleep she'd known for some time.

∼

The note was still on the kitchen table. Annie read it again before she threw it into the recycling – it wasn't a souvenir she wanted to keep.

And there were bigger things to worry about.

As if it could be any worse, her fears about the fallout from the previous evening paled in comparison with the reality. Hungover, wretched, she sat in front of the TV and watched in horror as channel after channel replayed her outburst on *News Tonight*. There were interviews with Justin Brooke, puffed up to his fullest pompous extent, sounding off about her 'unsubstantiated accusations', her 'unprofessional behaviour', while supporting the impeccable credentials of his parliamentary and cabinet colleagues.

Even Moira's dismissive response to the journalists waiting outside the Inquiry office did little to make anything feel better.

'I can assure you that I have no intention of asking for Ms MacIntosh's resignation. Unfortunately the stress brought on by the revelations of the abuse of many hundreds of children, coupled with the sudden death of a close relative earlier this week, led to what can only be described as uncharacteristic behaviour. We would like to apologise for what Ms MacIntosh implied on *News Tonight* last night, and to assure the media and the public that her comments did not in any way reflect the position of the Inquiry. My report is conducted strictly according to the conditions and protocols placed upon it. We work closely with the police and the DPP – all new evidence is shared and subject to the most rigorous scrutiny. Charges are brought only after thorough investigations have been carried out. The work of the Inquiry continues – I expect to be able to make a full report in a year's time. In the meantime I wish to thank my team, including Ms MacIntosh, for its tireless work in very trying circumstances. Most of all I wish to thank those who have given evidence to the Inquiry for having the courage to come forward. Thank you.'

Annie put her head in her hands and contemplated for a moment what her future might hold. Perhaps she should resign. She had put Moira in the difficult position of having to put her own reputation on the line in her defence. But without her hard-won career, what else was there?

Then, with characteristic resilience, she shook herself free of this negative thinking. It was time to shrug off this mood, to tear herself away from her obsessive perusal of the news. What was done was done. Nothing could change it now. It seemed to her that she had two choices: wallow in self-pity or get a grip.

Squaring her shoulders, she chose the latter.

An hour later, the door buzzer sounded in her freshly cleaned flat. On the screen she could see a young man in the uniform of the local supermarket. She let him in, helping him put bags of groceries into the kitchen.

She then slipped him a decent tip, which he acknowledged with a delighted, 'Wow, thanks', but as he turned to leave, someone appeared in the hallway.

'Annie MacIntosh? Duncan Sweetland, *Daily Mail*. I wonder if I could ask you a few questions about … '

'Get out of my flat, please. Now.' She stepped forward to usher him back through the door, but the boy from the supermarket was there before her, shouting in the journalist's face.

'Leave the lady alone, you bastard. You heard her. She don't want your sort in here. Get out!'

With the delivery boy pushing ahead, she was able to get the door shut and bolted, with Duncan Sweetland of the *Daily Mail* on the outside. He tried a few more times, ringing her bell and shouting through the letter box until an angry neighbour threatened to call the police. Watching from the window, she saw him leave the building, joining a small gathering of reporters and photographers on the pavement. This was even worse than she had expected. But one thing was certain – she couldn't stay imprisoned in her own home until the next big story came along to distract the media.

She considered her options. Moira was right – she did need to get away.

As she stood, thinking it through, her phone pinged an incoming text. Reluctantly, she picked it up. Scrolling through dozens of unread messages, she noticed one from the funeral directors in Kyle of Lochalsh. She pressed the button to return the call.

'Good morning Ms MacIntosh, we just wanted to discuss the funeral arrangements with you.' The soft Highland voice spoke soothingly. 'We know it can be difficult when the relatives live so far away.'

Of course, everything would be much easier if she just went back up north to arrange the funeral. It would help distract her from her moment of madness while the dust settled.

It was late morning by the time she had packed and made all the necessary arrangements for a stay in the Highlands. Suitcases and groceries were loaded into the car in the underground car park. But there still remained the problem of getting past the press.

Her appearance was the easy part. Casual clothes, loose, shaggy hair, bright lipstick, sunglasses. It was a good start. Surveying the results in the mirror, she looked nothing like the woman on *News Tonight*. To a casual observer she would pass much more readily as a pop diva than a lawyer approaching her middle years.

However, Duncan Sweetland had seen her this morning. He wouldn't be so easily fooled. She needed a smokescreen and she knew just what would work. She selected a number on her phone.

'Di, I need to get away, I'm going up north to sort out Janet's funeral and take some time out. Could you and Henry create some kind of diversion for me so I can get out of the garage?'

'Leave it with me, darling!' Her neighbour Di sounded thrilled – an actress, this part would be right up her street.

A quick glance in the rear-view mirror as she drove away in her Mini made Annie smile for the first time that day.

Henry, Di's excitable cockapoo, was barking frantically as he wrapped his lead around Sweetland's legs, while the rest of the press pack looked on in amusement. Di, blonde and glamorous, in a top showing far more cleavage than was decent, made a great show of trying to get hold of the dog while deliberately making matters worse. None of the media had noticed the garage door opening – she was free. A long drive to Plockton lay ahead.

PART TWO

Chapter 10
London
September, previously

They should have been on stage by now.

Cal and Charlie paced the underground corridor while above them twelve thousand fans clapped and stamped their impatience, screaming for 2CM.

Dougie, the tour manager, appeared.

'OK boys, all ready.'

Minutes later, as the intro music reached a crescendo, a roar of welcome greeted Charlie as he exploded onto the stage, kilt and dreadlocks flying. In contrast, Callum strolled calmly in his wake to take his place in front of the drummer. He waited, the band motionless as the fans had come to expect, until silence fell. Then he strummed the opening chords of "Island Nights".

The audience went wild.

Three hours later the house lights went up. The crowd slowly began to disperse as the band made their way through the low-ceilinged concrete corridors of the stadium to the dressing room. Charlie was livid.

'Fuck's sake, Cal, could ye no hae just done one more. They were gagging fer it, did ye no hear them? Is it Jo? I've telt ye, forget about her. There's plenty mair fish in the sea!'

'Fuck off, Charlie, you know as well as I do we were under-rehearsed. Much better to go out on a high than give them a fucked-up final encore. And no – it's nothing to do with Jo.'

Charlie was always revved-up after a gig – they all were – and usually looking for a fight, something to keep the adrenaline going before the inevitable post-concert plunge. Cal was his target tonight, for refusing to play a fourth encore.

In his role as singer, Charlie saw himself as leader of the band. He had been the ringleader when they ran away from home. 2CM, the band that had grown out of that dramatic beginning, was the name they eventually settled on after days of agonising over lists of possible names scribbled on scraps of paper, scored out, as they tried to settle on the right one. In the end, with a gig looming, Charlie suggested 2CM – their initials, Callum Mathieson, Charlie MacLean.

'Christ, you can't be serious!'

'Och, Cal, whit's wrang wi' it? It's modern, nane o' the teuchter rubbish you like – I mean, fuck's sake – Heskyr?' It was Callum's preferred name, after a lighthouse in the wild waters of the Minch. 'Whit does that tell anyone aboot us? Even if they could spell it. We're no yin o' thae Celtic bands, we're a proper rock band. Think UB40, U2. That's whit bands are called these days.'

Callum threw his hands up in surrender. 2CM. It had to be better than P45.

Now the two boys from Stornoway stood poised to make a breakthrough with their growing talent for writing and performing great rock and roll. They were six weeks into a European tour, ending in London, before heading out to the States to play New York and LA.

They had worked hard enough for it – 'ten years' hard labour', Charlie liked to say. 'Ye'd get less for murder.' Night after night playing pubs and halls, dropping in and out of one band after another until eventually they began to make enough money to form their own, always together, never letting go of the belief they had what it took to make it. Progress was slow, but after a couple of years the press began to take notice – so too had an enthusiastic Scottish A&R man. They were signed by one of the major record companies. Touring to promote their third and most successful album, *Go*, they were on the cusp of doing what every British rock band wanted most – breaking into the notoriously tricky American market.

They both had a quick shower and change of clothes before joining the party. The green room was another low-ceilinged concrete box. Apart from some sagging sofas that may once have been green, the only furniture in the room consisted of a table groaning under the weight of dozens of bottles – champagne, wine, beer, whisky. Charlie poured himself a large malt. Several more went down in quick succession while he exchanged banter with the A&R men, always the coolest in the record company, the ones who got closest to the artists.

More people arrived to fill the claustrophobic space – press, record company executives with overdressed, awkward wives, hangers-on of various persuasions and the best-looking of the women who had gone backstage at the first encore, ready to meet the boys.

'Aye, they canna resist a man in a kilt!'

Charlie spun one of the girls into a laughing embrace, kilt flying up to reveal nothing underneath.

'Oh here we go, the full Jim Morrison,' Callum sighed. The red-haired girl next to him laughed.

'What about you, Callum? Why do you never wear a kilt?'

Callum refused to be seen in a kilt, on stage anyway. Special occasions, and only north of the border, was his unspoken rule. Nor would he adopt the inauthentic accent Charlie had been cultivating ever since they first went to

Glasgow. Callum was perfectly happy with his own island voice and the clear pronunciation common in the Outer Hebrides, even if he was accused of being posh by the other members of the band and crew. In any case, as he'd discovered early on, his accent was just as much of a turn-on for the women as Charlie's kilt.

'I haven't got the legs for it.' He handed her a glass of champagne, and popped open a can of beer for himself. 'What's your name?'

'Amanda.'

'Need a piss, Amanda. Don't go away.'

Out of the suffocating green room he checked his pager – no new message, just the one she'd sent earlier – 'I can't. You know why.'

He let out a long sigh of resignation. It was exactly what he'd expected. His message, innocent enough, had read, 'Can we meet after the gig tonight?' – but he'd known the answer even as he sent it. Same as always. Still, hope, as someone once said, springs eternal.

Jo. She was around, of course. There was no way she could avoid it when they played Wembley. Doing the job the record company paid her for – looking after the journalists, arranging interviews, photos. Handling press and PR for 2CM.

Tonight, as every night, she kept her distance. The briefest glimpse at the other end of a corridor during the interval was all he'd seen of her – even after so many months, his heart leapt into his throat – seeing her dark bobbed hair, fashionable black trouser suit, white shirt. And that bright slash of red lipstick – her trademark. Shock felt like a punch in his stomach as their eyes met, then she was gone.

Amanda it was, then. A poor substitute, but better than another lonely night in another lonely hotel room. Especially on his birthday.

With a heavy heart he returned to the party. Amanda was waiting anxiously by the bar, exactly where he'd left her. Pretty. Nice clothes, posh voice. Better than many, since his one and only night with Jo.

Why? he asked himself. Why, of all the girls he could have had, had he fallen in love with the one who wasn't available? Jo, ten years older, married, with two kids. He knew she was in love with him, too. Even now, ten months later, the look in her eyes every time they saw each other betrayed her. It was the same look he felt in his own, full of love, longing, desire. Pain. But how could he expect her to leave her family for a twenty-four year old guitarist with no home, no stability, nothing to offer but his love?

Amanda reattached herself, taking his arm to let the other groupies know who was going back to the hotel with Cal Mathieson tonight. He pasted on a smile, tucking a stray lock of hair behind her ear, feeling her shiver of pleasure as his fingers lingered briefly on her cheek.

∽

Charlie was over the top even by his high standards – very drunk, with two women in tow. It was hard to tell which one had the bigger bust, although both exceeded Charlie's minimum requirement – DD.

'Charlie's on form tonight.' Ed Burrell, the band's manager, sidled up beside Callum. Burrell was well known as a heavyweight in the industry – they were lucky to be part of his stable.

'Aye, I can't decide whether to try and bring him down for a few hours or just leave him up there until the next gig.' Callum looked over at his bandmate, wrapped around the two skimpily dressed girls, eyes barely focused.

Burrell laughed. Leaving Callum to talk to the

managing director of the record company and his wife, he sought out the tour manager. Dougie was legendary – built like a bear with slicked-back dark hair, he was famous for an impressive collection of tour T-shirts, reflecting the hundreds of bands he'd worked with. He was a born fixer. Ed took him aside and murmured in his ear. Dougie nodded.

A short while later Callum was interrupted in the process of getting more familiar with Amanda.

'Here, give Charlie one of these. It'll chill him out. Just one, mind.' Dougie tucked a small plastic bag into the pocket of Callum's shirt.

'What is it?'

'Och, just some Es. They'll no' do any harm.'

The party was winding down. The managing director and his tedious wife went home to leafy suburbia at last, leaving just the usual suspects hanging around for the free booze and whatever other leftovers they could get their hands on.

Charlie, Callum and the three women shared a limo back to the hotel. That was how it was these days – limos, suites, all the trappings. The third album outsold the first two by three to one – success in anyone's terms. He knew his songs were a large part of the reason – big, bluesy ballads, guitar solos that screamed and sobbed his longing for the woman he loved. They were the darlings of the record company, the most successful band on their roster.

Callum just wished it all felt better. Or even as if it meant something.

~

In the lift at the luxury hotel near the concert venue, Charlie disengaged from his companions to drape himself over Callum.

'Dougie said ye'd got something for me,' he whispered in Callum's ear.

'Aye, but do you not think you've maybe had enough?'

'Fuck off, Cal! This is me, Charlie. I've never had enough!'

Callum was reluctant to give Charlie the whole packet. He hadn't seen exactly how many pills it contained but he estimated three or four. Callum had drunk a lot himself but he knew Charlie would have had a great deal more. He didn't want to take any chances. There was wild, and then there was Charlie. Never a great believer in any kind of self-discipline, lately his bandmate seemed to be out of control most of the time.

'I'll bring you it later in your room. I think they sometimes have cameras in these lifts.'

'Aye, true enough. Cannae be too careful, wi' going tae the US an' that.' Charlie mimed a suspicious look up at the ceiling of the lift, where a pinpoint of red light betrayed the presence of a small camera discreetly tucked into one corner.

'Good thinking, pal.'

～

There was a loud banging on the door. Callum and Amanda were enjoying a long kiss.

'Ye said ye'd bring it tae me!' Charlie hissed, shoving Callum back into the room and pulling the door closed behind him. 'Oh hello, darlin'.' Amanda sat up naked on the bed. 'I'll be coming for ye after I've seen tae thae ither lassies next door.'

'No, you'll not. She's spoken for.'

Callum found his shirt in the pile of clothing on the floor. He turned away as he extracted the bag of pills, taking out one, which he dropped into Charlie's waiting hand.

'Is that it?'

'That's your lot. Now fuck off.'

Perhaps if he had known those were the last words he would ever say to his childhood friend, Callum might have chosen better.

'Aye, I'm gone. Thanks, pal.'

He took another couple of the pills, downed one himself and offered the other to Amanda.

'What are they?' she asked.

'Ecstasy. Let's get loved up.' Amanda giggled and swallowed the pill.

Chapter 11
London
September, previously

The hammering on the door seemed to go on and on. Callum dragged himself awake through layers of sleep, worn out by the gig, the drink and the energetic sex of the previous night.

'Fuck off, Charlie, leave me alone.' He assumed Charlie would be looking for more pills.

Out in the corridor someone shouted his name.

'Mr Mathieson! Open the door, please.'

Callum hauled himself out of bed, wrapping a towel around his waist. Amanda groaned and turned over with a long sigh, burrowing deeper into the blankets.

Released, the door slammed open. Two uniformed police officers burst in, followed by Ed. His grim expression spoke of serious trouble.

'Callum Mathieson?'

A loud roaring seemed to fill his head. Callum sank down on the bed as the policeman continued to talk incomprehensibly.

'What's happened? What do you want? Why don't you bugger off and let me sleep?'

Ed stepped forward and sat down beside Callum. He laid his hand on Callum's arm, with a gentle squeeze.

'Cal, Charlie's dead. We don't know why … what's happened. I'm sorry, Cal … '

'Dead? Charlie ... dead? No, I've just seen him. He can't be ... '

Woken by the commotion, Amanda began weeping loudly. One of the officers closed the door against the gathering crowd of curious hotel guests and staff in the corridor, while the other began gathering up Callum's clothes from the floor.

'Get dressed, Mr Mathieson. We're taking you in for questioning. You too, Miss.'

As he picked up Callum's shirt, the pack of pills fell out of the pocket. There was still one left. Ostentatiously the policeman pulled on a pair of surgical gloves before he picked it up and slipped it into an evidence bag. Callum's heart raced.

'Fuck's sake! Will somebody just tell me what's happening, please?' His voice shook. Not yet fully awake, head thumping, he was barely able to take in what was being said.

'Charles MacLean died in his room this morning. We have reason to believe that sometime around 2am, Mr MacLean visited you in this room and returned with a pill matching the description of the one I have just found in your shirt pocket, which he took in the bathroom of his suite, witnessed by a Ms Wilson. She tells us that Mr MacLean was suddenly taken ill at around 4.30, shortly after which he collapsed. She called an ambulance while her friend Ms Andrews attempted CPR. The ambulance arrived at 4.45. All further attempts at resuscitation failed. He was pronounced dead at 5.30am. I am therefore taking you in for questioning on suspicion of supplying an illegal substance which may have caused the death of Mr MacLean.'

'No! Christ, no ... Charlie? No.'

The policeman read him his rights. Callum barely heard, mumbled his response.

Ed spoke up.

'As Mr Mathieson's manager I will be organising his legal representation. He'll have nothing to say until his solicitor is present. Nothing.' He looked hard at Callum.

Someone had tipped off the press. As Callum and Amanda were hustled out of the hotel into the waiting police car, the paparazzi were waiting. Callum was snapped again and again as reporters shouted incomprehensible questions. Everything Jo had taught the band about always being conscious of the paparazzi was forgotten. All he could think about was Charlie – dead – and that he might be responsible.

The solicitor was waiting at the police station. He insisted on being allowed some time to talk to Callum in private. They were given five minutes.

'OK, here's how it is. I don't know what happened and I don't want to know, but you're potentially in a lot of trouble. If this goes the wrong way the best you can hope for is supply, but the worst case scenario is they charge you with manslaughter.'

'Oh Christ ... '

'Right now they have nothing. They don't know what Charlie took or what the actual cause of death might be. Until they do they have no reason to hold you. They'll try to remand you on suspicion but I think I can deal with that. However, they found something in your pocket and they'll be checking on it right now so we don't have long. Just keep quiet and let me do my job, OK?'

Callum nodded, numb, not sure he really understood what had been said, or if he even cared what happened to him. All he wanted was to be left alone as he tried to process a truth that his mind refused to accept.

The interview was short. As good as his word, the solicitor challenged the police to show sufficient evidence for charging his client, or let him go. Switching to the attack, he made an issue of Callum's public humiliation, being taken out of the hotel in front of the press, accusing the police themselves of being the source of the tip-off. He would be making a formal complaint.

Throughout, Callum remained silent, eyes unfocused.

They were allowed to go, with assurances that he would stay close by until he was contacted again. Amanda left with them. In the car she tried to comfort him, taking his hand. He shook her off.

The only woman he wanted was Jo.

Back at the hotel it began to sink in properly, as once again Ed took over.

'I've informed the promoter and the agent. The rest of the tour is cancelled, but we have to limit the damage here as much as we can.'

'Has anyone spoken to Charlie's mum and dad? I should ... ' It was his first properly coherent thought since the police had arrived in his room.

'Yes, you should. The police will be on their way but I'm sure they'd want to hear it from you.'

Callum thought of all the pain and heartache the two of them had caused both families when they ran away from home. It was nothing compared to the damage he was about to do. He wasn't at all sure he had the courage. It would be the hardest thing he had ever done in his life. As he dialled the number he imagined George and Nancy, in the bungalow Charlie had bought them, high above Stornoway looking out over the cold grey waters of the Minch.

Charlie's mother answered, surprise evident in her tone. She didn't know yet.

'It's bad news, Nancy. I'm so sorry. It's Charlie ... Charlie's dead, Nancy, I ... ' He couldn't say any more. His own sobs were nothing to the howl of pain coming from the phone.

'Callum?' George came on the line. 'Just tell me, Callum, what's happened?' Callum could hear the doorbell ringing in the background. He pictured the uniformed police at the door, managing to control his voice long enough to say, 'Answer the door, George. It'll be the police. They can tell you more.'

The line was disconnected. Callum sat down heavily on the bed. Head in hands, he broke down and wept for his friend, for the family, for all the hurt and grief to come. He was barely aware of Amanda quietly gathering up her belongings and leaving.

There was no arrest, there would be no charges. Charlie had died of a heart attack. There was a congenital weakness – it could have happened at any time, but the quantity of alcohol in his bloodstream had almost certainly hastened his death. The tests had also found traces of a herbal sleeping pill present in his blood, which matched the pill found in Callum's pocket. It was a popular remedy readily available in any pharmacy and would not have contributed in any way.

Ed collapsed into an armchair, weak with relief. But for Callum, there was no consolation. Nothing changed the fact that at only twenty-seven, Charlie, his best friend, his soul-mate, was dead.

Chapter 12
Isle of Lewis
October, previously

At the family home in Stornoway the night before the funeral, Callum sat motionless in a chair opposite his sister Mhairi, a GP on Mull. She had often expressed her concern about Callum living the life he did, at a time when HIV was seen as a death sentence and rogue drugs were an ever-present risk, trying to impress on him the need to keep himself safe.

'So, Cal, tell me again – I need to get this straight in my head. The roadie put some pills in your pocket. You thought they were ecstasy but didn't really have any idea. You gave one to Charlie and this groupie you were with, and then you took one yourself? Is that right?'

'I know how it must sound to you, Mhairi – it's all fucked-up, you're right. But you have to trust the people around you. Ed told Dougie to give us something harmless so we'd rest. It'd happened before –'

'Are you completely out of your tiny mind, Cal? Just how dumb is it to take anything without really knowing what you're taking? All three of you could've died, not just Charlie. I know, it was his heart, it wasn't the sleeping pill. But still, just stick anything down your neck, is that how it is in that kind of life? I really thought you were smarter than that –'

'It's hard to come down after a gig, you're so high on

the adrenaline ... And I knew it wasn't ecstasy, because Amanda and I just fell asleep after–'

'... After casual sex with a complete stranger. For God's sake, Cal! Do you really care so little about yourself, never mind anyone else?'

Mhairi was rigid with anger.

'I know, you're right. I'll never forgive myself. In my head I know I didn't kill Charlie but I might have done, just as easily. Nancy and George are blaming me. They're not buying the heart thing at all – think it's some kind of a cover-up. Mum and Dad are treating me like a stranger. Fuck knows, I feel like a fucking stranger ... I don't even know who I am any more.'

'Oh, Cal ... '

Hot tears of grief poured down his face. Mhairi softened and took him into her arms, but there was nothing she or anyone else could do to comfort him.

Hundreds of people came to the funeral. There was a media circus, tabloid journalists mingling with the more serious music contingent, united in the bars around town. The eve of the funeral was like a carnival, fans and friends determined to give Charlie a hero's send-off. The piles of flowers around the door of the pub where they had played their first gig made Callum feel physically sick, as did the book of remembrance and all the rubbish being spouted by the locals who claimed to have known him.

He stayed home with his new best friend – Laphroaig single malt whisky.

The Church of Scotland minister, well known for his fire-and-brimstone sermons, was to preside, with only a short reading and a poem by Charlie's younger brothers.

It was as if he'd never had a life off the island, never been an international rock star. Devastated that he'd been denied the chance to say a proper farewell, Callum thought seriously about not going, but realised he wouldn't be able to forgive himself if he didn't – he owed it to Charlie to be there. He comforted himself by writing long letters telling Charlie all the things he'd never have said but felt all the same – that he loved him as a brother, just as much as he loved his birth brother, Dugald. That the times they'd had together would always be precious memories. That he was sorry for always being such a grumpy bastard in the mornings. That he wished he'd had a chance to say goodbye. That he'd give everything he had to turn back the clock and for his best friend to still be alive.

A slicing north-easterly wind blew off the Minch, straight into the churchyard, further chilling the congregation after an hour in the freezing kirk. It was another half-hour before Charlie was lowered into his grave, leaving the mourners free to retreat to the welcome warmth of the hotel by the harbour. Callum took some moments alone by the grave when everyone else had left, barely aware of the photographers lurking amongst the gravestones, without the decency to allow him even these precious moments to say his own, private farewell.

At the hotel he was reminded of the last time he had been in a press of bodies all trying to get to the bar – at the post-gig party on the night of Charlie's death. Dougie crossed the room and pulled him into a bear hug, tears in his eyes. Callum introduced him to Mhairi, leaving her to read the riot act about the dangers of casual drug use.

Then Jo was there, by his side.

'I'm so sorry, Cal. I can hardly imagine how hard this is for you. I wish I could ... '

He longed to take her hand and lead her away, somewhere quiet they could be alone together. If anyone could comfort him, it was Jo, hand on his arm, her touch burning through his clothes straight into his skin. But it was too late. If they'd ever had a chance together, it was long gone. Unable to look her in the eye, he merely nodded, swallowing his whisky in one gulp, turning away to find the remaining members of the band.

Danny and Pete, the drummer and bass player, were also hitting the whisky hard. Their future looked uncertain. Ed joined them.

'We need to talk, boys. There are contractual issues to sort out before we start to look for a new lead singer, but I'm sure if we get right onto it we can still salvage the tour of the States.'

'A new singer? The States? What the fuck are you on about? You can't be serious. Do you really think we can just carry on as if nothing's changed? 2CM, Charlie MacLean, Cal Mathieson, remember? Maybe it was a crap name but it was us, Charlie and me, our initials. Our songs. Charlie can't be replaced just like he was any other singer, he was half the band!'

Callum could barely believe Ed could be so crass as to bring this up now, Charlie barely laid in the ground.

'Cal, get real. Did The Who give up after Keith? Did AC/DC stop after Bon Scott died? No – this is a great band with a great future. Charlie would want you to carry on.'

'Do not fucking tell me what Charlie would want! Charlie would want not to be dead, that's what Charlie would want! Anyway, what the fuck are you suggesting, we find another singer called Charlie MacLean, we change the name of the fucking band? How in the name of fuck do you think this is going to work?'

Shaking with rage, fists clenched by his sides, Callum struggled to control the urge to hit someone, anyone, very hard.

Danny was starting to look thoroughly uncomfortable, but undeterred, Pete chipped in.

'There's this guy we used to play with, great voice, knows lots of the repertoire, We all think he'd be fantastic –'

' – Christ, you fuckers have already been talking about this! What, you thought you'd just land it on me, thought I'd just say fine, whatever you want? My God, I don't fucking believe this.' He shook his head, unable to understand how they could be so insensitive.

'Listen, you bastards, there is no band without Charlie, there is no tour. Charlie's gone. I don't want any more to do with it. As far as I'm concerned you can all go fuck yourselves, and if you think you can use the band name, think again. Just try it and I'll fucking sue the lot of you!'

He turned on his heel and stormed out of the hotel, tears blurring his vision. How could they be so unfeeling – not even to allow him time to grieve before they started putting pressure on him to carry on? What kind of people were they, that he'd been mixing with for all these years? What was wrong with him, that he'd never seen it?

Callum didn't stop until he stood at the end of the pier, oblivious to the bustle around him as the ferry arrived. A chapter of his life was over – he vowed to himself that he would never be part of that world again.

Chapter 13
Isle of Lewis
February, previously

'So there you are, Charlie. It's all a right fuck-up, as usual, but at least you're well out of it. There's nothing quite like death to boost a band's popularity, I'll give you that. I'm fucking loaded – the royalties just keep coming. But I wish Ed'd leave me alone. It was always us, the two of us. Our songs, our music. I'm not doing it without you.'

As he stood up from Charlie's graveside, Callum staggered, grabbing on to the new black marble headstone as he caught his balance.

Unsteadily, he meandered down to the gate of the churchyard. The half-bottle in his jacket pocket bumped against his hip. He paused for a mouthful of whisky before making his way back into town. The ferry had just arrived, passengers pouring out into the narrow streets. Callum threaded his way through the crowds, unseeing, barely aware of people stepping out of his way.

He had no plans for the day – no plans any day, no plans at all. Since his parents had asked him to leave three months ago, in despair at his foul-mouthed rants, his heavy drinking and his refusal to accept any kind of help, he spent his days idling around town, or mindless in front of the TV in his sparsely furnished flat.

His only routine was a visit to Charlie's grave every day. One by one, even the most sympathetic of his old school friends had fallen away. He knew he had become a figure of pity and derision. In a community used to hardship, with harsh weather, employment prospects and opportunities limited by the remoteness of the island, Callum was someone who had it much better than most – he was, or had been, a success beyond most people's wildest dreams. He was famous, he was wealthy, he was young, fit, strong – or had been before he started to drink. Not any more.

He couldn't blame his parents – they'd done everything they could. Even Charlie's parents had tried to help in the end. Tragic enough, that their own son had gone. They couldn't bear to see his best friend trying to drink himself to death too. But nothing anyone said or did made any difference. Not even Ed coming up from London to try and talk sense to him, get him into rehab and get his life back together. As the months passed, he was left to his own devices. Which suited him just fine.

Betty's was a café just off the Main Street. He went there most days. The staff tolerated him, just about. The owner was kind – she took it on herself to make sure he at least ate something on the six days a week the café was open. Sundays he didn't eat at all.

'Hello, Cal. How are you today?'

He took his usual seat in a quiet corner, tucked away at the back of the café.

'Aye, no' so bad.' It was his usual answer.

'I've some good lentil soup today. Will you have a bacon roll with that?'

'Just the soup. Thanks.' Callum sat, studying the photograph on the wall in front of him, a scene of fishing boats unloading their catch sometime in the last century. Sometimes he kept his brain occupied trying to count the fish, but never got much beyond twenty.

'I'm off now, Cal. Going to Glasgow to do a bit of

shopping, so you won't see me for a few days. My daughter Freya will be covering for me though, she'll take care of you. You'll remember her from school, I expect.'

He looked up into Betty's kind face and nodded, although he hadn't really heard what she'd said.

∼

'Callum? Cal, is that you? What's happened to you?'

The words took some time to penetrate his consciousness. He wasn't used to being spoken to, nor to hearing what sounded like concern directed towards him. Slowly he looked up.

The young woman was petite, pretty with an elfin face, freckled skin and dove-grey eyes. Her cropped blonde hair stuck up in random spikes as if her toilette constituted no more than running her fingers though it. He watched as her floral dress and chunky cardigan were engulfed under a striped apron made for a large butcher – its hem skimmed the tops of her Doc Martens as she wrapped the strings twice around her waist, tying them in a bow.

When he failed to answer, she pulled out the chair opposite him and sat down.

'I'm Freya, remember? We were in the same class at school. And I used to crew for you in the sailing club. Are you OK, Cal? Is there anything I can get you?'

Callum shook his head.

She continued to look into his face, her worried frown deepening as, to his acute embarrassment, he felt tears welling up in his eyes. Why could she not just leave him alone like everyone else around here?

'Oh Cal, you poor thing. This must be so hard for you – losing Charlie. It's not just that he was your best friend. You two were inseparable. It must feel as if you've lost part of yourself.'

A tear spilled over and tracked down his face. He felt it dribble into the rough stubble he could rarely be bothered to shave. Fuck. He wasn't going to start blubbing, was he? Just because for the first time someone gave words to the terrible emptiness that he felt? But it was too late. More tears followed.

Briefly she laid a small hand over his. His skin burned under the sudden contact. It had been a very long time since he'd known the comfort of human touch. He almost snatched his hand away. But as if she read his thoughts she released her grip with a gentle squeeze. She passed him a clean napkin.

'I'll get you a cup of tea. I'll be closing soon. Then we can talk. If you'd like.'

She stood up, clearing the remains of his lunch onto a tray.

At last Callum found his voice. It was low and gruff.

'Thanks, Freya. Aye, I would like that.'

With a quick smile she was gone, clearing tables, taking payment, chatting and laughing with the other diners, making time to bring him the promised tea, setting it in front of him with another sweet smile.

For the first time, Callum felt as if someone understood what he was going through.

Once he started talking, it was as if the floodgates opened. The words poured out – the pain, the guilt, the feeling that everything around him had turned to ashes, leaving him stalled and helpless, with no idea what to do about it. For the first time he admitted to himself, as much as to Freya, that he drank to forget, and gain a few hours of unconsciousness at night.

Freya listened carefully, offering occasional words of encouragement.

Eventually he'd said it all. There was nothing left to add.

Freya sat in silence for a few moments, looking down at the table with a thoughtful expression.

'It was never your fault, Cal. Charlie was responsible for his own behaviour – everyone is. And – well, I think he'd be furious if he could see you now, in this state. It's terrible, what happened, but are you planning on drinking yourself to death as well? Do you really want to join him? Imagine what he'd say about that. He'd say, "For fuck's sake, Cal, get a grip." And look at it this way – he might have been only twenty-seven, but so were Jimi Hendrix, Janis Joplin and Jim Morrison. "I'm up here with the stars!" That's what he'd say.'

Callum felt his eyes open wide with astonishment. Freya's finger traced a pattern on the tabletop, as if she felt embarrassed about her strange outburst.

'Sorry … it's just, after his heart attack, I read something about other musicians who died … all the same age. They call it the "27 club".'

Bizarrely, he felt a smile finding its way to his lips.

'I never knew. Aye, he would've liked that. Charlie and Jim Morrison. Jimi Hendrix. Janis. That would be some band. Yeah.' He felt the smile widen. The image comforted him, somehow. As did Freya's answering smile.

'Where are you living, Cal? Are you still with your mum and dad?'

'No, I'm in one of the flats near the harbour. I need my own space; it wasn't fair on them, having me at home in this state.'

'I pass there on my way to Mum's house. I'll walk you

back.' She stood up and held out her hand. He frowned, confused by the gesture.

'The bottle.' It was an order.

'Fuck off!'

'Come on, Cal. Give me the bottle.'

'I'll get more.'

'I don't think so. Do you want to get through this or not?'

He thought for a moment, seeing the determination on her face, weighing things up.

Then, with the merest suggestion of a nod, he handed her the whisky.

Standing, Callum couldn't help but be aware how small she was. She stood on tiptoes as she reached up, pushing the bottle to the back of a shelf behind the counter.

'You can have that back when you can enjoy a dram without drinking yourself into a coma. I'll be the judge of when that time comes.'

He laughed. It was the first time since Charlie's death he had heard that sound coming from his own throat. It sounded harsh, rusty.

Freya told him she'd come round to see him later, after she'd taken her mother's dogs for a walk. He didn't expect her. A couple of the other girls around town had tried to get close in the weeks after he came back. He'd soon let them know not to bother. Jo was the only woman he wanted, and that was never going to happen. Dimly, he understood that until he could find a way forward, he had nothing to offer except disappointment. On top of everything else, he didn't need to see pity, or revulsion, in anyone's eyes. Better to be alone.

She turned up with fish and chips. He tried to hide the

nausea brought on by the sharp tang of vinegar, picking at a few chips for the sake of politeness. The Irn Bru helped – with no whisky available, at least he could swig down some of Scotland's other national drink to settle his stomach.

'I don't feel very hungry,' he offered by way of apology.

'You look as if you don't eat much at all.' The accuracy of her observation was undeniable. Even Callum could see that his clothes hung off his skinny frame. His face looked gaunt in the mirror when he remembered to shave.

'So – you know all about my life since I ran away in search of fame and fortune. What about you?'

'Aberdeen – Uni. Chemistry. Then a year working in a lab until I realised I was in the wrong job. So I took a part-time course and retrained. Psychotherapy, counselling. I've come home to set up in practice here.'

Callum mulled that over for a moment.

'Does that make you some kind of a shrink?'

'Well, not exactly … '

But alarm bells were ringing.

'Is that what this is all about? Trying to drum up custom? Or maybe you just need someone to practise on? Is that why you're here? Am I some kind of a fucking project?'

He could feel the warning signs. Irrational anger occasionally swept through him. He knew it made him cruel and destructive. His mother had told him so, often enough, in the fraught weeks after the funeral. Those unpredictable rages had been the final straw for his parents. He thought perhaps he should just tell Freya to go, for her own good.

She had been looking down at her clasped hands. Now she raised her eyes, meeting his with a level gaze and a calm expression.

'I'd say you're a coincidence. A friend in need.'

Her words defused the tension. Touched again by her honest concern, Callum relaxed. Freya got up to leave.

'See you tomorrow?'

'Aye. Why not?' he said, thinking that for once there might be something to look forward to other than the next drink.

~

If he'd known how bossy she would turn out to be he might have thought twice. But almost before he knew it, she was taking over. Her regular visits came with offerings of home-cooked food – chilli, lasagne, simple meals to stimulate his appetite. He enjoyed watching her bustling around the kitchen, tutting over his lack of suitable saucepans and utensils. Gradually he noticed that those things mysteriously appeared, borrowed from the café. Other things changed with her presence. Jam-jars crammed with untidy bunches of wild flowers and grasses appeared on his table and windowsills. She hung some drawings and paintings on his bare walls, shyly admitting when he admired them that they were her own work. On one visit she suggested helping him clean his sparsely furnished one-bedroomed flat. Reluctantly he agreed. Helping him sort through his cupboard, she exclaimed at what she found hidden away at the back of the shelves.

'Do you even wear any of this stuff?' She held up a pair of expensive leather jeans that Jo had once made him wear for a photo shoot. It was unlikely that they still fitted. The black jeans that were all he wore these days were at least a size smaller.

He shook his head.

'Maybe time for a clear-out.'

'Aye, I expect you're right. I'll have a sort through it all ...'

She had to show him how the washing machine worked. He even caught her changing the bed one day, began to protest but stopped himself when he realised to his shame that he couldn't actually recall ever having put clean sheets on at all. Embarrassed, he helped her with the duvet cover, aware that the last time he'd done that job he had been helping his mother, years ago, before he first left home.

It was Freya's suggestion that he get his hair cut. When he reluctantly agreed, she frog-marched him to the hairdresser's, issuing instructions about length and style. The assistant who washed his hair massaged his scalp and for the first time in months he relaxed as the tension in his head and neck eased with the rhythmic pressure of the junior's fingers. Later, Freya stood beside him in the bathroom, watching as he shaved with a shaky hand. She passed little pieces of tissue to stick to the places where the razor nicked his skin. He was shocked by the sunken cheeks of the reflection that stared back at him through dull eyes. Without the shaggy hair and stubble, he was drawn and pale. Cal Mathieson, the rock star known for his smouldering good looks as much as his musical prowess, was a distant memory.

A few days later she turned up unannounced. His only other visitor, Tommy, was there, lounging on the sofa. His last link with the band, Tommy, also from the island, had been a member of the road crew. Prompted by Ed he had come home with Callum after Charlie died. They'd spent the afternoon reminiscing with the help of a few cans and the inevitable whisky.

Freya was furious. Before either of them knew what was happening, she'd poured what was left in the bottle down the sink, giving Tommy a ferocious tongue-lashing as she did so.

'What the hell did you think you were doing, bringing whisky? He's trying to stop drinking, you stupid ... Do you want to help him or not? Do you want to see him go the same way as Charlie? Seems to me you're part of the problem.' Tommy had slunk away, muttering something about 'interfering besoms ... ' on his way out.

Freya had turned to him then.

'What about you, Cal? Do you even actually want to get sober?'

Fighting to concentrate – she didn't know about the bottle they'd finished before she arrived – Callum eventually nodded.

'Well, it's got to come from you. I can help you, but I can't do it for you. Why don't you try AA meetings?'

'I'm not a fucking alky!' he answered, indignant. 'I just like a drink now and again!'

'The first step is admitting it to yourself. Let me know when you're ready to do that.' She'd left, closing the door quietly on her way out.

~

'I'm sorry, Freya. I've let you down.' He went to see her one afternoon the following week when she was helping out in her mother's café again. Freya hadn't been to visit since that evening, and he missed her, even if she was a bossy wee thing.

'No skin off my nose. You're letting yourself down.'

He didn't tell her about the effort it had taken to stay off the drink for four whole days.

'Well, I came to see if you'd like to go out somewhere tomorrow. I fancy a trip across to the west coast. It's years since I've been over there. What do you think?'

He could tell from the way her eyes lit up that she liked the idea. And in typical fashion took ownership of it straight away.

'OK. I'll borrow Mum's car and we'll take the dogs for a run on Dalmore Beach. They don't get enough decent walks, poor things. And you'll need a warm coat … ' He listened, amused, as she issued further instructions about suitable footwear and headgear, as if he were a boy, not a grown man. But it felt good to have her fussing over him again. Worth the effort of staying sober.

A robin. The thought sprang suddenly into his head. That was what she reminded him of. Bold, curious, bright-eyed. A welcome sight in the midst of a bleak winter. Leaving the café with a lighter heart and a stomach full of homemade soup and crusty bread, he heaved a sigh of relief. He'd worried that she wouldn't want to see him again after finding him back on the whisky.

It was the perfect day for an outing. With only a light breeze, the weather was bright and cold under a cloudless sky. They spent some time playing frisbee on the wet sand with Flo and Eddie, a pair of energetic Border terriers, before they set off for a long walk round the bay, talking with all the ease of old friends. Freya asked about his life in the band, encouraging him to talk about Charlie. She seemed to find his stories of their worst excesses, or at least the ones he was prepared to share, very funny. Freya had an infectious giggle. Callum couldn't remember when he'd last laughed so much, or felt so comfortable in the company of anyone else. Remembering Charlie, full of life, somehow seemed to bring him closer, and lessen the pain.

They stopped at a café on the way home. Ravenous, he ordered a bacon roll, followed by scones and jam washed down with mugfuls of strong tea. He caught her watching as he wolfed down his meal, a smile playing round her lips and dimpling her cheeks.

'Looks like your appetite's coming back.'

At that moment he realised he wanted to see those

dimples a lot more often. He didn't want her to stop caring about him. Maybe it was time to take this strange relationship to another level. Now that he was drinking less and eating more, being in company with an attractive woman was rekindling his interest in the opposite sex. He smiled back, holding her gaze until she looked away.

The following evening, Freya dropped by with some books she'd promised to loan him. As she turned to leave, he caught her arm, turning her to face him. But instead of leaning in for the kiss he was hoping for, she pulled out of his grasp.

'No, Cal.'

'But ... '

'No. I'm trying to help you, that's all. As a friend. Don't let's complicate things.'

'Freya, I'm very sorry, I ... ' He was appalled to think he had made her feel uncomfortable.

'It's OK, don't worry about it. See you soon.'

It was new territory for Callum. In the days of the band, all it took was a glance, a touch of the hand. Surrounded by eager groupies, he'd never known what it felt like to be turned down. He struggled to understand how he could have misread the signals so badly.

'Christ, Mathieson, you were aye a skinny kid, but now look at you. Do you ever eat at all?' Euan, another old school friend, ran a gym, tucked away in a back street behind the shops. Standing in shorts and T-shirt, Callum was painfully aware of the well-toned men working out around him. Self-conscious under Euan's head to foot scrutiny, he couldn't help but see the worried expression on the other man's face. 'You've no muscle-tone at all, man, and your stomach's concave. I can count every rib. Time to get you sorted out!'

Callum couldn't disagree. He'd thought the same himself this morning, a long critical look in the mirror leaving him shaken. It was one thing to be lean as a guitar hero – that went with the territory. This scrawny, wasted look was on another level altogether.

Freya could help in some ways – she already had. It was becoming easier to turn away from the whisky, and his appetite, as she had noticed, had returned to some extent. But his cooking skills were woefully inadequate, and not even the addition of bacon rolls and fry-ups to his daily intake was enough to restore the strong physique that used to drive Charlie mad with envy and the girls with – something else. In the sleepless night after his failed attempt to try his luck with Freya, it occurred to him that she might not actually find him all that attractive.

So – the gym. Euan was just the person to help. He suggested a healthy diet and an exercise routine.

'We'll start slow, build you up. No point rushing into anything – we want long-term results here. Three days a week for the first couple of weeks, and then we'll introduce weights, maybe a bit of running. There's a 10k at the end of July. We could make that a target. I'm doing it myself, so I could be your training buddy ... '

'What's a 10k?'

'A ten-kilometre run. For charity – kids with cancer. Don't you know anything?'

Callum didn't, and alarm-bells went off in his head. Ten kilometres? He doubted if he could run half of one, even for a worthy cause.

'Leave that to me. All I'm asking is commitment. D'you think you can give me that?'

He squared his shoulders.

'Aye. I'm all yours. Do your worst.'

～

'He's even got me doing yoga. Can you imagine? Fucking yoga! Me!'

Freya giggled. She'd dropped in on her way home from the art group for people with learning difficulties that she led at the town hall. Callum invited her to stay for supper – one of Euan's power meals, salmon with tomatoes, avocados and wild rice. They ate together at the kitchen counter, any awkwardness between them forgotten.

'You look better.'

'I have to admit, I'm feeling great. It's been a bit of a revelation, finding out that I actually quite like exercise. I always thought it was a bit … naff. All that lycra … '

Freya laughed.

'So, when can I expect to see you on the cover of *Health and Fitness*, smothered in spray tan and baby oil?'

An image flashed into his mind, of Freya, exactly as she had described him. There was a flirty and slightly indecent answer on the tip of his tongue. He bit it back, looking away as he tried to erase the picture in his head that was threatening to transmit itself to other parts of his anatomy.

'You should be so lucky,' earned another laugh.

'Well, now that you're into alternative therapies, how about you try art? It's really good for people with … all sorts of … issues … ' She tailed off. He realised that he was scowling at her.

'I don't think so.'

Freya was nothing if not persistent. 'Why not?'

'Because I wouldn't be any fucking good at it!' His tone was harsher than he'd intended, but he was annoyed. He hated being treated like one of her 'clients', as she called the people who attended her art therapy groups.

'That doesn't matter. It's the doing ... '

'Of course it fucking matters!' He recognised the warning signs and reined in his temper. 'Sorry.' It came out as a mumble.

'You don't always have to shine at everything you do. Some things are worth doing just for the pleasure of doing them.'

'I'm not interested in being half good at things. If I do something, I want to do it the best I can.'

'What about your music? You're a brilliant guitarist, couldn't you start playing again?'

Now she was straying into the no-go areas. God, this woman could be a real pain in the backside sometimes.

'Maybe.' He shut the conversation down, getting up to clear plates and stack the dishwasher.

'Will I make some tea? I've brought a new DVD – *The English Patient*. It got great reviews. Would you like to see it?'

'Yeah, great idea.' It would be a welcome relief from her probing at the sore places. He loaded it into the DVD player.

∼

'Sorry, Cal, I had no idea ... didn't know it would be so ...' A sob foreshadowed the tears that flowed as the credits rolled. Seeing how affected she was by the tragic romance of the film, Callum struggled against the desire to put a comforting arm around her, or let her know how moved he was, too. He waited as she found a tissue in the pocket of her dress and blew her nose.

'Aye, it was quite sad, wasn't it? Are you OK, Freya?' He kept his voice steady, his emotions under control.

His arms tightly folded.

She turned towards him with tears sparkling in her lashes and straight away he knew that if he tried to kiss her now, she'd let him. The desire to just do it, whatever the consequences, was strong. Instead, he gave her a cheerful grin and a brotherly pat on the shoulder, enjoying the confusion in her expression. 'More tea, before you get off home?'

Freya declined, gathering up her things. He accompanied her to the door. She stopped, hesitant, turning to face him with a puzzled expression. This girl would never make a poker player, Callum thought.

'Well, goodnight then, Cal. Maybe see you tomorrow?'

'Ah, sorry, I'm busy tomorrow. I'll call you. OK?' And then, just as she was about to go, he brushed her cheek lightly with his lips. 'Night, Freya, sleep well.'

He managed to contain his smile of satisfaction until the door was closed with Freya firmly on the outside. His lips tingled with the memory of her soft skin.

Two can play hard to get, he thought, enjoying this new game, teasing her, testing himself.

'There's something I'd like you to hear.'

He picked up his guitar. It occurred to him that she had never heard him sing, only recordings of the band. She curled up in the corner of the sofa as he began to play.

It was a while since he'd sung to anyone but himself. He was aware of a change in his voice. It was huskier than before, deeper. As he sang he allowed his emotions to lead the lyrics. In a mixture of English and Gaelic, the song described their day on the beach, their footsteps – large and small, the dogs' paw prints – the waves whispering on the shore, the gulls crying overhead. Lovers' initials in a heart, pierced with an arrow, drawn in the sand. This was not the kind of song he had written with Charlie, not a raw rock ballad like *Atlantic Shores*, but the older brother of that song – quiet, reflective. The work of a man coming to terms with life, observing the small pleasures to be found in the everyday. He was pleased with the maturity of it. It felt like his writing had come of age, reflecting the person he hoped he was becoming. As he let the last notes fade away, he looked up at Freya. Her grey eyes were moist, and full of wonder.

'Sorry, Cal, must go for a pee.' She fled the room, but not before he saw the tears she had only just been able to hold in.

Setting aside his guitar, Callum smiled inwardly. Got you there, he said to himself with quiet satisfaction.

Freya returned to the sitting room a short while later.

'Sorry Cal, I'm not feeling too great. I'll get off home now.'

'No problem, Freya. Sorry you're not feeling well. You seemed OK earlier, has it just started? I can get you a cab.'

'No really, I'll be fine. It's probably just time of the month … A walk in the fresh air'll do me good.'

She refused to give in to his insistence that he walk her home. Eventually, he let her go, promising to call the following day to make sure she was OK. Knowing that she was making an excuse because the boundaries she had set were beginning to crumble.

Chapter 14
Isle of Lewis
March /April, previously

'Don't, Freya. Do. Not. Fucking. Do. That.' Arms braced across the kitchen doorway for support, Callum shook with fury. Freya challenged him with a cold, angry look. She turned away, back to the sink, and taking a deep breath, squared her shoulders, upending the bottle. The whisky made gurgling sounds as it disappeared down the drain. Freya turned on the tap to flush it away.

'Fuck you, Freya. Fuck you. Stop interfering in my fucking life, get the fuck out of my fucking house and leave me the fuck alone.' He surprised himself, getting the words out so clearly.

Freya turned to go. Her expression was full of disappointment at what she had found when she'd turned up unannounced. Tommy and him, sprawled on the sofa, giggling stupidly as they made up random answers to the questions on *Eggheads* blaring out of the TV. Cans and bottles littered the coffee table. A packet of crisps had spilled most of its contents on the floor, where they lay half-trodden into the carpet that she had insisted he hoover only two days previously. Even with half a bottle of whisky inside him, Callum knew it wasn't a pretty sight.

'Aye, you tell her, man. Bossy bitch. She's only after your money, anyway.' Tommy had always tried to get rid of anyone who tried to get close to Callum.

But Freya was different. If he had to choose between the two of them, there was no contest. Freya would be favourite every time.

Glaring at Tommy on her way out of the kitchen, Freya pushed Callum aside, flinching as he sprang into action. He didn't touch her – it was Tommy's jaw his fist was aiming for.

'What the fuck? ... What was that for? What have I done?' Tommy's lip had split open, blood dribbling down his chin.

'Don't you ever, ever talk about Freya like that, you miserable piece of shite. You can fuck right off, right now.' His voice was low and menacing.

'Aw come on, pal ... '

Without a word, Freya bundled a protesting Tommy out of the flat ahead of her.

Callum stood frozen in the sitting room, unable to erase from his mind the look of pure fear on Freya's face in the moment he moved to hit Tommy. God, what had he done? She was a tiny wee girl. A full foot taller, almost twice her body weight, he had rebuilt his strength with his new-found gym-toned muscles. And she'd thought he was going to hit her. Was that the kind of man he was – a bully, someone who drank and took it out on women? The thought found its way through a mind befuddled with whisky, and brought him face to face with himself. He hated what he saw.

Then suddenly she was back – he hadn't even heard her come in. Pale and trembling, she faced him down.

'That's it, Callum. I've tried, I've done my very best, but if you're not prepared to help yourself, there's nothing more I can do. So fuck you too. You're on your own.'

'Freya, I'm ... '

She slammed the door, hard.

He wanted to go after her, take her into his arms,

comfort her, tell her how sorry he was. But fear of her response kept him rooted to the spot. It was some time before he moved, to sit down at the table, head in hands, and start to take stock of what he had become. Not the man he had been. That man was affectionate and respectful around women, qualities that had ensured his popularity amongst the girls who followed the band. The man for whom Jo, ten years his senior and mother of two children, had put her marriage in jeopardy. A streak of self-destructiveness, washed down with copious quantities of single malt, had erased that softness, making him cruel and ugly. Uncaring of the one person who mattered to him more than any other.

After a long, sleepless night, tossing and turning, engulfed in waves of shame as the effects of the whisky wore off, the scene replaying over and over again in his head, he dialled Freya's number with a shaking hand. Relief swept through him like a tsunami when she picked up immediately, as if she'd been waiting for his call.

'I'm so sorry, Freya – really, really sorry. Please forgive me. I didn't mean it. I can't do this on my own. I really need you. Can I see you, please?' The last words came out as a sob.

'On one condition, Cal.' Her voice was icily calm.

∽

'This isn't a game any more. It never has been. It's time you grew up.'

Pale and angry, Freya made her position crystal-clear when they met at the café after it closed. He'd had all day to think before she laid down the new rules of engagement. Grateful that she was prepared to see him at all, Callum signed up to them willingly – the alternative was unthinkable. The thought of never having the warmth of her company again, left alone, with only Tommy as his drinking buddy, filled him with dread. That life wouldn't be worth living.

But he knew that there was work to do to win back her friendship. Her contempt was searing.

'The day you frighten me again, Cal Mathieson, is the day I walk away for good. No more bingeing on whisky. No second chances. Period.'

Now he knew what it felt like to hang his head in shame.

So it was up to him. Straighten himself out, get on the twelve-step programme, take responsibility.

'And do it for you, not for me. You're a better man than this, a decent human being, if only you'll give yourself the chance. I know you lost Charlie, the band – I know everything blew up in your face. But you can choose to see that as an opportunity – not the end of something, but the beginning of something else. If you don't think you can, tell me now and I'm out of here, I won't waste any more of our time.'

He looked at her in silence for long moments, digesting what she was saying, realising how close she was to giving up on him.

'You're right, Freya. What happened yesterday – I'll never forgive myself. All this time I've been kidding myself I can handle it – the drink – but … ' he paused, remembering again the look on her face, 'well, obviously I can't. So I'll do whatever you ask. I'll join AA and I will get on top of this. That's a promise.'

Freya nodded, looking down. He realised that she was crying when a glistening tear dripped onto her hand. Impatiently, she rubbed her eyes. He moved to reach out to her, but she held her hands up to deter him.

'I don't want to see you again for a while. I need time to think this through. I'll call you when I'm ready. Will you please just go now.'

'But Freya ... '

'Cal, I mean it. Just go.'

Walking slowly back to his empty flat, Callum replayed this new scene over and over in his mind, piecing together what would have been obvious all along if only he hadn't been too stupid to see it. She cared about him. Really cared.

Perhaps as much as he cared about her.

Running took the place of drinking. It was Euan who stepped into the gap left by Freya's absence, taking advantage of warmer spring weather to get down to some serious training for the 10k run. For the next few weeks, bereft of Freya's company, he avoided Tommy's. It came as a relief when he heard that his erstwhile drinking buddy had found a job with the road crew of a band touring England.

Callum threw himself into his new routine. He soon found that the buzz he got from exercise was much better than the temporary pleasure whisky gave him, and came without the mood swings or the ensuing plunge into depression and self-loathing. He took satisfaction from seeing his body returning to its previous form, lean and strong. The man he faced in the mirror had brighter eyes and fuller cheeks. And shaved regularly.

It took an iron will to stay away from Freya. Every part of him yearned to see her, to pick up the threads of whatever it was that had been growing between them before he so carelessly threw it away. Instinct told him to wait, let her make the next move. It was difficult in a small town, but he avoided the places he thought he might run into her, spending long hours home alone.

With his father's encouragement he started reading again, as he had done in the band, whiling away the time in the company of fictional characters, as he had once filled days on tour, travelling between venues. And as spring gave way to an unusually warm summer, he began to write again, awakening dormant skills in an attempt to make sense of his life through songs and music. Alone with himself, sober, a growing sense of equilibrium took him by surprise.

∽

'Hi, Cal.'

His heart leapt. Returning one evening from the sailing club, he'd found her sitting on the harbour wall near his flat.

'Freya.' He tried to sound neutral. Not daring to say anything else in case he frightened her away, he sat down beside her – not too close, lest she hear the loud clamour coming from his chest.

'How have you been?' There was a slight tremor in her voice.

'Good. You?'

'OK. Busy. The practice is picking up, got some new groups going ... You look well, Cal. Have you ... ?'

'Yes, Freya, I have. I go to two meetings a week, I run every day, I've started teaching at the sailing school, I'm learning to cook a decent meal and ... but I've missed you.' A sideways look told him that she was pleased to hear that.

'You too.' Her small hand crept along the wall and came to rest beside his. He linked his little finger with hers. The erratic beat of his heart grew wilder.

'Very much,' he added.

'Yes. Me too. Loads.'

Allowing himself another glance, he saw that she was shivering. The warmth of the evening air had been blown away by a stiff breeze off the Minch. He let go of her finger and tentatively slipped his arm around her, drawing her close.

'You're cold, *mo gradh*. Snuggle up to me.' The Gaelic, my love, came from somewhere in the very depths of his soul.

His heart skipped a beat as she leaned in, shuffling closer until she was tight up against him. He burned all the way down the side where they touched. His mouth was dry, his breathing erratic. Yet part of him wanted the moment to last forever.

He turned to look at her.

'Can I kiss you?'

'Yes. I'd like that.'

Still he hesitated, searching her face for reassurance as he leant towards her. She smiled, and there were the dimples that turned him to jelly. Their lips met in a sweet, chaste kiss. When it finished, he drew back to look her in the eyes, saying what he knew now beyond any doubt.

'I love you, Freya.'

Freya's eyes shone with unshed tears.

'You too.' Her reply was a low murmur.

There was nothing chaste about the second kiss, initiated by Freya, full of raw emotion. 'I love you too, Cal.' Her voice shook.

Callum stood up, and taking her by the hand, led her to his front door, struggling to insert his key in the lock with a trembling hand.

'You need to be sure about this, Freya. Because ... this is serious. No more games. If we do this, it's for keeps. That's what I want – all, or nothing.'

'That's what I want too. From the very first moment

I saw you again, that's all I've wanted. I love you, Cal. It's been so hard, not seeing you.'

'I'm sorry, *mo gradh*, so sorry, putting you through all that ... But why? Why bother with me, when I'm such a fucked-up ... '

Freya silenced him with a finger on his lips.

'Cal, I've known you most of my life, ever since we first met in the sandpit at nursery. I remember your skinned knees, your stupid fights, your daft jokes. It was me that ran and got the teacher when you fell off the climbing frame and split your head open.'

Reaching up, she traced the faint raised scar on his forehead where he'd been stitched up after the fall. He caught her hand and kissed her fingertips.

'You were my first teenage crush – even when you treated girls like the enemy, to be avoided at all costs. I know you, I watched you grow up. You and that scruffy dog you use to have – Gnasher. The way you loved that dog ... I used to wish I was him ... fleas and all.'

The memory made them both laugh.

'When we used to go out sailing together – I don't suppose you even remember, but I do – your floppy hair, always in your eyes ... we must have been what, fourteen, fifteen? I thought you were gorgeous, even though you never even noticed me except to tell me to tighten a sail or something. And I saw what it was like with you and Charlie – you hero-worshipped him, like I hero-worshipped you. I even wondered at one point if I'd got it all wrong and you were gay ... and then you were just ... gone, on that school trip when you never came back. It broke my heart, to think I'd never see you again. So I went off to uni, thinking I'd get over you. I went out with loads of guys, but nothing ever lasted ... and then there you were, in the café. And I knew this was my chance. Even in the state you were in, I was never going to give up on you. These last few months I've watched you, I've seen the man you really are – still there even after the band and all that craziness ... That's the Cal I love, the man I want you to be always. So, there you are. Now you know.'

Callum felt tears welling up in his eyes. Freya. Everything he had always wanted had been there all along, right in front of him, and he'd never known. Even as his heart soared with love, he felt humbled by her words.

'God, Freya, I never realised – I don't deserve ... '

Freya silenced him, reaching up to kiss him again, her mouth on his making further speech impossible. Callum lifted her up and carried her into the bedroom, laying her down carefully on his bed, lying down beside her.

It was enough just to hold her in his arms finally, to breathe in her warm fragrance – shampoo and a fresh, floral perfume. He had never known anyone smell so good. He held her close, her head on his chest, their hands clasped over his wildly beating heart.

Freya raised herself up on one elbow to look down into his face. Taking hers between his hands, he kissed her, long and deep.

'I've dreamed about this for ever ... ' Freya sighed when she had breath to speak.

'Why didn't you ... ?'

'I didn't want it to be just sex. I want the real thing too. I needed to hear you say what you said ... '

'I should have told you months ago. The day we went to Dalmore Beach. That's when I knew how I felt about you.'

Round pearl buttons fastened the front of her dress. They kept slipping out of his fumbling fingers. Laughing at his clumsiness, Freya helped him finish the job, then, kicking off her sandals, she unfastened his belt.

'Multitasking. Clever, as well as beautiful,' he

murmured, making her giggle again.

He pulled his T-shirt over his head. Freya's sharp intake of breath, her dilating pupils, confirmed what he knew – how much better he looked now he was back in shape.

Moments later, when they were both naked, he held her at arm's length, devouring her with hungry eyes. The suntanned skin of her arms and face was dusted with golden brown freckles, fading into creamy paleness. His gaze lingered on the roundness of her limbs, the slight swell of her stomach, her breasts, surprisingly full, with dark pink nipples which rose to meet his lips as he bent to kiss them, one after the other. All the time he could feel her gaze following her fingers as they explored and caressed his most sensitive places. His breathing grew fast and shallow as desire intensified.

'You're so lovely, Freya. I want to make love to you, and I want to look at you, and I don't know what I want to do most. I kind of want time to slow down ... '

'I want you, inside me.' She was trembling, her voice low and husky.

'I'm scared I might hurt you ... '

'I'm not going to break, Cal ... ' Freya drew him closer, moulding herself to him. Still he paused, taking time for another long, loving kiss, relishing the moment, the anticipation.

And then he couldn't wait any longer. Rolling onto his back he took her with him, lifting her on top, quivering with excitement as she lowered herself down, guiding him inside with a long sigh in response to his soft moan.

'Wait – don't move ... ' He tried to think of anything to stop himself coming there and then. Somehow regaining control, letting Freya take over.

At last they were as close as it was possible to be, moving

in time to a rhythm they both instinctively understood as they surrendered to the pure joy of making love, in love.

~

'I've got something for you.' Freya dug deep into the battered leather satchel that accompanied her everywhere. From somewhere in the depths she withdrew a half-bottle of whisky.

'What? Is that … ?' Callum was confused.

'The one I took off you in the café, that first day … You can have it back now.'

Callum hesitated, then reached out to take it from her hand. She watched anxiously as he unscrewed the lid.

'Thanks, *mo gradh.*'

He sniffed the whisky, recoiling from the strength of the fumes. Turning, he carried the bottle into the kitchen and upended it over the sink, running the water to flush the golden liquid away. Carefully he dropped the bottle into the bin, returning to where Freya stood, frozen in place. Encircling her in his arms, he drew her close, feeling the answering pressure of her arms round his waist, her head on his chest.

'No more whisky, my love. You're all I need.'

'I love you, Cal. Have I told you that today?'

'I think you just did.' He lifted her effortlessly to sit on the kitchen counter, bringing her head level with his own, the better to kiss her.

Chapter 15
Isle of Lewis
July, previously

It was Freya who found the article. She pushed the newspaper across the table where they had just finished breakfast.

'Look at this, Cal. I didn't know there were schools that taught boatbuilding, did you?'

He took the paper and skimmed the article.

'What are you getting at? You think I could do this? Don't be daft, Freya. I can't build boats – I'm useless at that kind of stuff. Can't even put a shelf up, remember?' A recent attempt at DIY had fallen spectacularly off the wall, laden with books and one of Freya's eccentric floral arrangements.

'Yes, but you'd learn. Your uncle has a boatyard, doesn't he? It'll be in the genes somewhere. Anyway, you need to do something. You're much too young to be hanging around the house all day reading books.'

Part of him knew she was right, but he wasn't ready to admit as much.

'Stop bossing me about, woman. Save it for your art therapy class. And shouldn't you be there by now?'

'Oh damn!' Freya grabbed her bag and headed for the door, pausing only for a quick kiss on her way out.

Callum smiled to himself. They'd been together for a month already, yet still he woke up every morning thrilled to find her curled up beside him, tousled blonde head on the pillow next to his. Somehow he always got the blame for making her late in the morning, but she was just as ready to make love to him as he was to make love to her. They couldn't get enough of one another. The joy of making love with the woman he adored, after years of only knowing casual sex with strangers, was overwhelming. She was wrong if she thought he was reading books all day. Often he simply sat, daydreaming, thinking that he must be the luckiest man on the planet, to have her.

He read the article. Then he looked up the website. By the time she arrived home in the afternoon, he had called the college and discovered that there was still a place available to start in September. The interview, hotel and flights were booked.

'Wow.' Freya looked at him with a mixture of surprise and apprehension. 'I... do you think ... what about...? Falmouth – it's a long way ... '

'I'm only going if you'll come with me. I told you – all or nothing.'

Her answering smile told him everything he needed to know.

Callum couldn't remember ever feeling so nervous, not even on stage in front of a capacity crowd at Glastonbury. Being back at school again, for the first time in more than a decade, filled him with trepidation.

There were twelve students in the class, united by a common love of boats. One man in particular caught his attention – Patrick, Australian skipper of a tall ship looking to add boatbuilding to his CV, was about the same age and with his long, sun-bleached hair tied back in a ponytail, reminded him a little of Charlie.

The teacher, a talkative Welshman with a wicked sense of humour and a repertoire of bad jokes to equal Callum's, looked around at his new intake.

'I've seldom seen a less likely-looking bunch of prospective boatbuilders in my entire career.'

That put everyone at their ease.

Callum loved it from the start.

'But what about you, Freya? What are you going to do while I'm at school? You need something as well.'

'I might see if I can do some courses at the art school. I'd really love to develop my painting. But I'll look for a job, too ... '

He took her into his arms.

'Don't be daft, Freya, you don't need to work. It's my turn to look after you. Where would I be now, without you? There's enough money coming in from the royalties to keep both of us. Go to art school, please, it would make me so happy to know you're doing something you love. You deserve it.'

The course was exacting, much more so than Callum had anticipated – he had to work hard to understand the theoretical aspects and get his head round the maths, although to his immense surprise, the woodwork came as naturally to him as playing his guitar or sailing a dinghy.

Patrick and he quickly became friends, sharing the same taste in music and a similarly irreverent sense of humour. After a great deal of arm-twisting, Callum agreed to give his new friend guitar lessons. Patrick became a regular visitor at the idyllic cottage Freya had found, overlooking the Carrick Roads in Mylor, a few miles away from Falmouth. Freya seemed to enjoy having him around, delighted that Callum had found a friend that he could talk openly with about Charlie's death and his drinking in the aftermath. Patrick had had his own problems. On the tall ship, he taught sailing to troubled teenagers with drug and alcohol issues. It was a world he knew well. He put Callum's problems in context.

'The only thing you did wrong, mate,' he said during one conversation, 'was to be young. And dumb.'

'Good title for a song.' Laughing, they set about writing it.

~

In the small world of boatbuilding, it came as no surprise to discover that Dick knew Callum's uncle, Alastair. Ali was invited to come down from his yard near Plockton to spend a few days as a guest tutor, talking to the students about running a commercial yard.

Callum was appalled when he saw his uncle again for the first time in years. Crippled by rheumatoid arthritis, he had aged alarmingly.

Dick took him aside.

'I think you might be looking at your next career there, Cal. Ali won't be able to carry on much longer without help.'

Callum could see it himself. Beyond vague dreams about finding an old classic yacht to restore and sailing off round the world, he hadn't given much thought to what they would do after the course was over, but working with his uncle had its attractions.

Freya agreed. It would be a wrench moving away from the life they enjoyed in Cornwall, but as they talked it through, they agreed that much as they had come to love the west country, Scotland was home and always would be.

He talked to Alastair.

'I'd welcome the help, son, if that's what you want to

do. I'll not pretend otherwise.'

It was settled.

~

Falmouth knew how to throw a party. At the end of the course, the boat school set up a marquee down by the harbour, with the students' boats on show. A feast was laid on, accompanied by barrels of beer and cider, bottles of wine. Callum stuck to his usual water.

A local band wearing a strange version of kilts and playing an even stranger version of bagpipe music entertained the gathering, as well as a crowd of tourists attracted by the celebratory atmosphere. It was a beautiful weekend, a light breeze ruffling the bay, boats of all kinds making their way through the water. There was a carnival atmosphere in town as the holiday season got into its stride.

As the evening wore on, the music grew louder and the dancing wilder. Callum whirled Freya in a crazy waltz out of the marquee and down to the waterside.

'I need a break!' He threw himself down on a bench, pulling her down beside him. Gulls wheeled, screaming overhead in the golden light of the late evening.

He put his arm round Freya's shoulders, drawing her close and kissing her, one hand buried in her hair.

'Let's get married.'

Freya pulled away to look at him properly. Her eyes were wide with astonishment. Marriage had never been mentioned – although they were happy together, they'd never got around round to discussing it.

'Seriously? You want to get married?'

'Only to you, *mo gradh*. Aye, I do. I love you, Freya, and I'm pretty sure you love me too. We're great together. Why not?'

'Are you asking me?' Her look was challenging.

'Oh, I see.'

He got down on one knee, taking her hands in his.

'Freya, *mo gradh*, I love you. I want to marry you. Will you do me the great honour of becoming my wife?'

Giggling, Freya pulled him back up on to his feet, throwing her arms around his neck.

'Of course I will, Cal. I love you so much.'

Wrapped in each other's arms, locked together in a long kiss, they were oblivious to the small crowd of onlookers they had attracted, and to the flashing of camera lights.

Callum was rueful next morning. 'I maybe should have done that in private.'

The news was emblazoned on the front of three tabloid papers.

'2CM guitarist to wed.'

'Cal's romantic proposal.'

'Cal rocks Freya's world.'

The pictures told their own story. He should have known that the local stringer would be hanging around the party. He'd sold a few pictures before. This time he'd hit the jackpot.

They went home to Scotland. Not to Stornoway, but to the mainland, just north of the new Skye Bridge, where Alistair had his boatyard. Callum immersed himself in learning how to build his first Raasay 25, the racing boats his uncle had designed and in which the yard specialised.

He loved seeing how Freya thrived, given the opportunity to build her practice, dividing her time between part-time art therapy classes, counselling private clients and developing her own painting.

The wedding, at home in Stornoway, far from being the quiet affair Callum and Freya had hoped for, was hijacked. Freya's mother, summoning all her resources after years in catering, organised an impressive spread of local food for the wedding feast. Patrick, as best man, delighted the guests with tales of Callum's boatbuilding disasters and bits of gossip he had gleaned about Cal's days in the band.

There was a ceilidh, and dancing into the small hours. Late in the evening a fast RIB arrived to sweep them away across the Minch to a smart hotel in a remote corner of Skye for a week's honeymoon – making love, going for long walks, eating good food, reading, talking about the future.

On their last morning, Freya turned to him, smiling, her eyes alight with love.

'Do you remember when I found you and Tommy pissed that time? And I was so angry ... '

'How could I ever forget? I thought I'd lost you for good. Afterwards, when you were reading the riot act, you said I should see everything that had happened with Charlie as the beginning of something. Now I know what you meant. How do you feel about a family?'

'Children? How many? Two, three, more?' Freya teased.

'As many as we want.'

It was late morning. Clearing the debris of Sunday papers and breakfast out of the way, Callum took his bride into his arms yet again, smoothing back her spiky hair and nibbling her neck.

'Let's get started,' he murmured. 'Right now.'

He was twenty-seven years old. The age Charlie had been when he died. Two years ago he could never have imagined being where he was now – married to a woman he loved deeply, working at something he felt passionate about, deeply content in ways he had only ever imagined, and longed for. It felt like the right time to start a family.

∽

When Alastair fell in the boat shed, breaking his hip, everything changed. Sitting by his bedside in hospital after the emergency operation, Callum saw how frail his uncle had become. He was unlikely to make a sufficient recovery to return to the yard.

'What do you think, Ali? Time to lay down the tools?'

Alastair gave him a sad smile.

'Just been thinking the same thing myself, son,' his uncle replied. 'What would you say to taking over? You can build a Raasay 25 just as well as I can now, better, maybe. I'd be happy to hand it on if it's what you want – keep the business in the family. And if I'm totally honest, I never want to do a VAT return again!'

Nor did he wish to return to the remote cottage that he had lived in beside the boat shed. Sheltered housing suited him much better. Callum and Freya took it over – a home to make their own. Freya's vision, opening up the back of the house to the sea views, became reality.

The only sadness in their lives was the absence of a child. After eighteen months of marriage, when she had still not become pregnant, they had tests, discreetly, in a private clinic in Glasgow, to avoid attracting the attention of the press.

Callum's sperm count was low.

'I have to ask, Mr Mathieson, are you a drinker?' the consultant asked.

'Not any more, but aye, I have been. All the time in the band and then for a year after Charlie died. But I've stopped now. I'm in AA.'

'Good. I'm afraid that the drinking is probably responsible. It's not too serious, might just take you a bit longer. We'll test you every few months – it's something that varies, in any case. The count isn't too low, nothing we would treat at the moment. Stay off the booze, and keep trying.'

'No hardship there.' Callum looked fondly at his wife, relieved that nothing more serious had emerged, but devastated that his drinking was the cause of their problems.

They discussed the options.

'What if it doesn't happen, Freya? Would you want to go for artificial insemination? Or adoption?'

'No, I don't think so. It's your baby I want, Callum, not a baby. You know me, I'm not broody, I'm not always wanting to cuddle other people's babies – not very maternal, really. I'd love to have a baby that's ours, of course I would. But if it doesn't happen, we'll still be happy together, we'll have a wonderful life whatever.' Freya put her hand over his. 'And Cal, it is what it is, you mustn't blame yourself. You heard what he said, it'll happen, it may just take a bit of time.'

'Freya, I'm so sorry – it never occurred to me that it wouldn't be easy. We men spend most of our time trying not to get girls pregnant. And then … Me and my bloody drinking. I'll do whatever you want – foster, adopt, IVF. But … if it never happens, I promise you, I'll make it up to you. We'll have adventures – travel, sail around the world … and let's get a dog.'

Freya laughed.

'What a great idea!'

They got two, Border terriers.

'Cal Mathieson – Infertility Shock!'

The headline in the tabloid, above a picture of Callum and Freya leaving the clinic in Glasgow, was shocking enough. Being doorstepped outside the supermarket in Kyle of Lochalsh by Sean O'Brian, a reporter who had followed him over the years, nearly sent Callum over the top.

'Is it true Cal's firing blanks, Mrs Mathieson? Because he's an alcoholic?'

Freya stepped in before Callum could land a well-deserved punch. She bundled him into the Land Rover and drove away.

By then, she was already pregnant.

PART THREE

Chapter 16
Edinburgh
February 1970s

Janet woke to the unmistakeable sound of the front door crashing open against the sideboard in the hall. Heart thundering, she lay for a few moments, listening. The sound of Maddie's throaty laughter allowed her to relax. Not a burglar then – just her younger sister, back from yet another party in the small hours of the morning. With a sigh, she turned over, snuggling back under the warm duvet.

Sleep, however, was impossible. She couldn't help hearing the sounds from the adjoining bedroom – Maddie's voice, and another one – deep, masculine and, surprisingly, with an American accent. Not Ian, then, Maddie's long-term boyfriend and fellow art student. What on earth was her crazy sister up to this time?

The voices subsided as the bed-springs took up the conversation. Janet lay sleepless as the sounds of energetic sex from Maddie's room heightened to a frenzy, followed by a series of screeches and a muffled roar as the couple reached a climax. There was another gale of giggles from Maddie, followed by the deeper tones of her companion, before silence eventually fell.

It must have taken a full hour for her to drop off again, rage at her careless, promiscuous younger sibling slowly subsiding into resignation. Maddie would always do exactly what she wanted, whatever anyone else said or thought. Eight years older, Janet felt as if she had inherited all the sensible genes in their family. Even when she didn't have a day of marking fifth-year essays ahead, wild parties were not her choice of entertainment, and never had been. Meeting a friend at the Filmhouse to see a subtitled art movie was her idea of a good time. That was the plan for later. Perhaps they'd treat themselves to half a pint of lager and lime in the bar afterwards.

~

'Oh. Good mornin'. I'm real sorry, Ma'am. I was lookin' for … You must be Janet.'

Janet stopped in the doorway to the small galley kitchen. Most of the space seemed to be taken up by a man holding a jar of coffee in one hand and two mugs in the other.

Momentarily lost for words, Janet looked at the stranger in her kitchen, trying not to stare. It wasn't just that he was over six feet tall, wearing nothing but a pair of boxer shorts which did little to conceal the most impressive, muscular physique she had ever seen. Or his smile, revealing beautifully straight white teeth – American dentistry, she thought randomly. It was that he was the first black man she had ever met in person.

Putting down the mugs, he held out his hand. Not to acknowledge it would seem rude. She winced at the strength of his handshake.

'Lieutenant Stewart Fraser,' he introduced himself in a deep bass voice. 'United States Navy.'

'Hello. Yes, I'm Janet MacIntosh. Maddie's sister, as you so rightly surmise.' She heard herself, the pomposity of the words delivered in her best teacher's voice. Sometimes she wished she were more like Maddie, with her easy nature, able to chat with anyone as if they were her best friend. 'You'll be based in the Holy Loch, I presume?' There she went again, surmise, presume ...

He smiled again. 'That's right, Ma'am. For two more weeks, then I head home to Charleston, South Carolina. Back to school. Mind if I fix some coffee? Can I get you one too?'

Janet edged further into the room to fill the kettle and plug it in.

'School?' Surely he was too old for school. Well into his twenties, if he was an officer. And she was absolutely certain that none of the scrawny youths she taught would look so ... mature, in their underwear.

'University. The US Navy's payin' my way. I give them two years, they give me an education. Good deal, huh?'

Janet couldn't help liking him. His manners were delightful, for a man wearing next to nothing in a stranger's kitchen. So unlike Maddie's usual one-night stands, monosyllabic latter-day hippies with the lank hair, pale skin and bad teeth common to many a Scots youth. Maybe for once Maddie hadn't got it quite so wrong. But if this tall, handsome American naval officer was going back to the States, this could only be a fling, like so many of her sister's casual encounters, usually revenge for something Ian had done to 'piss her off'.

'Stewart, have you not made that coffee yet? What are you doing, roasting the beans? Honestly ... '

Maddie appeared from the hallway, her shock of Pre-Raphaelite red locks tumbling around her face, wearing only a white T-shirt that obviously belonged to her new friend. Even in this state, she looked fabulous. In the close proximity of the kitchen Janet couldn't help but be aware of the effect she was having on Stewart. Quickly she finished making her morning tea and retreated to the privacy of her bedroom, leaving them to return to Maddie's. This time she turned the radio up to mask the sounds she preferred not to hear.

There was no opportunity for further conversation with Maddie that day, and unable to face another night at home, feeling like a spare part, Janet stayed at her friend's house. A sense of loyalty she hardly understood prevented her from telling her friend why – instead she made up a cock-and-bull story about a broken boiler.

Chapter 17
Edinburgh
February 1970s

'Maddie?' The flat was silent. 'Maddie?' Janet called out again. With a sense of relief she dropped her bag on the hall sideboard and closed the front door behind her.

The bathroom was even more of a shambles than usual, wet towels draped over the bath, water dribbling in a slow stream from an unclosed basin tap. Sighing, Janet began restoring order while she planned what she would say to Maddie when she finally came home. With her Finals only weeks away, Janet was worried that her sister wasn't doing enough work for her degree submission. The responsibility of looking out for her younger sister weighed heavily, but since the death in a plane crash of their parents some years previously, she had no option but to try her best. If only Maddie were a bit less – well, Maddie.

Wiping down the bathroom shelf, she knocked a silver foil blister packet onto the floor. Picking it up, she recognised Maddie's contraceptive pills. She had been the one to suggest Maddie go to the family planning clinic when her sister and Ian started sleeping together. Now, examining the packet, it came as no great surprise to see that Maddie paid scant attention to the directions she had been given. Interspersed with the empty bubbles were others which still held a little pink pill. Including the last two days.

'I despair, Maddie. I really do.'

Janet sighed, propping the packet up against the mirror to remind her sister to take the next one.

∼

It was early evening when Maddie reappeared, shedding her coat and scarf over the sofa as she threw herself down on the cushions with a long exhalation of breath.

'God, that was a narrow escape!' Her face was flushed as if she'd been running in the cold February wind.

'Why? What happened?' Alarm sounded in Janet's tone.

'Stewart. I just got back from seeing him off at the station. Thank God he's gone. He was gorgeous, but talk about intense! I thought he was going to start blubbering when the train was pulling out – telling me how wonderful I was, he'd never met anyone like me, would I go and visit him in the States? I mean, for God's sake, it was just a bit of fun! I had to find out ... you know, if it's true what they say about black guys ... ' She caught sight of Janet's face, wearing a look of sheer horror, and grinned. 'Let's just say I wasn't disappointed ... but honestly! I don't need all that heavy stuff. And you're just as bad. Lighten up, man!'

Janet shook her head and not for the first time wondered what planet her sister thought she was living on.

'Maddie, does it ever cross your mind that you could get yourself in a lot of trouble with these games you play? Never mind about poor Ian, treated like a doormat. Stewart seemed like a really nice man, surely he deserves better than this. You can't go around playing with people's feelings. It's just not right.'

'Oh no, here we go again. Big sister lecture, blah blah! What do you know, anyway? When did you ever have a boyfriend!' Maddie's voice was shrill.

'Never.' Janet told herself not to escalate the argument but she was too angry to hold back. 'And why not? Because ever since we lost Mum and Dad I've had you to look after, as well as finish my degree, get a job, do all the cooking, the housework, the shopping ... While you do exactly what you want, when you want, with whoever you want ... You're so selfish, Maddie, and now you're on course to fail your degree because all you want to do is go out having a good time and sleeping around! God, if Mum and Dad could see ...'

'Don't you dare! Don't bring them into this ...'

The argument ended as it always did, Maddie howling with grief at the loss of her parents when she was only twelve, Janet feeling she had to comfort her, while inside, a tiny voice that she seldom acknowledged whimpered, 'What about me? Who looks after me? Why do I have to be the strong one all the time?'

The first letter arrived two days later. Tidy handwriting on Basildon Bond notepaper, rubber-stamped with the insignia of the US Navy, postmarked Dunoon.

'Oh God, it must be from him!' Maddie threw it aside on the kitchen table.

'Aren't you going to open it?'

'What would I do that for? I'm never going to see him again. Chuck it in the bin, will you Janet? I'm off, I'm meeting Ian to walk to college. See you later!'

Never quite knowing why, Janet took the letter and put it away in a shoebox in the bottom of her wardrobe. More followed as the weeks passed, Basildon Bond replaced by flimsy airmail stamped with American postage. Reconciled with Ian, Maddie showed no interest, and in the end Janet stopped putting the letters in front of her, putting them away one after the next in the hope that one day her sister might come to her senses and want to read them.

Chapter 18
Edinburgh
1970s

'So they failed you? Well, I won't say I told you so, but it's hardly a surprise, is it? Honestly Maddie, what a waste. Four years, thrown away. With nothing to show for it.'

Janet struggled to keep her temper under control. She'd have given anything to have the chance to go to art school, but in the aftermath of losing their parents, had instead trained to teach English, conscious that their small inheritance would not last long, and that she would need a steady income to support them both while Maddie finished her studies. Even with a full grant, it had been difficult to make ends meet, between the cost of art materials and books mounting up every term and Maddie's unerring ability to spend her grant the moment it arrived. And all for nothing.

'I can go back, repeat the final year. It's no big deal.'

'No Maddie, you can't. It's not an option. You won't be able to get another grant, and I can't afford to keep you in paints and booze for another year, so forget about it. Get out there and find yourself a job. It's time you started paying your way around here. I've done all I can, but you're old enough to look after yourself now.' Too angry to wait for her sister's response, she left the room and took herself out for a long walk round the Meadows.

The flat was quiet when she returned. There was a pot of stew simmering in the oven, vegetables prepared ready to be cooked. The table was laid for two, with a bottle of wine – cheap, but perfectly drinkable – alongside a bunch of Sweet Williams in a vase. In all the years they had lived in this flat together, Maddie had never once cooked for her. Janet was astonished.

'I made supper.' Maddie came into the kitchen, stating the obvious.

'So I see. What a lovely surprise, thank you.'

Maddie turned on the heat under the potatoes.

'I didn't know you could actually cook, Maddie.'

'I did home economics at school. I suppose I just remember from then.' Maddie was uncharacteristically subdued, but Janet decided to make the most of a rare half-hour of freedom from domesticity to finish preparing a lesson for the following day.

Maddie poured them both a glass of wine as they sat down to a surprisingly tasty stew with mashed potatoes and carrots.

'I hope this isn't a one-off. You're a very good cook, Maddie. This is delicious!'

'Hmm. Well, I might be doing a bit more cooking from now on, if ... ' Maddie fell silent.

'If what?'

There was a long silence. Then Maddie carefully set her cutlery down on her plate and took a long pull from her wine glass.

'I think ... I think I might be pregnant ... '

She burst into tears.

It was love at first sight. Janet leant over the crib and gazed down at her niece. Wrapped in a blanket, all that was visible was a dark halo of hair framing a perfect little brown face.

'Can I hold her?' she asked the nurse who was quietly tending to Maddie, still drowsy after giving birth.

'Yes, of course. And I expect Mum would like a proper look now, wouldn't she?'

'I am here, you know, you can talk to me.' Maddie was her usual waspish self.

With infinite care Janet lifted the baby out of the cot and watched as the dark blue-brown eyes fluttered open and seemed to meet hers with a questioning look. The tiny rosebud mouth began to make sucking motions.

'Hello, darling. Welcome to the world. You're so gorgeous! Are you hungry?' Carefully she sat down on the bed and handed the tiny bundle to her mother.

Maddie held the child to her, her expression unreadable. 'Has Ian seen her?' she asked at last.

'Yes. I'm afraid he's gone, Maddie. He was so upset.'

'Well, I should have known. I kept hoping, you know, it would be his…'

The nurse coughed discreetly, and withdrew to attend to something on the far side of the room.

'You should have been honest with him for the start. Letting him imagine it was his baby – that was just cruel, Maddie.' Janet had tried everything she could to get her sister to take responsibility, in vain. Maddie dropped her gaze and nodded. It was too late to change anything now.

The baby began to whimper, bringing the nurse back to the bedside.

'Let me help you with the feeding. Some mothers take to it straight away, others need a bit of help.'

'I'm sure I'll be fine. I've read all about it.'

The nurse looked doubtful.

The baby had no trouble at all. Her little pursed lips found the nipple and suckled noisily.

'Ow! It hurts!' Then as she grew used to the sensation, Maddie gazed down on her daughter with a look of pure joy, and a tenderness Janet had never seen before on her sister's face.

'She's so perfect. My baby. A little girl. I can't quite believe it.' Maddie took one tiny hand in hers and traced the little fingers. The baby let go of the nipple, milky bubbles around her mouth, and drifted off to sleep again. Tears of happiness spilled from Maddie's eyes, but she could not tear her gaze away from her daughter's face, even when the nurse took her away to settle her in the cot so they could both rest.

'I'll take a breather while she sleeps,' Janet said.

Outside the room, she stopped for a moment to try to bring her own emotions under control. The sight of the baby in her sister's arms, sucking at her breast, struck somewhere deep inside her, leaving her feelings in turmoil. She was intensely envious. At the same time, she felt a connection to the child she had never foreseen, a fiercely protective feeling, a determination to always be part of her life. Supporting her sister through the long months of pregnancy had brought them closer together, leaving Janet feeling fully invested in a sense of family.

'What are you going to call her?' Maddie was bathed and rested, sitting up in a chair to nurse the baby – Madonna and child.

'I thought maybe Annie. After Mum, you know? Annie MacIntosh, Janet as a middle name, what do you think?'

Janet flushed with pleasure.

'I'd like that.' Even if all she inherited from her grandmother was her name, at least maybe some sensible Janet genes would rub off on her niece.

~

Life changed out of all recognition as Annie joined their household. By the time she came home from hospital, Janet had decorated the box-room as a nursery with a frieze of bright cartoon animals marching round the pale yellow walls, mobiles hanging from the ceiling over a cot painted in rainbow colours. There was a nursing chair for Maddie and a new chest of drawers full of all the things the baby would need for the first year, with a changing mat on top and a shelf full of soft toys above it.

'It's perfect, Janet. Thank you so much.' Maddie was moved to tears of gratitude by her sister's willingness to take this new member of their strange little family in her stride. Until Janet asked the question she knew her sister didn't want to hear.

'Aren't you going to let Stewart know he's a father?'

'No! I'm not. Absolutely not. I don't want him to have anything to do with this. It was my mistake and I'll deal with it my own way. I don't want him involved, Janet. Please, promise me you'll never let him know. Promise!'

Reluctantly, Janet agreed. The letters still arrived, fewer now, but still regular enough. Always first to pick up the mail in the morning, Janet continued to put them away in the shoebox, even more determined to keep them now so that one day Annie would be able to find out who her father was. It was clear that Maddie had no intention of ever telling her, and for Janet, whose role as doting aunt suited her very well, the possibility of Stewart perhaps wanting to take part was less than appealing. She was perfectly capable of looking after both her sister and Annie, especially with the extra money that came with her promotion to deputy headmistress.

Motherhood suited Maddie. She threw herself into the task of bringing up her daughter with an enthusiasm she had never brought to her studies at art school.

'All my friends are dead jealous.' They had just returned from a warm Sunday afternoon walk in the Meadows where they'd run into a group of Maddie's old college chums enjoying a barbecue on the grass. Annie was passed around between them, gurgling with delight as each new friend fussed over her.

'So they should be, shouldn't they, Annie?' Janet had felt pangs of jealousy as well. They were hardly a normal family, but Janet had come to regard Annie almost as much hers as her sister's. They both glowed with pride at Maddie's friends' admiration of Annie, pretty in a smocked gingham dress that her mother had spent hours making. But Janet was more than happy to reclaim her niece at the first possible opportunity.

∼

To her eternal regret, it was Janet who first suggested nursery. If she could have foreseen the consequences, she would never have mentioned it.

'She's so bright, Maddie. It would be good for her to have other children to play with – it's not as if she has brothers and sisters. And kids do so much better at school if they have some nursery experience before they start.'

Even Maddie could see the logic. But with Annie at nursery in the mornings, Maddie was bored. She began to look for ways to fill the empty hours. A friend suggested a theatre design course. They enrolled together.

'How was it?' Janet demanded, keen to hear all about Maddie's first day. 'Do you think you'll enjoy it?'

'Oh yes. I think I will, I really do. There are some great people on it. I feel as if I'm really going to fit in.'

Janet was delighted. At last, Maddie had found something that might lead to a career.

But a week later it emerged that it wasn't the career possibilities that Maddie was interested in.

'Janet, this is Ruadhri.' It was a long time since Janet had seen that flush on her sister's face, or the bright sparkle in her eyes. The man behind her in the hallway reminded her of a grizzly bear, with his shaggy dark hair and moth-eaten fur coat, looking at Maddie as if he wanted to devour her.

'Hello Ruadhri.' Politeness demanded at least that. But there was a concern much greater than Ruadhri's ursine presence. 'Maddie, where's Annie?'

'Oh my God! I forgot all about her! She must still be at nursery!'

Janet's heart sank.

PART FOUR

Chapter 19
West Highlands & Edinburgh
April

Crossing the border into Scotland, Annie let out a whoop and punched the air, remembering how her mother used to do the same on their rare visits north. Somehow her heart always lifted coming back to Scotland, the land of her birth.

She found herself thinking about Maddie – contrasting the chaos of her mother's life with the success of Janet's. How was it possible for the two sisters to have been so different? Janet used her education to full advantage, with her successful teaching career followed by her growing acclaim as an artist. Annie could not have wished for a better role model than Janet, or a worse one than her own mother. She counted herself lucky to have followed in her aunt's footsteps – she could so easily have gone the other way.

In a call to the funeral director she set a date for Janet's cremation. It was so important to get the memorial service right – Janet had been a crucial part of Annie's life. The service must reflect her truthfully. Annie was determined to make it a worthy celebration of her aunt's life.

It was late evening by the time she parked the Mini outside Janet's house in Plockton. At the end of a short terrace of fishermen's cottages on the edge of the village, it enjoyed spectacular views across an inlet scattered with small islands towards soaring mountains in the distance.

It was a beautiful night, bright and clear, with a little lingering warmth after an unseasonably warm day. Annie felt the peace of the Highlands settle around her. She took a moment to enjoy the fresh sea air.

A large ginger cat appeared from the side of the cottage, acknowledging her with a long look and a quiet miaow. Janet's cat, Boris, she realised, wondering who had been feeding him. And what would happen to him now?

The key was under a flowerpot. Boris followed her as she ferried bags from the car into the kitchen. He jumped up onto a chair which, judging by the ginger hair covering its cushion, was for his exclusive use.

A red Rayburn warmed a kitchen full of bright pottery and paintings, a riot of primary colours and interesting objects. Annie felt as if Janet would bustle in from her studio any minute, put the kettle on and sit down for a chat. Tears sprang to her eyes to think she would never see her beloved aunt again.

She was still putting things away when there was a knock on the door. Without waiting for an answer, Fiona let herself in. She cut a striking figure, her grey hair tied up in straggly bun, wearing one of the bright knitted sweaters she made to sell in the local craft shop. Thick oven-gloves protected her hands from the heat of a casserole straight from the oven.

'I made this for you. You'll need something after the drive. I see Boris is settled back in; he's been in with me the last few days – he always did share his affections between Janet and me. He's a lovely cat. Janet adored him.' Fiona put the casserole in the warming oven with the ease of someone completely at home in Janet's kitchen.

'Thank you so much – for everything. It's been good to know the house was in good hands. I don't know how long

I'll stay – at least a couple of weeks, I expect. The cremation is booked for next Thursday and there'll be a memorial and a wake in the village the next day. And there's so much to sort out, with the estate and so on. Glass of wine? I was just about to open a bottle. I don't know about you, but I could use a drink.'

Fiona was happy to accept, and they spent some time reminiscing about Janet over a glass of Merlot and generous helpings of hot casserole.

The spare room was already made up with fresh white linen. Annie filled a hot-water bottle against the chill of the night, but even after the long journey, sleep was elusive.

Sometime after midnight she got up for a glass of water. Standing at the kitchen window, she looked out over the sound. Moonlight silvered the water. The mountains in the distance stood in silhouette against an indigo sky, a full moon hanging above them, casting an eerie blue light on the summits. The beauty of the scene held her transfixed.

Boris came to investigate, made curious by her stillness. His miaow released her from the spell. Together they went upstairs to bed, where the cat's quiet purring lulled her into a deep, dreamless slumber.

In the studio the following morning, Annie surveyed the scene – hundreds of paintings stacked up around the walls. There were a few works in progress, never to be finished. The sight of the unfinished canvases on their easels, palettes ready beside them, was heartbreaking.

It was impossible to know where to begin. She would contact the gallery – the owner would know how to sort and catalogue them.

Choking back tears, Annie left the timber building,

locking the door behind her.

Sorting out Janet's affairs was going to be harder than she had imagined.

Taking refuge in practicalities, she spent the remainder of the day, with Fiona's help, working through Janet's address book, letting people know about the funeral arrangements and contacting those who needed to know of her aunt's demise. In the afternoon she found the details of Janet's solicitor in Edinburgh and called her.

The solicitor was adamant – it would be much better to meet face to face, so Annie could sign documents relevant to the estate before the process of confirmation could be undertaken. All the necessary paperwork would be ready in a couple of days. And yes, as executor it was fine for her to stay in the cottage.

Annie made an appointment to meet the solicitor in Edinburgh the following week.

The solicitor raised her eyebrows when she met Annie in reception.

'Yes, I am that Annie MacIntosh.' She might as well get it over with. The story was still rumbling on, though she had seen no headlines in this morning's newspapers. Her fifteen minutes of fame would, she hoped, soon be well behind her.

'I'm very sorry for your loss.'

'Thank you.'

'I expect these past few days won't have been easy for you, on top of your aunt's death.'

'I've no one to blame but myself.'

'Well, I have to say, if what you did exposes a cover-up and accelerates bringing more perpetrators to court, it may be no bad thing.' Annie was grateful for the support of a fellow lawyer. 'Anyway, you're here to discuss the estate so let's do that, shall we? And I've organised some sandwiches to be brought in shortly – you'll have had a long drive.'

It appeared things were simpler than Annie had thought.

'Yes, the will is straightforward, as you will see. Janet was highly organised, good at admin. I wish they were all this simple.'

There were a number of bequests to charities she supported, and sums of money to people who had worked for her. Some of the paintings were to go to particular galleries by prior arrangement – the rest to be sold and the proceeds to be shared out amongst various charities, with a trust fund for art education. Annie was to keep whichever paintings she chose for herself. Some money was left to Fiona, more to another elderly neighbour in the village. There was a special request for Boris to live out his days with Fiona. The rest, the cottage and a substantial sum of money, was left to Annie.

'That much? I had no idea.' Annie was humbled. 'She always lived so simply, I just assumed there wasn't much money. Goodness.'

Annie hadn't given her financial situation much thought, but as she walked along Princes Street, Edinburgh Castle dark against a clear sky, she reflected on her position – better off than she had ever imagined, and the owner of not just one but two homes.

A homeless man was sitting on the pavement on the corner of Hanover Street and George Street.

'Support your local vagrant!'

Smiling, she dropped a twenty-pound note into his cap.

Chapter 20
West Highlands
April

It was a pleasure to wake up in the peace of the cottage – her cottage, Annie thought, with a mixture of pleasure and sadness – on the morning of the memorial.

Lying in bed watching the reflections of sunlight on water dancing on the ceiling above her head, she mulled over the events of the last few days. She told herself that she ought to feel more adrift than she did, having worked so hard for so long on the Inquiry, but oddly she didn't miss the day-to-day doing of it at all. Mark, she realised, had hardly figured in her thoughts since his departure only a week before. Being so busy getting ready for the cremation and today's ceremony explained some of it. But she imagined it was also that she felt so peaceful here, away from her high-stress London life.

Putting on a pink dress she had bought in Edinburgh, she watched through the window as a white-hulled boat skimmed across the sound. She wondered if it was Callum's – it looked like the boat she had seen tied up at his pier.

The service was well attended. Friends and neighbours were there, as well as former colleagues from Janet's teaching years, some gallery owners and a number of fellow artists. No one wore black – everyone was dressed in the bright colours Janet had favoured.

Following her aunt's instructions, Annie had organised a humanist ceremony. There were warm eulogies and poems, amusing stories from different times in Janet's life. Fiona spoke movingly of the friendship that had grown between them, only to be so suddenly cut short.

Annie had steeled herself to speak. She described the importance of her aunt's place in her own unorthodox childhood and the debt of gratitude she felt for having had such a powerful role model in her life.

There was music Janet had loved – Mozart, Joni Mitchell, Purcell. Everyone agreed it was a fitting send-off.

Fiona hugged her as they left the village hall to make their way to the hotel for the funeral tea. 'You've done her proud, Annie. It's just as she'd have wanted.'

'Well, I was lucky she left such clear instructions. I'm amazed at how many people turned up.'

Jamie and Claire Anderson Butler, owners of the London gallery which represented Janet, were staying overnight. Annie arranged to meet up with them in the hotel that evening for supper so they could discuss future exhibitions – there was talk of a retrospective soon.

Jamie and Claire were at a window table in the bar, an open bottle and three glasses in front of them. Annie made her way through the crowded room to join them.

'Wine?' Jamie held the bottle poised over her glass.

'Oh, please.' Annie thought a drink might help her relax, and the emotion of the last few days to settle.

'Annie, you didn't tell me about the band!' Claire was pink with excitement. Jamie smiled and rolled his eyes.

'What band?'

'Cal Mathieson and Friends! They're playing tonight, here! I thought you must have laid it on just for me.'

'No, I can't say I knew anything about it. But let's bring dinner forward if you want to see them.' It occurred to her that a bit of live entertainment might be exactly what she needed, too, after the stress of the past couple of weeks.

'Oh yes please. Jamie, go and tell them.'

As Jamie went off to rearrange dinner, Claire turned to Annie.

'I was such a huge fan of 2CM. Must have seen them a dozen times. Most of the girls I knew were Charlie fans, loved the kilt and all the crazy dancing. But it was always Cal for me – I was a sucker for the dark, brooding ones, loved a man with a bit of mystery about him. I didn't know he lived up here, he just seemed to disappear after Charlie died. You must know him, I suppose.'

'I only recently met him, actually. I had no idea who he was. Don't expect too much, Claire, he's just a scruffy boatbuilder these days.'

Annie went on to recount the story of her meeting with Callum. Claire's eyes grew wider and wider.

'My God, Annie, I used to have daydreams about him, just like you're describing. He rescued me from car wrecks, burning buildings, floods! He'd sweep me up in his arms just as I was about to be engulfed in … whatever, … and then our eyes would meet, our hands would touch, and it would always end in the full Mills and Boon clinch! And it really happened to you! My teenage self hates you! I hate you!'

Annie laughed at this version of her rather more mundane meeting with Cal Mathieson, former guitar hero.

'If it's any consolation, there was no romantic ending. He was pissed off, having to rescue some stupid southerner who'd run herself off the road in unsuitable shoes, when he had a boat to varnish. Although he was very sweet about me crying all over him. I just got a bacon sarnie and a bumpy ride back to Inverness in a breakdown truck – with no heating!'

∽

There was a small raised platform at the back of the bar. Callum sat on a stool at the front of the stage, cradling his guitar on his knee. He introduced the other members of the band, Jack and Steve, both surrounded by an array of instruments.

The audience responded warmly as Callum strummed a chord and said a few words about what they would be playing. The opening number was a traditional folk song underlaid with a drumbeat that gave it a contemporary twist. Claire had managed to find them a table as close to the stage as possible without actually joining the band. Chin propped in her hand, she sat gazing adoringly at Callum.

Annie would hardly have recognised him. He'd had a haircut since she'd last seen him – her practised eye knew expensive hairdressing when she saw it – and he was clean-shaven, revealing his bone structure and the startling colour of his eyes, accentuated by the blue of a denim shirt worn loose over black jeans. She had to agree with Claire, seen like this he was a better-looking man than she had thought at their first meeting. Much more like a glamorous former lead guitarist than an unkempt boatbuilder.

The set was a mix of their take on traditional songs with others by contemporary musicians, from David Gray to Hozier, interspersed with a few new pieces written by Callum and Steve.

Callum was the main vocalist. He had a rock singer's voice, rich and gravelly, while his playing reminded the audience why 2CM had been so successful – he was nothing short of brilliant. Even Annie could hear it.

Claire leaned over and whispered in Annie's ear. 'This is such a treat! You lucky thing, having Cal on your doorstep! I might have to move up here myself!'

The first half ended with a Dave Matthews song, one Annie knew as a favourite of Mark's – 'The Space Between'. It was a bold choice for a local pub band. Callum handled it effortlessly, the complexity of the song stripped down, guitar leading with drums and keyboards in the background. It went down well, cheers and applause slowly dying away as Callum announced, 'We're taking a short break, but then we've got a special treat for you. See you in ten.'

The lights came up. Callum set his guitar on a stand and stood up to leave the stage. Catching sight of Annie, his face lit up in a smile of recognition.

'You've got to introduce me!' Claire was beside herself with excitement. 'I think he's even better-looking now! And his voice – wow! Gorgeous!'

Jamie frowned at his wife.

'Calm down, Claire, you're making an idiot of yourself. Remember we're up from the big city, we're supposed to be the epitome of cool. You'll notice none of the locals have their tongues hanging out.'

The band returned to the stage with the pretty girl Annie recognised from the photos she had seen in Callum's study. Kirsty had long dark wavy hair and bright blue eyes just like her father's. In a short floral dress, bare legs, thick socks and heavy-soled Doc Martens, her look was charmingly girlish. Her voice was sweet and powerful at the same time, with a suggestion of the same husky edge as Callum's. They performed a few songs, sometimes in unison, sometimes in harmony, sharing a rapport that made the other band members seem to fade into the background.

Callum took the microphone.

'The next song was a big favourite of someone we've

recently lost – a friend, a neighbour and a truly talented artist. On behalf of us all I offer sincere condolences to her niece, Annie, who is here with us tonight. Janet once told Freya that this was her favourite poem, and I have to concur. In my opinion you'll never find better words to describe how it feels to be in love. So I would like to dedicate "My Love is like a Red, Red Rose" to Janet.'

With Kirsty singing in harmony, they performed a poignant version of the Burns song her aunt had loved. As the final chords died away, Annie fumbled in her pocket for a tissue to wipe away her tears. Callum acknowledged her with a sad smile.

'What a lovely thing to do,' whispered Claire. Deeply moved by the words of the song and Callum's introduction, Annie nodded her agreement.

Kirsty stepped forward, holding the microphone in both hands. A wavering spotlight found her on the stage.

'I've been working on a new song I want to sing for you tonight. It was one my mum really loved, so this is for her. And my dad, Cal.' The look she gave her father was full of love. 'I hope you all enjoy it.'

Annie knew the opening chords, although to begin with she couldn't place them. But as Kirsty began to sing in her sweet, husky voice, she recognised a Bonnie Raitt song about unrequited love, a lament so eloquent with pain it tore the heart apart. Kirsty's version was astonishing for someone so young. She sang from her soul, as if she had lived all the emotion contained within it. Haunted by the beauty and sadness of Kirsty's song, Annie suddenly thought of Mark's letter. Was that how he had felt? Somehow, she couldn't imagine it.

The last notes sounded on the keyboard. There was a stunned silence in the room, as if there had been a collective holding of the breath. Kirsty stood alone in the spotlight.

Then the applause began, cheers and whistles, some people leaping to their feet. Everyone knew they had been witness to something extraordinary.

Seemingly overwhelmed by the response, Kirsty looked down at the stage, shy, smiling and saying, 'thank you, thank you', until Callum, moisture shining in his eyes, stepped into the spotlight and put his arm around her. For a few moments they stood, hugging, oblivious to the audience and the band, Callum saying something only his daughter could hear. Then, visibly composing himself, he turned to the mic.

'Ladies and gentlemen, give it up for my lovely, talented daughter, Kirsty Mathieson!' There was a catch in his voice. Annie and Claire exchanged a glance. The tears that had welled up in her eyes were there in Claire's as well. Annie was reconsidering her initial impression of this man. He had emotional depths that he wasn't afraid to reveal.

As the applause finally died down, and people began to retake their seats the stage lights came back on as Callum sat down again, picking up his guitar.

'Well! How the hell are we supposed to follow that?' There was a ripple of laughter. 'I can only think of one song. It's by the master, Paul Simon. "Father and Daughter".'

He began to sing, accompanied at first only by his guitar until the others picked up the melody, joining in quietly on drums and keyboards. Kirsty picked up her flute and punctuated the chorus with a few haunting notes. There were tears in her eyes as her father sang the lyrics about a father's love for his daughter. By the end of the performance, Kirsty once again in Callum's arms as the audience stamped, clapped and whooped, there was hardly a dry eye in the house.

'Come and have a nightcap.' Jamie led the way to a table in the corner of the snug behind the main bar.

Callum and Kirsty appeared in the room, heading towards them.

'Stay calm, Claire!' Jamie warned his wife quietly out of the side of his mouth.

Callum stopped by their table, smiling. 'Hello, Annie, I just wanted to say I hope the funeral wasn't too hard for you. I'm sorry for not being there. I'm afraid ... well, I'm not so good at funerals.'

'No apology needed, really. In fact it's me who has to thank you, for what you said about Janet. It was so kind. Will you join us?'

Declining Jamie's offer of a drink, Callum drew up more chairs. Annie made the introductions. To her relief Claire was able to control her previously expressed intention to 'grab him and kiss the face off him!' Kirsty accepted their complimentary comments about her performance with a pretty blush. Callum looked on with pride.

'We saw you on TV. You were, like, awesome!' Sadly, offstage Kirsty's language lacked the poetry of the lyrics she sang.

'Maybe, but it almost cost me my job,' Annie told her ruefully.

'No way! All you did was, like, tell the truth, right?' Kirsty's face was a picture of indignation.

Annie smiled, aware Callum was listening to their conversation.

'The thing about truth is sometimes it just has to come out in little bits. I went too fast for them. I jumped the gun. What I did was wrong, unprofessional. I had to get away for a while to let the fuss die down.'

'Can I talk to you about it sometime? I'm, like, thinking I might become a lawyer too.'

Callum's mouth all but fell open in astonishment.

'Really? First I've heard of it! When did this happen? And, please, Kirsty, will you stop saying "like" every other word. You know it drives me crazy!'

Kirsty blushed again.

'Well it was like, when I saw Annie on the news that night I just thought, like, what a cool thing to do, helping those kids and bringing people to justice if they prey on, like, people who can't look after themselves. It's like, you know, massively cool.'

Annie laughed.

'It's not always like that! I'd love to tell you about it but you'll need to promise to limit the "likes". Otherwise you'll drive me round the bend as well.'

'Great, get Cal to fix up for you to come next weekend. And Cal, I'll stop saying "like" when you stop singing bits of song lyrics all the time. It drove Mum crazy, and it's driving me, like, totally nuts!'

She bounced off to join a squealing group of girls on the other side of the room. Callum watched her go, shaking his head, smiling.

'Do you?' asked Annie.

'Aye, well it's a bit of a bad habit of mine. I can't help it. My head's full of lyrics – there's not much room for anything else in there. I might have been Einstein if I didn't remember all the words of every song I've ever heard.'

Claire watched Kirsty go.

'How do you keep up with her?'

'I just wing it. I'm the single father of a teenage girl, and I've lost the instructions.'

They all laughed.

Conversation turned to the gig, Callum easy company, amusing and self-deprecating, Claire flirting for all she was worth, to Jamie's bemusement. They talked about contemporary Scottish painting – the gallery's specialism. Remembering the art books and catalogues in the study, Callum's knowledge of the artists and movements came as no surprise to Annie. It emerged that he was friendly with a couple of the painters Claire and Jamie represented.

Unable to contribute much to the discussion, Annie suddenly felt waves of exhaustion rolling over her. At the first break in the conversation, she made her excuses.

Callum said he had to get Kirsty home for an early start back to Edinburgh next day. They left the hotel together. Kirsty, reluctant to leave her friends, promised to be out in 'like, five more minutes'.

'You'll be on your way back to London, I expect, now the funeral's over?' Callum made it more of a question than an observation.

'I'm not sure. I've taken a bit of a sabbatical. I still have a lot to sort out here, and it's best to let the dust settle after *News Tonight* ...'

'You know, there's plenty of people around here really admire you for what you said. He looked like a sleazy bastard, that politician.'

Annie laughed. 'Too right. You've got him in one. It was good to see you again, Callum, I never really thanked you properly for the other day. And I really enjoyed the gig. I loved your song for Janet. I was very touched. And Kirsty was fantastic – what a talent.'

'Thank you. I expect I'll be seeing you around the village. If you can bear it, come and talk to Kirsty about being a lawyer – I'd be very pleased if she did something academic. She can always sing, but another string to the bow wouldn't be a bad thing.'

'True. Choice is good. I'd be happy to help.' She took her house key out of her bag. 'Goodnight, then.'

'Can I drop you off?'

'That's very kind, but actually I need the walk. It's only five minutes and it's such a beautiful evening ... '

'Of course. See you soon, then.'

Callum stepped forward, and to Annie's consternation, kissed her cheek, a light brush of his lips leaving her skin tingling. She hadn't known they were on kissing terms.

'Goodnight.'

Annie walked home, Callum's woody scent lingering in the air around her.

Back at the cottage, searching through Janet's CD collection, she found a copy of the Bonnie Raitt CD that featured "I Can't Make You Love Me" – it had been a favourite, she remembered. She listened to the original, remembering Kirsty's sweet version, and Callum's emotional response. She wished she had Kirsty's talent. She wished there were someone in her life that she truly loved. And she wished above all that she had known the love of a father.

Chapter 21
West Highlands
April

Someone was knocking on the front door. Annie woke with a start, stumbling out of bed. It was broad daylight. Grabbing her silk dressing gown, she shouted, 'Just coming' as she ran downstairs. Boris followed close on her heels.

She opened the door, holding her robe around her, expecting the postman. Callum broke into a broad smile. Whatever he started to say was drowned out in a cacophony of hysterical barking from the dogs in the Land Rover parked behind him. Annie stepped aside to let him in, as Boris retreated, indignant, into the kitchen.

'Sorry, they get very excited around cats. Stupid mutts.'

Annie tied the sash of her robe, glad that the chill of the night air meant she'd put on pyjamas. Callum's presence in her kitchen was unsettling. He brought with him the scent of the open air, of walks along the beach in the fresh breeze. Straight out of bed, her untamed hair was wild around her face, the warmth of her duvet still clung to her skin. Adding to an uncomfortable sense of exposure, the drying rack above the range was festooned with her laundry – socks, tights, a nightdress and several sets of lacy lingerie in the pinks and mauves she favoured. She saw him take it all in, quickly averting his gaze to one of Janet's paintings.

'Coffee?' she asked, to mask her discomfort.

'No, really, I should go … '

His evident unease told her he felt as uncomfortable as she did.

'Honestly, it's fine. I should be up anyway ... '

'Well, OK, but I'd prefer tea, please. I'm on my way back from the village, came to give you this. I meant to send it to your office but I kept forgetting. Sorry to arrive unannounced.' He laid the lavender cashmere scarf on the table.

'Oh! I'd forgotten all about it. Thank you.' She glanced at the kitchen clock, horrified to see it was already after nine. She must have slept for the best part of ten hours, twice her London norm.

'You'll not be needing a scarf today. Twenty-one degrees, according to the forecast, light winds. Perfect sailing day. I was planning to take *Sweet Dreams* out round the bay. Would you ... maybe you'd like to come with me?'

Annie had never been sailing. The offer was tempting – it would do her good to get out and do something new, after the emotional upheaval of Janet's funeral. But sailing?

'You'll love it or hate it. Either way, we won't go far, I can get you back on dry land if you don't like it. Up to you.'

'Actually, you know what? I'd love to. Will I come to your place or would you like to wait here while I get ready? Oh, and what should I wear?'

'I'll wait for you. Jeans, trainers, and something warm, fleece maybe.'

'Fleece? Don't be silly, I'm from London. We don't wear fleece, we wear cashmere.'

His laughter set them both at ease.

'Aye, maybe you do, but you'll not be warm enough.'

She went to shower and dress leaving Callum drinking tea under Boris's suspicious gaze.

A slow smile crept over Callum's lips as he surveyed Annie from head to foot. She had chosen skinny jeans and a fitted T shirt, a pink cashmere sweater tied round her shoulders. New trainers gleamed lurid pink and yellow.

'Very ... London.'

'I did warn you.'

'Aye. So you did. Well, you'll do. We'll take a picnic. I've got some stuff at home but I don't know what you like. Fancy London stuff I imagine. What have you got here?'

They raided the fridge for fruit and cheese. Chaource and papaya, Beaufort and kiwi fruit.

'I guess this is confirming your worst suspicions.'

'Just a bit.' He grinned. 'But I must admit, I've got a weakness for good French cheese. Especially these two. Not always easy to find, up here.'

Annie set down dry food and a bowl of fresh water for Boris, and despite her earlier comment, found a warm fleece jacket hanging in the lobby.

'Oh, and you'll need sunglasses.'

She found some in her bag and put them on, looking to him for comment. He nodded his approval.

'You'll be far and away the most glamorous crew in the Western Isles.'

∼

'Welcome aboard.'

Callum held his hand out to steady her as Annie stepped from the pier on to the side deck of the yacht. The dogs leapt aboard behind her.

He passed down the bags of provisions before boarding himself, setting the boat rocking in the water. Annie stepped down into the cockpit. Looking around, she admired the bright varnish of the woodwork, contrasting with the silvery weathered planking on deck.

A set of double doors opened at the forward end of the cockpit, leading the way below deck. Callum went inside, sitting on the step down into the cabin. As she passed him the bags, she marvelled at the way everything was stowed away into lockers and racks. There was even a coolbox, into which he poured a bag of ice to chill the bottle of wine Annie had brought, milk, cheese and cold meats. There was a cooker, two burners with an oven below, and a small round sink.

'It's so cosy. I'd imagined something much more spartan.'

'I don't do spartan. All the comforts of home. Come below and have a look.' He moved aside to let her pass.

To her surprise, Annie found she could stand up with room to spare. There was a berth on either side of the cabin, upholstered in a muted plaid fabric, with cushions and throws lending a homely air. The shelves above were crammed with books and charts. An old-fashioned lamp hung under the pointed skylight. On one side of the white-painted bulkhead at the forward end, there was an antique map showing a group of islands, on the other an open door revealed a forward cabin. Annie could see sail bags and ropes stacked up on its two further berths.

'Wow! It's fantastic! I love it!' She was enchanted by the boat's tidy practicality, all life's necessities carefully stowed away in the tight space. The craftsmanship was obvious in the quality of the joinery, glowing in the sunlight flooding through the skylight.

'I'd no idea what to expect. It's like a little house. Can you sleep in it? Did you build it? How long did it take? How far could you go in a boat like this?'

Callum smiled at the barrage of questions.

'I'm really glad you like her. I didn't build her, but I

restored her. Been working on her on and off for a couple of years. I just launched her last month, can't decide whether to keep her or not. She's very seaworthy. A boat like this could cross oceans. But first I need to get used to her, see how she handles.'

Why are boats female, Annie wondered?.

He found lifejackets for them all, dogs included, and took her through the safety procedures – 'Stay in the cockpit so you don't fall overboard. One hand for the boat at all times.' Then he fired up the outboard motor and cast off the mooring lines, steering the boat out of the bay.

Clear of the rocks and shallows, Callum raised the sails and cut the engine. Peace descended as the wind took over. The boat picked up speed and took off across the sound towards Skye, settling into a comfortable rhythm, at one with the wind and waves.

The bridge came into view as they cleared a headland. Annie used her phone to photograph the mountains and the majestic Skye crossing, turning the lens on Mick and Keith, comical in bright turquoise life-jackets, curled up together on the cockpit sole.

'Do you mind?' She pointed the camera at Callum.

'As long as it's not going to end up on social bloody media.'

'Promise. I can't stand all that stuff ... '

'Kirsty never stops. Her whole life seems to be dedicated to taking the perfect selfie. Drives me nuts.'

Annie took two quick snaps, hoping he hadn't noticed that the second was a close-up.

'This is wonderful! Now I see why people love sailing!'

'Good. I'll not be needing to take you back then. This is a perfect day for it – flat sea and a good breeze, doesn't get better than this. We're doing ... ' he read the numbers on a screen on the coachroof 'six knots, even towing the dinghy.'

She wondered if that was a good thing, but Callum seemed pleased with it, so it must be.

He exchanged a wave with the man on another boat that sailed close past them.

'That's one of mine.' It was the same as the boats she had seen in the shed, white sails bright against the clear blue sky, red ensign streaming out astern as it sped away southwards towards the bridge.

'Going well. Sandy's really got the measure of her.' There was a note of pride in his voice.

'Right, here's the passage plan. See those wee islands up to the north there?' He pointed to a small group of islands some way off. 'We're going halfway across the sound towards Raasay, to give you a sense of being in more open waters. Then we'll tack back and tuck into the anchorage there. They're lovely islands. We'll have our picnic, and we'll take the dogs ashore for a walk. Sound OK to you?'

'Aye-aye, Captain,' Annie punctuated her reply with a smart salute.

He barked with laughter.

'Respect – I'm not used to that.'

She settled back to enjoy the ride, content to watch as Callum steered with a light touch on the tiller, occasionally loosening or tightening a sail, reading the changes in the wind. In leather sea boots and a red sailing jacket over black jeans, dark hair swept back by the wind – Annie noticed a few strands of silver lit up by the sun – he looked like a man completely in his element. His clear blue gaze constantly shifted from the sails to the water to the horizon.

'Want a go?'

'I wouldn't know what to do.'

He showed her, explaining the different points of sailing. He spoke quietly, with clear and simple instructions. Holding the tiller with her until she grew used to the subtle movements required to keep the boat sailing steadily, he let go when he was confident of her grasp of what to do. He settled down in the corner of the cockpit out of the wind. Mick and Keith fought for best position on his lap.

'You've got a real feel for this. I'm impressed.'

'You're a very good teacher.'

'You're a very good pupil. Some people never get the hang of it. I teach at the sailing club – kids, mostly. But I do a couple of yacht master courses every year, to keep my hand in. Been doing it for a few years. I enjoy teaching.'

He began to sing, almost under his breath. "Sweet Dreams", a song she knew.

'So that's where the name comes from.'

'Of course. Great name for a boat.'

Annie thrilled to the feeling of the hull carving through the water under her hand, sails taut in the breeze and the hiss of the wake rushing past just inches away.

'Hold your course, but look out to the port side – your left.'

Two dolphins, racing along beside them, broke the surface of the water with a whoosh of breath, then dived together under the hull.

'Oh no ... I'm going to hit them!' she screamed, letting go of the tiller.

Callum put out a hand to steady it and pressed a button on the auto helm screen mounted on the coachroof.

'There, hands-free. Now you can watch the dolphins. And you won't hit them. They're much faster than us.'

The dolphins, joined by several more, swam with them for the next few minutes, diving under the bow, racing alongside, playing in their wake. Torn between watching and trying to capture them on the phone camera, Annie rushed from one side to the other, squealing with delight at each new appearance. Callum kept watch, pointing out the ones she'd missed. Only the dogs seemed unimpressed.

Then they were gone – swimming away, only an occasional fin cutting the surface of the water here and there as a reminder of their presence in the deep water around them.

'That was the most wonderful thing I've ever seen! Are they always here?'

'Aye, you often see them, but you never take it for granted when they come to play. It's part of the magic in these parts. There's so much wildlife here – whales, basking shark, otters, sea eagles, more kinds of birds than you can imagine, but the puffins are best. And seals, of course, hundreds, thousands of them. It's part of why I love it.'

'I never imagined . . . ' Words failed her. How could she ever have imagined this, embroiled in the sad life of an abuse inquiry that occupied her thoughts most of the time?

He talked her through altering course, making for the north-western end of the islands. The boat sat up straighter, and Callum went below, leaving Annie at the helm. Nervous, she concentrated hard on the headland he had pointed out, keeping the boat sailing steadily towards it, only partly aware of the whistling kettle. A short while later Callum came up from below with mugs of tea and chocolate biscuits.

'Traditional.'

'What, not rum and hard tack?'

'Not on my boat. I'll take over – have a break.'

Annie sat back, sipping tea, fully relaxed for the first time in as long as she could remember as she relished the enjoyment of doing something so far removed from her normal life, in such good and, she had to admit to herself, attractive company.

A beacon atop the north-westernmost of the islands led them into a narrow gap, barely thirty metres across, between the two. That opened out into a wider pool, where they dropped anchor. Callum switched off the engine and *Sweet Dreams* swung round to settle in the current. They were quite alone – except for dozens of seals. Lying on the rocks or swimming in the lagoon, the seals watched them from a safe distance, sleek heads rising out of the water, huge dark eyes fixed on the boat. Annie was transfixed.

'What do you think?' Callum spoke quietly beside her, eyes on the seals. 'The Crowlin Islands. One of my favourite anchorages.'

Annie had never known a place so remote or so peaceful. Silence fell between them as they soaked up the atmosphere.

The islands rose up on either side. A bend at the entrance made it seem as if the land had closed in behind them. Only to the south was it possible to see out past the headland behind which the Skye bridge was just visible in the distance.

Callum broke the spell.

'It's perfect here, really well-sheltered. Lunch first, or a trip ashore?'

Keen to get closer to the basking seals, Annie replied without hesitation.

'Ashore.'

He helped her climb over the side of the yacht into the rubber tender.

Dogs leaping ahead through the heather and bracken, they climbed to the top of the hill, where they found a little lochan, mirror-calm, reflecting the bright sky. They could see for miles – Callum pointed out Raasay and Rona to the west, with the mountains of Skye behind. The Applecross peninsula stretched out to the north, the Cuillins and Kyles of Lochalsh to the south.

The sun glistening on the water was intensely bright. It was warm on land, in the early spring sun.

'This is amazing, Callum. I wouldn't have missed it for anything.'

'Glad to see you enjoying it so much. I know it's been a tough time for you. There's nothing like sailing to put things in perspective. And you weren't seasick – that's a bonus.'

'Quite the contrary, I'm starving! Did you mention lunch?'

Chapter 22
West Highlands
April

'So you were born in Edinburgh? How come you ended up in London?' The cockpit table held the remains of a splendid lunch of salad with cold ham and cheese, sourdough bread and fresh fruit. Callum helped himself to a last piece of Beaufort with an oatcake, sitting back to listen to her answer. The ease that had grown between them on the trip across the sound had settled into a comfortable companionship. Conversation flowed easily.

Annie smiled.

'My crazy mother. Maddie. Well named. Only sensible decision she ever took in her life. Although I expect it had more to do with running after a man' – she couldn't bring herself to say his name – 'than any consideration for my welfare. But at least I went to a multicultural school, as opposed to being the only mixed-race kid in an Edinburgh primary.'

London. A two-bedroomed flat in Swiss Cottage, on the edge of a huge, modern estate. An architect's vision of how social housing should look. The reality, a stepped crescent that stretched away into the distance as far as the eye could see, had quickly deteriorated into just another concrete jungle. Lately it appeared regularly in films and TV dramas as a sink estate inhabited by drug dealers and violent criminals. It was on a downward trajectory all the time they lived there.

Annie remembered her nursery school, filled with the sounds of chattering children. She had a clear image of playing in the sandpit with her best friend Sandra, a girl with hair so blonde it was almost white, and a boy with a name she never learned to pronounce, with skin so black she saw her own as pale by comparison. He was born in Africa, he told her proudly.

'Is that where the lions live?'

He made claws of his hands and roared. Annie laughed.

'Yes, and tigers –'

'—and alligators?'

'—and great big noisy elephants –'

'—cheeky monkeys!'

'Slithery snakes!' They collapsed in fits of the giggles, shouting out the names of all the animals they could remember and then making up more when they ran out, until the nursery teacher came to see what all the fuss was about. At story time she showed them a book of cartoon animals, the pages cut in half laterally so that you could match the top of the tiger with the legs of the elephant, making up a whole zoo of strange new creatures. The classroom rang with the shrieks and gurgles of delighted childish laughter.

It was one of her earliest memories. She still had a copy of the book – *Animal Lore and Disorder* – which she had found in an antique fair years later. The memory brought a smile to her face.

But then it faded as she thought of her life at home – Ruadhri, impatient, angry and unpredictable as his work in theatre design dried up. Maddie's exuberance fading as the relationship deteriorated into shouting matches, slamming doors, thrown crockery. The dark times, when the shouting became beatings, her mother on the floor, crying hysterically as blood poured from her nose. Police visits, warnings, social workers. By the time she was old enough to have a true grasp of how bad things were, she also understood how close she'd come to being taken into care.

~

'It wasn't the happiest childhood. Mum's boyfriend ... ' she shook her head. There were no words to describe her feelings about that part of her history. 'It was Janet who made it all bearable. She was my guardian angel. She often came to see us ... I suppose she was checking up on things, she really worried about Maddie ... and she'd take me out to do all the things that Mum never wanted to do – trips to the zoo, the museums, the parks – away from all the tension at home. And of course she couldn't help being a teacher – she was always bringing me books and telling me I had to work hard at school. Not that I needed to be told. By the time I was ten I already knew education was my ticket out of the mess my mother had made of her life – I was damned sure my own was going to be different.' She paused and laughed. 'Once I told Janet I was going to be a banker when I grew up. Don't know what happened to that one ... '

'I can't see you as a banker. A lawyer, yes, but not someone moving money around for a living.'

'Sounds like you don't have much time for bankers.'

'To be honest, I'm not sure I've ever met one. Apart from the local bank manager. Just blind prejudice, probably ... ' Annie smiled at his embarrassed expression. 'But ... your dad? What about ... didn't he ... ?'

'I have no idea who my father is. My mother refused to tell me anything about him. The only thing I can be sure about is he was ... is ... black. Obviously.'

'And your mum never ... that's hard. Sorry.'

'It's fine. I ... Anyway, I'd just finished my A-Levels. Ruadhri was long gone by then, just Mum and me. But she was in a bad way – drinking heavily, drugged up on antidepressants and sleeping pills. She'd stopped trying to work by then – she'd been such a good designer, used to make the most gorgeous wedding dresses ... but it all fell apart. And then one night he turned up – I told her not to let him in ... ' She broke off as the memory of that night coursed through her, setting her insides churning, even all these years later, aware that Callum was watching her closely.

~

'Don't answer it, Mum. Please.'

Maddie ignored her, rushing to answer the door. Annie could hear the murmured conversation on the doorstep. Then there he was, in the sitting room, Maddie behind him, an uncertain smile on her face. Annie's stomach turned over with revulsion. She kept her expression cold.

'Hello, Annie. You're all grown up since I last saw you.'

There was no mistaking the look in his eyes. She'd seen it before. Disgusted, she left the room, shutting her bedroom door firmly behind her. She pushed a chair under the handle. She could hear them next door, a reunion of sorts, her mother crying out, Ruadhri's cruel laugh. Shaking with fear and revulsion, she drowned out the sounds with loud music in her headphones.

In the morning he came into the kitchen where she was making coffee. She was wearing flannelette pyjamas, a grubby towelling dressing gown belted tight around her waist. Novelty slippers – tiger feet.

'I don't think you should be walking around half-dressed like that, Annie. It's a bit much for a man to take.'

'Don't you dare ...'

She took her mug off the counter and made to walk past him, back to her room. He grabbed her arm, looming over her, stale whisky breath in her face as he tried to kiss her.

'Take your filthy fucking hands off me,' she hissed, pulling away, spilling scalding coffee on her hand.

Maddie was standing in the hallway. She'd seen it all. She took a step into the kitchen, blazing eyes fixed on Ruadhri.

'Get out. Now.' Her voice was barely more than a whisper.

'Oh, come on, Maddie. It was just a bit of fun.' Ruadhri tried to laugh it off.

'Get out. Before I kill you.'

'Jesus Christ, Maddie—'

She took another step towards him, fearless with rage.

'OK, OK, I'm going. As if I'd want to stay in this witches' coven anyway.'

Moments later he had grabbed his bag and slammed the front door.

'Oh God, Annie, I'm so, so sorry. You were right, I should never have let him in. To think of him, looking at you like that ... putting his hands on you ... I could kill him ... I should have killed him. I'm so sorry, it's all my fault –'

'Of course it isn't, Mum. None of it's your fault, it's him, he's a ... a ... ' she couldn't say it, not to Maddie, when she was so vulnerable. 'But are you OK, Mum? Maybe you should go out today, so you're not here if he comes back. Why don't you go up town? Get a friend to go with you –

do some shopping. Buy yourself something nice. Or go and see that film you said you wanted to see at the weekend.'

'Good idea, Annie. I think I might.'

Unable to get the events of the morning out of her mind, Annie had called home from school at lunchtime, but there was no reply. Pleased, she'd let herself think that Maddie had taken her advice.

There was a study period after school, so she arrived home later than usual that afternoon.

The flat was in silence. Normally the radio would be blaring as Maddie prepared tea.

'Mum?' she called.

She went into the kitchen. An empty plastic bag lay on the counter. She recognised the name of the off-licence.

Maddie was on her bed. The bottle had fallen from her grasp, spilling whisky over the bedclothes. The sharp, smoky smell filled the bedroom. Some white pills lay scattered on the duvet cover. She looked peaceful. Annie knew straight away, but tried to revive her anyway, crying, screaming, trying not to know that her mother was cold, lifeless, gone.

Annie brushed away the moisture in her eyes.

'Sorry ... my mum died – overdose. No note or anything ... ' She broke off, choking back the tears that so often ambushed her as she revisited the hurt. No note, no explanation, no goodbye.

Callum reached out and laid his hand over hers, clasped together on her knees, knuckles white. His touch was warm and comforting. For a brief moment she tried to imagine how it would feel to lay her head on his chest and cry out all the grief that she had kept under tight control for years. But she shook herself out of it and sat up straight. He took his hand away.

'God, Annie, you haven't half been through it. What happened to you then?'

'I already had my place at the LSE.'

'LSE?'

'London School of Economics. I went into student accommodation, then after I graduated Janet helped me find a flat. Putney, south of the river – I'm still there. I suppose I just worked my way through it ... the grief and everything ... I focused on getting my degree.'

'A first, I bet.'

She smiled her agreement.

'And then I did my articles with a radical law firm and the rest just fell into place.'

'I hardly know what to say.'

'There's nothing to say. It's life – everyone has bad stuff to deal with. I mean, look at what's happened to you ... Charlie, your career, and then to lose your wife so young ... '

He nodded, looking out across the sunlit bay. The boat began to swing round as the tide changed. For a few moments they were quiet, lost in their own reflections.

'Tea?' Callum broke the silence. Annie was beginning to recognise that this was much more than his preferred drink. The ritual of tea-making gave him time to contemplate, gather his thoughts.

'Freya ... ' he began, his gaze fixed on the shoreline. 'We were at school together, then we met up again in Stornoway. It was a few months after Charlie died ... ' He described the aftermath, his grief at the loss of his best friend, his career as a musician. The words came easily. It was far in the past –

nowadays he could talk about it with no difficulty.

Talking about losing Freya was a different matter entirely.

How many times had his sister tried to get him to see a bereavement counsellor, or at least talk to his GP? And yet he had never felt the need. 'It's grief, Mhairi,' he had said. 'I don't want to be medicated, or talk to anyone. What is there to say?'

But somehow, now, hearing about Annie's life, the losses she had suffered, he felt able to open up about his own feelings.

'Freya was amazing. Just seemed to understand what I was going through, how to help me deal with it. Tough love, though.' He paused, smiling, remembering how she had walked away after finding him drinking once too often. 'Wouldn't let me get away with ... made me face up to things ... Charlie, the band, my own ... sense of responsibility. She was a psychotherapist, knew exactly what she was doing. Funny, for a while I thought I was in control but I had no idea ... ' He stopped, the familiar wave of loss and longing snatching his breath away. Annie sat quiet on the opposite side of the cockpit, looking out at the seals on the rocks, giving him time to collect himself.

'It was inevitable that we would end up together. Like ... coming home. Finding my soulmate, my destiny. And then losing her ... ' He stopped again, concentrating on the words. He was barely aware of Annie now. This was something he needed to articulate for himself.

'Losing Charlie ... that was hard. But losing Freya was something else altogether. All those words you always knew – bereaved, mourning, loss – you don't know what they really mean until it happens to you. It's visceral, grief. Like ... like having your heart torn out. A chasm opens up beside you, where your other half should be – no, not half, more than half. We were more than the sum of our parts. There was Freya, and me, and then ... us. In all our years together, we never spent a single night apart. And yet the strangest thing happens ... even though we spent almost twenty years together, I can't remember her voice, I can't picture her face. People say that's common, but it's so hard, painful ... maybe it's because you're so close. You become ... not one, but a unit. Alone, you're a stranger to yourself. Even now I don't really know who I am, first person singular. I'm still working on that. And of course, having to hold it together for Kirsty. If it wasn't for her I don't know how ... '

He fell silent again, the memory of those early weeks and months of aching loss crowding out the ability to say any more. Still lost in thought, he took a mouthful of tea, finding it had gone cold. Turning in his seat, he poured the remains overboard, tucking the empty mug into the corner of the cockpit seat beside him. Annie remained silent, understanding that he was really talking to himself.

'And then there's all the love that you still feel ... so powerful, like at the beginning when all you can think about is ... her ... but now it's got nowhere to go. It's hard to hang on to the memory in an honest way – you edit out all the bad stuff and suddenly it seems you're grieving for someone she never was.' He smiled. 'We were like any other couple, Freya and me, always bickering, finding more and more ways to drive each other mad. She'd turned it into an art form. Bossy doesn't begin to describe her. And I'm no saint, either. I don't know how she put up with me – I'm a moody bastard, unpredictable, messy, disorganised, never able to take a decision. Swearing all the time. I must have been a bloody nightmare to live with. But the illness ... the cancer – well, you forget all the other stuff. Then it's just about the love. Wanting to do everything I could for her. It would have been far easier to go through it myself than watch Freya ... fade ... Oh Jesus.'

It was impossible to go on. Dimly aware of Annie reaching out, now it was his turn to feel the comfort of another person's touch, a brief gesture of sympathy.

'I can hardly imagine it, Callum. I'm so terribly sorry. I ... I've never loved anyone like that, the way you describe it ... It's different, I suppose, losing a parent, an aunt ... '

Callum glanced at her, saw her expression of concern.

'I'm sorry, Annie, dumping this on you.'

'Please, you have nothing to be sorry about. It's good that you're able to talk about it. I know how hard that is.'

'Aye.' He didn't tell her that she was the first person he'd ever talked to about the pain that was usually beyond words.

It was time to change the subject. 'I'd better go ashore again. I expect the dogs need a pee by now.'

'I'll come too. I need to find somewhere I can ... well, you know, I need to go ashore too.'

Callum laughed, dispersing the solemn mood.

'Sorry, I forgot to show you the heads.'

He led the way below and showed her the tiny compartment between the cabins, complete with fold-down wash-basin and running water, and told her how it worked.

'Much more civilised.'

Afterwards they went ashore again, to the other island, where a ruined cottage nestled in a shallow valley.

It was as they climbed up out of the sheltered hollow they became aware of the wind. They walked up to the highest point and looked out over the sound. The calm waters they had enjoyed in the morning were now a threatening grey, white-capped waves chasing each other down the channel. A yacht off the coast of Raasay was beating southwards, heeled over, sails reefed down.

'Goodness, it's all changed,' Annie observed nervously.

'Hm. It's just an offshore wind, happens in the afternoon when the land heats up. It'll die down later. It's just a bit rougher than I'd have expected. Wind over tide. We should have started back earlier – my fault, talking too much.'

'And me – it wasn't just you!' A glance at her watch told Annie they had talked for more than three hours.' Can we not sail in these conditions?'

'Aye, we could, that wee boat's tough, she'd take anything weather-wise, but I'm more worried about you – it won't be very comfortable going back, we'll be rolling around a lot, beam-on to the waves. It can make you feel a bit sick.'

Annie felt queasy just thinking about it.

'What'll we do?'

'We're well sheltered here. Our best bet is to stay put. This'll have gone down by the morning. Unless you need to be back tonight. Do you? Any hot dates lined up?'

Annie thought about Boris, the nearest thing she'd had to a date since she arrived in the village. She quickly dismissed him from her list of concerns – he was a cat, a born survivor, and she'd left plenty for him to eat. What did she have to get back for? Another evening alone, a few too many glasses of wine, maybe a look at the emails she'd been ignoring ever since she came up to organise the funeral. Nothing. And besides, she was really enjoying herself, on the little boat with all its home comforts, and Callum. As far as Annie was concerned, there was no rush to get back.

'No, it would be fun to stay here. An adventure.'

'Good. That's settled.'

∽

Back on board, Callum searched through the lockers in the galley, triumphantly producing a foil pack.

'I knew I had something stashed away – will this do?' He held out the packet. Chilli con carne, Annie read.

'Perfect.'

There was still plenty of salad and fruit, a big bar of chocolate – even some biscuits for the dogs.

'At least no one's going to go hungry.'

Early evening brought a rapid fall in temperature. The galley stove gave welcome warmth to the cabin as Callum heated the meal.

'We'll eat in the cockpit – there's more room.'

'Won't it get too cold?'

Callum fetched the throws from the cabin, wrapping one round Annie's shoulders.

'That'll help.'

Snuggled into their blankets, they settled down to eat surprisingly good chilli.

'Everything tastes good when you're sailing. Even if it comes out of a packet.'

Annie could only agree. 'It's delicious.'

Resuming their earlier conversation, they talked about family. Callum's parents had both been teachers, now retired. His brother was a professor of history in Edinburgh, his sister a GP on Skye.

'I was the rebel. Running away to be in a band. Just after my O-Levels – I was supposed to be going to Edinburgh University to do English, but we were in Glasgow on a school trip to see the Burrell Collection. Charlie saw an ad in the window of a music shop – a band was looking for a guitarist and a singer. It was a spur of the moment thing, crazy ... When I think now of the pain I caused the family it makes me ashamed. Nothing like being a parent yourself to give you a reality check.'

'I was a rebel too. Only in my case that meant being a good girl, doing my homework, working hard at school. Reading – I was always reading. My mother used to call me a "wee swot" But I knew I had to get to university, have a proper career. I must have been about ten when I took a long hard look at Mum's life and knew it wasn't for me. Nothing like having a screwed-up mother to give you a reality check, either.'

Callum smiled.

'And now look at us. Rebels together ... '

He broke off suddenly. In the silence, a strange keening sound drifted across the water.

'Listen!'

'What's that? It's really eerie.' A rush of adrenaline made her skin tingle and sent a shiver down her spine.

The dogs sat up, ears pricked, growling deep in their throats. Callum rubbed the neck of the closest dog, soothing him.

'It's only the seals. They're singing for us.'

The sun hung low over the craggy mountains of Skye. While Callum took the dogs for a last trip ashore, Annie cleared up and stowed everything away, relishing a quiet moment alone in the boat. In the calm water of the anchorage, it felt safe and secure, a cosy home on the water.

Dusk was well advanced, with only a brilliant strip of orange to show where the sun had slipped out of sight, when the shore party returned. The seal songs continued intermittently. Seabirds called out with plaintive cries.

The peace of the anchorage intensified as night fell.

Below, Callum closed the companionway doors, shutting out the chilly evening air. He performed some alchemy with paraffin and meths, lighting the Tilley lamp which glowed with a soft yellow light, hissing quietly and giving off welcome heat. Drowsy in the warmth of her blanket, Annie stretched out on the port-side berth, head propped up on a pile of cushions. The boat rocked gently in the current.

'Tiring, this sailing business,' she murmured.

'We should probably get some sleep. We'll head off early, we'll catch the last couple of hours of favourable tide if we leave about seven.'

He opened a locker behind the starboard-side berth.

'Fuck it.'

'What's wrong?'

'No sleeping-bags. I wasn't planning an overnight trip. They're back at the house.'

'Oh. Well, I'm perfectly warm.'

'You won't be. There's only twenty millimetres of planking and a coat of paint between you and the Atlantic Ocean. It'll be cold, this early in the season.'

She yawned, snuggling deeper into the blanket.

'I'm fine, really.'

'Aye, well just keep wrapped up. Wear everything you've got. Hat, scarf, gloves, the lot – you'll need it. I'll leave the Tilley on until it burns down. D'you want a dog to keep you warm?'

A picture of the dogs ashore, rolling in something that looked suspiciously like a dead fish, formed in Annie's mind.

'I don't think so, thanks. I'd much rather have Boris ... softer.' And more fastidious, she thought.

'You're welcome to him. Cats – horrible creatures. I'm allergic.'

'Aw, shame. Boris is lovely. Like a living teddy-bear.

My new bestie.'

'Beastie, more like.'

Annie smiled sleepily. Her eyelids began to close.

Trying not to wake her, Callum arranged her scarf higher round her neck, drawing it up around her ears. He wrapped himself in his own blanket, pulled on a woollen hat and made room on the end of his berth for the dogs, before he too allowed himself to drift off.

∼

'What's wrong, Annie?'

Annie was moving around restlessly. The lamp had gone out, leaving the cabin in inky darkness.

'Sorry, I didn't mean to wake you. I'm just so cold – absolutely freezing!'

He could hear her shivering.

'You should have had a dog. But I've got two, and I'm cold as well.' He hesitated before he spoke again. 'Don't take this the wrong way, but we'd be much warmer if we slept together.'

'There's hardly enough room for one in this bed! How are we going to do that?'

Callum chuckled. 'You'd be surprised what we boatbuilders have up our sleeves.'

He lit a lamp above his berth and reached into a locker below it, producing some sections of board which slotted into the space between the two sofas. The back cushions fitted on top of the infill boards, creating a berth across the width of the cabin.

'Clever!'

They moved closer together, rearranging cushions, blankets and dogs until they lay side by side in a cocoon of covers, Mick and Keith sealing the bedclothes tight around their feet. Callum switched the light off, plunging them once more into velvety darkness.

Annie's shivers subsided slowly. Tentatively Callum put his arm around her, drawing her closer, breathing in a faint hint of the spicy scent he remembered from their first meeting. Annie eased herself closer still and he felt her warmth seeping through their layers of clothing.

He began to sing, very quietly, a line of a song she didn't know, the lyric about two people warming each other, just as they were.

'What's that?' she asked

'Hall and Oates. "Sara Smile." My mum's favourite.'

'Nice. Sing a bit more.'

He sang a few more lines, keeping his voice soft and breathy.

'It's lovely. Is that your annoying habit then?'

'Aye, I've got one for every occasion. Are you getting any warmer?'

'Mmm, I am, thanks.'

He tucked the blanket tighter around her shoulders.

'OK?'

He could feel her relaxing as she warmed up.

'OK? I know women who would kill to be in my place right now.' she murmured, her voice sleepy.

'Names and addresses, please.'

'Claire Anderson-Butler, Beauchamp Lane Gallery, London.'

Callum laughed. 'That flirty woman! I don't think so.'

He drew her closer still, something stirring in his stomach as she snuggled up. Spooned together, the gentle rocking of the boat and the breeze sighing in the rigging lulled them back into a peaceful sleep.

Chapter 23
West Highlands
April

Grey dawn light filtered through the skylight above her head. Suddenly awake, it took Annie a moment to remember where she was. But as the boat rocked gently in the current, Callum stirred in his sleep, tightening his arm around her. She felt the warmth of his breath on the back of her neck. It felt good to lie in his embrace, snug and sleepy.

One of the dogs wriggled at her feet, rolling onto his back with a long sigh. The movement woke Callum.

'Morning, Annie,' he murmured. 'Sleep OK?'

'Mmm, I did, thanks.' She had slept surprisingly well, snuggled up with a man she hardly knew.

'I need a pee. And so will the dogs. I'll take them ashore, give you some privacy.'

By the time they returned, Annie had restored the cabin to its normal state, the blankets neatly folded on the sofas, infill sections stowed away in their locker. The kettle came to the boil, whistling on the stove. They breakfasted on papaya, with bread and cheese, washed down with mugs of tea.

As Callum prepared the boat to leave, Annie struggled with her lifejacket. She'd managed the previous day, copying how Callum put his on, effortlessly shrugging it over his shoulders and fastening the buckle. For some reason now the damned thing wouldn't cooperate.

'It's twisted. Let me help you. Turn round.'

The feeling of his hands brushing her shoulders as he smoothed the straps sent shivers down her spine. He turned her back to face him and fastened the buckle. As their eyes met, Annie became acutely aware of his hands, close to her breasts. She dropped her gaze, suddenly shy in the intimacy of the moment, wondering if he was conscious of the effect he was having on her.

'There, that's it. The other strap goes between your legs and clips in beside the buckle. I'll let you deal with that yourself.' His tone was matter-of-fact but she could hear the smile in his voice.

'I really loved this, Callum. I'm so glad you asked me.' She kept her tone light, trying to defuse the tension in the atmosphere.

'It's been great, hasn't it? Maybe you'll come out to play again sometime.'

'I'd love to. As long as you remember the sleeping-bags next time.'

'Did you not like sleeping with me, then?' His tone was teasing.

'I'm very grateful you took pity on me. I thought I was going to freeze to death.'

'It was no hardship for me, Annie.' Suddenly serious, he held her gaze a fraction longer than was comfortable. She looked down to avoid his eyes.

'Anyway, I suppose now I can say I've slept with a famous rock star.' She hoped the comment sounded the right light-hearted note.

'Former rock star,' he corrected her. 'And I'd be careful about that. I've got form there. People might get the wrong idea about you.'

His comment made her giggle.

Comfortable together again, the conversation

resumed – books, films. Life. As the boat made steady progress back towards the entrance to Loch Carron, they slipped effortlessly from one topic to the next. Laughter often bubbled up as they found that they shared the same sense of humour.

'I've really enjoyed this, Annie. It's been great to have someone I can talk to. It gets a wee bit lonely up here without Kirsty, that's why she still comes home so much. Sometimes I go weeks without having a proper conversation.'

'I wondered about that. What keeps you here, with Kirsty away?'

'There are only two things I'm any good at in life. One is performing – been there, done that, got the scars. Never again, not like in the band. The stuff I do now suits me fine. The other thing I can do is build boats. I love it, you saw that the first time we met. And I've got everything I need here. I couldn't imagine doing it anywhere else. This is my home. So I suppose loneliness is a price I pay.'

The sea was calm again, the conditions perfect. As they made their way back across the sound, he taught her how to trim the sails. Watching her at the helm, Callum commented on how easily she had taken to sailing. Some of the people he taught never got it at all, but Annie was one of those rare students, a natural sailor. For someone who had never set foot on a sailing yacht before, her grasp of how the wind and the sails worked together seemed to be completely instinctive.

Annie's thoughts were elsewhere.

'Can I ask you something?' Suddenly it seemed important to know.

'Depends.'

'It's quite personal.'

'Try me.'

'Have you ... has there been anyone else ... since ... ?'

He looked at his hands, twisting his wedding ring, a simple gold band. When he met her eyes, his expression was serious.

'I shouldn't have asked.' she said.

'No, it's fine. There was someone, a few months back. It didn't work out.'

'Oh.' She felt a stab of disappointment.

'It was just – it was much too soon. She was divorced, looking for much more than I could give. It would never have worked, we're all wrong for each other. I think it was Cal the rock star she was interested in really, and that's not me. And Kirsty couldn't stand her.'

'That must have been hard.'

'Aye, it's not just about me. If I ever have another relationship it has to be right for Kirsty too.'

He made it sound unlikely he ever would.

Feeling she was on tricky ground, she changed the subject, paying attention to the boat again.

'We seem to have slowed down. Am I doing something wrong?'

He studied the water around them.

'No, it's the tide – it's turned against us – not much, only about a knot, but it's good that you noticed it – shows you're really getting a feel for this.'

'I'd never have expected it, city girl like me. I always thought having a good time was a hundred-pound theatre ticket and a posh restaurant. I'd no idea you could have so much fun for free.'

'Free? Have you never heard what people say about sailing? It's like tearing up fifty-pound notes in a cold shower.'

'Well, the wind's free, the wildlife's free, all this amazing scenery is free.'

'I can't argue with that. Right, time to take the sails down – we'll be turning into the bay in a moment. Turn her up into the wind and hold her there.' He started the engine.

Not only did she understand the instruction, Annie carried it out perfectly while he dropped the sails. Then, standing beside her ready to take over, he talked her through taking *Sweet Dreams* towards her berth. As the boat came to rest against the pier, he stepped ashore with the lines.

'Well done, you're a natural. You make a great first mate.'

Callum followed her into the kitchen. The constraint that had grown between them earlier had returned on the drive back to the village. Now it hung heavy in the air.

He put the bags down on the table and waited, awkward, while Annie took off Aunt Janet's fleece jacket.

'Tea?' Her voice sounded unnatural, brittle.

'Ehm … no. No thanks. I should get going … farm shop and so on. Kirsty'll be home for the weekend – eats like a horse. So … ehm … '

Annie nodded and smiled.

'Well … thanks. I really loved it … sailing and … the dolphins, the seals … even your singing! It was such an adventure.'

'Aye. Well, sorry I fucked up, should have got you back … '

'Callum, really, I didn't mind at all. It was fun. I enjoyed every minute.'

'Good. So … will you come to supper on Saturday? Kirsty'd like it … and so would I.'

'Yes, of course. I'd love to. What time?'

'We eat early – sixish, if that's OK. Anything you don't eat?'

'Tripe.'

He smiled. Annie couldn't resist smiling back. There was something infectious about his slow grin and the way it seemed to light up his eyes.

'I'll take it off the menu, then. So – see you Saturday.'

He hesitated. Just for a moment she thought he was going to kiss her, but he turned and was gone, through the door and into the Land Rover, before she even had time to acknowledge her disappointment.

Chapter 24
West Highlands
April

Annie jumped at the sound of a knock on the door later that morning. Fiona stood on the doorstep, Boris in her arms.

'I thought I'd better bring him back – he came over to mine last night when you didn't come home ... '

Boris took up his usual place with a reproving glance in Annie's direction.

'No, I ... we ... got stuck, out on the islands ... the wind ... '

'You went out sailing with him then, did you? Cal Mathieson.'

'You sound as if you don't approve.'

Fiona gave her a long look.

'How much do you know about him, Annie?'

'Not much ... I know he was in a band, I know he was married and his wife died ... '

'Do you know about the drinking?'

Suddenly it fell into place. Tea. Water.

'Is it a problem?'

'I'll say. He's an alcoholic. You don't want to see him when he falls off the wagon – he's a nasty drunk, unpredictable – Jekyll and Hyde.'

'Is he violent?' Ruadhri flashed across her mind.

'Not to women, although he has a vicious tongue, but he's had his moments with some of the men around here ... '

'Well, I was lucky then. He was ... charming.'

Fiona's laugh was hollow.

'Aye, he can be that. When it suits him. I'm just saying, be careful, Annie. He's not all that he seems. My friend Cathy ... they went out together a few times. Until he started drinking again – he binges, whisky, two or three bottles at a sitting, drinks himself into a coma. It's not pretty. Cathy had hoped ... well, it would never have worked anyway, she wasn't the right type for him, too interested in who he used to be. But she's not over him, he really messed her up, blowing hot and cold all the time. She never knew where she stood. So ... I'm just warning you.'

'Well, there's really no need. We went out for a sail, that's all, it wasn't a date or anything. I'm going back to London next week. Anyway, after Mark, I've had it with men. The last thing I'm looking for is a relationship.'

There was a scepticism in Fiona's expression that Annie chose to ignore. It was none of her business.

'Come over and have some lunch, if you'd like. I've got some good beetroot soup on the go. And I made bread this morning too.'

Annie accepted the invitation, thinking how much she'd miss these casual social events. In contrast to London, where dinner parties and theatre visits were arranged months in advance, and spontaneous was just a word.

Over lunch Fiona suggested that she take a break from organising Janet's affairs.

'Why don't you just relax? Have a sofa day with a pot of tea and a good book. I've just finished a great read – it's set in the Highlands, really draws you in. You can borrow it if you like ... '

'Sounds like a good idea. I think I might just do that.'

It wasn't the kind of book she read, normally. Annie preferred crime and psychological thrillers to historical romance, but much to her surprise, it turned out to be exactly what she needed – pure escapism. She finished it in one sitting, falling into bed late that night to dream of kilted warriors chasing redcoats through the Highland glens.

∽

'Whoa! I'm sorry! Are you OK, Annie?'

Outside the post office next morning, checking a message on her mobile, Annie collided with Callum in full running gear – lycra shorts, grey T-shirt stained dark with sweat, trainers. A backpack. His hair was swept back, forehead beaded with moisture.

He held her at arm's length, checking to make sure she was alright.

'I'm fine, honestly.' Annie smiled, reassuring him. 'I'm impressed! Have you run all the way from the boatyard?'

Breathing heavily, he bent over with his hands on his knees.

'Three times a week.' The answer came out in a gasp.

Annie considered her own lacklustre attempts to keep fit. Getting off the tube one stop early, but only if she had time. A stroll round the common with Di and her dog on Saturday morning. She had an expensive gym membership, although it had been so long since she'd used it that she wasn't sure if she could still find the way there. Perhaps if she ran six miles, three times a week, she could shed the extra kilos that stood between her and a size twelve.

'You put me to shame.'

'I wouldn't recommend it. Fucking torture. And I'm probably buggering up my knees, down the line.'

'Why do it? I'd imagine boatbuilding keeps you fit enough.'

'Not really. Lots of standing around, not much to get the heart going.'

His mention of hearts drew Annie's attention to her own, which seemed to be beating faster than usual.

'Well, I'd better not get between a man and his fitness routine – and Boris'll be wanting his breakfast.'

As she turned to walk the short distance back to the cottage, Callum fell into step beside her, his breathing back to normal.

'I told Kirsty you'd be joining us tomorrow night. I hope she'll not wear you out – she's a bit full on at the moment – all "like" and "awesome" – it's doing my head in.'

'I'm sure I'll manage. Half the kids in my office are the same. I'm looking forward to getting to know her – she seems like a lovely girl.'

'Aye, well, she gets that from her mother.' Callum shrugged his backpack off his shoulders and extracted a water bottle. He drained it in one long gulp.

'Do you need to fill that up?' They were at Annie's front door.

'If you wouldn't mind. It usually lasts the run, but it's so hot today … '

Ducking under the low lintel, he followed her into the kitchen.

Talking about it afterwards, they agreed that it was inevitable.

As Annie reached out to take the water bottle, their hands touched. Not much was said. Words were superfluous as the atmosphere turned electric.

'Annie … '

'Yes.'

It was impossible to know which of them made the first move, but their arms were around one another and the kiss that began tentatively soon became urgent. Annie ignored the voice in her head saying 'don't do this' as she slipped her hands under his T-shirt, feeling the warm skin underneath. When they broke apart to catch their breath, he was trembling as much as she was.

Their eyes met. His thumb traced the shape of her mouth. He took her hand. Still watching her, he brought it to his lips, kissing the inside of her wrist. Her stomach flipped over.

Briefly, her analytical brain took over. How often must he have done that in the past, to how many other women, never mind his wife of eighteen years? But it was too late to think about that. And in any case, she was way past caring.

The second kiss was gentle, just a soft pressure as their lips met, becoming more forceful as they surrendered to the feeling of pure pleasure. It was some time before it ended.

'I wanted to kiss you the moment you answered the door all sleepy in your jammies.'

'Me too. Wanted you to ... I don't know how I managed to keep my hands off you all that time on *Sweet Dreams*.'

He brushed her hair off her face, tucking it behind her ears, laughing softly.

'Why did you?'

'I could hardly walk home if it didn't work out, could I?'

Callum's smile widened.

'Aye, well, you might have got a wee bit wet. But it was never going to be a problem. I very much want to take you to bed again. Would that be OK?'

He kissed her, very gently.

'Yes please. Without clothes.' Her answer was delivered in a shaky voice, her body tingling in ways that left her breathless.

~

In the golden sunlight filling her room, Annie helped him take off his T-shirt, admiring his lean frame, his chest lightly dusted with black hair that drew a line down the centre of his abdomen, disappearing under the waistband of his shorts.

He had a tattoo. A band of script in a language she didn't recognise, round his upper arm, dark against pale skin. Annie had a rule about men with tattoos. Mentally she rewrote the contract to include an exemption clause for Callum.

'What does it say?' She traced the letters with a trembling finger.

'Not a fu … clue. I was completely off my face when it was done. Japan, it was … on tour. Charlie's idea. He had one the same. I expect it says "stupid wee tosser" – but maybe not.'

Annie giggled, trying to imagine what his life had been like, but couldn't, never having let go control of her own. He took her back into his arms.

'Goodness, you're very … strong. And quite sweaty … '

He laughed, a quiet chuckle.

'I'm hoping to get sweatier … '

'Maybe I can help with that … '

'You already are.' His voice was lower, deeper – almost a growl. Her heart fluttered in a way she had only ever read about in romantic fiction, but never really understood. Until now.

Annie wrapped her arms around him, feeling the hard muscles under the smooth skin of his back. Callum caught up the hem of her top, pulling it up over her head. He dropped it on the floor, stepping back to look at her.

His pupils dilated, blue eyes on brown skin and pink lace. He reached round her to unfasten her bra. It joined the heap of discarded clothing at their feet. They kissed again, skin to skin.

'Heather honey. Golden brown, sweet,' he murmured, cupping her breasts, thumbs stroking her nipples. Feeling weak at the knees, she slipped shaking hands under the tight waistband of Lycra shorts that left nothing about his state of arousal to the imagination.

Holding her wrists, he stopped her.

'Are you sure, Annie? We don't have to do this ... if you're not ... '

'Yes, I am. Completely sure. If you are.'

He released her hands. Then gripped them again.

'But what about ... '

'It's OK. I ... have ... '

Hands free, she helped him unpeel his running shorts, stepping back to admire him, tall, lean and apparently completely comfortable naked under her scrutiny. Watching her, penetrating blue eyes alight with excitement. She shivered with anticipation and removed the rest of her clothing. Her jeans and pants joined the pile on the floor. For long moments, it was his turn to look at her, a long gaze that seemed to give off its own heat as it moved between her face and her body, then back.

'You're so lovely,' he murmured, holding out his hand. She gave him her own, and let him lead her to the bed. They lay down in the shaft of warm sunlight spilling across the duvet.

'It's been a while. I'm not going to be much good at this.'

He was right. Annie was as ready as he was, but it was

over all too quickly.

Afterwards they lay entangled, using all their senses as they took time to discover one another with hands, lips, tongues. Callum, fit from the physical work he did, was not thin as she had first thought, but strongly built with hard muscles and broad shoulders, only a slight softening around his waist showing that he was in his forties rather than his twenties. Using just his fingertips, he caressed her in long, rhythmic strokes.

'If I was Boris, I'd be purring.' It was a low murmur as she languished under the pleasure of his touch.

'If you were Boris, I'd be sneezing.' Annie giggled.

Callum's hands continued their voyage of discovery. 'It's a boatbuilder thing. Touch. Fingers can tell you a lot. These curves – they're absolutely perfect. You're very beautiful.' Somehow, although she had never thought so, she felt it.

She tried it herself.

'What's this?'

There was a long indented scar on his shin. The dark hair had not regrown around it, leaving it exposed and livid red.

'Oh that. Caught it with an adze.' Remembering the shock as the sharp tool cut straight through his jeans into his leg, the frantic drive to hospital, bleeding profusely, as Freya screamed at him to keep the pressure on the wound. The towel she had snatched from the bathroom soaked through and turned red.

'Nasty. Lots of blood.'

She stitched it together again with tiny, fluttery kisses. Callum shivered as her lips brushed over the sensitive skin.

'I'd no idea a scar could be so ... erogenous.'

'I'd no idea this was going to happen. Life's full of surprises.'

'I have a confession ... When we ran into each other I was on my way to see you ... I haven't been able to stop thinking about you ever since ... ever since I bottled out of kissing you yesterday ... '

'So you were ... '

'You're the first ... since Freya ... I haven't ... '

'Not Cathy?'

He sat up, extricating himself from her arms.

'You've been talking to Fiona.'

'She made it her business to warn me about you. Drinking and stuff.'

He nodded, looking down at the white bedlinen.

'Aye. She's never liked me, that woman. The drinking ... ' He twisted round to meet her eyes ' ... I'm an alcoholic, Annie. A recovering alcoholic – I go to meetings, AA ... occasionally I fall off the wagon.'

'I'm sorry. I hadn't realised ... '

'I deal with it. Fiona's husband was a drinker, I think he used to hit her, maybe that's why ... but she's had it in for me ever since I went out with Cath – some friends set us up, her a divorcee, me ... alone. It was never going to work, though, no spark, no chemistry ... I should have said so from the very start, but I was ... lonely, I suppose. We went on a couple of dates, but ... it was nothing like this, Annie. I never – she was small and blonde, like Freya. But she wasn't Freya ... so ... I couldn't ... didn't want ... no, we never did this. It would never have felt ... right. But now, with you ... '

He broke off. Annie saw the sadness in his eyes. Whatever Fiona might think, whatever problems he might have, in that moment she knew that Callum was at heart a good man. With a hand on his cheek she turned his head towards her and kissed him, taking his lip between her teeth as desire began to stir again.

'I'd almost forgotten how good this feels,' he

whispered, deep inside her as they moved together, finding an easy rhythm as if they'd been lovers for years, not hours.

It occurred to Annie that she had never really known before. He talked to her – did she like this, or this? Oh yes, both, everything, very much. Don't stop, please. Was that OK? She must tell him if he was too rough, he didn't want to hurt her. Her normal reserve dissolved as she was swept up in his uninhibited enjoyment. As her guard came down and her confidence grew, she followed his lead, discovering ways to make him groan with pure pleasure.

'What's that?'

Callum was singing, just under his breath. There was a lyric about swimming in a sea of blankets.

'Just a song. About you, actually. It's called "Your body is a Wonderland."'

He smiled as she laughed aloud.

'How can you sing like that?'

'Like what?'

'Just … straight off. I don't know the songs but they sound right.'

'Perfect pitch. Not many of us. One in ten thousand. Think yourself lucky.'

'Oh, I do. Imagine, if you were out of tune.'

Nothing like this had ever happened in Annie's life. Her relationships had been affairs of the head much more than the heart. Dating. Getting acquainted, tastes and preferences. Sex was something she considered carefully, weighing up the pros and cons before she reached a decision. There was a businesslike quality about her dealings with men, unwritten contracts, unspoken rules. A formality.

Never before had she simply fallen into bed with someone she barely knew. No discussion, no agenda, simply giving in to a powerful attraction. Spontaneous was delightful. Callum brought out responses that were uninhibited, sensuous. She could hardly recognise this version of herself – an entirely new sensory appetite seemed suddenly to have awakened, leaving her whole body hungry for more.

'I can't, Annie. Not so soon.' Her fingertips traced the line of soft dark hair running down the centre of his stomach.

'Really? Want a bet?'

Goodness, had she just said that? Annie the ice maiden, as a former partner had once called her, complaining towards the end of their short-lived affair that she never took the initiative in bed.

Callum could. And did.

'Greedy besom. You're just using me for your own sexual gratification. Shameless.'

She collapsed by his side, giggling. Shameless? Besom was the name her mother had called her when she was naughty.

Callum wrapped himself around her, warming to his topic.

'Of course, I should have known what type of a woman you are, killer heels, painted toenails … frilly knickers … '

'Yeah, and I know your type as well. Sex and drugs and rock and roll, you're all the same, you old rockers.'

'Who are you calling an old rocker? Forty-five isn't old! Anyway, I've never denied it. But you, pretending to be a respectable professional woman, while all the time, you're … you're … '

'Careful what you say next. I am a lawyer, remember … '

' ... gorgeous. That's what I was going to say. Gorgeous ... '

'That's OK then.'

' ... for a brazen floozy.'

They were helpless with laughter. Especially after she discovered how ticklish he was. How was it possible for a man to be ticklish and sexy at the same time?

Sexiness had never figured as an attribute she looked for in men. Now she asked herself why the hell not. Nor had she ever known a man who made her laugh so much, in bed or out. There was a lot to be said for both. And he made her feel sexy, too. Exhilaratingly so. Shameless, as he said. And loving it.

Later, after a shower, Callum lay back, drowsy in the warm sunlight, watching as she smoothed moisturiser into her skin. Remembering the pleasure he used to take in the little intimacies of married life.

'Are you coming back to bed?'

She didn't need to be asked twice.

'Would it have made any difference? If you'd had a nice cosy sleeping-bag, instead of a scruffy boatbuilder and a couple of smelly dogs to keep you warm, I mean.'

'I don't think so. This was going to happen, wasn't it? Sleeping together on the boat, that was lovely. Really lovely. But if we hadn't, I think it would still have happened.'

'So do I. Never any doubt.'

'When did you know for sure?'

'When you asked if there'd been anyone else. Earlier, when we woke up, I thought ... I wondered what would have happened if I'd made a move, kissed you or something ... '

'I'd have liked that, if you had.'

'Things might have got a bit out of control.'

'What do you mean?'

'Well, it's been a long time since I woke up with a woman in my arms. I'm just a man, after all. Why do you think I had to go ashore in such a hurry?'

'Oh. Goodness. If I'd realised ... well, I might just have ripped your clothes off there and then.'

'Now you tell me!'

They laughed, trying to imagine sex in the tight space of the cabin on *Sweet Dreams*. Annie snuggled up, head on his shoulder as he drew her close. She breathed him in – her shower gel, sex, a slight tang of sweat and whatever it was that was uniquely him – a wonderful combination.

Dust motes danced in the sunlight. Relaxed, Callum drifted in and out of sleep. Annie watched him, memorising every feature, the pale colour of his skin, hands and face reddened by the sun and wind of the past two days, the dark growth of his stubble, the soft fullness of his lips. When he opened his extraordinarily blue eyes and turned to look at her, her stomach seemed suddenly full of butterflies.

All of a sudden her recent conversation with Moira came to mind. Now she understood what Moira had meant.

Callum. Widowed. Unselfconscious, at ease in his own skin, comfortable and natural around her. A man who clearly liked women, a generous and tender lover, caring about her pleasure as much as his own, then making her laugh too. Definitely third category. Remembering what Moira had said about widowers, Annie wondered how to make a casserole.

Hunger drove them down to the kitchen a little later. Boris haughtily accepted a bowl of food. He ate with disapproving looks at Callum, drinking tea and eating fruit cake at the kitchen table.

'I need to go home to feed the dogs and change, then there's a place up the coast I'd like to take you tonight – great food, local seafood mostly. Would you like that?'

'Yes, please.'

If he had suggested they walk over hot coals to get there she'd have agreed without a moment's hesitation.

~

Annie offered to drive him back, but he decided to finish his run. He needed time to think, to try to assimilate what had just happened. Running would help clear his head. With a last kiss, he left the cottage, just as a well-known local gossip was passing the door.

'Aye-aye.' It was an expression Callum knew well could mean anything from 'hello' to 'what's going on here?' The intonation in old Arthur's voice made his meaning perfectly clear.

Steady! Callum told himself – slow down, one step at a time. Oh, but Annie …

As he ran he replayed scenes from the day in his mind. Discovering Annie was like opening a parcel to find many layers of tissue paper, each one revealing a little more as she allowed him to see beyond the person she kept hidden behind her cool demeanour, until he uncovered the warm, passionate woman beneath the layers of wrapping.

What would Freya have said? He contrasted the long, slow build-up of his relationship with his wife to today's explosive coming together with Annie. Both wonderful, both utterly different.

Was it all just about sex, the first time since Freya had become ill? It wouldn't be surprising, after all. Yet they seemed to connect on so many levels, not only physical. He trembled as he thought about her, shaking his head with disbelief as he realised that they had made love three – or was it four? – times in the course of just a few hours. He was behaving like a man half his age.

But to be touched, caressed, held again, as a lover. To hold a woman in his arms, to make love after so long – to laugh again, feel again – strong emotions, other than sadness and loneliness – he hadn't known how much he needed this.

Turning into the driveway, he cautioned himself against letting it happen too fast. Stay calm, don't rush into anything, he counselled himself. Knowing he already had.

He showered again, shaved, dressed with unaccustomed care, choosing a faded denim shirt to wear over his favourite black jeans. On automatic pilot, he fed the dogs. Trying to behave normally, all the time he was impatient with longing to turn around again, back to Annie.

An hour later he was outside her cottage. She had changed too. A soft pink cashmere cardigan, pale jeans and silk shirt suited her perfectly. She looked, as he had said earlier, gorgeous. As he helped her into the car, he caught the scent of her spicy fragrance. All his resolutions crumbled.

Chapter 25
West Highlands
April

'Well, it's out now,' Callum announced as he started the engine. He'd come in the SUV so they would be able to talk.

'What?'

'Us. The whole village knows – I ran into Arthur as I left. Might as well have announced it with a loud-hailer.'

'Oh dear. Will that make problems for you?'

'Only if Sean O'Brian gets wind of it.' He told her briefly about the tabloid stringer who had stalked him over the years. 'What about you?'

Annie shook her head.

'No one's interested in me. I've had my fifteen minutes of fame. I'm nothing more than chip-wrapping now.'

There were things about the media that Callum, for all his quiet life in the West Highlands, understood much better than his metropolitan companion.

'Aye, maybe.'

Their route took them through the village and out along the waterside to the head of Loch Carron, where they turned back along the north shore. High mountains rose up all around them as they headed inland. Turning off onto a single-track side road, they met very little traffic as they climbed up the twisting route, higher and higher. Steep drops fell away to one side, precipitous scree-clad mountainsides rose high above the road to the other.

'Is he real, or just for the tourists?' A stag, antlered head held high, stood on a rocky promontory below them.

'Stuffed, I expect. Oh, maybe not.' The magnificent beast turned and ambled away, out of sight behind a rocky outcrop.

Near the summit, Callum pulled into a lay-by so Annie could admire the view. As it had the previous day, the wind had risen in the afternoon and now blew steadily over the mountain tops.

From their high vantage point, swathes of the Western Isles lay at their feet. Callum stood behind her, holding her close. He pointed out the different islands. They could see the north end of Skye, with Raasay and Rona in front across the Inner Sound. To the south lay the Crowlin Islands, where they had lain at anchor two nights before. The Cuillins were jagged peaks at the southern end of Skye. To the north, faint on the far horizon, Callum pointed out the Outer Hebrides – Harris and Lewis.

'That's where I'm from. Stornoway.'

'Stornoway.' She repeated the name in a dreamy voice. It had such a romantic ring.

The sky was silvery blue in the early evening sun, the sea deep indigo, slashed with the white crests of waves breaking in their restless dash southwards. The breathtaking beauty of the Western Isles left her speechless.

'Lovely, isn't it?' Callum murmured in her ear.

She could only nod in agreement. It was lovely. With Callum standing close behind her, sheltering them both from the wind with his warm jacket, it was perfect.

Another car pulled up beside the VW. A couple got out, nodding and smiling as they passed. Annie caught a few words on the wind.

'Is that not ... '

'Aye, and ... lawyer ... *News Tonight* ... '

On the shore at the foot of the mountains, the whitewashed walls of the Applecross Inn gleamed in the golden light. Trestle tables outside were occupied by hillwalkers, tourists and the occasional smoker. Released from captivity in the back of the car, Mick and Keith ran barking down to the shore to join other dogs playing on the beach, splashing in the shallows, tossing seaweed in the air.

A chalked sign outside the door of the pub announced forthcoming events.

'Oh! I'd forgotten Steve and Jack are playing tonight. You'll enjoy that,' Callum told her.

The bar, wood-panelled under a low ceiling, reflected its seaside location. Fishing floats and nets hung from the beams, the walls displayed black and white photos of fishermen landing their catch. There was a hum of conversation interspersed with ripples of laughter. The barman greeted Callum with a wide grin and took an order for drinks – white wine for Annie, mineral water for Callum.

'And a bowl of spinies, if you have any.'

'Coming right up, Cal. Take the table in the window there.' He handed them menus.

'Spinies?'

The waiter brought a dish to the table. Annie eyed them suspiciously, bright orangey-crimson shrimp-like things curled up in tight circles. Callum eased one out of its shell, dipped it in mayonnaise and held it up to her lips. It was delicious – sweeter than lobster and meltingly tender.

'Mmm, lovely.'

'Squat lobsters. One of Scotland's best-kept secrets,' Callum told her. 'No one else seems to want the little buggers, they take all the lobster and the langoustine, but not the spinies. Fine by me.'

The squat lobsters didn't last long.

Callum brought the dogs in to lie under the table,

benefiting from a few scraps from their supper of seafood with salad, chips and chunks of homemade bread. Annie sipped her wine, enjoying the atmosphere as the pub filled up in anticipation of the band.

Steve and Jack arrived laden with instruments. Annie was introduced to Jack's wife. Jenny, a large, blonde woman, red lipstick matching the roses in the flamboyant print of her dress, was also from the south of England. Extra chairs were found, more drinks brought. Callum shuffled his chair round the table to sit beside Annie.

Jenny and Annie fell into conversation about the Highlands, comparing notes – things they enjoyed about Scotland, and missed about London. An opportunity in social work had brought Jenny to the Highlands some years back, and having met Jack and settled down, she had never wanted to leave. 'I fell in love with the place, almost as much as the man!' she said with a smile.

All the time Annie was acutely aware of Callum's warm presence at her side. They were playing footsie under the table, enjoying the secret contact between them while they talked to the others. Callum entertained the group with the story of a boat that had been brought to the yard for repair after an unfortunate encounter with a rock off one of the islands. There were gales of laughter – the shipwrecked mariner was well known locally – this was not his first brush with the same rock. Annie played along, chatting with Jenny as if Callum were nothing more than a friend as he stroked her knee under the table, his hand inching slowly up her thigh, making it ever harder to concentrate on what Jenny was saying.

'Will you do a couple of numbers with us, Cal?' Steve asked, as Jenny began to question her about the Inquiry. Her attention was distracted when she saw Jack's eyebrows raised in surprise at Callum's answer.

'I know what I said before. But that's what I want to sing – and don't tell me you don't know it. You play it yourselves often enough.'

Steve looked abashed. The three men went off to sort out instruments. Jenny took advantage of their absence to ask the question she had obviously wanted to ask all along.

'So you and Cal, are you ... ? You seem ... close. Sorry. Just tell me to mind my own business!'

Annie smiled.

'I don't know what we are, or even if "we" are "we" at all. It's just dinner.'

'Oh yeah?' Jenny sounded as unconvinced as Annie had been unconvincing. 'Well, I for one hope it's more than dinner. If ever there's a man who needs to find a good woman, it's Cal. He's been alone long enough now. He needs to start having some fun again before he gets past it!'

Thinking of the fun they'd had that day, Annie smiled to herself. Callum was very far from past it.

Callum returned to join them at the table. Jenny's knowing smile told him what she had guessed. He took Annie's hand.

'You don't mind, do you? If I do a couple of numbers with the boys?'

'Of course I don't. I love hearing you sing.' They exchanged a private look, thinking of him singing to her in bed earlier. He brought her hand to his lips, kissing her fingertips as he held her gaze. Annie was conscious of people watching. Jenny looked away, a smile lifting the corners of her mouth.

Steve and Jack began to play a medley of traditional Scottish tunes. Both musicians played a range of instruments – guitar, fiddle, banjo, penny whistle, chanter, bodhran. The audience responded with enthusiastic applause.

'We have a wee special treat for you tonight,' Jack announced after a few numbers. 'Cal wasn't expected, but we found him here having his tea and he's agreed to do a couple of songs with us. Cal Mathieson, everyone!'

Smiling in acknowledgement of catcalls and whistles, Callum went up to join them on the small platform, picking up a borrowed guitar.

'This is unrehearsed, so forgive me please, if I'm a bit rusty. Thanks, guys, for inviting me to play.' He strummed a chord, adjusting the tuning. As he did so he talked about what he was going to sing.

'I was out sailing with a friend a couple of days ago, and in the afternoon the wind got up. It made me think of this song by Jacques Brel – you'll probably know the Bowie version – "Wild is the wind".'

The song was not about the wind at all, but about deep, passionate love. Callum's interpretation was slow and soulful, the emotion accentuated by some delicate fiddle work from Jack. As it built to its climax, his eyes sought out Annie in the crowd. Letting the final notes die to a whisper, he smiled and inclined his head in the slightest of nods.

Jenny leaned closer. 'Just dinner?'

Annie felt herself blushing, aware of the curious glances cast in her direction. She shrank back in her seat, hiding behind Jenny.

The next song came as a complete surprise.

'Out on the boat with someone who has never sailed in these waters, it was as if I was seeing the Western Isles for the first time myself. Charlie and me wrote this when we were at a really low ebb – we didn't seem to be getting anywhere, we were skint, and most of all, we were homesick. This is the song that changed everything. I'd like to dedicate it to the memories of Charlie and Freya. And tonight, I'm singing it especially for Annie. "Atlantic Shores".'

There was an audible intake of breath from the audience.

Jenny grabbed Annie's hand and squeezed it tight, as Callum began to sing 2CM's best-known hit for the first time since Charlie had died. Even Annie knew it, but she had only ever heard the loud rock version that had dominated the charts in the weeks and months after Charlie's death. Callum sang it stripped bare, like a lament, the rasp in his voice accentuating the feeling of longing for a home far away, while his guitar wove its intricate notes together with Jack's fiddle to evoke the sound of the birds on the wind and the seals singing in the bays.

> *'I hear the wind-blown breakers roar*
> *Bursting in foam on Atlantic shores*
> *Crying your name to a dirty sky*
> *Why can't I let the memories lie?'*

Callum matched the rhythm of the bodhran with his clenched fist beating time over his heart. Watching Annie across the room, he fought to stay in control of the tide of emotion threatening to overwhelm him. He sang the song he'd vowed publicly and repeatedly never to sing again, for Annie, to let her know how much she already meant to him.

The audience could barely believe what they were seeing – it was a magical performance, full of passion. For those who knew the history behind it, an unforgettable moment.

At thirty-nine years old, never having felt anything like it before, Annie finally acknowledged what was happening to her. Watching Callum as he came to the end of the song, his eyes fixed on her own, she felt as if the ground had gone from beneath her and she was spiralling downwards, out of control. Falling. In love.

Chapter 26
West Highlands
April

'I'm not sure I should have done that.'

Callum negotiated the car up the steep mountain road out of the village. Darkness was falling. The headlights picked out the grassy verge and occasional unnerving pinpricks of light reflected in the eyes of grazing sheep.

Stunned by a rush of emotions completely new to her, Annie was intensely aware of everything about him – capable hands on the steering-wheel – how had she failed to notice his wrists before, broad and strong, dark hair on pale skin? Who knew that wrists could be the source of such powerful waves of desire? The tones of his voice – soft, gruff, deep, musical – caressed her ears. His body gave off a complex mixture of scents – musk, wood, shaving-foam, shampoo. Breathing him in, she felt strange – lightheaded, somehow outside herself.

They'd left the inn soon after his performance. The reaction was ecstatic, everyone thrilled to have seen something so special, Callum breaking his own taboo with so much passion.

'Why not? It's your song, and it was … wonderful.'

It was the best she could manage. She wanted to tell him how deeply moved she had been by his singing. But she couldn't think of the right words.

'Aye, but now the pressure'll be on to keep doing it. I'll

have Ed back on my case trying to get me out on tour again, revivals, all the fucking nonsense. I'm not ready for that.'

'No, I understand, from what you said on the boat.'

'I never asked, did you ever see us play, back in the day?'

'Me? No! I was the one at home with my revision. Some of my school friends used to go to concerts. One of them threw her knickers on stage at a Take That gig once – she was only fourteen. I was horrified, little prude that I was. Definitely not the knicker-throwing type.'

'Aaaaw. So would you not throw your knickers for me, then?' He took advantage of a straight stretch of road to turn with a grin.

'I think I already have,' she replied, meeting his eyes, smiling too. And my heart and soul, she thought. He stopped the car in the middle of the road, reaching across to gather her into his arms for a long, lingering kiss.

Overcome with shyness again as they arrived back at the cottage, she led the way into the kitchen. For a moment they stood quietly, just looking at each other, then Callum brought her hand to his lips, kissing the inside of her wrist. Her stomach flipped over.

'Don't do that unless you're ready for the consequences.'

He smiled, eyes alight as they met her own. Slowly and deliberately, he did it again.

'I'm ready, Annie. Are you going to ask me to stay?'

'I'd love you to stay. Please stay.'

They shared a long kiss, full of the promise of more to come. Annie began to tremble, her body alive to every slight touch, every breath.

Callum felt himself shaking too.

'I'd better settle the dogs for the night – they can sleep in the car.'

'Don't let them near my cat.'

Outside, he waited impatiently as the dogs sniffed around the grassy verge. He tried to calm his breathing, knowing that even if he wanted to stop this now, he couldn't. Whatever was happening was out of control – he could only roll with it, see where it went.

Inside, Annie searched her reflection in the bathroom mirror for signs of the turmoil she felt, amazed to see she looked the same as usual – maybe just a little brighter in the eyes.

They undressed, slowly, taking their time to rediscover one another, trembling with anticipation.

Earlier in the day they'd enjoyed great sex, joyous, playful, uninhibited, both of them eager to find ways to please the other.

This time was different. Annie felt adrift in uncharted waters. Making love, in love, she let go all sense of control and allowed herself just to be, to feel, to respond.

There was a change in Callum too. A sense of urgency that he hadn't felt for a very long time, back in the earliest days of his marriage, was driving him. Knowing how much he wanted her made Annie want him even more – more than she had wanted anything in her life. Without ever knowing it, she had always been waiting for this – falling in love.

As they came together again, it was as if another, deeper part of her opened up. With that same sense of weightlessness, her body answered his in every detail. It was as if she wanted to absorb him, totally, to be absorbed. So fused together were they, it was impossible to know where one ended and the other began. Willingly, she surrendered every part of herself, crying his name in a place where the physical was indistinguishable from the emotional in a tidal wave of feeling.

Afterwards, slick with sweat, stunned, gasping, they lay facing one another. He took her hand, kissed it, and held it against his heart.

'Annie – what are you doing to me?' Callum's voice was soft, full of wonder.

'Nothing you aren't doing to me.' She traced his lips with her finger. She wanted to tell him how she felt, but the words weren't big enough to say it properly. All she could do was show him.

For a while they lay recovering, talking, laughing. Kissing and caressing again.

'I don't know if my heart's strong enough for this.'

'I'll be gentle with you next time. I think you'll be OK.'

'Next time? You're insatiable, woman! Who do you think I am, Superman? You're maybe expecting too much.'

There was compelling evidence to the contrary.

'Actually, I think you might be wrong.'

He was. Annie was lost again.

'Superman,' she murmured later, when her heart-rate had slowed to something closer to normal.

It was possible, she discovered, to be helplessly in love and helpless with laughter at the same time.

'Malt whisky – one of the pale ones from Islay maybe. Ardbeg. Lagavulin.' The words sounded beautiful, spoken in his soft Stornoway accent. He gazed into her eyes, trying to describe their colour.

'What about you? Black hair, blue eyes, pale skin – where does that come from?'

'I'm a Celt – it's common.'

'There's nothing common about you, Callum. You are a very rare Celt.'

'Or you. An exotic flower. That's what I thought the

very first time I saw you, soaking wet in those ridiculous shoes.'

Annie remembered those 'ridiculous shoes', kicked off under the bed in another life. Now that she'd met Callum, she wasn't at all sure she wanted that life any more. Not if she could have this one.

Sleep caught up with them. Annie nestled closer, wishing a part of her could stay awake not to miss a moment, but feeling herself surrendering to a delicious sense of peace as he began to relax beside her.

They slept, spooned together like before, but this time as lovers, naked in linen bedsheets. Once or twice during the night, Callum woke, drawing her closer, marvelling at how well they fitted together, how good it felt not to be alone.

At other moments, half-waking, Annie was thrilled by the feeling of lying warm and secure in the arms of the man with whom she was already deeply in love.

Chapter 27
West Highlands
April

Boris had taken up residence on the crumpled duvet. Claws sheathed, he patted her cheek to remind her it was time for breakfast. Annie opened her eyes to see Callum, fully dressed, sitting at the side of the bed under the cat's malevolent stare. She blinked, blinded by the bright morning light. Callum bent to brush her lips lightly with his.

'Hi.'

Annie smiled sleepily. His eyes were bright, hair tousled, unshaven. Her heart felt brimful of love. She stretched luxuriously.

'Hi. I didn't even know you were up. You look very wide awake. Where have you been?'

'I couldn't wake you. You looked so peaceful.' His smile set her pulse racing. 'I went to the shop. I've made tea. And I bought croissants, with heather honey.'

She sat up, tucking the duvet around her breasts, constrained still, despite everything they had done together. She took the mug of tea he offered. Boris jumped off the bed and left the room, tail twitching.

'I'm not used to this.'

'A bit of spoiling never did anyone any harm. You deserve it.' His expression grew serious. 'You'd better see this before anyone else shows you.'

A Scottish tabloid carried a page of pictures under the headline 'Cal in love?'

There was a series of grainy shots, obviously taken on a mobile phone the previous evening. Getting into the VW at the car park. Callum, hand on the small of her back as they went into the Inn. In the next picture he was feeding her squat lobster from his fingers as he looked straight into her eyes. The intimacy between them could not have been clearer. Toasting one another over dinner, holding hands across the table. They hadn't been able to take their eyes, or their hands, off each other, she remembered, seeing the evidence in pictures. Whoever had taken the photographs had even managed to get one of him looking at her from the stage, half-smiling, eyes alight – her own expression stunned, snapped at the very moment she recognised the depths of her feelings. The two of them leaving the bar, Callum's arm round her shoulders, his other hand up to deter a girl with a selfie stick.

There was very little by way of a story – the pictures spoke for themselves – but what there was made uncomfortable reading. Subheaded 'Simpson Inquiry lawyer Annie on hot date with Cal' it went on to describe Callum's unplanned participation in the gig and the fact that he had sung "Atlantic Shores", dedicated to Annie. It concluded that they looked 'loved up'. The fact was undeniable.

'The couple we saw at the viewpoint. I saw them in the bar later. Bastards!'

'I'm really sorry, Annie. I've grown used to this stuff over the years, but I hate to see you dragged into it as well. Bloody mobile phones, everyone's paparazzi now.'

'It's just tabloid nonsense. Nothing to do with us really.'

Annie was determined not to be unsettled by it. If this

was the price of being with Callum, so be it, she'd pay.

'Exactly. That's the only way to deal with it.'

Callum spread honey on a piece of croissant and offered it up to her lips, licking the stickiness off his fingers. She did the same for him, smiling into his eyes. Feeding each other was another way of making love. Everything Annie ate seemed to taste of him.

He set the tray aside. She watched with caressing eyes as he stripped off his clothes. Slipping back under the duvet, he gathered her into his arms. Their lips met again, a kiss that reignited the flames that had threatened to consume them the night before. They knew each other so well already, what they liked, what to do. Sticky with honey, they made love, slowly, with exquisite tenderness. Annie's eyes filled with tears of emotion as they reached a shuddering climax. Callum kissed them away.

The sound of rain driving against the windows woke them some time later. The weather had broken with a vengeance. Callum threw off the covers, reaching for his watch.

'I've got to go. Kirsty'll be here in a couple of hours. Sixish, we'll have supper early.'

With a last kiss, he was gone.

Going downstairs, he began to sing – *Here comes the rain again* ... Leaving one Annie, her honey taste still on his lips, singing the song of another. Smiling, Annie lay, luxuriating in the warm bed with its musky scent of sex.

Chapter 28
West Highlands
April

It was just after six when Annie parked her Mini in the driveway of Callum's house. An afternoon spent catching up with all the messages and emails she had been ignoring, brought her briefly down to earth with reminders of a life that felt very far away.

In Janet's bookshelf she found a well-thumbed copy of *The Poisonwood Bible* and started to read. But concentration was impossible, and she allowed her thoughts to drift. In the warmth of the kitchen, daydreaming, reliving the last few wonderful days, her stomach seemed to turn somersaults as she thought about Callum. The way he held her hair back so he could kiss her neck. The way he felt in her arms, the way it felt to be wrapped in his. His singing. The sounds he made making love. His laugh, his eyes, his lips. All of him.

A few nights ago he had asked her what her plans were now that the funeral was over. Now she asked herself the same question. When would she go back to London? Should she go back? Or was there a future here: a small legal practice, perhaps, as a family lawyer? She imagined herself in her own office in one of the small Highland towns – giving up her highflying ambitions – leading a quieter life.

Perhaps a life with Callum.

She hardly dared have the thought. It was too soon,

nothing had even been said. She knew how she felt, but what about Callum? It would be foolish to ignore the possibility that for him it was all about loneliness, the opportunity to have some fun, enjoy a bit of healthy sex after so long on his own. Yet everything seemed to suggest he felt the same way as she did. It was surely more than sex. For her at least, it was falling in love.

She dressed for the evening with particular care – cream cashmere, black jeans, suede boots. Loose hair framed her face in a halo of tight curls. The merest suggestion of pink in her lipgloss was all the makeup she wore, along with a generous spray of the scent he'd said he liked so much as he had breathed it in the previous evening – Fragonard, Belle de Nuit.

Everything that had happened in two short days, so unexpected, had left her feeling incredibly alive – nerves strung tight, senses fine-tuned.

The rain had let up briefly, but the temperature had dropped. The early spring seemed to be back on hold.

Shivering in the damp, chilly air, she rang the doorbell.

'Door's open!' Kirsty yelled from inside.

'Annie! It's, like, awesome to see you! Cal's getting changed, I've to like, look after you.'

Annie felt uncharacteristically awkward. What do you say to a teenage girl when you've just spent the last two days in bed with her father? And fallen head over heels in love with him?

'Hi Kirsty, great to see you. How's school?' Mentally, Annie imagined Kirsty rolling her eyes. What a lame start.

'Oh, you know … it's cool, some of my teachers are, like, awesome.'

'And Edinburgh – do you like being there, so far from home?'

For God's sake, relax, Annie screamed at herself,

inwardly.

Kirsty's face clouded.

'Yeah, it's cool, like I get on with my cousins, and Dugald and Sally – they're good – Dugald is Cal's brother, you know? – but I miss Cal, and my mum ... you know about Mum?'

'Yes, I do. I'm so sorry Kirsty. I lost my mother when I was young too, not as young as you, but I know how hard it is.'

'Yeah. It so is.'

Oddly, this exchange broke the ice. They had found common ground, albeit in sadness and loss.

And then Callum appeared, and her heart leapt in her chest. He had changed too. New jeans, deck shoes on bare feet. A coarse ivory linen shirt was loose over his waist, protected by a striped butcher's apron. Hair brushed back, clean-shaven, had it not been for the apron he would have looked a lot more like Cal, ex-rock guitarist, than Callum the boatbuilder. As it was he looked like a celebrity chef. And father of Kirsty.

'Wow.' It was only his eyes that spoke, but she heard them loud and clear.

'Wow yourself,' her eyes replied. How could she ever have thought he was anything other than stunning?

He kissed her cheek, holding her arm for a little too long, as if he didn't want to let go. Aware that Kirsty was watching them closely, Annie hoped she hadn't seen the paper.

She had brought a bottle of wine on Callum's instruction. 'I spend a good deal of my life in pubs. I don't have a problem with people enjoying a drink around me.' Flowers for Kirsty, not knowing what a teenage girl might like – fortunately she had chosen well. Kirsty, suddenly subdued, took the fragrant bouquet and delicately sniffed a peach-coloured rose. 'They're lovely. We never have flowers these days. Thank you. I'll put them in water.'

Callum took advantage of his daughter's brief absence to kiss Annie on the lips and sing *'Darling, you look wonderful tonight'* quietly into her ear. She laughed.

'So cheesy!' she mouthed at him, making him grin sheepishly.

'But you do. Beautiful.'

Delicious smells came from the kitchen. Annie wondered why being around Callum made her so hungry. As promised he had cooked chicken, seasoned with lemon, herbs and garlic. It rested on the worktop beside the Aga, with a tray of roasted vegetables. He poured her a glass of wine, mineral water for himself and Kirsty.

The flowers were placed in the centre of the table, cleared of its usual debris and set for three.

'You two go and talk while I finish off in here.'

Annie and Kirsty sat near the welcome warmth of the wood burner while Callum continued to potter about in the kitchen, cursing the dogs for getting under his feet.

Kirsty had a thousand questions, fired at random. Annie replied as best she could, relaxing as Callum's daughter's enthusiastic chatter put her at ease. As Kirsty ran out of steam and began to focus, Annie suggested how to prepare for a career as a solicitor. She remembered her own conversations with Janet, as she tried to decide on her future. It seemed that Kirsty was looking for exactly that sort of guidance.

'So did you do law at university?' asked Kirsty, eventually.

'No. Some people prefer to do a first degree and then do the legal bit afterwards. Gives you more choice.'

'What did you do?'

'Politics and Economics. At the LSE in London. It was great, I really loved it.'

'I'm sure I'll have lots more questions, if you don't mind the odd text.' They exchanged mobile numbers.

In the kitchen, Callum laughed.

'Aye, the odd text. If you can figure out what she's talking about you'll be doing a lot better than me.'

'Oh, Cal! Keep up! Texting, messaging, it's what we do now. You're such a dinosaur.'

'There's no excuse for not writing stuff properly. Emojis, numerals! Where's the poetry? Where's the romance?'

Kirsty rolled her eyes. 'Silly old fart.' The words were just loud enough for Annie to hear. She and Kirsty exchanged glances, giggling conspiratorially. Annie breathed a quiet sigh of relief. It was going to be OK.

Dinner more than lived up to its promise. To follow the chicken there was locally made ice cream which Annie tried to resist until Callum pointed out that the flavour – heather honey – was his favourite. She concentrated on not meeting his eyes. Kirsty gave him a penetrating look, helping them all to a generous bowlful, with homemade raspberry coulis. It was delicious.

Annie helped clear up, all together in the kitchen, enjoying Kirsty's giggle, Callum's barking laugh – being part of their little family.

A car horn sounded outside.

'That's Louise.' Kirsty was going to her friend's house. 'Is it alright if I stay over, Cal? We've got loads of catching up to do.'

'Aye, OK, just remember you need to be back for the early train tomorrow.'

She kissed Callum, then Annie, much to her delight, before she hurtled out of the house, a flurry of long legs and short skirt.

'Amazing,' Callum observed. 'Not a single "like".'

He hadn't heard the conversation before he appeared in the kitchen. He topped up her wineglass, poured himself more mineral water.

'She likes you. You'd soon know if she didn't.'

Annie felt ridiculously pleased. She hadn't even considered how much it would matter.

Darkness came early in the poor weather conditions. Callum lit lamps.

'Music. Tell me what you like.' He studied lists of artists on the screen of his phone.

'You choose.'

He selected a playlist. A Dave Matthews track began to play. Callum pulled her to her feet.

'Come and dance with me.'

'Oh no, I'm a useless dancer. Don't make me do this, please!' Annie begged.

'It's dancing, not rocket science. Just let your body do what it wants to do.'

He began to dance. She watched the way he moved, loose-limbed, sensual, letting the music dictate the moves. So sexy. She imagined him on stage, girls screaming in the audience, in a charged atmosphere. It was easy to picture.

'I can't do that.' It was a wail of protest.

'Yes, you can. You were doing it this morning. And last night. And most of yesterday.' He teased.

'That was different. That was sex.'

'My point exactly.' He moved close. 'Just follow me, do what I do.' He turned her round, so he was behind her. Hands on her hips, he guided her until she relaxed and began to move with him, stomach fluttering with the sensuality of his touch, his body close against hers. Remembering, anticipating. They danced to a song full of love and lust, sung in a low, growling voice reminiscent of his own.

'Could you always dance like this?'

'No way! We had lessons. Charlie and me, we started out with four left feet. Useless. Ed told us nothing turns the women off faster than bad dancing. He got us a choreographer.'

'Another illusion shattered.'

'At least Kirsty doesn't get to accuse me of dad dancing.'

'You're so good at everything. Dancing too.'

'No I'm not, I'm only any good at things I enjoy. Performing, boatbuilding, sailing, cooking. That's about it. Otherwise, what's the point? Oh, and sex, although I think I might be a bit out of practice there.' His eyes were full of mischief.

From her short acquaintance with Callum, Annie knew he excelled in all of them. Especially the last.

'Out of practice? I think we've covered everything legal. What else have you got in your repertoire?' She smiled up at him.

He raised his eyebrows and grinned. 'We'll see.'

Her stomach seemed to be performing backflips.

Another track came on – Bowie, "Let's Dance". She was really enjoying herself now.

'I haven't danced for ages,' Callum told her. 'I always loved it. Not as much as Charlie, he was some kind of dervish, completely wild, all flying hair and kilt – nothing on underneath – but it was great, on stage.'

'Must have been fun being a rock star.'

'Aye – sometimes.' His tone suggested otherwise. Callum watched as she let the music lead her.

'You've really got it now. I knew you could do it. Just needed to loosen up a bit.'

If she was any looser, Annie thought, she might fall over altogether.

'I've got a great teacher. Sailing, dancing ... '

The track changed again. Slow, this time, a lyrical guitar, a slow drumbeat, a voice like whisky and honey.

He took her into his arms to dance close, slow and sensuous, moving together easily as he sang the words softly in her ear. The song was about the end of a love affair, full of sadness, Callum's voice singing the words just for her, sending shivers down her spine.

'It's so sad.'

'It's only a song.'

His hands were on her hips, holding her close. Their thighs brushed together – she could feel his arousal, her response fluttering somewhere deep inside.

As they danced Annie became aware that he was leading her towards the rooms at the back of the house. Teasing her, spinning it out, dancing through the kitchen, round the island, back into the sitting room, out towards the passageway.

Secure in the arms of the man she loved, she allowed herself to be led to the bedroom.

The door was ajar. Callum nudged it open with his elbow. The lights were on, either side of the wide bed, its patchwork quilt folded back over white bedclothes. They crossed the threshold into the room.

Without warning, he froze into complete stillness. Alarmed, Annie looked up into his face. He was terribly pale.

She stepped back, keeping a tight hold of his arms.

'Callum, what is it? Are you OK?'

He looked straight through her, not answering.

'Callum, please speak to me, what's wrong?'

His eyes focused, meeting hers briefly then looking away. His expression was inward-looking, unreadable.

'I can't do this.' It was barely a whisper.

She understood, instantly. Freya had been gone for more than two years. But her presence was everywhere in this room. She released her grip on Callum's arms and stepped back out of the bedroom.

'It's OK.'

Callum's head dropped.

Unsure what to do, Annie returned to the living room. Another slow, romantic tune was playing. She couldn't see how to turn it off.

Callum appeared beside her, stopping the music. They stood in the ensuing silence, silent themselves, reflected side by side in the window. Callum was motionless, head bowed, occasional tremors passing through him.

'I should go.' Annie whispered, willing him to return from whatever dark place he had gone, ask her to stay.

Instead he simply nodded.

∼

Back home – with no recollection of the drive down the narrow, twisting road in the dark and rain – she poured herself a large whisky and sat by the stove in the kitchen, waves of emotion breaking over her. Part of her wanted to believe everything would be alright. Another part, the analytical lawyer, knew it wouldn't. She gulped the whisky, hoping that the burn at the back of her throat would somehow anaesthetise her against the stabbing pain of her thoughts.

She replayed every moment, remembering each tiny detail. Standing in the bedroom, realising that even if he could have taken her to that bed to make love to her, she couldn't have let him. Not there, in the room he had shared with his wife.

She should never have let herself get involved. But

she was involved. She knew how deep her feelings were – had truly believed Callum had been falling in love with her – everything that had happened suggested he felt as she did, that something real was happening between them. Then she remembered him telling her about the woman he had gone out with before her – what had he said? 'It was much too soon.' It was still much too soon. Perhaps it always would be.

She felt such a fool. It wasn't as if she hadn't been warned. How could she have invested so much in him, so quickly? She'd been honest with him – had told him that she'd never been in love. She was now. She'd always kept so much of herself in reserve, afraid of being hurt, of allowing herself to be vulnerable. Was it simply that she had never met the right person? Until Callum.

Mark had accused her of being cold, detached, putting work before anything else. It was true, she always kept a distance. All her life, from the moment she'd recognised her mother's instability, she had known she had to be self-reliant, strong, in control. Independent.

These last few days, for the first time ever, she had dropped her guard and opened up to Callum. She'd thought she could trust him, convinced by his calm demeanour, seduced by his tenderness. A man in control, in touch with his feelings. She was wrong – he was vulnerable, messed up, still in mourning.

In love, but with his late wife, not with her at all.

Boris jumped off his chair. On silent paws he crossed the kitchen to sit by her side, looking up into her face, uttering soft miaows. Dim grey dawn light was seeping through the window. A glance at the clock told her that she had been sitting for hours, her thoughts spinning round and round, always coming back to the same place – whatever she thought had been growing between them had been no more than an illusion.

It was over before it started.

Taking the whisky bottle with her, she went to Janet's room – the rumpled sheets of her own bed, so recently the scene of the most perfect, tender loving she had ever known, were more than she could bear.

Sleep was impossible. At best she dozed for a few minutes, woken by every slight sound, imagining, longing for it to be Callum, coming to say he was sorry, everything was OK, he loved her. Knowing the whisky wasn't helping, she drank it all the same, searching for oblivion. Trying to stop the images running through her head – Callum at the helm of the boat, driving, pointing out the islands across the sound, eyes meeting hers as he stood on stage, naked in bed, beside her, inside her, holding her close as they danced together. The smell of him, the taste of him, the way he felt in her arms. It was all over. It had never been hers in the first place.

As the light strengthened she gave up the struggle for sleep. Weak and drunk, she stumbled into the shower, standing braced against the walls under the gushing water until it ran cold, wishing it would just wash her away.

∼

Nursing a cup of cold tea at the kitchen table, her heart leapt in her chest at the sound of a knock on the door sometime in the late morning. Not Callum. Fiona stood on the doorstep, in the rain.

'Annie, what's wrong? Has something happened?'

The tears she had been refusing to shed would not be held back any longer. Her body was racked with great, gasping sobs, as Fiona held her, talking quietly and soothingly until she calmed enough to be able to talk. And then she spilled out the whole story.

'Well, I hate to say so, but I did warn you … I was afraid

this might happen. He's a very attractive man, Annie. But it's like Cathy said – he doesn't know what he wants now Freya's gone. She said it was as if Freya was always there whenever they were together. Like trying to compete with a ghost. Let it go, Annie. I saw the paper yesterday – you really don't need that stuff, it follows Callum around all the time, even now. You're in no state to deal with this. Look what you've been through these last weeks. You need to think of yourself just now. You really don't need a screwed-up man like Callum, and all the baggage he carries.'

Annie knew Fiona was right, though it did nothing to lessen her feeling of empty desolation.

'I came to see if you wanted some supper with me tonight. Bring Boris.'

Numb, Annie agreed, rather than face the evening alone.

'Try and get a rest this afternoon. And put the whisky bottle away. Scotland is too full of ghosts who imagined that it solved anything. Callum knows all about that himself. I'll see you later.'

Annie tried to think more constructively. Everything Fiona had warned her about had come true. Perhaps it was for the best that it ended before she got in any deeper. She would go and see him, talk it through.

Outside the cottage, the rain-storm intensified as a black squall raced in from the Atlantic.

The Land Rover was parked in the driveway outside the cottage. Her heart thudded – he must be here. But there was no answer to the ring of the doorbell, no barking, no welcoming shout from Kirsty. She tried the door. Locked. As was the back door. The firmly padlocked boat shed held no sign of life. Then she saw that the other car was gone. He wasn't there after all.

Driving back to the village she tried to hold on to the resolve that had taken her to his house. She despised herself for falling to pieces, reminding herself she was not a lovesick teenager, but a woman approaching her middle years – she ought to behave like one. Go round and have a sensible conversation like a proper adult, tell him that on reflection she thought it best they draw a line under the events of the past few days, put it behind them.

In his absence, she acknowledged that despite everything Fiona had said, she had been longing to see him again. The lovesick teenager wept bitter tears.

By the time Annie arrived back at the cottage, she had reached a decision. What was the point of hanging around here, miserable, waiting to see him and say ... what? That a relationship that hadn't even started was over? That she didn't want to see him again? That it had all been a mistake? No – there was only one thing to do – get the hell away from here, put the whole sorry mess behind her and move on. This was what happened when you acted impulsively – it all went horribly wrong.

Within an hour she had thrown her cases into the back of the car and cancelled her arrangement with Fiona.

Rechecking the desk for any paperwork she would need in order to complete the forms for the solicitor, she found an old shoebox tucked away at the back of the bottom drawer. It was tied with a purple ribbon, 'Letters' written on the lid in her aunt's tidy handwriting. Hastily Annie untied the ribbon and opened the lid. Inside were bundles of envelopes. She recognised her own scrawling handwriting and remembered the long letters she had written to Janet right up until the point when email seemed to take over as a much more immediate means of communication. She replaced the lid and retied the ribbon. The shoebox joined the cases in the back of the car.

Chapter 29
West Highlands
April

'Cal! Where are you, Cal?'

Although Callum could hear Kirsty calling for him, he didn't – couldn't – answer.

Sometime late in the evening he had found himself in the shed, pulling back the tarpaulin covering the 42' classic McGruer and retreating to the shabby cockpit. Only weeks after the boat had been delivered to the yard, Freya's cancer was diagnosed. Until now it had stayed under wraps.

'Cal, are you in here? I'm going to miss the train!'

He was huddled in a corner of the cockpit amongst the dust and peeling varnish. Head in hands, waves of memory washed over him, stunning him with grief as if it had only just happened. Feeling as if all his wounds were open and bleeding. Charlie, Freya. Freya.

The wine Annie had brought barely touched the sides. He drank it straight out of the bottle, down in one. It had no effect at all. He craved whisky – but there was never any in the house. He faced this crisis cold.

'Cal!'

Kirsty's voice was closer now, echoing in the high rafters. He could hear her on the ladder propped up against the hull. Her head appeared above the side deck. She climbed aboard.

'Cal, Dad, what's wrong?' She sat down beside him in

the cockpit, taking his cold hand in hers.

'You're freezing, how long have you been up here?'

He said nothing. The answer was – ever since the wine bottle was empty. All night and most of the morning.

'Dad,' she only ever called him that if she was worried about him, 'Dad, you've got to talk to me. You're scaring me. What's wrong? Have you been drinking?'

Still no reply.

'Dad!' she shook his arm, desperate to get him to look at her.

Dully, his eyes focused on his daughter.

'Sorry, lass – just having a bit of a … moment. I'm OK.' He mumbled, mouth too dry to form the words clearly.

'No, you're not, Dad. You're freezing cold. Come back in the house – tell me what's happened. Is it Annie?'

He shook his head, slowly easing his stiff body out of the corner. She helped him to stand up and carefully guided him down the ladder and back to the house. Only when he was sitting by the stove, wrapped in a blanket with a mug of warm tea in his cold hands did she try again.

'Right. Now talk to me.' It was an order, so reminiscent of her mother. Tears formed in his eyes.

'I miss her so much,' he whispered.

Kirsty burst into tears, and sank down into his lap, sobbing. He pulled her close, stroking her hair as he allowed his own tears to flow unchecked.

'I'm sorry, lass. Sometimes it just hits me like a tidal wave. I don't want you to see me like this, it's not fair on you. I'm supposed to be the strong one.'

'Cal, we have to look after each other. That's what she wanted. It was one of the last things she ever said to me, "Look after your father."'

Her sobs grew louder, and they held each other, remembering Freya, comforting one another, crying together. Somehow, it helped. It was cathartic, holding his daughter, Freya's daughter – their child, the most important part of his life.

Callum slowly warmed up. Kirsty made him eat some breakfast.

'I've missed the train.' she said. 'But it doesn't matter. I'll go back tomorrow. You can phone the school, it'll be fine.'

'No, Kirsty. I'll drive you back. Get your stuff together. I'll change and get the dogs.' He called his brother to let him know.

On the way south, conversation possible in the relative quiet of the VW SUV that had been Freya's car, they talked more.

'But it must have had something to do with Annie, you were getting on so well I thought I'd better make myself scarce. I miss Mum too, Cal, you know I do, but I worry about you, all alone. I thought – hoped – you and Annie might ... '

'So did I, Kirsty. But it's not so simple as all that.'

'What's not simple, Cal? Mum's gone, we both loved her, we both miss her. But life has to go on. You're too young to be buried away out here on your own. I saw how you were with Annie ... '

He started to say something but Kirsty carried on.

' ... and don't tell me its not true, I saw the paper at Louise's. I don't mind, Cal. I hated that Cathy woman you went out with, she was just on the make. But Annie – well, she's lovely. So smart – funny, intelligent – beautiful. I thought she was perfect for you. I was so happy when I saw you together last night. She really fancies you, it's so obvious. And you feel the same, don't try to tell me otherwise.'

Kirsty's meaning was perfectly clear – she was giving

him permission.

'She's a lovely woman, and I won't deny we had a great time together. But I … I'm just not ready, lass. I think I'm moving forward and then I just get overwhelmed with feelings of … Freya's still here, she's all around. I still talk to her.'

'I know. I do too. When Annie brought the flowers I had to go away so I could have a wee cry, just seeing flowers in the house again. We always had flowers when Mum was alive, she loved flowers.'

Callum had bought flowers every week, right up until his wife's death. It had never occurred to him that Kirsty had noticed either their presence or their absence.

'I'm not ready, Kirsty. That's the truth. I don't want to hurt anyone. Cathy was hurt, whatever you thought of her. She's a nice enough woman, she deserves better. And Annie certainly does, God knows she has enough on her plate – she's just lost her aunt and her partner, all at the same time. The last thing she needs is a stupid bugger like me messing with her head.'

'It'll be OK, Cal. Maybe you just need to give it a bit of time.'

He groaned aloud. He had to deal with it, properly, like a man, go round tomorrow and talk to her, explain that he couldn't embark on a serious relationship as long as he felt it was a betrayal of Freya.

In Edinburgh, Dugald and Sally agreed.

'You'll know when the right time comes, Cal.' He had always been able to talk to his sister-in-law. Sally was a common-sense woman, used to dealing with the emotional fallout of living in a house full of teenagers – and his brother.

'You just have to go with your instinct. But Cal, maybe you should start to think about clearing out some of Freya's things. It's not really healthy to leave everything as if she might just walk back in the door any minute. I'll come up and give you a hand if you like – it won't be easy.'

~

Calmed by the evening and a fitful sleep in the madhouse that Dugald and Sally called home, he walked the dogs on Salisbury Crags the following morning, hoping that a brisk march up the steep path would help clear his head. Overnight rain had washed the air clear. The Scottish Parliament, an odd arrangement of boat-shaped buildings, lay in the valley below him, Holyrood Palace austere behind. The Castle brooded, silhouetted above the Old Town against the bright sky. Out in the distance, beyond the elegant Georgian terraces of the New Town, the blue waters of the Forth sparkled in the sun, the hills of Fife rising up across the water.

By late morning he was back on the A9, heading north.

Driving, he reprised his few days with Annie, cursing himself for starting something he should have known he couldn't follow through, but remembering how good she had felt in his arms, how much he had enjoyed her company. Miserable, he thought about how much they had laughed together. It was unusual for him to meet someone who had no idea who he was, or had been. Annie took him as she found him, with no expectations of Cal Mathieson, rock star.

He'd known it when they went sailing together – Annie was someone he could fall in love with. The attraction had been there from the moment she answered the door that morning. A quickening, the reawakening of something he'd thought he would never feel again, after Freya. He remembered the feeling when he first kissed her, stomach turning over, not just with desire, but with something else, a sense that something important was happening. He was sure Annie had felt it too – from the way she trembled, the look in her eyes. She was not a woman who did anything lightly. Beneath her reserve, one of the things he found so attractive about her, she had thrilled him with her growing warmth as she let her guard down. He recalled the intensity of their lovemaking, both of them stunned in its aftermath.

And there was no mistaking her response the last time they had made love. In his not inconsiderable experience, women didn't cry when they were having casual sex. There had been nothing casual about anything that had happened between them. Annie's tears had struck deep into his heart.

It was not just sex – they connected on a level somewhere far beyond the physical. The time on the boat, getting to know each other, had been a revelation. He had never opened up to anyone else about his feelings, not since Freya. But with Annie, talking had been as easy as breathing.

Everything had been perfect – until he'd tried to take her into the place he now recognised was a sanctuary, the place where the spirit of his wife still lived.

Until he came to terms with the fact that Freya was truly gone, he would not be ready for another relationship. That was what he must tell her. Annie would surely understand.

Nearing home, he took the back route through the village towards her cottage, heart thumping at the prospect of seeing her again, dreading what he knew he had to say.

There was no red Mini outside. The cottage was locked up, empty.

He knocked on the door of Fiona's house. She stood firmly in the doorway. The ginger cat on the window-ledge fixed him with a baleful stare.

'She's gone back to London. Left a couple of hours

ago. You probably passed her on the road.'

'Did she say when she'd be back?'

'No, but judging by the state of her I don't suppose it'll be any time soon. You need to sort yourself out, Callum Mathieson. You can't just use people whenever you feel like it. Annie was newly bereaved, vulnerable. You took advantage of her. You should be ashamed of yourself, flashing your rock-star looks around whenever anyone takes your fancy. Cathy's still not over you. Think about what you're doing. Everyone round here knows how much you loved Freya, you have nothing but sympathy, but it doesn't give you the right to hurt others.'

Callum opened his mouth to defend himself, changed his mind.

Fiona carried on.

'Anyway, I don't think Annie intends to come back, she's asked me to see about getting the cottage rented out as soon as confirmation of the estate comes through. But if she does I suggest you stay well away.'

'She's a grown woman, Fiona. I'm sure she knows her own mind.'

'Aye, and you're a grown man, but you don't seem to know yours, do you?'

He turned on his heel, unable to deny the truth of her last statement.

Callum drove off, up the road towards the boatyard. But as the turning came into view, he put his foot hard on the accelerator and drove on, across the Skye Bridge and up to Portree, to buy the whisky none of the local shops would sell him.

Chapter 30
London
April

'Annie – don't give up on him, please. He just needs time. Kirsty x :)'

She had stopped at a service area somewhere south of Glasgow. The text lit up her screen. She read it, and bit her lip against the onset of further tears.

'It's OK, Kirsty. I'm on my way back to London. Take care x' She couldn't think of anything else to say in reply.

Back home, her flat felt cold, unwelcoming – its stylish minimalism impersonal, sterile. She missed the warmth of the range, the clutter of Janet's colourful collection of pottery and paintings, and she longed for Boris's warm furry body on her lap. Even with the heating turned up and the lamps lit, there was no cosiness in the environment that had suited her so well until only three weeks previously. It was as if she had changed into another person altogether, a creature newly formed, out of its shell, exposed and vulnerable. She needed to find herself again before she went under.

Between her chilly sheets she lay, sleepless, reliving the past three weeks, wishing she could turn back the clock and do it all again, differently, leaving herself intact. At the same time, she feared it was too late. She was already in pieces.

∽

Up north, Annie had simply ignored the messages piling up in her inbox. In Putney next morning, with a cup of coffee on the desk in front of her – she promised herself she would never drink tea again – she began working her way through the list. Only a handful were of any interest, including two from Claire at the gallery suggesting possible dates for Janet's retrospective.

'Annie! Great to hear from you, are you back? I didn't expect I'd ever see you again, not with the distractions on offer up there!'

Claire had a disgustingly dirty laugh.

Annie tried to be businesslike, talking about the paintings and the proposed exhibition. Claire was having none of it.

'Why don't we discuss it over lunch? Then you can tell me all about it.'

The last thing she was going to do was meet up for lunch just to satisfy Claire's salacious curiosity about what Callum was like in bed.

'I don't have time before I go back to work, Claire.' It was a lie. She hadn't made any such plans yet.

'Oh come on, Annie. Just share a little I can take to bed with boring old Jamie.'

'Claire! That's a terrible thing to say.'

'I saw those pictures of the two of you online. Don't try and tell me nothing happened. The sparks were just about jumping out of the screen. What was he feeding you, anyway? Oysters?'

Claire cackled at her own wit.

Online ... oh no, that hadn't occurred to her.

'I really don't want to talk about it, Claire. It was just a bit of fun, but I've got more to do with my life than hang around with an ageing rock star.'

If she kept saying it, maybe she would eventually feel it.

'Well, if he's free I might have a go myself!'

Annie felt sick.

In the end they agreed a date for Janet's retrospective, eight months hence. Annie came off the phone, shattered. Her flimsy carapace wasn't yet fit for purpose.

Moira was a different matter. She was the only person Annie could face seeing.

'I'm coming over tonight, after work. I'll bring the wine, takeaway will do, pizza, anything.'

Moira breezed in, caught Annie up in a tight hug, saying, 'God, I've missed you!' and launched straight into business. 'We've all missed you – the office has almost ground to a halt.'

She looked at Annie closely.

'You look great. Have you put on weight? It suits you.'

Annie knew that if she had, she certainly wasn't eating enough now to maintain it. Her appetite had deserted her completely. She picked at a slice of pizza while Moira demolished the rest. But they were equally matched in the consumption of the wine.

'Anyway, we're really struggling without you. David Robertson has stepped in, but frankly he's an arse, not fit to lick your boots, never mind try to fill them. We're already falling behind – no one has your ability to see straight to the point. I'm so glad you're back – wondered if you're ready to get stuck in again. I'd like to see this get to court before half the perpetrators have died off. Work from home if you want.'

After the last few days, it felt good to be back in her comfort zone. If anything could help her get over her heartbreak, she knew it would be work. But she hesitated.

'Can I sleep on it? It's just ... well, I'd like to get Aunt Janet's stuff sorted out – I didn't really have much time when I was up there and the estate was much bigger than I had expected – I know once I'm back in the office I'll have no time at all ... '

'How much longer do you think you need?'

'A week? And if anything urgent comes up, I could handle it from home ... '

Reluctantly, Moira agreed.

'So how did it go up there? Seems as if you've been away for ages.'

'Oh it was ... you know ... '

Annie was uncomfortably aware of Moira's piercing gaze.

'Are you going to tell me or do I have to get you even more pissed than you already are?'

It was no good trying to hide anything from Moira. They knew each other too well. Annie told her all about it.

'Cal Mathieson? Of 2CM? Wow. Not your usual type. Much too flashy. You always go for the professionals, the cerebral ones.'

'Maybe that's where I was going wrong,' Annie observed, with a wry smile.

'I always loved 2CM. Charlie in his kilt!'

'I feel like I've made a complete fool of myself, Moira. I didn't know who he is, I thought he was just a bloke who builds boats. He's not flashy at all. Quite the opposite. He lives very quietly, looking after his daughter, working in his yard. He plays in a local band. He's a really lovely man. But still in love with his late wife. You didn't tell me that when you told me your widowers theory.'

'He doesn't fit the profile. There are always exceptions. Poor you. You didn't need that on top of everything else.'

'I should never have let my guard down. It's all such a mess, Moira.'

'It'll be alright, Annie. You've survived a lot worse. Just chalk it up to experience and move on.'

'That's what I keep telling myself.'

∽

Next morning Moira rang with some gossip about Justin Brooke, the home office minister Annie had challenged on *News Tonight*.

'Between you and me, Annie, he's keeping his head well below the parapet. A couple of weeks ago he was talking about taking you to court, but he's completely quiet now. I think he may have been called in for a police interview. Fingers crossed – a major scalp would give everyone a lift right now.'

As they were speaking, a new email pinged its arrival in her inbox. She didn't recognise the address, raasayboats@btinternet.com. Then she did – she felt as if her heart had stopped.

'Moira, I have to go. Something's just … I'll get back to you.'

My dear Annie,

I don't know where to begin. I came to see you but you'd already gone. There was so much I wanted to say, to try to explain.

I owe you a huge apology. I should have realised I was letting everything move too fast. Fiona said you were really upset, tore strips off me for starting something I couldn't follow through. I deserve it. The last thing I ever meant to do was hurt you.

However, I have to face up to the truth, which is that I'm not ready to get involved in another relationship yet. I don't know if I ever will be. It's not just that I loved Freya so much. Without her it's as if I've lost any sense of direction – I don't know who I am. I still feel like a married man, even though I know she's gone. I can just about hold it together for Kirsty, and if I stick to my routines I can pretend everything's fine, but it's not. I had no right to involve you in my emotional wreckage, especially when you were having such a difficult time yourself.

None of which means what happened wasn't the best thing that's happened to me for a very long time. You brought something out in me that's been buried for so long. I thought I could be that man, I really want to be that man, rather than the screw-up I am.

I thought I could handle it, thought I was ready. But I got scared by how quickly everything seemed to be running away from us. Then when I was about to take you to bed at home it was as if I ran into a brick wall. I think I went into some kind of shock.

I hope eventually you can forgive me. I'm not sure I can forgive myself.

Take care, Annie. You are a lovely woman, with so much to give. I hope you find someone to love you the way you should be loved. In different circumstances I truly believe it could have been me.

Yours aye, with apologies and regret,
Callum

The last glimmer of hope that he would turn up at her door, take her in his arms and make everything right again was laid to rest. There was a finality about his message. It struck deep into her wounded heart, and she cried, alone, in mourning for a love she truly believed could have grown and flourished, whatever problems might have lain in the way.

Agonising over her reply, she struggled to get the right tone.

Dear Callum,

There really is no need for any apology. We are both adults and we went into whatever it was with our eyes wide open. I loved spending time with you – there are no regrets.

I came by the house on the way south. I should have waited to see you, but I admit that I was in shock too. I needed to get away. Email is a particularly sterile form of communication, but it's the best you and I have right now.

As to relationships, I can barely imagine how hard it is for you having lost someone you expected to share the rest of your life with. One romantic weekend, however pleasurable, could never change that. Nor would I ever be able to take the place of someone you loved, and still love, so completely. If I stirred up painful memories then any apology must come from me.

Whatever happened between us, I can't see how it could have a future. I love Scotland, but my life is here in London, just as yours is there, in the boatyard, in that beautiful place, with your daughter and your music.

I'll always be grateful to you for taking me sailing and showing me things I'd never imagined. The dolphins and the singing seals were magical. I'll never forget any of it. And you introduced me to a world of music I never paid attention to before – I will be a lot more open-minded in future.

Please, look after yourself, Callum. I'm no therapist, but it seems to me that maybe you need to let yourself grieve.

And Kirsty – please tell her I am always happy to talk to her about her future or anything. And it's probably none of my business – but I just want to say, as the daughter of an alcoholic mother – please don't let Kirsty ever go through what I went through.

Annie X

She looked at that miserable 'X', wondering whether to leave it or delete it. It fitted with the lightness of tone she was trying to convey, but by comparison to the kisses they had shared, it seemed utterly feeble.

She left it.

It wasn't what she wanted to write. Her inner teenager screamed in her head, just tell him the truth, tell him you'll be there however long it takes, tell him how you really feel. Fight for him. Her thirty-nine-year-old self told her inner teenager to 'shut the fuck up' as she hit 'send'.

She called Moira back.

'You know what, Moira? I'm ready to start again now. How about I come in tomorrow?'

Moira whooped down the phone. Gratefully, Annie threw herself back into the familiar world of work. Back to what passed for normal.

Chapter 31
West Highlands
April

Callum was sober at last.

Missed at AA, not answering his phone, one of the other members recognised the danger signs and spoke to Jack. He and Jenny called round, to find Callum sitting staring out of the window, drunk, morose, unwashed, sick. Filled with self-loathing.

'Bugger off, Jack. Leave me alone, I'm fine.'

'Ye're no fine, Callum. Look at yerself. Ye need tae sober up, ye need tae eat. And ye need to dae it right now, because Kirsty will be home soon and ye canna let her see this. Think aboot it, Cal. Dinnae dae it for yerself, dae it for her. Ye're all the lassie's got. Dinnae let her down.'

Jenny poured the remainder of the whisky away and heated up some soup, the only food Callum could tolerate. She and Jack stayed over for the next few days, making sure he stayed sober, making him eat, restoring a semblance of order.

Grateful, a chastened Callum focused on Kirsty. Jack was right. She must never see him like this – he owed it to Freya as well as himself.

Annie had replied to the email he'd sent as he'd started on the first bottle. His hands were still shaking as he opened her message. He read her reply, so much more eloquent than his own attempt. For a while he sat, reliving every moment they had spent together, wondering if it really was irretrievably over, reading and rereading the words on his screen. Hating himself for screwing up so badly, for drinking again, for being the fuck-up he'd been before Freya and was in danger of becoming again. Then he printed it off and folded it carefully into an envelope, putting it away in his desk – other than memories, it was all he had.

~

Sally drove Kirsty home from Edinburgh. Talking to Callum on the phone, she heard it in his voice – he was in trouble.

They talked late into the night. He listened to her advice. She persuaded him he had to make changes, start the process of moving forward. Suggested rehab – he said he'd think about it.

Kirsty too knew something was badly wrong. He didn't want to burden his daughter with his problems, but with a persistence so like her mother's, she wore him down.

'All I want is for you to be happy, Cal. I can't bear to think of you here on your own. You need to make changes, like Sally said. It'll help you. I don't want you starting to drink again, Cal. I can't lose you, too.'

Annie's words came to mind as he held his sobbing daughter – he had to be strong for her, get himself under control.

~

It was Kirsty's idea – he should build a studio, start recording some of the songs he'd been writing.

The architect friend Freya had used when she first remodelled the cottage was more than happy to come round to discuss further changes with Callum. He thought the alterations would be reasonably straightforward. He would get something drawn up as quickly as possible, delighted Callum was thinking about recording again, hoping it could all be done within four or five months.

Callum steeled himself. He began the heartbreaking business of clearing the room he and Freya had shared after she was unable to climb the stairs to the master bedroom. For the best part of a week he lingered over the task, considering each piece of clothing and the memories it held, jewellery he had bought for her, indulging her taste for large, bright handmade pieces, student work from the art college degree shows they had loved to see each year.

Her wedding ring. He took off his own – Freya's fitted snugly inside it. She'd had such tiny hands. He tied both rings together with a length of sailmakers' thread, and made a small wooden box to put them in, wrapped in tissue paper. When the studio was started, he would bury the box in the new foundations, so they would always be there together.

Clearing the room was like walking through a minefield, never knowing what he would uncover to cause the next explosion of memory and pain. Yet in the process he began to see that Annie was right. He had never allowed himself to grieve. Staying strong for Kirsty had been his focus. He had lost his wife, but Kirsty had lost her mother, she needed all her father's love and support. He had developed the habit of suppressing his own feelings, refusing to give in to the tears that he always felt would never stop if he allowed them to start. Until that night with Annie, there had been no point at which he had confronted his own need to mourn his wife. He only thought he had, because he felt so bereft all the time.

Little by little he allowed the tide of emotions he had

kept buried since Freya's death to break. Some were so overwhelming, all he could do was cry. So he cried, finally confronting his pain, and then let himself remember all the good times before she had become ill. As he did so he relived the months after they'd first met again in Stornoway, when she had guided him, helping him come to terms with losing Charlie.

He understood now that he'd stayed in the room where she spent her last months, the bed in which he'd held her hand as she drew her final, faltering breaths, to keep her close. This was where they'd spent most of their time together, sharing an intimacy of a kind never imagined in their years as lovers, but one which, as her carer, he treasured just the same. Refusing to consider suggestions that he should employ a nurse to assist with the increasing demands of her physical deterioration, he was determined to see her through her final weeks and days, assisted only by the palliative care nurse and the advice and support of his sister to help him on the rare occasions when he felt the responsibility might be too much. Until in the final stages, as fervently as he had longed for her to live only months previously, he longed for her to be released from the ravages of her illness.

He could barely believe now that he might have considered, even for a single second, bringing Annie into this room. It was, he supposed, a measure of how caught up he was in the moment, in the excitement of an incredible physical and emotional release after his long years of numb shock and aching sadness in the empty space he occupied without his wife. He remembered what Sally had said, about it being as if Freya might return. It was what he had been hoping for, longing for. Somehow he had believed, in some deep part of his unconscious mind, that while all her things were still around, they would be ready for her when she came back. At last he understood he would never be able to move forward until he accepted it would never happen.

The master suite upstairs, with its huge windows facing out across the view, became his new refuge. It held precious memories of the ebb and flow of life before Freya's decline into illness. Kirsty was conceived in this room. Its four walls were witness to everything that had passed between his wife and himself. Gentle, sleepy morning sex; to other times when they just wanted a good hard fuck. As a couple, lovemaking had always remained an important part of their relationship. The daily exchanges of normal life, from inconsequential chat to blazing rows – Freya a silent sulker, Callum volatile and explosive. Tearful, tender reconciliations – they never fell out for long. Nights when Kirsty crawled in beside them, her hot little body driving them to opposite sides of the bed as their daughter lay spreadeagled, fast asleep between them. Laughter, lots of laughter. Recollections he embraced and treasured, part of the landscape of his life as a husband and father.

The changes he made to the room were lightly done, but revealed anew the clever architecture – exposed beams under a vaulted ceiling, tall windows with their views of dramatic mountains. He applied fresh taupe-coloured paint, bought new furniture, rearranged pictures. Lying between crisp linen sheets, he looked around, allowing himself to take pleasure in a space that reflected his own style. Comforted by the knowledge that Freya would have approved.

Only one of Freya's paintings hung in the newly painted bedroom. It was his favourite, the one piece in which she herself had ever truly believed.

'Would you like to see it, Cal?' Freya had been working hard in her studio for a couple of days, simmering with excitement in a way unusual for her

'Of course, *mo gradh*, always.'

It was a square canvas, quite small – her preferred format. Otherwise, she had broken all her own rules. It was divided equally in half, something she was taught never to do, the bottom section painted in red ochre, the upper part cerulean blue. What made the painting was the part where the two blocks of colour met. There was a blurred edge, no more than an inch wide, where the two colours merged in tiny interlocking strands. He stepped in close. From a distance it looked hazy. Only close up was it possible to see how the colours kept their separate identities, joining together in fine whorls and rivulets.

'What do you think?'

'It's lovely. So subtle. Landscape?'

'If that's what you see. But no. It's us.'

'Us?'

It was before Kirsty was conceived. They had almost given up hope of ever having a child. Just the two of them. Individuals, their combined lives meeting halfway in tightly woven strands.

'Yes. You're the blue sky, I'm the red earth.'

'Oh, Freya.' He took her hand, lost for words, tears pricking his eyes.

Together they stood for a while, considering what she had painted. Then Callum stepped forward and turned the canvas through ninety degrees on the easel, so the bands of colour were vertical. He returned to stand beside her.

'OK, now I see it. We stand side by side, you and me. Neither one on top of the other. Well, sometimes ... quite often, actually ... '

Freya laughed and hugged him, but she preferred it as she had intended. For once he didn't have a lyric to sing. Nothing came to mind that was anything other than trite. Unworthy of such a precious moment.

For the rest of her life, the canvas lived in the bedroom, a barometer monitoring the weather of their love, turned through three hundred and sixty degrees according to how either one of them felt the balance to be on any given day.

Callum hung it vertically, his favourite interpretation – his cerulean blue to the right, Freya's red ochre to the left.

Kirsty was thrilled with the results of his redecoration. She insisted her own room was given the same treatment, although she promptly replaced her old childhood clutter with a more up-to-date version on its tastefully painted walls.

∽

A new order came in for a Raasay 25. He threw himself into the task, working long hours before falling exhausted into bed to sleep deeply until he got up the next morning to do it all again.

One night, he dreamt of Freya as she was when they had first started living together, full of life and energy. They were walking on Dalmore Beach, her arm linked through his. 'It's OK, Cal,' she was saying, over and over again. He woke, remembering and somehow comforted.

Other nights, Annie appeared fleetingly in his dreams. He re-read their emails – he had made his sound so final. There was a lightness of tone in Annie's response – maybe he had, after all, misread her. Maybe what happened between them had just been a bit of fun for her, whatever Fiona said. Perhaps, he told himself, she'd just needed comfort, on the rebound after breaking up with her partner.

But that wasn't what he truly believed. He regretted the silence between them, missed the intimacy they had shared, however briefly. Longed to be close to her again, hated himself for having behaved so carelessly. He wondered if he should do something, make contact. But until he had something better than apologies to offer, he felt it would be a mistake. Without any clear idea what to do, doing nothing was the easiest option.

Work began on the studio. A team of Polish builders worked long hours and took the same pride in their work as he did in his own. The boatyard rang with the sounds of screeching power tools from both house and shed for six days of the week, overlaid with the thumping beat and searing guitar solos of 2CM at the height of their recording career. It was the builders' music of choice.

Chapter 32
London
Summer

Within the first few weeks Annie had caught up on the backlog that had built up in her absence. She worked tirelessly. Moira grew concerned.

'Give yourself a break, Annie. You're working yourself into the ground.'

Annie was thin, any weight gain from her three weeks in Scotland long gone. It was, she told herself, the one consolation of having a broken heart – she could get into clothes she hadn't been able to wear for years.

The confirmation came through. Fiona called to let her know tenants had been found for the cottage, a young Polish builder, his wife and their new baby. It felt like cutting off a lifeline, but she agreed, signed the contract. It felt like another step towards putting Callum in the past.

In July, just as Parliament went into recess, the allegations of a police cover-up in the care home scandal were strengthened by a newspaper investigation. There was a flurry of activity, more interviews and press conferences as Annie and Moira worked long hours together, building up a picture of depravity that horrified them both. It was, for Annie, as if she'd never been away. She told herself that Callum had been nothing more than a blip, a temporary lapse of judgement, brought on by the grief of losing Aunt Janet. Life was back to normal.

∽

Chris, a colleague, had theatre tickets for a new play – they were like gold dust. He invited her to join him. It was a date, her first since Scotland. Dressing, she tried to summon up a sense of enthusiasm. Chris had booked early supper at a fashionable new restaurant in the West End. The food looked spectacular, but tasted, as all food did to her now, of nothing. He was neatly dressed in matching casuals, carefully manicured. She found his fashionably cut blond hair and freckled skin deeply unattractive. Dull, over-eager, he reminded her of a Labrador puppy. His was one of those home counties braying voices, and he had a habit of laughing at his own, not very funny, jokes.

The play was incomprehensible, the simulated emotion wooden and predictable. She fought to stay awake after the interval, and threw herself into a cab with a sigh of relief as soon as she could get away, avoiding his attempt to kiss her goodnight, promising herself she wouldn't do it again.

That night she dreamed of the Applecross Inn. Callum was waiting to go on stage. He was holding her hands – she could feel the roughness of his skin, the little nicks and scars from his tools. He wore scruffy black jeans, stained with glue and varnish, and a grey T-shirt, the fabric soft and warm. The wood-panelled bar resonated to the sound of laughter, of half-heard conversations in soft Highland accents. Callum was speaking quietly in her ear, words whose meaning she couldn't quite catch. Leaning close, she breathed in his musky scent. Strands of his hair caressed her cheek. She woke, trying to remember his words, her mind chasing down fleeting memories of the dream, the feeling of her hands in his, his mouth against her ear, his physicality. Knowing all the time what she should do was fight those feelings, to get him out of her head if she was going to get over him.

Yet try as she might to put him out of her mind, reminders of Callum were everywhere. Songs he had sung would catch her unawares, glimpses of tall dark-haired men made her heart leap. Cursing her stupidity, she nevertheless downloaded albums she knew he liked, immersing herself in the music, searching for solace in the lyrics, always hearing the songs in Callum's husky voice. She listened to the 2CM albums, tuning out Charlie and listening for Callum's guitar, his vocals. Often they sang about home, the islands, Scotland. She grew to love their music. The third album was the one she loved best – Callum's love songs were like arrows piercing her heart – his version of "Ae fond Kiss" almost impossible to listen to, so accurately did it tell the story of their own brief romance. Painful though they were – he must have been in love when he wrote them, she thought – those songs captured her heart too.

One night, after an evening spent home alone with a few too many glasses of wine, she Googled him, just to see his face.

Even twenty years after the demise of 2CM, there was a deluge of information – biography, discography, gossip. You Tube clips of the band – Callum always behind the whirling dervish that was Charlie in full flight – head down over his guitar or thrown back as he sang, moving in time to the music.

2CM had won a Brit award – Callum supporting Charlie – or perhaps it was the other way round – as they made their way up to the stage – a cringe-making, drunken attempt at a speech.

There was footage of him on stage at a benefit concert, with Clapton, Robert Plant, and yes, that was Bruce

Springsteen. How exciting for him, playing in the major leagues.

Awful kiss-and-tell tabloid stories – 'My three-in-a-bed romp with Charlie and Callum', 'Cal broke my heart', 'Mathieson NOT dad to Cheryl's baby'. His name linked with glamour models, page three girls, soap stars. There were endless pictures of him leaving hotels, nightclubs, with scantily dressed, overly made-up women. Mentally, she filed these stories in the part of her mind where she kept all the reasons she should get over him and get on with her life.

But having started, she couldn't stop.

On the cover of a German music magazine a young Callum looked up from beneath his eyebrows, straight into her soul. It was a black and white photograph, except for the eyes, a flash of blue. Stripped to the waist, a line of white underwear showed provocatively beneath the waistband of his jeans. The headline summed him up – 'hottest man in rock and roll'. Her body longed for him.

Paparazzi shots, thousands of them. Devastated, ashen-faced, as he was led out of a hotel by the police the day Charlie died. Alone by Charlie's grave, head down, defeated.

How awful, to have gone through the horror of Charlie's death in the full glare of media attention, never having time alone to grieve, always at the mercy of tabloid snappers and scribblers. No wonder he drank.

A later date – he was leaving a church hall somewhere with a group of other people – the caption read 'Cal in AA'.

Even his attempt at recovery was documented.

It made her think about the role drinking played in her own life. It had been a good day – a drink to celebrate, or just to round it off. A bad day – several glasses of wine to make up for it, settle the nerves. Going out – a drink first.

Dinner – a bottle of wine. She was in no position to judge anyone else on their drinking. Even now there was a glass of wine on the desk beside her. Neither a good day nor a bad day, just another day to be endured.

She went into the kitchen and poured the remains into the sink, returning with a glass of water.

On the screen of her laptop Callum was down on one knee somewhere by a harbour, holidaymakers in the background, watching as he held the hands of a lovely young blond woman, her head thrown back, laughing. A second in the same place, the two of them kissing, her feet off the ground as he held her in a tight embrace. Freya. Pure envy made her lightheaded. His wife. So unlike the women of his rock star days – cropped hair, bare of make up, wearing Doc Martens and a pretty dress. 'Wedding Bells for Cal and Mystery Woman', screamed the headline.

With a start she noticed the date on those pictures. The day Callum was asking Freya to marry him in Falmouth, she was partying hard in London, celebrating Tony Blair's first election victory in 1997, with a roomful of delirious New Labour campaigners. She remembered dawn breaking over the Festival Hall that day. *Things can only get better* ... her twenty-one-year-old self was singing, over and over again, along with the ecstatic crowd, waiting in the brilliant early morning sunlight for the arrival of the new prime minister.

Perhaps they would, but when?

How strange – a bad boy of the music scene, down on one knee, making an old-fashioned proposal of marriage, while the earnest bluestocking good girl that she had been was behaving badly at a party, falling into bed with a fellow activist and waking up to regret it.

There were wedding pictures. Callum in full dress kilt, all black, socks fallen down over his boots, looking heartbreakingly handsome. She'd have married him, she thought, jealousy twisting her stomach in knots. Freya looked radiantly pretty, in a gorgeous cream lace dress, a crown of flowers woven into her cropped blonde hair. She was tiny beside him.

Someone had recently put up a video on Facebook. Captioned 'In loving memory of my best friend Freya', it was a video clip of the newly married couple dancing the first waltz. He smiled down into his wife's face as he held her, his kilt swaying. Freya was laughing, barefoot, standing on his boots.

She told herself to turn the bloody computer off, stop torturing herself, but she couldn't.

There were later pictures. With Freya again and a baby wrapped in a white blanket. Callum carried his daughter with exquisite care. Freya held his arm as they walked towards a waiting car.

Somewhere that looked like the Mediterranean, a forest of masts bristled in a marina. Callum, deeply tanned, in navy shorts, deck shoes and a white T-shirt emblazoned with the line drawing of a yacht, stood on a podium next to a blond man in the same kit, brandishing a bottle of champagne. An impressive silver cup stood on a table in front of them. 'Skipper Patrick Barber celebrates another *Sweet Caledonia* victory in the Regates Royales with tactician and rock guitarist, Cal Mathieson.'

And then the latest pictures, in Applecross, the two of them together. One of them falling in love.

Unable to bear any more, she closed the lid of her laptop, desolate in her loneliness and longing for something she had never had and now believed she never would. Tears poured down her face.

Being in love was the most painful thing she had ever experienced. Now she understood why she had always taken such care to avoid it.

Annie hated this weakness in herself. It was an emotion foreign to her – she couldn't understand why the strategies that had always worked in the past, self-discipline, an iron will, were failing her now.

But it could never have worked, she told herself.

Firstly, because he was an alcoholic. She knew too much about dependency to want it in her life again, however well controlled. Even setting his drinking aside, his history alone made him quite the wrong sort of partner for someone like her. The succession of suitable men who had preceded him were the kind she needed, if any – men who had led careful lives, lawyers, academics, government advisors. Career-minded, focused – not men like Callum who, until Freya had taken him in hand, had simply let life happen to him, careless of consequences.

Most importantly, she told herself, they had so little in common. How could she, her life steeped in politics and the law, even for a moment entertain the idea of a partner for whom current affairs meant no more than the direction of the tide?

Yet her whole being ached for him. For the incredible moment of complete surrender she had only known once in her life, with Callum. The moment of melting together, fusing into one entity, unforgettable in its intensity. She wondered, not having anything to compare it with, if it was something that only ever happened once in anyone's life. And did Callum's question, 'what are you doing to me?' mean that even though he had been happily married for many years, it had never happened to him before, either?

As the weeks went by, Annie tried in vain to convince herself it had only ever been about physical attraction, the amazing sex.

Over and over again, she asked herself the same question. How could she have allowed her icy core, the very thing that had given her the strength to get through a difficult childhood and the life she had built for herself, to melt so completely, leaving her so exposed?

Sometimes, longing to hear his voice, she thought she should call him, or at least send a message. But she held back. The email he sent after her return to London offered no hope. Pride, and the last vestiges of dignity to which she clung as her other resources deserted her, would not allow her to expose her weakness. Instead, she told herself she would get over him in time. She had to believe that if she was patient, if she held fast to a semblance of normality, normality would return.

Chapter 33
Cannes
September

It was late September. Giving in to pressure from Moira to take a holiday, Annie spent a week in a villa in Mandelieu on the Côte d'Azur as a guest of Steph, an old university friend. Benefiting from her holiday, Annie felt that at last she was making progress. She was beginning to feel more like herself, as good as she could remember since leaving Scotland. Warm sun, good food and lazy days around the pool had conspired to engender a sense of wellbeing for the first time since life had turned upside down. Steph and her husband Graham were welcoming and good company, as were their two teenaged boys, Toby and Ralph. There was a succession of visitors and houseguests. An Italian colleague of Graham's was showing an interest, singling her out at mealtimes and on walks. He suggested that she visit him in Milan. Recently divorced, he was attractive, intelligent and amusing. Flattered, Annie wondered if she might take him up on his offer. She told herself she was really beginning to get over Callum. Ready for something else in her life. Moving on.

On her last day, Steph suggested a trip to Cannes. They spent the morning window-shopping on the Rue d'Antibes, where the cool and fashionable refreshed their wardrobes in designer boutiques with astronomical price-tags. They shared a delicious seafood platter and a carafe of rosé in a restaurant on the Croisette. The Mediterranean was a rich turquoise blue on the south side of the tree-lined promenade. They amused themselves people-watching, marvelling at a fascinating parade of wealth and eccentricity – designer dogs in handbags – elegant, stylish couples – elderly ladies with immaculate coiffures, dressed despite the still warm September air, in furs – all promenading to be admired, amongst crowds of teenagers intent on their mobile phones.

After lunch they set off for a walk around the old harbour. Banners announcing the Regates Royales, a race series due to start the following week, snapped and fluttered in the breeze. The marina was a hive of activity, suntanned crew on the decks of classic yachts organising sails and lines, ferrying supplies, cleaning and varnishing. Good-natured banter passed between the boats in a variety of accents, antipodean predominant. Annie was enchanted. The yachts were beautiful. She could imagine the snug spaces below deck, that particular feeling when the wind filled the sails and they took off with no more than the hiss of the water along the hull and a foaming wake to mark their passing. Like sailing on *Sweet Dreams*.

By the side of the Palais des Festivals, the biggest and brashest of the power-boats were lined up – a telling display of what a large disposable income could buy. Only one yacht was moored amongst them – mast towering higher than any other in the marina. With her long overhangs and golden dragon carved into the bow, her silvery teak decks, shiny varnish as smooth as glass, she brought to mind a thoroughbred in a field of carthorses. A red ensign lifted in the breeze, suspended from a gilt-topped flagstaff at her stern. A walkway stretched from the aft deck to hover suspended just above the quayside, where a basket full of sandals and deck shoes indicated that the crew was aboard.

Annie stopped to admire her, entranced. There was a name etched into a polished brass plate capping the end of the boom. '*Sweet Caledonia 1927*,' she murmured. It snagged at her memory.

'If you could have any one you wanted, which would it be?' Stephanie asked. She had stopped to admire several million euros in the form of a vulgar grey power-boat with black-tinted windows. 'I think I might go for this one. It's so cool.'

'Oh Steph, no, that's not a boat, that's the wet dream of a man who's worried about the size of his dick! Look, this is a proper boat. I'd have this one – if I had the money.'

'Good choice.'

The accent was unmistakably Australian. An athletic-looking bronzed man with sun-bleached hair, wrap-around sunglasses and zinc cream on his nose stood behind them. Annie blushed to think what else he had overheard, wishing she hadn't drunk quite so much wine with her lunch.

'And you're probably right about the small dick too ... '

They all laughed.

'Do you sail?' he asked Annie.

'Only once. It was a much smaller boat than this, though.' Almost as an afterthought she added, 'In Scotland.'

'No kidding! Whereabouts? West coast, if you were lucky. God's own sailing up there. That's where she comes from.' He indicated the classic yacht. 'The Clyde. Built by William Fife in 1927.'

'I was further north. Plockton, near Skye. Do you know it?'

'Yeah, I do. Boatbuilder mate of mine has a yard near Plockton.'

Her heart flipped. The Australian carried on

'Yeah, I'd be up there with him if it wasn't for the shitty weather. Cal, great guy, good mate.'

Now she remembered where she'd seen this man before. He was in one of the photographs she had seen online. Without the zinc cream.

'We went to boat school together. Great sailor – he joins us sometimes for the races. In fact, he'll be crewing in a couple of weeks for the racing at St Tropez.'

'St Tropez', Annie repeated, numb. Her heart raced. Callum might so easily have been here.

'Yeah, he's our tactician. No one can read the wind like Cal. We've really missed him the last couple of years.'

Neither she nor Steph had any idea what a tactician might be, but there was something about the Australian's infectious enthusiasm, together with his bleached blond good looks, that kept them chatting.

'So, are you telling me you race in one of these?' asked Stephanie.

'Yeah, this one. I'm skipper. Biggest cutter ever built by the Fife yard. Wins all the prizes, now we've replaced the mast.'

They dutifully looked up and admired the beautiful shining spar.

'It was Callum I sailed with. In his boat. *Sweet Dreams*.' She said it quietly, the temptation to see him through the eyes of someone who knew him well proving too much to resist.

'No shit! How is he? Haven't seen him for a while – he hasn't been down since … you know he lost … ?' Annie nodded. 'I've been a bit worried, to be honest. That's why I invited him for the racing – he needs to get out, meet people, have fun. How's he doing?'

Annie felt a sharp stab of envy at the thought of Callum meeting people, having fun. She'd seen too many lovely suntanned female crew members, no doubt very much interested in a bit of fun.

'I don't really know him very well.' In a sense it was true, she realised. 'I was in Plockton organising my aunt's funeral. He was very kind and invited me out on his boat. He seemed OK.' She knew that wasn't true – he was anything but OK.

'Is he playing again? I hope so – too much wasted talent if he isn't.'

'He played at the pub a couple of times. He's … ' she remembered Applecross with a longing that took her breath away, '…amazing.'

'Amazing? Is that the best you can do? Fucking dynamite! Cal Mathieson, he's one of the best guitarists ever to come out of the UK!'

Annie nodded – she didn't trust herself to speak.

Stephanie gave her an odd look.

'I think we'd better go. The others'll be wondering where we've got to.'

'It was good talking to you guys. Patrick, by the way, Patrick Barber.' He held out a tanned hand and they shook.

'I'm Annie MacIntosh, and this is Stephanie Peters. Good to meet you too. And please, say "Hi" to Callum from me when you see him.'

'Hey, come back tomorrow, I'll show you around. I'd do it now but I've got a crew briefing.'

'Love to, really, but I'm flying home tomorrow.'

Stephanie made an excuse. She would much rather have looked around the power-boat.

They turned back up the quay towards the Croisette.

'Annie, you've been holding out on me. You never told me you know Cal Mathieson. 2CM! I always loved them. Charlie and his kilt! Sex in pleats!'

Annie gave her the abbreviated version, just a date, leaving out the broken heart. At least Steph hadn't seen the pictures.

Chapter 34
West Highlands
September

To Cal, raasayboats@btinternet.com
  G'day Cal,
  How are you, mate? Just met a friend of yours down on the quay – Annie MacIntosh. She said to say hi. When you come down I want a full explanation – how come you had that gorgeous woman on your boat then let her go? What's wrong with you, you daft Scottish bastard?
  See you at Marseilles airport on the 5th.
  P.

To Patrick, skipper@sweetcaledonia.fr
  Patrick,
  If I ever need advice about my love life from a promiscuous Ozzie with the track record of a rabbit I'll let you know.
  See you on the 5th. Flight lands 18.30.
  Cal.
  PS. Did Annie seem OK to you? What was she doing there? Was she with anyone? Did she say how long she was staying?

Two weeks later, Patrick had to repeat every word Annie had said, describe how she'd looked, what she had been wearing – a dress … (long, short? I dunno, somewhere in between, mate ... gold sandals I think - or maybe that was the other woman ...). With the scant information Patrick was able to provide, Callum tried to picture her, white linen bright against her brown skin, the dress loose and unstructured the way she liked her clothes, comfortable, unshowy. A floppy sun hat, natural straw, he imagined, perhaps a scarf tied around the crown ... painted toenails of course ... Did she seem happy?

'For fuck's sake, Cal! Why don't you just call her, go and see her yourself?'

'I can't. I've burnt those bridges already.' And he told Patrick all about it.

Chapter 35
Norfolk
December

Through long winter evenings in front of a log fire, Annie and Moira spent Christmas in Norfolk. They took bracing walks on windswept beaches, entertained friends and neighbours in a festive round of dinner parties and boozy lunches, while comfortable as always in each other's company.

On a rare quiet evening, Annie was washing up after supper when Moira called her through to the sitting room

'You might want to see this.' A programme was just beginning. The title, *Where Are They Now?* scrolled down the screen. In the opening shot a woman, dressed in a stylish padded coat and bright scarf, walked along a beach against a background which made Annie's heart lurch.

'That's ... '

'Good evening. I'm Karin Latimer. Thank you for tuning in to *'Where Are They Now?'*. For the second in our series I'm here in the Highlands of Scotland to meet Cal Mathieson, who needs no introduction as the guitarist with 2CM, the band we all loved so much before Charlie's tragic death in 1995. After more than twenty years out of the spotlight, fans will be thrilled to learn Cal has been back in the studio and is about to release a new album – his first solo work.'

Heart racing, Annie sank down on the sofa beside

Moira. The next scene was in an interior she knew well.

The presenter, an attractive dark-haired woman, looked painfully thin and angular in a short black dress and thick black tights. Dark pink lipstick gave definition to artificially full lips, and she wore the kind of heels Annie knew Callum would not have been able to resist remarking on. Crossing her long legs to show off her skinny thighs, the woman continued.

'Cal, thank you very much for agreeing to talk to us. I understand this is your first interview in more than twenty years. It is well known that you've guarded your privacy very closely in that time. In the past you insisted you would never perform again. What changed your mind?'

And then Callum filled the screen.

He looked drawn and tired, blue eyes downcast as he considered his reply. There were more silver strands visible in his hair. Annie felt as if she had been stabbed by a sharp blade in her guts.

'Good morning, Karin. I'm flattered you've come all this way. Especially in such unsuitable shoes.'

Hearing him speak in his deep voice, his soft island accent, twisted the knife deeper. She moved to the edge of the sofa, closer to the screen.

Karin laughed. Callum smiled his crooked grin.

He was wearing the denim shirt he had worn the night they went to Applecross – the one with pearl buttons. Annie's fingertips tingled with the memory of how they'd felt as she unfastened them slowly, one by one, a kiss for every button. Their anticipation, building with each button, each kiss. On screen, the colour of the fabric accentuated the blue of his eyes, exactly the same shade as the sky outside the window behind him. Sunshine illuminated the distant mountains and cast deep shadows in their folds. The water was calm. She could just make out the mast of *Sweet Dreams* tied up alongside the pier. A wave of longing for a place that had never been home, but that she now realised was embedded deep in her heart, flowed through her veins. But the ache of longing to be back there, in that room with Callum, was much, much stronger.

He was sitting opposite the presenter in one of the leather chairs Annie remembered sitting in herself. Callum cradled a bright pottery mug in his hands – tea, she knew – strong, milk, no sugar.

'This is not something I ever expected to do again. After Charlie's heart attack I thought my days as a musician were over. However, when we got together, Freya … my … late wife, encouraged me to start playing again. These days I gig with local musicians – you could say I've rediscovered my pleasure in making music – recognised the part it plays in my life. Last year … I began to sing some of the songs Charlie and I wrote together in the 80s and 90s. Up until then I hadn't wanted to perform that material but … now I think they deserve to be heard again, although I'm interpreting them very differently.'

'Hmm. I understand the treatment is generally acoustic. Would you say that was down to the influence of the traditional musicians you've been playing with?'

'Aye, it's certainly made me look at different ways of making music.'

He went on to talk about songwriting, about the rich seam of work, from Dylan to Adele. He warmed to his topic, eloquent in describing how he chose the songs, how much respect he had for the songwriters.

The camera cut to Karin watching him speak, smiling and nodding. There was footage of the band live on stage in the hotel where they'd played on the night of Janet's celebration. Callum was singing a Daryl Hall song, 'Someone Like You'. Head thrown back, he performed the song as she remembered from the clips she had watched of 2CM, using his hands, his facial expressions, to convey the emotion, his physicality enhancing the passion of the lyrics. It was a performance more suited to an arena than the local pub, almost as if he had gone back in time to his days as a leading member of one of the biggest bands in the country.

'I'd forgotten how good he was. Is.' Moira said quietly. Annie nodded.

'The hard part has been making the choices. For every song you choose there are hundreds more you're leaving out. So we've done what would have been called a triple album in the past – there are forty songs altogether. But don't try and listen to them all at once, or you'll think I'm a right miserable git.'

He looked into the camera with a wry smile.

'I'm sure no one who spends any time with you would think so!' Karin smiled that simpering smile again, recrossing her legs.

Annie wanted to kill her – slowly and painfully.

'So far you haven't had a name for the work. It's about to be released. Can you tell me what you've decided to call it?'

'Well, the working title was *Songs of Love, Loss and Longing* which will probably give you a clue as to what to expect. But it's really called *First Person Singular*. His smile was sad.

Annie felt as if her heart was breaking all over again. For his pain, as well as her own.

'So would it be right to say this is a very personal album?'

'Aye, you could say so. I lost my wife to ovarian cancer. I agreed to do this to raise funds for the charity that helped us during her illness.'

'I am so sorry. It must have been very hard for you

to lose your wife so young.' Her sympathy sounded false, saccharine. 'You have a daughter, Kirsty. She's fifteen, is that right?'

'Aye.'

'I'm told she sings with you sometimes.'

'Aye, she does some gigs with the band, just for fun. She's still at school, about to do her Highers.'

Annie saw his expression soften as it always did when he talked about Kirsty.

'Will she be following you into a career in music? I've heard there's been some interest in her already from one of the record companies.'

'No, that's not her ambition. She wants to become a lawyer.'

'Yet the clips I've seen on YouTube show she has obviously inherited a lot of musical talent from her father. There was talk recently of a romance between yourself and the Simpson Inquiry lawyer, Annie MacIntosh – is it perhaps her influence that's got your daughter interested in law rather than music?'

'Oh God! What a bitch,' Moira exclaimed. Annie shook her head, horrified.

Callum was visibly shocked by the question. His expression froze. He took a moment to recover himself, sipping from his mug and setting it aside, before calmly replying.

'My daughter knows her own mind, and I don't discuss my private life.'

'Of course. Forgive me.' Karin pasted on another insincere smile.

Moira squeezed Annie's hand.

'Finally, Cal has agreed to preview a couple of songs for us. So we'll go and join Steve McIntyre and Jack Fergusson in the studio. Cal, thank you so much for agreeing to speak to me. It's great that you're writing and recording again. I wish you every success with the new work. I'm sure it'll raise a lot of money for Ovarian Cancer Research, a charity we should all support.'

A number came up on screen with details of how to download the album and how to donate to the charity, while the camera followed them to the back of the room. The interviewer walked close beside Callum, laughing at something he said, touching his arm.

Seeing the woman touch him made Annie feel sick to the pit of her stomach.

To her confusion, the passageway towards the study and bedroom now led into a new extension, where a room dominated by a large mixing desk opened into a recording studio. Steve and Jack were already there, surrounded by their instruments.

Visibly more relaxed as he stood in front of the mic, Callum strummed a chord in the way she remembered so well, and introduced the first song – "Atlantic Shores", the acoustic version he had performed in Applecross. The band had done more work on it – there was a poignant instrumental section where guitar, fiddle and bodhran interwove in an evocation of the sounds of the sea, the wind and the shoreline, before the final verse in which Callum sang of the harsh beauty of the seascape and the song of the seals amongst the islands. The changing shape of his hand as he formed the chords, the slight squeak of his long fingers on the strings, transported her back to Applecross

'Is that what he sang for you?'

Annie nodded.

'Beautiful.'

The next song was one she didn't know. Callum looked straight into the camera, adjusting the tuning on his guitar as he introduced a new song.

'Anyone who's lost someone they love will recognise what this song's about.'

You never fold on a winning hand, but I couldn't tell
though I had gold, it never seemed as grand as when it all fell

The lyric told the story of coming to terms.

I'm growing used to another skin cos I recognise
I spent too long in the one I was in, with no compromise

Once again she could see how much of himself he was putting into the performance, using his hands to emphasise certain lyrics, the introspection of the song reflected in the expression on his face, as he went into an intricate guitar solo. Jack's drumming was a slow heartbeat.

The song concluded –

I'll start again for the very first time

He set his guitar aside. Accompanied by the electric violin and drum, he kept time with his clenched fist beating out the rhythm over his heart.

As he sang the line over and over again, the sound fading out as the credits rolled, Callum looked up, straight down the lens. Annie felt as if he knew she was watching, as if he were sending her a message. Unconsciously she had laid her own hand over her own heart.

Moira looked at her, motionless in her seat, staring at the screen as a trailer ran for the next programme.

'Oh God, Annie, I'm so sorry. I'm a bloody insensitive fool. I shouldn't have put it on.'

'No, it's OK, Moira, it was so … so good to see him.' Her voice wavered. And then she broke down. Moira held her as she cried heart-wrenching sobs.

Annie had tried with everything she had to believe she was through the worst, that she had put the past behind her. But seeing Callum, hearing him sing, the strength of her emotions confirmed what deep in her heart she already knew. The past, those few precious days with Callum, was where she still longed to be.

Chapter 36
London
January

New Year brought a fresh perspective. This can't go on, Annie told herself with renewed resolve. Get a grip, stop obsessing about Callum. It was never meant to be. Get over it.

In the spirit of new beginnings, she cleaned and tidied her flat from top to bottom, throwing out old clothes, clearing kitchen cupboards. Finally she tackled her study, the job she had been dreading most, sorting her untidy desk, filing months-worth of paperwork, tidying out the drawers.

The shoebox took her by surprise. In all the turmoil after coming back from Scotland and re-immersing herself in work, she had completely forgotten about it. Now her mouth turned unaccountably dry as she set it down on the newly cleared desktop and untied the ribbon holding it shut.

Under bundles of her own letters she found another envelope, simply addressed to 'Annie', in Janet's handwriting. A letter that her aunt had meant to send but never got round to, perhaps? Curious, she drew out two handwritten pages. The first was on old-fashioned

Basildon Bond writing paper.

Dundas Street,
Edinburgh
July 1979

My Darling Annie,
Your mother has just left, and it breaks my heart to think I will be seeing you much less now – she is determined to follow Ruadhri to London and nothing I say will make her change her mind. I am so worried about her, and about you. But I have to tread carefully – Maddie is quite capable of stopping me seeing you at all, and I couldn't bear that.

I expect that it will be many years before you see the contents of this box – even I don't know what the letters say. It took some persuading for her not to destroy them – she was furious when she found out I had kept them. I promised her I wouldn't open them and I have kept that promise only because I knew that nothing would be gained by my doing so. She made her choices long ago. I hope she will have told you about your father, but knowing her, probably not. I'm sorry – it's something you should know, but at least you can decide if you want to read his letters yourself and know that whatever Maddie may have told you, he was a decent human being. If their romance had just been a casual fling for him, as it was for her, he'd never have written to her for over a year with no response.

At least financially I know that you will be OK. I persuaded the trustees to release Maddie's share of the inheritance because she has you to care for, and I will do my very best to make sure you get the kind of education and opportunities you need. I love you so much, and I'm devastated that you are going to be so far away.

All I know about your father, except that he was a tall, handsome man with delightful manners who deserved better than to be treated like a plaything by Maddie, is in this box.

> *I love you very much, Annie, and I will always be here for you.*
> *Your loving aunt,*
> *Janet.*

There were more letters, in a hand she had never seen before, under a small artist's sketchbook which she recognised as the kind her mother had preferred, soft-covered A5. Annie set it aside, suddenly afraid of what else she might find.

She sat back, heart thudding as she realised that she was finally about to find out about her father, whatever kind of man he was. But first she had to know more about Janet's reasons for keeping the letters secret for so many years. The second sheet, written much later, was on different notepaper. With a start, she realised that it was the same as she had used herself, from Janet's desk. This letter was very recent, written only a few months before she died.

> *My Dearest Annie,*
>
> *If you are reading this, it's probably because something has happened to me. I know my health is not what it was, and while I may have many more years to enjoy the life I've made for myself in the Highlands, I am also aware that nothing is certain in life. Turning seventy has made me reflect, and I would hate to leave a mess behind me.*
>
> *I should have given you this box years ago after Maddie died, but there never seemed to be a right time. I was afraid of upsetting you, when you seemed to be coping so well, making a life for yourself. I'm so proud of you and everything you have become. Your strength is extraordinary, equalled only by your intellect.*
>
> *Watching you grow and become the person you are, I couldn't think of a good reason to unsettle you with thoughts of a father when your life seemed perfectly full without ever having known*

him. I have searched my conscience but after so long, I stand by my decision, right or wrong. Now it's for you to decide.

I hope you have a good life, Annie, full of love and happiness and all the good things that you deserve. I love you and will continue to see as much of you as I can. Perhaps one day whatever you find here will make you want to meet Stewart – in some ways I hope so. You have grown up to be a truly remarkable person, and if you ever do meet your father, I hope he will see that and be proud of the part he played in bringing such a fine woman into the world.

With all my love,
Janet.

Stunned, Annie sat back in her chair, holding the letter, trying to make sense of it.

Knowing that she was about to meet, if only through letters, the father she'd so often tried to imagine sent chills down her spine. Part of her wasn't even sure she wanted to know after all this time.

It had been some time since she'd had a drink. Now, she opened a bottle of chilled white wine, pouring herself a large glass as she prepared to meet her father. Carefully she began to extract the remaining contents of the shoebox.

~

The letters, dozens of them, were all still sealed in their envelopes, sorted by the dates on the postmarks, earliest on top. There was a small parcel. Curious, Annie opened it to find a jewellery box containing a ring – gold set with diamonds in a Celtic knot. Lastly she turned to the sketchbook. She opened it with a shaking hand.

The first drawing was a portrait – a young black man, reading in a chair, one long-fingered hand holding his book, the other, index finger extended, supporting his chin. His look was one of quiet concentration, eyes down as he read, full lips slightly apart as if he might have been saying something, or reading aloud. His hair was cropped close to his head, revealing a strong neck and a finely shaped skull. Annie's heart thudded in her chest as she saw a likeness of her father for the first time. She knew her mother's style – this was a good drawing. She hoped the likeness was true, if this was all she was to have. The second drawing, sketchier and less detailed, nevertheless confirmed the same shape of head, the same long-fingered hands – just like her own, she knew – but in this one he was smiling, eyes looking straight out of the page, crinkling up at the corners just the way her own did.

Maddie had scrawled across the bottom of the second page 'Stewart'.

The first letter must have been written very shortly afterwards.

USS Canopus
2/21/75

Darling, Beautiful Maddie,
I am still in shock. I met you, made love with you and had to leave you, all in forty-eight hours. I am back on board ship surrounded by hundreds of men in uniform talking in loud American voices, and all I can see is you, so lovely with your wild red hair and your hippy clothes, and all I can hear is your soft Scottish voice. I can see you dancing at the party in your amazing dress –that dress, wow! I can see you pretending to be a southern belle – and doing it so well you even had me convinced, and most of all I can see you naked in bed – but I don't want to dwell on it because I ache for you, for your touch, for your kisses. I'm useless here. My senior officer had to say my name three times before I heard him – now they're all sure I met someone in Edinburgh and they keep asking me who she is. Mine, is what I want to tell them, all mine.

I can't get you out of my head, Maddie. I guess I'm under your spell.

What I wanted to say to you when you left this afternoon is simply this; I know we have only had a very short time together, but I also know without any shadow of doubt that I love you, with all my heart.

Stewart

Annie put the letter down. In some obscure way she felt as if she were invading her father's privacy, reading letters only ever meant for her mother's eyes. Yet she knew her mother had never read them. No one had. They were all unopened in their envelopes, some written on old-fashioned writing paper, most on flimsy blue airmail.

And they deserved to be read – more followed, love letters from the man about whom she had known nothing, only that her mother had told her their short affair had all been a mistake, with Annie as the unintended consequence.

The next one mentioned the ring.

Glasgow train
2/28/1975

My Darling Maddie,
Ashore in Glasgow today I saw this ring and thought it was perfect for you. Will you marry me?
It would make me the happiest man alive.
I'm on my way back to the ship, and I am hoping with every part of me you will call this week to tell me that you will come back to the States with me. I know I'm rushing you, but we had something together that is so special. I feel really sure we can make it work. I know there's another man in your life, but how real can that be compared to what we had? Could you have been the way you were with me, if you were really in love with him? I can offer

you a good life here, you can carry on with your art and once I'm qualified we could have a house with a studio and you can paint while I save the world!

Seriously, Maddie, I never believed in love at first sight, but now I know it's real because I loved you from the very first moment I saw you. I know it wasn't the same for you, but I believe you could love me and I swear I would never give you reason to doubt my feelings for you, which only seem to grow stronger every day.

I want you, I want you, I want you.

Wear my ring, Maddie, and come to the States with me. I want you to be Mrs Stewart Fraser.

I love you, with all my heart,
Stewart

Tears pricked in Annie's eyes at the thought of this young man, her father, so desperately in love with her careless, feckless mother, not having known her for long enough to know her true nature, her wild, self-destructive side, her lying, her cheating. Would it have been different if Maddie had ever read the letters? Might she have been persuaded by the sheer force of his love to go to him and give it a try?

She thought of her own situation, the ache of the love she still felt for Callum, knowing that it would never be returned.

'Poor Stewart. I know just how you were feeling. But you were probably well out of it. And so am I,' she said to the father she had never known.

Charleston
South Carolina
3/28/1975

My Darling,

I guess now I must accept that because you never called and have not replied to any of my letters I haven't convinced you to come Charleston yet. But I don't give up so easy, Maddie, so I'm just going to keep on trying.

I'm working in a law firm in the town here, ahead of starting at law school in the fall. I do bits of research and stuff, really interesting. We deal with a lot of civil rights cases here. It makes me all the more determined to follow that path in my own practice once I qualify.

I think you'd like it here. There are lots of artists living in these parts, I've got to know some of them through an old college friend. We also have a couple of Scottish girls in town! Two of the guys from the Holy Loch base are here, with girls who came home with them, married now and settling down nicely. So you wouldn't be the only one. Sarah, one of the wives, is having a baby. I have been trying to imagine the babies we would have together, Maddie. I would want them to have your wild red hair, your cute little nose, your freckles, your naughty laugh. From me – well maybe my height, my brains (modest, always), my ability to love unconditionally. We'd have beautiful babies, please come and let's try.

I won't give up on us, Maddie. I think of you all the time. I wish you were here in my arms, as you always are in my heart.

Please write and let me know you've been reading my letters.
Love always,
Stewart

There were many more letters, written over several months. Mostly they acknowledged the absence of any reply from Maddie, but as she read them through in order, Annie became aware of a change in tone over time. She could sense they had become a conversation he was having with himself, recounting events taking place in his life as he went from working in the law office to university in Savannah. He told amusing stories of his friends and family. With one he had enclosed a photograph of himself – so like the drawing – with his parents, two sisters and a shaggy dog of indeterminate breed, sitting on the steps outside a white clapboard house, exactly as Annie had imagined it would look from his descriptions. She set the picture aside with the drawings.

Gradually he had written less often, until the final letter.

Savannah
4/27/1976

Dear Maddie,

It's over a year now since we met and since I fell head over heels in love. But now, after more than a year of silence from you, I can only conclude that what my family and friends have been telling me all along is true – I will never see you again, because you never did feel the same way as me.

It's hard for me to say this Maddie, because I love you so much still, and if you walked into my life again I would be the happiest man alive. But I know now it's never going to happen. I have been living on dreams for the last year but now I have to move forward. I've turned 25, my studies are going well and I have to think of my future.

I've met someone, Maddie. For the first time since I first saw you I have feelings for another woman – she's studying law like me and she's a fine person, steady and true, and very lovely. Her name is Melissa. We sing in the choir together and lately I've been walking her back to her dorm. I can tell that she has strong feelings for me. I admit, I am drawn to her, but as you know I still hope I might hear from you. I am torn, but it's not fair for me to hold back any more so here is what I have decided to do.

This letter goes by airmail tonight. By my reckoning you will have it in a week's time. If I have not heard from you by letter or by telephone by the time three weeks have passed, I will know you don't want to see me and I will never write again.

Please write me, Maddie, if only to let me know for sure.
With love,
Stewart

Setting the last letter aside, Annie laid her head on her arms and wept – for the terrible waste her mother had made of her life, for the awful sadness of a young man, in love and hoping against all the odds that his dream of a future with her mother would come true, and for herself, discovering after half a lifetime, that contrary to what her mother had always allowed her to believe, she was the daughter of a fine, loving man. They had never been given the chance to know one another. From everything she had read, she felt sure he would have been a wonderful father and husband. How different a life they might have had as a family. She had other aunts, she realised, maybe cousins – perhaps half-brothers and sisters, and yet they didn't even know she existed. Her mother, selfish to the last, had denied her all of this, her birthright. Had Maddie had her way, she would never even have seen these letters – they would have been destroyed, and with them any possibility of ever knowing anything at all about her father.

It took no time at all to find Stewart Fraser, Attorney at Law, in an internet search. A successful civil rights lawyer, his career was well documented. Within an hour Annie knew that he had indeed married Melissa, that they had two sons and a daughter – half-siblings, she thought, with a fizz of excitement. The oldest, Samuel, was only four years younger than herself. She pored over pictures of her father with all the fervour she had those of Callum. A handsome, strongly built young man became an imposing forty-year-old at the height of his career, silver appeared in his hair in his fifties. He was tipped to become a judge, there had been talk of a political career.

The most recent picture showed what little hair remained to be steely grey. He appeared in formal dress at a charity event. Annie noticed that he was using a cane for support. She frowned.

The accompanying article almost brought her heart to a standstill. It described his dramatic collapse in court two years previously. Helicoptered to hospital, resuscitation, triple bypass surgery ... she had almost lost her father before ever finding him.

Draining her glass, she found Moira's number on her phone. The call was picked up on the third ring.

'Are you busy?' She heard the tremor in her voice as she told Moira what she'd found.

'God, Annie! That's incredible. What are you going to do?'

'I don't know. I just don't know what to do. Maybe Janet was right. I've done without a father for my whole life. Do I even need one now? I'm going to try to sleep on it, think it over. I'll wait until after the opening of Janet's exhibition. Got to get through that first. Then ... well, I'll see how I feel.'

'Very wise. You don't want to rush into anything. I'll see you at the opening on Monday. You can let me know what you've decided then.'

Chapter 37
London
January

Karin was late, forty minutes and counting. Callum called her mobile, got voicemail, texted.

'2 mins :)' her message came back. Another ten passed. Impatient and angry, he sat in the bar as instructed, nursing a mineral water, tempted just to leave. But she had said it was important and might help the charity, so he supposed he ought to find out what she had in mind.

He cursed himself for his stupidity in agreeing to meet her, tonight of all nights. In London to meet up with Patrick for the boat show at the O2, he had tried to fit too much into too little time, forgetting how long it took to get around. He hated being here – the city held only bad memories from the past.

As he waited, his anxiety about perhaps seeing Annie again gripped his guts, unsettling him further. He tried to imagine how it would feel – was it just an illusion, had their affair been no more than a quick fling? Or did the fact that more and more often he found himself thinking about her, remembering how real their connection had felt, mean that there was more to it than that? That there might be a chance, if she felt the same way, to move things forward to a new level? To let their fledgling relationship grow wings and fly ...

Karin rushed into the bar, all apologies and air kisses,

not an iota of sincerity about either.

'Let's give this private view a miss. I'm gagging for a drink, and then we could go straight to the restaurant. I had to pull a few favours to get a table, but we need to be prompt at eight or they'll give it away.'

'No! I need to go to the exhibition – it's important. The artist was a good friend of my wife's, so let's go, now.'

They were lucky to get a taxi on such a miserable foggy night.

In the cab she chattered on about a programme she was doing – he tuned her out, trying to imagine what Annie would feel, if she was even there. He hoped they might get a little time together, he would suggest they meet and talk, get a sense of where things stood, try to repair the damage. His mouth was dry and his hands clammy as the taxi drew up outside the brightly lit gallery, already full of smartly dressed people and loud chatter.

Karin saw someone she knew and went off to perform a few of her trademark air kisses, eyes scanning the room to see if there was anyone more important around.

Claire rushed to Callum's side, proprietorial, flirting. She congratulated him on the new album, settling in for a long chat. He looked around the gallery, taking in the bright abstracts that were full of a sense of home.

His heart lurched as he caught sight of Annie on the far side of the room in front of a large painting in the familiar colours of the Western Isles. It was as if everything around him went into slow motion. Excusing himself, he made his way over to her side.

He really hadn't known how it would feel to see her again. In reality, he felt completely overwhelmed as memories of them together assaulted his senses. He had a brief moment to look at her before she was aware of him. She was too thin, but beautiful in the soft heather colour of her clothes, copper-tinged dark hair framing her face. Taller than he remembered, he noticed that she was wearing heels, not as high as the ones she'd been wearing when they first met, they still accentuated the curve of her calves, her slim ankles. She turned as if she had felt his presence beside her, his body calling out to hers. Her eyes widened with surprise, and something else he couldn't read – shock, perhaps.

With his hand on her shoulder he kissed her cheek, breathing in the scent he had almost forgotten. All his senses tingling, his heart thudded so loudly he was sure she must hear it. Somehow he fought back the strong urge to wrap her up in his arms, bury his hands in her hair, kiss her properly, like the first time.

There was no doubt in his mind now. He longed to hold her. To say all the things that needed to be said. Instead he smiled politely as she introduced her friend and they exchanged handshakes.

Then they were alone together.

It was awkward. They exchanged irrelevant small talk, as if they were nothing more than acquaintances. He complimented her on her appearance, hoping she would understand what he really wanted to say – 'It's so good to see you. You're so beautiful. I should have told you, all those months ago, how I really feel … ' But Annie was formal, remote – the polite, reserved woman he had rescued from the crashed car, not the warm, passionate one whose tears of emotion he had kissed away the last time they made love. He tried to be natural, but it seemed the distance he had put between them was too great.

And then, all at once he realised he knew nothing about her life here in London. Perhaps she was with someone, one of the affluent-looking men in the gallery. In Callum's mind, her life had frozen in time after she left the Highlands. How stupid of him, why would he for one moment imagine this sophisticated, metropolitan woman would have no life beyond the time she had spent with him? The brief relationship he himself had ended so abruptly, so brutally.

A wave of uncertainty engulfed him. The ease that had grown between them all those months ago just wasn't there. He had destroyed it. He struggled to find the words he wanted to say.

'I was looking forward to … ' he began. And then Karin appeared, grabbing his arm, pulling him away with astonishing rudeness, barely acknowledging Annie beyond a cursory glance, a fake smile, before pushing her way through the guests to the waiting cab.

He should have shaken her off, should have said, 'Forget it, I'm not interested in whatever this idea of yours might be'. In retrospect, he would have done so many things differently. But instead, full of miserable uncertainty, he allowed himself to be led away. He had only the briefest moment to glance back. Annie was watching him go, her expression giving nothing away.

Late January London was raw in the harsh grip of freezing fog that night. The Anderson-Butler gallery, tucked away behind Bond Street, was brightly lit amongst the dark office buildings around it.

Annie had treated herself to a new dress for the opening – a soft heather-coloured silk shift with a long cashmere cardigan, a couple of shades darker, against the chill of the winter night. Her hair was loose – recently cut, it was carefully sculpted into a cloud around her face. She wore a little make-up – soft brown shadow, pink lipstick. She talked to Jamie, complimenting him on the way the paintings were displayed. He prided himself on having spotted Janet's talent early on in a mixed show at the Royal Scottish Academy.

'Thanks, Annie. That means a lot, coming from you. It's great for me too, seeing them properly hung. When they were all stacked up in the studio, you couldn't get a true sense of where she was heading. But when you see the progression in her work, it's clear she was really finding her feet in pure abstraction. I'm convinced she'd have been a major figure in Scottish painting, given a few more years. Wilhelmina Barns-Graham, Barbara Rae, that sort of stature. So tragic she died before she was properly recognised.'

The quality of the paintings sang. The colours transported Annie to the Western Isles, stirring up painful memories of her time there, and everything that had happened. Studying the paintings, she could see how the magical light, the muted colours, had worked their way into her emotions. The canvases brought it all back, that short, intense period that had changed her so completely.

The gallery filled up as more invitees arrived. A few red dots began to appear on the wall as paintings were snapped up by eager collectors.

Annie chatted to friends as they arrived, repeating what Jamie had told her and pointing them towards works she thought they would like.

Perhaps it was the heightening of her senses stirred up by the paintings. Standing with Moira in front of an abstract seascape, a tremor suddenly ran through her as her body somehow became aware of him even before she heard his voice – deep, and soft.

'Hello, Annie.'

She turned. In a glance she saw how much more grey showed in his hair. Dressed for the city rather than the boatyard, his usual scruffy fleece had been replaced by a slim coat in a soft fabric with a grey pile lining – stylish, metropolitan. Open to reveal a grey T-shirt. And the inevitable black jeans and boots. Bearded, his trimmed stubble was also peppered with silver.

But his startling blue eyes were just the same. Annie felt her pulse accelerate, blood pumping through her veins.

'Callum. How lovely to see you.' It took a monumental effort to keep her voice steady.

He leaned forward to kiss her, the merest brush of his lips against her cheek. One hand rested lightly on her shoulder. His beard rasped briefly against her skin. She shivered with a memory of the last time she had felt it. Surely he must have been aware of her trembling intake of breath.

Seeing him again, everything became quite simple. She wanted to put her arms around him, lay her head on his chest. Hear his heartbeat, feel his warmth, his arms around her. She didn't care about his problems – she just wanted him. To be with him again, whatever the cost, whatever difficulties might lie in the way.

Despite her best efforts, she knew in that moment that she was still as hopelessly in love with Callum Mathieson as she had been all those months ago.

Feigning a calm she did not feel, she introduced Moira, who quickly caught sight of someone she needed to talk to on the other side of the room, discreetly leaving them together.

'How have … '

'You look … '

Their words collided.

'You first.' Callum smiled, holding her gaze until she had to look away. In all these months, she had been unable to make the picture form in her mind, the wide mouth, his smile. How could she have forgotten how good he looked, when he was never out of her thoughts?

'No, you.' She needed time to get her breathing under control.

'You look lovely.' She remembered with a pang the last time he had told her so. 'Shorter hair, suits you.'

'You look well, too.' It was the best she could manage. 'I ... I didn't expect to see you here tonight.'

'My charity is a beneficiary of the sale. Because of Freya, you know ... being a friend.'

Annie remembered Ovarian Cancer Research was one of the charities mentioned in the will.

'Of course. Thank you for coming.' It was all wrong, stiff, formal. All she wanted to do was to tell him how she felt.

'I was looking forward to ... ' he began.

They were interrupted. A tall, angular woman approached and threaded her arm through Callum's. Annie was shocked to recognise the woman who had interviewed him on the TV programme.

'Cal, the taxi's here. We need to go, they won't keep the booking. So sorry, have to drag him away,' she added, acknowledging Annie for the first time with a fake smile.

'Annie ...'

His companion was having none of it. As Karin led him away, he looked back and their eyes met again. But she couldn't read what his expression was saying.

Back in her flat, Moira put a glass of water into Annie's shaking hands.

'OK, listen, Annie. It's time you took a proper break. Why don't you go and find your father? Go to the States. You need to get away from here for a while, get your head sorted out.'

Annie nodded, tears splashing onto her sleeve. 'Yes. I do.'

She had thought she was in repair. But no – she was in pieces again, right back where she had been all those months ago. Any remaining sticking plasters that had been holding her together had fallen off.

Chapter 38
London
January

The paparazzi were out in force for the opening of the new restaurant in Shoreditch. Cameras flashed as the crowd of hopefuls waiting outside parted for the new big thing in music TV, Karin Latimer. She paused in the entrance and turned with a big smile, pulling Callum round to face the snappers.

The restaurant was a noisy crush of people, there to be seen. Underdressed, overdressed women, men with sculpted facial hair in impossibly tight jeans. Too many reminders of his old life, the parties, the openings, the froth and nonsense. The oldest person there by years, he felt like a fish out of water.

Uncharacteristically, Karin had booked a quiet corner table. They sat down and ordered drinks. A plate of something reminiscent of seafood appeared in front of them. Dried fish skins – the trendy alternative to a bowl of nuts. Disgusting. He thought of sharing squat lobsters with Annie in Applecross.

'OK, so tell me about this idea.'

'So my producer has asked me to make a series. It'll be called "From Cornwall to Dingwall" – great name, huh? – and I'd like you to come on board as a consultant. It's about the local scene, who's playing where, all the little venues, like the hotel you play in … '

Callum struggled to concentrate on what she was saying, preoccupied still by his all too brief encounter with Annie.

' ... an analysis of the live music scene around the country. I thought you'd be able to help us find artists to showcase – you'd be really good, with your experience.'

'Doesn't sound like something I'd like to do, and I can't see what it's got to do with the charity. The whole point is those gigs are small, intimate, just for pleasure. No pressure, none of the nonsense.'

'But that's exactly the point! Local audiences enjoying local acts. Like the footage of you we filmed for the programme – that was so good. All the atmosphere of a great pub gig.'

'People go to the pub if they want to see a great pub gig – they're hardly going to stay home and watch it on TV.'

'Yes but there's so much hidden talent playing those gigs, and if we don't put it out there then No one ever gets to see those acts other than the ones lucky enough to be there. Your daughter, Kirsty, for example – I saw the YouTube footage of her singing a Bonnie Raitt song ... '

Suddenly Callum was fully aware of what she was saying.

'OK ... Hold on a minute ... Just hold on. I get it now. This is about Kirsty, isn't it? This is bugger-all to do with the charity or any of the other stuff you've just been banging on about. This is about cherry-picking to get to the wee gems. I didn't even know anyone had put Kirsty up on YouTube, or it would've come down – fast. Those gigs – they're about the place and the circumstances. That's the whole point of live music. It happens in the moment. Kirsty sang the song because it was one her mother loved. She sang it for me. It was never meant to go beyond those four walls ... '

'Welcome to the twenty-first century, Cal. Nothing is

fixed in time and place any more. Any public performance can go viral. That's what makes it so interesting. And you more than anyone know Kirsty is a really exciting singer, she could easily go all the way. If we could showcase her and a few others like her coming up through the local scene ... '

'No! Absolutely not! Kirsty's too young to get caught up in this stuff. She's going to university, and then she can decide what kind of career she wants, but she's not going to be manoeuvred into anything. For God's sake, she's only just sixteen!'

'Sixteen. Same age you were when you and Charlie ran away! Anyway I thought she knew her own mind, Cal, isn't it her decision?'

He was angry now, struggling to control his temper.

'I know her better than anyone. I'm her father. She wants to be a lawyer. Now, sorry, but I've wasted enough time on this bullshit. If you'd told me what you really wanted in the first place I could have saved us both a lot of time and trouble. I can't believe I've wasted time on this ... nonsense instead of spending the evening with ... '

'Yeah, I saw the way you were looking at Annie MacIntosh. I thought it was over.'

Callum stood up, shaking with anger.

'You've got a lot to learn about what's important in life beyond your own career, Karin. I hope I won't be seeing you around.'

The pictures of his hurried departure were discarded – they didn't fit the story.

He caught the first available taxi back to the gallery. It was in darkness.

∼

Patrick was in the hotel bar talking to some boat show exhibitors. The volume of conversation and laughter told Callum that they were already a few drinks in. Callum joined them, bringing another round, with a double Laphroaig for himself.

Patrick looked at him with concern.

'How'd it go, mate?'

'It was a fucking disaster.'

Callum threw himself into a chair. Before Patrick could stop him, he swallowed the whisky in one gulp. It tasted so good. He signalled the barman to bring another.

'So you saw her, but it didn't work out the way you hoped?'

'I saw her for no more than a minute. Not only was there no time to have any kind of conversation, she now thinks I'm seeing that bloody Karin woman. I've totally fucking screwed up again.'

'Can't be all bad. Karin's a bit of alright herself.' Patrick tried to lighten the atmosphere.

'She's a total bitch. And if you mention fish, or sea, believe me, I'll punch your fucking lights out. Best friend or not.'

'OK, OK! Back off, mate. So what do you want to do now? Dinner?'

'No. I want to get absolutely fucking hammered.'

'I don't think so, Cal.' Patrick knew what he was dealing with. He'd seen Callum on a bender once before. It wasn't something he ever wanted to see again, however much he'd had to drink himself. A waiter approached with another whisky on a tray. Patrick took it and swallowed it down before Callum could get his hands on it.

Later he emptied the minibar in Callum's room.

'Fuck you, Patrick.'

'You'll thank me in the morning.'

~

Callum woke suddenly. Someone was knocking on the door. Room service. He'd ordered an early breakfast. Still half asleep, he stumbled out of bed.

'Annie! How did you ...'

He held the door wide. She came in, her scent setting his pulse racing as he closed the door and turned to face her.

She slipped off her coat, draping it over the back of a chair.

'Annie ...'

He couldn't quite believe she was here. Kirsty, he thought, she must have found out where he was staying from Kirsty.

Still she hadn't said anything. He moved towards her.

'Don't talk, Callum. I just want to look at you.'

He had nothing on. He'd answered the door stark naked.

The caress of Annie's eyes warmed his skin. Then she reached down, pulling her dress up over her head. It fell in a silky heap on the floor. Her underwear followed. Wearing nothing but her high-heeled shoes, she looked so much thinner, her breasts full above the slenderness of her waist, nipples dark against the rich honey colour of her skin. He drank her in with thirsty eyes, feeling the blood rushing to his groin.

Annie stepped out of her shoes as she stepped into his arms, hair brushing his cheek, her scent enveloping him in its delicious spiciness as she pressed herself against him. She was trembling, exactly as she had the first time.

'Love me, Callum. Fuck me. Fuck me, and love me.'

'Yes, Annie. I love you. I do love you. Yes.'

He grasped her hips and lifted her easily, her legs wrapped around him as they fell back together onto the bed. She was so hot, so wet, so ready. Then he was deep inside her, desire heightening as she gasped and cried out.

'Oh Callum.'

It wasn't Annie's voice.

The face wasn't Annie's either. It was Karin's.

'Christ. Oh Christ.'

On the point of orgasm, Callum woke, shuddering, horrified.

The knock on the door came again.

'Room service, sir.'

Fragments of the disturbing dream still haunted him as he sat on the plane, impatient for the short flight to be over.

A furious Kirsty met him at Edinburgh airport.

'Cal!' She waved the *Daily Record* under his nose. 'Please, please tell me you aren't seeing Cruella de Vil. I will never forgive you, and neither will the dogs!'

His heart sank as he saw the close-up of his grim face alongside that of a smiling Karin outside the restaurant.

They were halfway home by the time Callum had calmed her down and convinced her the paparazzi pictures were no more than that. Then he told her what Karin had really wanted.

'First of all, Kirsty, promise me you won't let Louise put anything else you do up on YouTube. That's how you lose control. It's what brings the Cruella de Vils around. It's you she's interested in, not me. I answered for you. I told her you weren't ready to get into the music industry yet – you want to go to university, you want to become a lawyer. But am I right? Is going to university what you want? Or just what I want for you?'

'It's what I want. You know I love to sing, but it's just

something I enjoy, like, you know, hanging out with my friends, going to the movies, all that stuff. It's not, like, I'm one of those talent-show girls, you know, like, "this is my dream, it's everything to me, I never want to do anything else." She mimicked an imaginary contestant. 'That's not where I'm coming from.'

'Good.'

'And anyway, I promised Mum.'

'What did you promise?'

'That I'd finish school, go to university or music college, and then make up my mind. She wanted me to have choices about my life, and she said the best way was to get a proper education first. So, I promised. And I will.'

Callum reached across and squeezed her hand as tears welled up.

'*Tapadh leibh*,' he murmured softly. Partly to Kirsty, mostly to Freya. Thank you.

Chapter 39
South Carolina
February

Annie's flight landed at Atlanta in the late evening. She disembarked, shattered, still without any clear idea what to do. There were no guidelines, no protocols to lead the way. Since she had found out about her father, she had been frozen in indecision. Friends offered advice. Mostly their answer was simple – do nothing, you've managed all these years without a father, do you really want one now? You can't just turn up after forty years and say "Hi Dad, I'm your daughter", can you?'

Moira had suggested the opposite – take the initiative – just ring his doorbell and introduce yourself. None of it helped. But at least she was on the move, taking action. Another day in London torturing herself with thoughts of Callum and that dreadful woman would have driven her insane.

Clear of immigration, she checked in at an airport hotel. There was no connecting flight to Charleston until next morning.

Sleep was elusive. She ate a salad, all that could tempt her from the high-calorie offerings on the room service menu. The TV offered hundreds of choices. She watched an episode of *Outlander*, because it was set in Scotland and the scenery was magnificent. There was a love scene in it that made her cry. Something about it recalled the tenderness with which Callum had held her. Was he now holding Karin, just as tenderly? The thought was unbearable.

She put on her headphones and played his songs, as she had hundreds of times since she had downloaded the new album. Listening to him was painful – the songs resonated with her own sense of loss – but it was a connection. Sometimes she believed he was thinking about her when he made the recording, though it was obvious that the lyrics were mostly about his love for Freya. She could picture him singing, head back, eyes closed, hand over his heart. Lulled by the music, her body finally gave in to a deep sleep. Callum was singing about his broken heart.

Annie arrived in Charleston in the early afternoon. Her hotel was downtown near Stewart Fraser's office, in the area around the County Courthouse. Even now, undecided how to approach him, she had given herself the rest of the day to think about it. But at least she was close. She had time to kill beforehand.

The concierge recommended a walk along King Street. It was ages since she had done anything like this – being a tourist, window-shopping, stopping for coffee and a pastry in a café. The weather was delightful – warm and sunny.

The shops were lovely. Eye-candy, Janet used to call the stuff they sold, things you didn't need but really wanted. She bought a silk scarf in the pinks and mauves she liked, and a silver pendant she knew Moira would love.

One shop caught her eye, making her smile. It sold pet supplies, the window a gaudy display of ridiculous accessories in bright colours. How many dogs actually needed a pink tutu, or a tartan baseball cap? Would Boris give up his hairy cushion for a purple velvet daybed? She doubted it. But personalised dog-collars ...

'Yes, one to say Mick, the other, Keith,' she repeated to

the middle- aged pet lover behind the counter.

'Like the Rolling Stones?'

'Exactly.'

'What size of dogs?'

'Oh. I don't know ... '

The shop owner showed her a book of all the dog breeds.

Annie, amazed to discover how many different kinds of dog there were, flipped the pages until she found them.

'They're like this.'

'Oh Borders, great dogs. Not yours?'

'A friend's.'

'Cool names!'

Annie chose the gaudiest collars on offer, gold leather with the names emblazoned in turquoise and purple rhinestones. The shopkeeper wrapped everything up, offering Annie a card to add a note to the package.

Hi from Charleston. Couldn't resist. Now you'll be able to tell them apart.
Annie X

She addressed the envelope to Callum and Kirsty Mathieson – the shop owner looked at the address, and exclaimed

'Scotland! I'd just love to visit Scotland. Is it as beautiful as they say?'

'And then some.'

By the time she stepped out of the shop into the bright afternoon sunshine, she was a hundred and fifty dollars lighter. Her heart felt a little lighter, too.

~

Finding her father turned out to be easy. In the end, it just came down to chance.

Sitting with her laptop in the hotel lobby, Annie caught up with her emails. Reception was busy. A conference – on family law, she noticed with interest – was ending. Groups of attendees passed through the lobby. She was aware of a smartly dressed African American woman looking at her as she passed. Their eyes met. The woman said something to her companions before returning to Annie's table.

'Excuse me, but are you Annie MacIntosh?'

'Yes, I am, how did you … '

'My name is Melissa Jordan Fraser … '

'Stewart, I don't care about the game, there'll be other games. Just do what I ask and get your ass over here now … No, I can't tell you why, just it's important … No, it's a surprise … When did I ever give you a nasty surprise? Yes … Yes. In the lobby. See you soon. Love you.'

Melissa ended the call.

'He'll be here soon.'

'Thank you, Melissa. I didn't know what I was going to do – I had some half-baked idea about making an appointment to see him at his office … I don't know the rules for this.'

Knowing she was finally about to meet her father, her pulse began to race. She fiddled with her handbag, fluffed up her hair, smoothed it down again.

'There are no rules. Relax, honey. It's all gonna be fine.'

Melissa had explained how she recognised Annie.

'We were watching the BBC online – Stewart still loves to watch stuff from the UK. There was a piece we were both interested in – there've been cases over here too so we were following what was happening with Simpson – typical lawyers, huh? – and then we saw you on a programme, *News Tonight* –'

'– Oh, God, no. Please tell me you didn't see that. It wasn't my finest hour.'

Melissa smiled, and carried on.

'You were magnificent! But I thought Stewart was ill again – he was grey in the face, shaking. And I could see it at once, the shape of your head, the way you use your hands when you're making a point, your eyes. You are so like him, but you are the image of our daughter, Marcia. You could be sisters … ' Melissa heard what she had just said.

'Gracious! … You *are* sisters!'

Annie's felt her heart skip a beat, imagining the sister she would also soon meet. A sister! She'd always longed for a sister.

'Of course, I knew all about him and your mother – when we first met he was such a mess, poor guy, still so much in love with her – or with the idea of her anyway. I very nearly gave up on him … '

Annie thought of the letters he had written to her mother for all those months. She knew exactly how her father had felt.

'Anyway, that's another story. So he looked you up online, found your date of birth, born in Edinburgh, Scotland, father unknown, mother Madeleine MacIntosh. I thought he was going to have another heart attack, I truly did … Ever since then he's been wondering what to do – could he just walk into your life and say, "Hi, I'm your daddy!"? We didn't have any way of knowing if you knew, or what your mom might have told you. We just didn't know what to do next. And now here you are. You've found him.'

'This must be so hard for you, Melissa – to find out your husband has another child … I'm so sorry … '

'Oh honey.' Melissa reached across and took her hand. 'No one's to blame here, especially not you. He was a young man, single. Your mother told him she was taking the contraceptive pill. We all thought sex came without consequences in those days – free love and all that. The Germaine Greer, Erica Jong era.'

Annie nodded – she'd read both authors, recognised their influence on her mother's generation.

'And besides,' Melissa continued, 'like you, I guess, I've seen it all in my line of work, and believe me, nothing shocks me, not any more. And I know if he'd had any notion, Stewart would have stood by your mother. He asked her to marry him, long before she would have known she was carrying his child. I know my husband all ways up, he's a fine man.'

'I knew that as soon as I read his letters. It nearly broke my heart, to find that the little my mother told me was a lie. I'm so glad he found someone who made him happy.'

'We've made each other happy. He can tell you himself.'

Annie followed Melissa's gaze to the hotel entrance. She recognised him at once, the tall, stooped man in the doorway. Her father. Shaking with emotion, she stood up as he approached them. Recognition dawned on his face as he drew close enough to see her clearly. He stopped, shocked into stillness.

For a long moment they stood immobile, just looking, taking in every detail. Not knowing what to do. Fighting to keep her emotions under control, she held out her hand. He grasped it in his own, drawing her towards him as he said in a beautiful bass voice, 'I can't hardly believe this ... '

He wrapped his arms around her, drawing her into her first ever fatherly embrace.

'I don't know what to call you.' Her voice, full of unshed tears, was muffled against his jacket.

'The other kids call me Dad. How about that?'

∽

Annie had worried, beforehand, that they might not have anything to say to each other. But in reality, there was so much to talk about it was hard to know where to begin.

Melissa decided to go home, leaving them to get to know one another. Father and daughter found a quiet corner in the bar.

'I have to ask about Maddie. Is she … ?'

Looking down, unable to meet his eyes, Annie shook her head. A huge sigh escaped him, and his shoulders dropped.

'How?'

She looked up again.

'I don't really know for certain. There was an inquest. The verdict was misadventure, which covers everything if the coroner isn't absolutely sure it's … intentional. I want to believe it wasn't, but … There was a man – Ruadhri – who came and went, for years. He'd just left her again when it happened – she was really low. But was it deliberate? I don't know.'

'Oh, Annie. To think … That you had to go through something so terrible … I am so very sorry.'

'You should know, though … she was a good mother to me, especially when I was little. When it was just the two of us we had such fun together. I know she loved me, and she did the very best she was able. But she had … issues, always. Men. Jobs. Money. Drink, drugs. She was … volatile, you just never knew which version of Maddie you'd be getting, one day to the next.'

'What did she tell you about me? And please, Annie darlin' – be honest. I need to know.'

Annie looked down at her hands, clasped together on the table. She took a deep breath, and looked up into his eyes.

'She told me she'd made a mistake. You were a mistake. I was a mistake.'

He caught his breath and covered her hands with his own. His cheeks were wet with tears. Annie's eyes welled up too.

The more she told him, the more he recognised of the young woman he'd fallen so hopelessly in love with. The mother of his child, a child he had longed for them to have together in the dark months following his return to the US.

'I read your letters. I hated to invade your privacy, but … I had to know. What a waste, so much love, and she just threw it away. I'm so sorry. It's part of why I wanted to find you, to tell you how sorry I am for what she did.'

'Annie. Oh my darling Annie. No need for that, not for a single thing. What a fine woman you are. Maddie did what she did. That can't be changed. But between us we made you, and now I've met you, I would never, ever change that. Thank you for coming to find me. I didn't know how to begin, I've written so many letters – thrown them away, I've picked up the phone so many times and hung up again. You've got more courage than I ever had, and I thank you for it. Now, I want to get to know you. Tell me all about you, Annie, and your life.'

They talked and talked. By midnight, she could see he was tiring and the barman made it clear he wanted to close up.

Plans were made to meet again next morning, but even so it was so hard to part. Annie walked with him to the lobby, both momentarily silent, lost in their own thoughts. A cab was waiting outside. They embraced in the doorway. Stewart climbed into the car, winding down the window.

Annie stood on the sidewalk.

'Dad.'

'Yes, darlin'?'

'Just "Dad".'

It was hours before she slept. For once it wasn't thoughts of Callum that kept her awake – it was images of her father, his huge smile and shining eyes, the feeling of being enfolded in his arms. The knowledge that she was his flesh and blood. The joy of having someone in her life who was simply called Dad.

Chapter 40
West Highlands
February

Callum and Patrick roared with laughter as Nicole Kidman, all seven stone of her wringing wet, leant out of the cockpit of the speeding yacht and plucked Sam Neill, twelve stone and waterlogged, out of the sea with one hand.

'Oh, God, gets me every time.' Patrick wiped tears of mirth from his eyes. 'I love sailing movies, especially the ones made by someone who's never sailed in their life. If I ever go overboard again I want to be rescued by Nicole Kidman. Last time it took three deckhands and a hoist to get me back on board! Got any more?'

'I think we've watched them all now.'

Callum and Patrick were spending a wet Saturday watching DVDs on the newly installed screen in the sitting room, lounging on the sofa eating pizza and crisps. Kirsty had gone off to Louise's in disgust, not prepared to share her Saturday with a couple of 'overgrown adolescents'.

With *Sweet Caledonia* in Southampton for mechanical repairs, Patrick had taken time off to visit Callum and his goddaughter, Kirsty.

'You weren't in great shape at the boat show, mate. Thought I'd come and check up. I like what you've done to the place.'

The programme of redecoration had continued downstairs. The living area was transformed with fresh paint and stylish, contemporary furniture. The old wooden dining table was replaced with a new one Callum had made, glass top over a base fashioned from a driftwood tree trunk he'd found on the shore, the old chairs given a new lease of life, repainted by Kirsty. Freya's pictures still hung on the walls, rearranged to show them in better light, along with a new canvas, one of Janet's, the colours of the sound outside the windows in more benign mood.

Callum looked around, liking what he had achieved. It was the same house, but different, reflecting his own style.

'Once I started it was hard to stop. I guess I needed to do it. I was worried about Kirsty at first, but she loves it – she thinks it's "like, massively cool".'

In fact Kirsty, had said much more than that.

'It's time, Cal. Anyway, it's not the things that matter, they're just stuff. Mum is inside us, it's how we remember her that counts, that's all. And if it helps you, do it.'

'Wiser than her years, my daughter. She may look like me, but the best of her is all Freya.'

Mick and Keith padded in from their bed in the utility room, hoping it was time for supper.

'What the hell are they wearing?' Patrick bent forward to read the collars. 'Christ, do you think they know you're taking the piss?'

'They were a present. From Annie. From the States.'

'What? If she's trying to send you some kind of a message she's chosen a strange fucking way to go about it.'

'Aye, well. At least it was contact of some kind. Better than nothing.'

'You haven't given up then?'

'There's nothing to give up. I … I should just let it go.'

'You always were an idle bastard, Cal. You're in love with the woman, it's so obvious. Why don't you go and find her?'

'Because I made such a fucking mess of it all. All I'm any good for is building boats and writing songs. Unless I've got someone telling me what to do, I'm a useless fucker. Fiona said it – I don't know my arse from my elbow. Charlie, Freya, they did the thinking for me. I don't deserve Annie. I'm no good for someone like her. Why would she want me, anyway? She's a lawyer, a professional, someone with a proper life, high profile, a big future. The last thing she needs is another toxic relationship. You've no idea how tough she's had it – what she needs is some nice, regular, boring bloke without all the shite I carry around.'

He opened a can of Coke, took a long pull.

'And anyway, I've got a boat to finish.'

'Fucking excuses, Cal. Everyone's afraid of getting hurt but how can you just let it go? What if she finds someone else? She's a grown woman, she can make up her own mind what she wants. And from what I saw in Cannes – the way she looked when she talked about you – it's the same look you have when you talk about her. Send her a message, do something, you stupid bastard, for your own sake as well as hers.'

'Oh fuck off, Patrick. Leave me alone.'

Patrick sighed.

'Anyway, what about you? How come you've not found anyone yourself? There've been plenty of women interested enough – that hot German girl this summer – she was right up for it. God knows what they see in you, but I suppose you're not that ugly, for a fucking Australian.'

'You never saw it, Cal, did you?'

'Saw what?'

'Freya. It was Freya I wanted. If she hadn't been with you … well … I've spent years trying to find a woman like her. You've no fucking idea what a lucky bastard you are. And now Annie. You've got another chance, Cal. Don't let it pass you by.'

He dropped Patrick off at the station next morning – they had stayed up late, talking about the past. He was still reeling with shock at Patrick's confession. It had never crossed his mind that his friend had fallen in love with his wife.

Driving home, he thought about Freya, remembering how much she had given up to look after him, her plans to start her own business, to make her own mark. How selflessly she had applied herself to his recovery, always putting him first. Accepting the fact that his drinking had jeopardised their chance to have the family she wanted – an only child herself, she had longed for a brother or sister for Kirsty.

He had relied completely on Freya to lead the way, make the decisions, shape their lives together.

A lesser man than Patrick might have tried to take Freya from him. He'd never have let it happen. He'd have fought for her with everything he had. Because he loved her so completely.

So why wasn't he fighting for Annie?

Fiona was working in her vegetable plot. She glared at him as he opened the gate into the garden. So did the cat on the window ledge.

'What do you want, Callum?'

'I'd like to talk to you, Fiona, please. Just ten minutes – it's important.'

Fiona stood up from her weeding, straightening her back with a groan.

'I'll put the kettle on.'

When he left her cottage an hour later he knew what he had to do. He mulled over parts of the conversation.

'Why did you not tell me she came to look for me before she left?'

Fiona had looked defiant.

'Because I didn't trust you. She was in pieces. I thought it was best for her to leave. Anyway, what difference would it have made?'

'What difference? All the difference in the world. I wouldn't have drunk myself into oblivion for a start. I'd have gone after her. I knew straight away I'd made a mistake, but it wasn't too late then, not if we'd been able to talk about it, work out a way forward. As it is – well, we've wasted months, not knowing what to do.'

Fiona looked down, fiddling with her teaspoon.

'I know what you think of me, Fiona. But I did something wrong, and I want to put it right. So will you please, please just think about what Annie might want. Let me have her address so I can go and talk to her. If the best I can do is make a proper apology, that'll be an improvement on where things are now.'

'Surely you have her contact details already. Why don't you just email or text or something like any normal person?'

'Because this is too important for a stupid electronic message.'

Fiona sighed heavily as she went to get her address book. Reluctantly she scribbled down Annie's details on a scrap of paper. Callum looked at it, nodded, folded it carefully into his wallet.

'Thank you.'

'Please don't go if you're not really serious. Don't screw it up again, Callum.'

'Fiona, you said to me at the time that I didn't know my own mind, and you were right – it really struck home.

But that's not the case now.'

Fiona and Boris watched as he walked away down the path.

~

'Cal, I've had an idea.' Kirsty emerged from the studio.

'Hmm?'

'Will you do that song, the one you've been working on? I'd like to record it.'

'What for? I'm not even sure it's finished yet.'

'Go on, Cal, please. I need to do this before I go back to school. Patrick wants the video of us all and I'd like to include the song.'

It wasn't the whole truth. She didn't tell him about the plan she and her godfather had agreed.

Callum didn't feel in the least like singing. He wanted to get online and book a flight. But Kirsty looked so disappointed when he refused that he sighed, sat down and picked up his guitar, humming a few bars to warm up his voice. Kirsty was already set up to record – she made a few adjustments to the balance as Callum began to play the introduction.

When you're fast losing hope
and it's all too much to bear ...

He stopped, shook his head at something he wasn't happy about, then began again.

Kirsty opened her phone, selected 'video' and pressed 'record' as the music worked its usual magic on her father, head down, lost in his playing.

Chapter 41
South Carolina
February

Stewart took them both back to the quiet area of Charleston where he and Melissa lived. It was a three-storey town house a short walk from his office in a historic area of town, looking much as it would have done two hundred years ago. The street was cobbled, the houses clad in timber sidings, painted in pastel colours, with brightly coloured shutters.

Stewart's house, cream walls contrasting with dark blue window frames, stood side-on to the cobbled street in a lush shaded courtyard garden, with a tinkling fountain at its centre. They entered through a door on to a wide verandah facing out over the garden.

Annie was charmed by the architecture.

'These houses are very old, by our standards. We were lucky, we bought it in the early 80s as a fix-er-upp-er. No way we could afford it now!'

The interior was an oasis of calm, with hardwood floors linking the open-plan spaces leading to a smart kitchen in which glass-fronted white cabinets contrasted with shiny granite worktops. They sat in plush chairs in the sitting room, where three floor-to-ceiling windows afforded a view across the verandah out to the garden. The smells of freshly brewed coffee, floor polish and exotic flowers added to the sense of peace in the house.

They talked all afternoon.

In the evening the rest of the family, grown up with families of their own, came to meet her. There were nerves on both sides. Marcia and Joseph, her younger half-brother, were open and welcoming. Samuel, closest to her in age and the eldest of the three, was cool and polite, but Annie could see that he struggled to accept the fact that he was no longer the firstborn child of his father as he had always believed himself to be. Taking advantage of a quiet moment to talk to him alone, she suggested they meet and talk. He looked at her for a long moment, telling her he would think about it, give her a call in a day or so maybe.

But Samuel's suspicion was the only awkwardness in an introduction to a world that was otherwise generous and open-hearted in a way that left her astounded and deeply grateful. Everyone was at pains to make her feel like just another member of a big, noisy, opinionated, combative but above all loving family. Despite Melissa's protestations that as a guest she was excused table-clearing duty, she found herself in the kitchen helping Marcia load the dishwasher after dinner. They talked about work as they looked for common ground. Listening to Annie's description of her working life and the Inquiry, Marcia, head teacher of an elementary school, shared her thoughts about some of the troubled children under her care who came from disadvantaged and sometimes abusive backgrounds.

'My aunt Janet was a head teacher as well. Such a coincidence.'

'Isn't it? And strange that you and me are both doing the kind of work that brings us in contact with kids like this.'

'Nature or nurture. The perennial question.'

'Well, maybe we just answered it, sister. Different sides of the world, different mothers, same father, same concerns. Says something, huh?'

Annie was certain that whatever else came of finding her family, she and Marcia would always be friends.

∼

Stewart appeared in the doorway, carrying a stack of plates, and stopped in his tracks. They were so alike, his two daughters. Same height, same build, same shoulder-length hair standing out around their faces, same full lips and almond eyes. Annie's skin was a few shades lighter, Marcia had inherited her father's deep ebony. But no one would question that they were sisters.

'Are y'all having a silly old fool moment, Dad?' Marcia saw the tears in his eyes.

'Darn right I am.'

He folded both his daughters into a bear hug.

'I always wanted a sister, Dad. Thank you for giving me one. Welcome to the mad world of the Frasers, Annie.'

∼

Melissa suggested she come to stay at the house. Annie wasn't sure, her natural caution urging her to take it slowly, but Melissa was insistent and Stewart was thrilled by the idea, so she moved her bags into Marcia's old room and joined the household.

'But I don't want to impose. A week, at the very most, if you can put up with me for that long. Then I have to go back home, to work.'

Semi-retired after his heart attack, Stewart was able to spend much of his time with Annie, though he wished it were more.

'I missed the first thirty-nine years. There's so much to make up.'

The next few days were a whirlwind tour of the city, with Annie admiring its historic atmosphere and enjoying the wonderful food on offer in its bars and restaurants. She met her extended family – aunts and uncles, cousins. Their graciousness left her humbled, although some of the younger children found her strange accent hilarious. They set about teaching her how to talk like a proper South Carolina person.

One day they drove out into the countryside, where she was introduced to the dark side of Deep South history, visiting plantations and seeing at first hand the slave quarters where Stewart and Melissa's ancestors would have lived while they worked the cotton and indigo fields.

'No wonder you were interested in civil rights, Dad.'

'Yeah. It still ain't perfect, but things have sure changed around here.'

'I can hardly believe this is my history, too. It seems so remote, yet it's only a few generations ago.'

'I'll give you a list of what to read. You'll be surprised, Annie, to know how tied up your Scottish ancestry is with what happened here. Why do you think my name is Fraser?'

'Oh no … To my shame, Dad, I've never even thought about it. Do you mean … ?'

'Yeah, exactly. The Scots had a long history of involvement with slavery. I'm planning on writing a book about it when I finally retire.'

'I'd like to help with that. I feel I have so much to learn about who I am. I've only ever known half the story.'

'It warms my heart that this matters to you, darlin'. And to know that something real good came out of Maddie and me.'

They hugged each other tight.

'I hope you know how wonderful it is for me to have found you. To have a family! Ever since Aunt Janet died, I've felt so alone. And now I know I'm not. It's ... '

Words were lost in tears, as Stewart produced a clean linen hankie, first to mop up her tears and then his own.

～

One afternoon, they were drinking coffee on the verandah after lunch.

'Dad, what I still don't understand is why you persevered with my mother for so long, with nothing coming back. Why did you go on writing for all that time?'

'It's a question I asked myself, day after day, week after week. And you know, the answer is, setting aside the thought that sheer persistence might just wear her down, it was also ... I always had this feeling there was something more, something else. It was just at the back of my mind, if only I could see it. And now I think – somehow ... this probably will sound real dumb ... somehow ... at some level I knew about you.'

Annie took his hands, stroking them with her thumbs.

'She did both of us so much harm. She denied us the chance to know each other. There were so many times when I really hated her – for being so careless about people, their feelings. She was so destructive. But you know, Dad, when I look at you and see what you have here – Melissa, the family – I'm so glad she didn't ever answer you, because she'd have destroyed you, just like everything else that was good in her life.'

'Maybe so, but it was you who bore the brunt. You grew up without a father. That makes me angry. You deserved better.'

'I've come out of it OK. I learned in the school of hard

knocks, that's what we call it back home. I'm strong, I'm self-sufficient, independent ... '

'Lonely? I'd like to think there was someone special in your life, Annie. I was blessed. I got a second chance at love. I grabbed it with both hands, and I thank God I did. But you? I've known you for a whole week now and you've never once mentioned a husband or a partner, kids. Do you want to tell me?'

Annie sighed. She'd hoped if she never said anything, neither would he.

'No one just now. I was in a relationship that ended last year, the night before my *News Tonight* meltdown. A contributory factor, you might say. Then I met someone up in the Scottish Highlands, after Janet's funeral.' She paused, thinking how to say it. 'I thought there might be something there, but ... '

She couldn't continue. Those damned tears welled up again.

Patiently, her father encouraged her to tell him about it. Right up to the point when she fled London, the tabloid pictures of Callum side by side with Karin Latimer pursuing her all the way onto the plane.

He was silent for a while. Then he began, in a soft voice ...

'I can still remember the very moment I fell in love with your mother.' He paused. 'It was the night after we first met. It was at a party, she was wearing this fabulous silk dress and she looked like some Hollywood film star from the 40s. Just stunning. We spent two days and nights together and I just kind of knew this was ... I already had an idea that I was getting in too deep, but then it was too late.

'I was reading. I thought she was sleeping, but then I saw she was drawing me. I felt it, like a physical thing. I was falling, spinning around. I was still sitting in my chair, with my book, but everything looked different. I could barely breathe. She came and sat in front of me, to do another drawing. I could see her properly then – she was so beautiful, you know? – serious for once, concentrating. It was like being caught up in a tornado. Falling in love. Before that, I guess I could have walked away. But that moment changed everything. I was lost. I'd like to think that was the night we made you. In love, on my side anyway.'

Annie thought of Applecross, the physical feeling of falling as Callum met her eyes from the stage, singing just for her.

'I had the same feeling. That's why it's so hard – you know. It could have been me talking. That was just how it felt, for me ... I have those drawings of you – best she ever did.'

She laughed, mirthlessly, her eyebrows knitted in pain.

'There's a picture of me, too, at the moment it happened. It was all over a Scottish gossip paper. Callum ... ' it was ages since she'd said his name, it felt strange, forming the word in her mouth, 'he's quite famous – used to play in a band – someone was taking pictures of us on a mobile – a cellphone.'

She paused, and for a few moments they both sat in silence.

'What should I do, Dad? This never happened to me before. I was caught at such a difficult time. I wish it had never happened. It just hurts so much.'

Stewart put his arm around her and pulled her close, stroking her hair. Melissa had come out onto the terrace to join them. She had heard the last part of the conversation. She watched as her husband comforted his eldest daughter the way he had comforted Marcia, nursing her through the heartbreak of teenage romance gone wrong, and again through the break-up of her first marriage.

Melissa spoke then, softly and gently.

'Why don't you just go ask him how he feels, Annie?'

Stewart met her eyes across his daughter's head. They exchanged a smile, full of almost forty years of love.

'You'd better listen to her, Annie. If anyone knows about this, it's Melissa.'

'Yes, but he's seeing someone. I saw them together just before I came away, it was all over the papers – '

'So it must be true? Ask him, Annie. Find out for yourself. Make contact.'

'I did.' She told them about the dog collars. It sounded ridiculous.

'Hm. Unorthodox, but I suppose it's better than nothing.' Melissa was laughing. Annie had to laugh too. What had she been thinking?

~

'Annie. Can I come in?' It was Melissa, knocking lightly on the bedroom door later that evening.

'Of course.' Annie shifted to one side of the bed and Melissa sat down. She had an iPad in her hand.

'I thought you might want to see this.' she said, clicking on the screen and handing the tablet to Annie.

It was the front page of a UK music magazine. Karin Latimer had a wide smile on her face, her left hand held up to show off a sparkling engagement ring. Annie felt sick.

'Scroll down.' Melissa said quietly.

The article was headlined 'Fairytale Romance for Karin' and went on to break the news of her engagement to the lead singer of a successful Irish boy-band. Heart soaring, Annie scrolled down again to the picture of the happy couple at their engagement party in a smart Shoreditch restaurant, just three days previously. She scanned the pictures of the partygoers. Callum was nowhere to be seen.

Looking up from the screen, she caught Melissa's gaze resting on her with fondness.

'Go see him, Annie. Give it your best shot. Don't give up. If you really love someone, you do everything you can. It might work out or it might not, but if you don't try, Annie, you'll never know.'

Chapter 42
Charleston
February

It was the day before Annie's return home. Her extended family of relatives had left after a magnificent lunch prepared by Melissa, Annie her willing helper, learning how to cook delicious South Carolina food alongside Marcia and Joseph.

A dinner date with Samuel had gone some way to ease the tension between Annie and her half-brother.

'I can't say I'm happy about it,' he confessed. 'But no way is it your fault, and ... well, what can I say? You seem like a decent sort of person. To start with I thought you might be on the make, somehow. But I talked to Dad about it. It's a hell of a story.'

'Does that mean you intend to write it?' Samuel had aspirations to give up the day job, running a real estate business, which he hated. He confessed that he had struggled as the eldest child in a high-achieving family, feeling the weight of his parents' expectations on his shoulders. Real estate was never his calling, just the latest in a long line of failed attempts to establish himself.

'Well, I guess that would depend how you felt about it.'

'Hm. I'll get back to you on that.'
He laughed.
'Looks like you're learning the lingo.'

Now he came into the kitchen with a tray laden with glassware.

'Hey guys, let's have a drink in the den. And watch a movie.' said Samuel. 'It's a family tradition after a big lunch.'

'Take your father,' Melissa suggested. 'Get him out from under my feet while I finish off in here.'

The den was one room Annie had not yet seen. Down in the basement, exactly as she had imagined from TV shows, through a passageway full of skis, bikes, golf clubs, baseball bats and all the paraphernalia of a family who enjoyed having fun.

'Dad's little secret.'

Marcia opened the door to a large wood-panelled room. Annie stood on the threshold, silenced, in a state of amazement. There were two huge tartan sofas arranged at right angles around a low table, covered in a clashing tartan cloth. The walls were fitted out with shelf after shelf of Scottish tat – Loch Ness monsters, kilted pipers, Jimmy hats, models of Edinburgh Castle, pennants. There were shelves of books, music and DVDs. All about Scotland. There was even a glass case containing a kilt, Fraser tartan, she assumed. A targe with two crossed swords filled the wall above it. A moth-eaten stag's head hung over the door.

'You had to see this. Until you've been in this room you don't really know this guy.'

'It's – em ... '

They were all laughing, Stewart a little shamefaced.

'They get me something, every birthday, every Thanksgiving, every Christmas. It started as a joke. I think it's a bit out of control now.'

'Well, you're always on about your Scottish ancestry. This is your wee "hieland hame".'

More laughter at Joseph's comment.

They arranged themselves in the big squashy sofas,

Stewart between his daughters on one, the boys on the other, with Melissa, who joined them, kitchen tasks complete.

'What'll we watch, Dad?'

'Let Annie decide. She's the guest of honour.'

Annie chose *Local Hero*.

They watched the movie, which they all knew well. They told her about a family visit years earlier, touring around Scotland in a motorhome, visiting the Fraser grave at Culloden.

The film came to its conclusion. Bereft, Mac looked out across the city from his swanky apartment, listening to the ringtone, picturing the phonebox in the tiny Scottish village he has fallen in love with. Tears formed in Annie's eyes. The scene always made her cry. This time it made her ache with homesickness. Stewart squeezed Annie's shoulder and she glanced round to see tears in his eyes too. They exchanged a private smile.

'Time to go home,' she murmured.

She would be back for Thanksgiving. Stewart and Melissa would come to London in the summer. Marcia had a conference to attend in the fall – she would stay with Annie. She promised to think about Samuel's idea for a novel based on her parents' time together. It was only *au revoir*, not goodbye.

Annie and Stewart sat in a booth in a coffee shop at Atlanta airport. It was too early to go through the gate, and anyway, they wanted this time together, just the two of them, for a proper goodbye. Annie switched her phone on for the first time in days. It beeped the sound that told her she had a new text.

'Kirsty' came up on the screen. Her heart skipped a beat.

'Do you mind, Dad? It's from Callum's daughter.'

It was a video. She pressed the arrow to start play.

She recognised the bank of springy grass at the side of Callum's cottage, with the boat shed in the background, brightly lit by the sun. One of the dogs appeared on the screen, chasing a frisbee. Her heart leapt as Callum came into the shot with another man – Patrick. They were dressed for the cold, padded jackets, scarves. Patrick's hat was pulled down over his ears. Callum's dark hair flew around his face in the breeze, silver threads catching the sunlight.

Tail wagging furiously, the dog brought the frisbee to Callum. He and Patrick began to play, throwing the frisbee back and forth while the dog, soon joined by the second, joined in, leaping and barking around them. Sunlight caught the gaudy stones spelling out the names on their collars. The sound of the men's shouts and laughter and the dogs' barking came quietly though the phone, followed by a much louder shout from Kirsty,

'Cal, don't tease them!'

Annie struggled for a few moments with the phone, as Callum's unmistakable voice came through the speaker at full volume. A couple at the next table looked round, startled. She pressed the pause button and plugged in her headphones. Then she went back to the beginning and held the phone so Stewart could see it, offering him one headphone so he could listen too. They huddled together to watch.

The camera followed Callum and Patrick, Callum and Kirsty, Kirsty and Patrick, as the phone was swapped around. At one point the film panned across the view of the mountains of the Applecross peninsula in the background, then out towards the Inner Sound, sparkling under the bright wintry sky, towards Raasay. Callum sang "Atlantic Shores".

As the song ended, there was a close-up shot of Callum, Patrick and the two dogs sitting on the bench at the back of the boat shed.

'Hi Annie. Mick and Keith and Cal and me just wanted to say a big thank you for their collars. Cool! Hope you like my little movie. Cal wrote a new song for you, coming up next. Oh, and g'day from Patrick too.'

Annie's heart leapt as Callum appeared again on the screen, alone with his guitar in the new studio she recognised from the TV programme. He strummed a few chords and began to sing.

When you're fast losing hope and it's all too much to bear it's time to cast off ...

The screen went black. The batteries had died.

'That's Callum?' Stewart asked.

She nodded, wiping away tears.

'He wrote a song for you, Annie, darlin'. You know what you have to do.'

She nodded again.

'Let me know what happens.' He held her tight in a bearhug. 'Skype, remember?'

The plane landed late, kept in a holding pattern over Heathrow for the best part of an hour. Another hour to think. There had been no way of charging her phone on the plane – the port at her seat didn't work. But even without having heard all of the song, she knew what she was going to do next.

PART FIVE

Chapter 43
Driving North
March

'Edinburgh, Glasgow, I don't mind which.'

Annie quivered with impatience at the sales counter. The woman seemed to be taking forever, checking her screen to find the first available flight to Scotland. Jittery after the sleepless flight, the long delay in landing – having made up her mind, she wanted to be on her way.

'I could give you the 10.15 to Edinburgh. There's one seat left. Would that work for you?'

The price was exorbitant, but she didn't care. She would land in just over an hour, pick up a car, should be in the village by late afternoon.

She went straight to the car-hire desk – all they had left in Edinburgh was a gas-guzzling SUV.

'I'll take it.'

She handed over her credit card.

The flight to Edinburgh landed early, a brisk following wind seemingly speeding her on her way. But by the time she picked up the car doubts were beginning to crowd into her mind.

What was she doing? Setting aside the fact that this was utter impulsive madness, she was tired, jet-lagged – in no state to go driving on those Highland roads – inevitably, the weather conditions were atrocious.

And what if he wasn't there? Worse, what if he was there but didn't want to see her?

Squaring her shoulders, Annie switched off that part of her brain, and drank a double expresso by way of preparation for the journey.

As soon as she started the engine she plugged her phone in to the charger. It was so far into the red zone that nothing happened until she was in the snarl-up of traffic on the way to the Forth Road Bridge. Then it pinged into life. Glancing at the screen as she crawled through the slow-moving jam, she saw several messages from Moira – 'Please call ASAP'.

'Annie, great. I was getting so worried, thought you must surely be back hours ago.'

'I'm in Scotland. Don't ask … '

'Oh. I'd hoped to see you later today. Are you … ?'

'Yes. I have to. I can't see any way forward unless I settle this in my own mind. There have been developments … Dad and Melissa were brilliant, you'd love them, they took it all in their stride. They were so welcoming – lovely … so glad I went. I've got this huge family – a sister, two brothers, cousins, aunts – the full enchilada, as my dad would say! I can't wait for you to meet them!'

'That's wonderful. I'm so pleased for you. I look forward to meeting them too … but Annie, just to give you a heads-up – we're not supposed to know, of course, but I've heard through the grapevine – there are going to be arrests tomorrow – it'll be in the news first thing. We got them. Brooke, lots of them – it'll be carnage.'

'No! Really?'

'We did it, Annie. We got them.' There was a catch of emotion in Moira's voice.

For the first time since leaving the States, Annie was able to think of something other than Callum. This was her life too, everything she had worked towards for years. She shook with emotion.

'Annie? Can you still hear me?'

'Yes, I'm sorry, Moira, I just … I can't believe it. The whole list?'

'Most of them, yes.'

Annie felt tears pricking in her eyes, thoughts rushing backwards and forwards. It was by no means over, but it was a start. And a vindication of all their hard work, an outcome that would start to restore the self-respect of the many victims, bring them a sense of closure.

'It's the most amazing news, Moira. Thank you. It's the best homecoming I could have possibly imagined … ' Almost, anyway.

'Annie, there's something else. I really wanted to discuss it with you in person – but … it might all depend on what happens – when you see him.'

'Moira, I'm driving. Just spit it out, for God's sake!'

She executed a tricky manoeuvre around standing traffic waiting to exit the motorway at Dunfermline.

'The Scottish Government – there's a similar thing up there. They're setting up their own inquiry – asked if I could recommend anyone to head it up. Edinburgh-based. I thought of you, Annie. No one would be better qualified … Oh dear, sorry, I didn't want to do this on the phone … '

Stunned, Annie's mind went completely blank. This was much too much to take in.

'Annie?'

'I can't even think about it just now. I'm on my way up north – that's all I can think about. I'll call you. I just need to know where things stand, you know … '

'I understand, Annie. Drive safely, and good luck. I'll

be thinking about you.'

~

Three hours at the very least, she calculated. Another three hours to think.

Moira's call had shaken her. Could she face the idea of another inquiry, further immersion in the awful stories of abuse, of exploitation by the powerful of the powerless? Had she not done enough? But the chance to expose what had happened, to champion the victims ... as Moira had said, no one would be more qualified. And Edinburgh-based – a homecoming, of a kind. Was it what she wanted, needed? Or should she go back to America, start a new life with the support of her family – what was really left for her here, if she was wrong?

Perth was another snarl-up, traffic tailing back from the roundabouts. Then the A9, slow as ever, queuing behind lorries followed by a mad scramble to overtake at the short sections of dual carriageway. All in teeming rain and sleet, muddy spray, and seemingly endless roadworks. It took all of her concentration.

She could see brighter skies as she turned west, traffic cones and queues of vehicles left behind as tree-clad mountains soared high above the road. At Spean Bridge she stopped to drink more coffee, tidy up and brush her teeth. Changing into warmer clothes, her heart thudded erratically.

Deep breaths, she told herself, rejoining the road for the final stretch towards the village.

Over and over again as she drove the last few miles, she rehearsed what she needed to say. There would be no room for weakness or for any lack of clarity. She was tired of living half a life. She owed it to herself to settle it.

With Stewart's help she had tried to unravel what had happened that evening at the gallery. Could all her senses, which had told her Callum was as nervous and excited about seeing her as she had been stunned when she saw him, have been so completely wrong? She recalled the feeling of his lips brushing her cheek – a shiver had passed through her and, she was sure, through him as well. Could she trust any of it, or was it just another way of refusing to address the reality – he was simply neither ready for another woman in his life, nor the right person with whom she should even contemplate a relationship?

But now she tried to consider the reality.

Trying to imagine a future in which she headed up a Scottish inquiry – the MacIntosh Inquiry – she thought of the fallout if she were involved with a man who, darling though he was of the Scottish press, nevertheless had a past littered with hostages to fortune – drugs, drink, women. It could, and would, all be used against her at the first sign of trouble. How would she be able to deal with it? And what else was there likely to be that she did not yet know about him?

What was not in doubt was how much she loved him.

It had been wonderful to talk it through with her father. He had helped her piece together the pattern her life had fallen into, her failure to commit, to allow anyone to come close. He pointed out to her the very obvious truth – relationships are built and conducted according to how they are observed in childhood. With only a dysfunctional, alcoholic mother as guidance, it was no surprise Annie had struggled to form lasting partnerships as an adult.

Her need to protect herself had overridden all other considerations. Until she fell in love.

Stewart and Melissa helped her understand much more about love. Not the falling in love – which, she realised now, was the easy part. It happened, if it was meant to, almost by itself, as it had happened to her. It was what followed that mattered, and that was what she was ready for now, after all the failures of her past. A man she could commit to, support, look to for support. A partnership. Callum. Of course it would never be perfect. Of course there would be difficulties. Her father and stepmother had talked about their own marriage, openly and honestly, the ups and downs, the sadness and the joy. The commitment it took to make it work.

Callum could commit – she knew that. He was capable of loving very deeply, of following through on love whatever it took. He had shown it unequivocally in his love for his wife. And he would always love Freya – she was a major part of the man he was.

What she needed to know now was – could he love her? As she was ready to love him? Unconditionally.

'Go and find out. If you think there may be something there, trust your instinct. For your own sake, go and see him. If you don't try, Annie, you'll never know.' She repeated Melissa's words to herself.

'And Annie, whatever happens, you ain't alone any more. You're my daughter. I love you. I'm here for you, whatever. So is Melissa. Remember this – we're your family – here to catch you if you fall. That's what families are for.'

In an attempt to focus, she rehearsed again what she planned to say.

By the time she remembered she still hadn't heard the rest of the song, there was no signal on her phone.

Chapter 44
West Highlands
March

Sick with nerves, heartbeat loud in her chest, Annie drove past the daffodil-bright verge towards the sign she first saw a year ago. Her hands were shaking as she passed between the gateposts.

She parked the Mercedes in front of the cottage.

There was no one in, not even the dogs, although she could hear barking somewhere close by – the beach, perhaps. She walked round the side of the cottage, past the Land Rover and the VW. As she got closer to the boat shed she could hear the whine of a machine. The sound was almost drowned out by the accelerated thudding of her heart. He was there.

A gusty wind blew rags of cloud across the sky. The light was constantly changing, as though some unseen hand were switching the sun on and off. Out across the water a squall made its way down the sound. A rainbow arced across to Raasay in the distance. The sea was rough, a confused maelstrom of grey waves, white foam blowing from their crests.

She stood outside the boat shed, on the pier, watching the weather, watching *Sweet Dreams* straining at her mooring lines. The screaming of the gulls overhead echoed the screaming of the machinery inside the shed.

She could still just turn and go away. He'd never know

she'd been here.

One of the dogs – Mick, according to his collar – rushed to meet her, barking with his customary enthusiasm. She crouched down to ruffle his ears.

The noise of the machine changed note, gradually dying away. In the silence that followed, she turned back to the shed.

Leaving Mick to scamper off in search of his twin, she rang the ship's bell. She waited. Nothing. She rang again, trembling. Faintly, from inside she could hear another sound – singing. Blood coursed through her veins as she tugged open the door.

He was at the bench, fitting a plank into the vice. Dressed in a grey sweatshirt and black jeans – covered in sawdust – tucked into his heavy boots. Bearded still, dark stubble against pale skin. His hair was tucked out of sight under a black woollen hat, pulled down over his ears, a set of goggles askew on top of his head. A dust-mask lay on the bench beside him. He wore headphones. She could see the wires that led to the phone in his pocket. Annie smiled. Without an audience, his singing along to the music in his ears was as bad as anyone else's. She recognised a Dave Matthews song. A favourite, she remembered.

For a while she stood, watching, listening, allowing herself just to look at him again, unnoticed. Her heart wrenched as he moved in time to the music, the way he bent his knees and the swaying of his hips – moving the way he had the night they'd slow-danced to a sudden stop, months before.

Chapter 45
West Highlands
March

One of the dogs was whimpering downstairs.

Callum eased himself up on the pillow, hoping it would stop. Knowing it wouldn't – he'd forgotten to let them out. Forgotten their routine altogether – a last run around outside, barking at invisible foxes, imaginary rabbits. A dog biscuit as they went into their crate for the night. Unaccustomed to being loose in the utility room at bed-time, they were fretful, whining.

He'd have to do something about it before the barking started.

The bedside light was still on, casting a soft light on Annie, sleeping by his side. A slight smile played around her lips, one arm was thrown across his stomach. He couldn't resist bending to kiss her mouth, just that little smiling corner. The smile deepened, though her breathing told him she hadn't wakened – hardly surprising after her long journey from Atlanta, all the way to the Highlands.

Gently, he moved her arm aside as he inched over to the edge of the bed. As quietly as he could he pulled on his jeans, unable to take his eyes off Annie's sleeping form, skin dark against the white sheets, hair spread in loops and coils over the pillow – so lovely. He felt he had to pinch himself, to believe that she was really there. He pulled the duvet over her bare shoulders lest the chill of the night air wake her.

The dogs greeted his arrival with enthusiastic yips and wagging tails, barrelling through the doorway into the garden, rushing across the grass towards the shed. Their normal evening route.

It would be at least ten minutes before they came back.

There was still some residual warmth in the sitting room, the woodburner making clicking sounds as it cooled. He stood in front of the windows, looking out at the view. The moon was almost full, riding high over the mountains of Skye, silvering the waters of the sound. The dark sky was brilliant with stars, the mountains bathed in eerie blue light. In the bay a seal – or perhaps the otter – left a glittering wake across the water.

Callum stood looking out at the familiar sights of home. The woman he loved lay sleeping upstairs. Still barely able to believe that she was here, he relived the hours since her arrival – making promises, making plans, making love. In the morning when they woke they would make love and plans and promises again, and for years to come. No longer in repair, he knew he was ready now to commit, to love again. His heart felt brimful of joy.

Unaccustomed sounds from downstairs woke her – the scrape of the back door, Callum's quiet voice, the dogs whining. They hadn't even brought her cases in – she had nothing here except the clothes she arrived in, discarded around the room. Annie cast around for something to wear, finding Callum's T-shirt, soft cotton with his lingering scent causing waves of renewed desire as she pulled it over her head. She smiled, thinking of all the times she had worn his clothes, right from their very first meeting, when he had wrapped his coat around her as protection against the driving rain.

She made her way quietly downstairs, hesitant in the darkness of an as-yet unfamiliar part of the house.

Callum stood, silhouetted against the moonlit bay. Silently she picked her way through the kitchen, unable to tear her eyes away from his tall figure, pale light glistening in the silver strands of his hair, the outline of his broad shoulders, his long straight back.

'Callum?'

He jumped, and turned to find her there behind him. Annie – wearing the T-shirt she had helped him remove earlier. Pale against the darkness of the interior, against the darkness of her skin. Callum took her into his arms, unable to speak as a tidal wave of emotion overwhelmed him.

Holding her close, he let his body tell her again – I love you, I want you. Tightening her arms around him, her body answered – I want you too. I love you too.

ANNIE MACINTOSH TO HEAD INQUIRY INTO SCOTTISH CARE HOME SCANDAL

Politics Scotland

EXCLUSIVE!
DOWNLOAD THREE FABULOUS NEW SONGS FROM CAL MATHIESON!
Music Today

PLAYLIST

'The Space Between'
The Dave Matthews Band

'My Love Is Like A Red Red Rose'
Eddi Reader

'I Can't Make You Love Me'
Bonnie Raitt

'Father and Daughter'
Paul Simon

'Sweet Dreams (Are Made of This)'
Eurythmics

'Sarah Smile'
Daryl Hall and John Oates

'Your Body Is A Wonderland'
John Mayer

'Here Comes the Rain Again'
Eurythmics

'Wild is the Wind'
David Bowie

PLAYLIST

'Wonderful Tonight'
Eric Clapton

'When the World Ends'
The Dave Matthews Band

'Let's Dance'
David Bowie

'Slow Dancing In A Burning Room'
John Mayer

'Ae Fond Kiss'
Eddi Reader

'Things Can Only Get Better'
D:Ream

'Someone Like You'
Daryl Hall

'Going Home (Theme of *Local Hero*)'
Mark Knopfler

'In Repair'
John Mayer

ACKNOWLEDGEMENTS

In Repair has been a long time in the writing. The creation of any first novel is inevitably a matter of trial and error, and this one is no exception. This version is somewhere around the fifteenth attempt, and even now there are many things I would change.

I wish to thank the many people who helped along the way. The late Andy Mackie, former lecturer in creative writing at Queen Margaret University in Edinburgh, as well as a good friend, became my first editor after a chance discussion at our art class. I owe him a huge debt of gratitude for his words of encouragement, for making me believe in myself as a writer and for teaching me how to avoid pitfalls and black holes – he was the best creative writing tutor I could ever have had. It was Andy who made me ask myself the question, 'how many courses do you need to do before you believe in yourself as a writer?' and find the answer – no more, just do it. 'The best writing is re-writing,' he used to say – edit, edit and edit again. I am so sorry he is no longer with us to see *In Repair* finally published.

My enthusiastic early readers gave invaluable help and encouragement. Monica Loudon, a lifelong tee-totaller turned Cal into a recovering alcoholic overnight when she observed that he was 'nice enough but a bit boring'. Belinda Robertson loved every version and spurred me on by asking for more and more – and a happy ending, please. Norma Austin-Hart, whose own writing far outshines mine, gave me a target to aim for. Iain Clark, former drummer for Uriah Heep and Cressida, gave me valuable insights into life in a touring rock band. Jacquie Roberts kept me right on the workings of a child abuse Inquiry. Alice Perkins and Jack Straw offered warm encouragement and convinced me to go for publication. Nick Price and Andy Murray, both romantics at heart, confirmed that Cal was a believable character and that I wasn't just writing for women. I want to thank Andy in particular for becoming the voice of Cal with his wonderful songs.

I am also deeply grateful to The Edinburgh Writers' Club, whose members didn't laugh when I suggested I might be one of them and whose support for writers at all levels and in all disciplines is widely appreciated. Moniack Mhor gave me a place where I could just be a writer amongst other like-minded souls. I am especially grateful to The Scottish Association of Writers and in particular Rosemary Gemmel for awarding me the Pitlochry Quaich in 2019.

As I neared completion, Sophy Dale cast a professional publisher's eye over my work and strengthened my belief in my story-telling. Tom Johnstone's editing skills saved me embarrassment with bad spelling, grammar and amateur punctuation. Helen Bleck, for her input as editor and proof-reader. Jim Hutcheson turned a scruffy Word file into the elegant volume you see today.

I must also acknowledge two complete strangers from across the pond who have no idea of their influence in the creation of this story. I devoured all eight volumes of Diana Gabaldon's *Outlander* series over the course of a particularly cold, wet Scottish summer, and found myself in awe of the world she created around her two main protagonists. I wondered if I could write something as compelling, and *In Repair* began to take shape in my head. Another American, John Mayer, is the main inspiration for Cal – a brilliant guitarist and lyricist who loves performing with other musicians, a man who apparently faces up to his demons and who is, of course, drop-dead gorgeous! Thank you for the music, the loan of your good looks and for your unintended assistance with the formation of one of my main characters.

Above all, my eternal gratitude goes to my late, beloved husband John Preston, for his long-suffering patience as I disappeared into a fictional world with characters who occupied all my free time and much of his for what turned out to be the last two years of his life. He was always my fiercest critic, but at the same time he was hugely proud of me for sticking with it, and while he was always ready to criticise, it was only because he wanted me to be the best writer I could be. 'That'll do' was never good enough for him in any part of his life, my writing included, and my work massively improved as a result. Thank you, my beloved, for your tough love, for your unwavering support and for being the love of my life. Everything I understand about love I learned in our forty-two happy years together. Everything I understand about grief comes from losing you.

The long delay in publishing came about partly because after John died in 2017, I was unable to write for a long time. Grief robbed me of the desire to create, and for a while everything I tried to write seemed pointless. However, it would have been even more pointless to abandon all the work I had done, and gradually, my

...nfidence returned as I picked up the pieces again. ...week of retreat at Moniack Mhor gave me the space ...needed to knock *In Repair* into shape, and it was that ...rsion that was recognised by the SAW Conference ...pen novel competition in 2019.

In Repair is the first of a trilogy of novels featuring Cal Mathieson and Annie MacIntosh. I have no ambition to be known as a romantic novelist, so I try to write about their love against the backdrop of real life with all the problems it puts in the way of a happy ending. The sequels, *Under Pressure* and *Echoes of Love*, will take them into dark places where their love is tested by events from the lives they lived before they met. Like any couple who meet later in life, Cal and Annie have baggage that can't be erased, and my preoccupation is with how this affects their relationship and whether that relationship can survive the ghosts of the past. Prepare for some greater jeopardy than simple doubt in the next two books!

Roz Preston
July 2025

CAL'S SONGS

To listen to the songs mentioned in this story, click on the links below. These have been interpretated by Andy Murray with lyrics by Andy, John Preston and Roz Preston.

4-tunes.com

rozprestonauthor.co.uk